THE HISTORY OF US

Jonathan Harvey comes from Liverpool and is a multi-award-winning writer of plays, films, sitcoms and Britain's longest-running drama serial.

Jonathan's theatre work includes the award-winning *Beautiful Thing* (Bush Theatre, Donmar Warehouse, Duke of York's; winner: John Whiting Award; nominated: Olivier Award for Best Comedy), *Babies* (Royal Court Theatre; winner: *Evening Standard* Award for Most Promising Playwright; winner: George Devine Award) and *Rupert Street Lonely Hearts Club* (English Touring Theatre, Donmar Warehouse, Criterion Theatre; winner: *Manchester Evening News* Award for Best New Play; winner: *City Life Magazine* Award for Best New Play). Other plays include *Tomorrow I'll Be Happy* (Royal National Theatre), *Corrie!* (Lowry Theatre and national tour; winner: *Manchester Evening News* Award for Best Special Entertainment), *Canary* (Liverpool Playhouse, Hampstead Theatre and English Touring Theatre), *Hushabye Mountain* (English Touring Theatre, Hampstead Theatre), *Guiding Star* (Everyman Theatre, Royal National Theatre), *Boom Bang a Bang* (Bush Theatre), *Mohair* (Royal Court Theatre Upstairs) and *Wildfire* (Royal Court Theatre Upstairs). Jonathan also co-wrote the musical *Closer to Heaven* with the Pet Shop Boys.

For television Jonathan has created and written three series of the BAFTA-nominated *Gimme Gimme Gimme* for the BBC, two series of *Beautiful People* (winner: Best Comedy, Banff TV Festival), the double-BAFTA-nominated *Best Friends, Von Trapped!* and *Birthday Girl*. He has also written for *Tracey Ullman's Show*, *Rev* (winner: BAFTA for Best Sitcom), *Shameless*, *The Catherine Tate Show*, *At Home with the Braithwaites*, *Lilies* and *Murder Most Horrid*. To date he has written over one hundred episodes of *Coronation Street*.

Jonathan's film work includes *Beautiful Thing* for Film4 (Outstanding Film, GLAAD Awards, New York; Best Film, London Lesbian and Gay Film Festival; Best Screenplay, Fort Lauderdale Film Festival; Grand Prix, Paris Film Festival; Jury Award, São Paolo International Film Festival).

But perhaps most telling of all, he also won the Space-hopper Championships at Butlins Pwhelli in 1976.

His novels are *All She Wants*, *The Confusion of Karen Carpenter*, *The Girl Who Just Appeared*, *The Secrets We Keep* and *The History of Us*.

JONATHAN HARVEY

The HISTORY OF US

PAN BOOKS

First published 2016 by Pan Books
an imprint of Pan Macmillan
20 New Wharf Road, London N1 9RR
Associated companies throughout the world
www.panmacmillan.com

ISBN 978-1-4472-9820-5

1 3 5 7 9 8 6 4 2

A CIP catalogue record for this book is available from the British Library.

Printed and bound by CPI Group (UK) Ltd, Croydon, CR0 4YY

Visit www.panmacmillan.com to read more about all our books
and to buy them. You will also find features, author interviews and
news of any author events, and you can sign up for e-newsletters
so that you're always first to hear about our new releases.

For anyone who has fallen out
and fallen back in again

ACKNOWLEDGEMENTS

Continued thanks to Wayne Brookes, Camilla Elworthy, Jeremy Trevathan and all the team at Pan Macmillan who publish my books and seem to think they make sense! Also to my agent Gordon Wise for keeping me on the straight and narrow, and to Michael McCoy for handling all my other writing.

A few fabulous people bid considerable amounts of money for some of my favourite charities to have characters named after them in this book, so thank you to Karen Paterson for bidding money for Moodswings Network. Moodswings is a Manchester-based charity that gives information, advice and ongoing support to people with mood disorders and other forms of emotional distress. Also thank you to Jem Pammenter-Fry and Mark Reynolds, who bid money for The Food Chain. The Food Chain is a London-based charity that aims to ensure that people living with HIV can access the nutrition they need to get well, stay well and lead healthy, independent lives.

This is a story about friendship, so thank you to all the friends I've had along the way. Some have hung around longer than others, but none are ever forgotten. And to my mates on

Alderson Road in my teenage years, hopefully none of us has ended up like the characters in this book!

And finally, thank you to my partner Paul Hunt for keeping the faith and egging me on whenever I thought I couldn't finish this book.

BILLY

London, 2015: That Night

Dear God,

It was only when I got home that I realized there was blood on the knee of my jeans. A circle of what looked like red tar that drooped a bit at the bottom, making it look almost like a heart. I took them off and put them in the washing machine, then sat in the kitchen eating tonight's cold lasagne. It was very oily. Some of it dropped onto my dressing gown. I think the blood will be easier to get out than the oil.

I don't think I need forgiveness for what happened tonight. It happened. It must be your will. What a sublime coincidence. Or maybe divine intervention?

Ellie Goulding is playing on the radio.

I hate Ellie Goulding.

I switch her off. Dead.

I will go through to the bedroom and join her. I will sleep, I'm sure.

Amen.

KATHLEEN

London, 2015

Sky. And more sky. Such an expanse of it, pregnant with clouds yet somehow it looks hollow, something is missing. It feels so odd that it's not there any more. How apt that today of all days I strain my neck up and the tower block that once obliterated the clouds has evaporated.

Of course, it's not really evaporated; it was knocked down in the mid-nineties, when it was found to be riddled with asbestos. We'd not known that before, though the council had been at pains to inform us that we shouldn't hammer nails into the walls to hang pictures. But who hangs pictures at nineteen? It was just our home. We thought there was a quirky beauty in the fact that it looked like it had been cobbled together by a Seventies toddler, plastic brick by plastic brick. We found something charming in the notion that it always felt like even a moderate gust of wind might send it toppling onto the estate below.

I lived here with my friends Adam and Jocelyn. We'd run away to London together. Or had we? Had we really run away? Were we really that brave? Or did it just feel like we had? A new beginning, a new life. And yet today I go to Jocelyn's funeral. It's like the flats have been erased from the picture. And now she has too.

As I stand in this grubby corner of Paddington, almost choking on the fumes of fried chicken and petrol, I try to picture us up there in our bird's nest. Planning, dreaming. What lives we thought we'd lead. Images and half-forgotten memories ping into my head from our days here: the Jamaican man in the corner shop assuming I was Scottish. Playing pool in the pub on the corner of the estate. The endless queue at the long-gone phone box, which was . . . just here. Right where I'm standing.

It's disorientating when things change so much.

The corner shop with the laconic Jamaican guy is now a pretentious-looking restaurant. The grubby shack of a cafe where I first saw curried goat advertised, but didn't dare eat, is now a betting shop. Our favourite pub has been rebranded from a down at heel spit-and-sawdust boozer to something called The Friendly Fox. I bet they do a nice Thai red curry. That sort of place always does. The whole area seems cleaner, sanitized, boring.

Some kids zoom past me on those annoying little scooters, laughing.

The laughter. I look up again. Oh yes, the belly laughter. The hours spent watching old Hollywood movies up there on a video player the size of a sideboard. It's probably the benefit of nostalgia, but we really didn't seem to have a care in the world. Other than working out where the next laugh was coming from. Or the next Hollywood rental.

We certainly didn't think it would end like this. With one of us falling from another high building. A calm bright day like this, I'd imagine. An advert-blue sky. Clouds like whispers. And down she fell. I wonder how long it took? I remember jumping from a high diving board as a child. The fear before doing it. The exhilaration during. The distortion of noise as I dropped. I wonder if it was like that.

Poor Jocelyn.

I look for evidence that the flats used to be here. In their place now are smarter low-rise blocks in tasteful beige brick. If beige can be said to be tasteful. So often that word is used to describe something as being dull. I don't like that. Beige is almost interesting. I think grey is duller. Or a cross between the two. Greige. The windows of these flats are vertical oblongs, long and narrow. Who thought, twenty years ago, that narrow was a good idea for windows? Clearly some architect did. I keep looking. Jessica Fletcher's got nothing on me.

Bingo.

As I walk along I finally see my evidence that our former life was here. In between two of the blocks is a sweeping helter-skelter of a concrete walkway that takes you to a further group of flats that are slightly higher up. That walkway used to lead to our block, Harmony Heights. The campest-sounding block of flats in London. There was a car park of sorts underneath. I experience a frisson of excitement as I recognize it. It feels like a bit of us is still there. I stare at it for so long, hoping that if I don't blink, it will suddenly reappear: that carbuncle of white flats, soaring twenty-odd storeys high. I'm disappointed when it doesn't.

Ah, the confidence of youth. The hours I spent staring out of the window, onto the Lego set of London, all the sights. These days I'd be so scared of the height of the place I'd keep my distance, just sit on the bed, squeal if anyone went to open a curtain.

And then I remember. I only came here for a nostalgic five minutes. I've probably been here for the best part of half an hour.

I look at my phone. *Shit.* If I don't hurry I'll be late.

I'd planned on walking. It's about an hour from here. I don't particularly like walking, but the claustrophobia of the tube is something I need to be anaesthetized in order to consider.

But I could just have one in The Friendly Fox. For old times' sake. My friend has died. It's called Dutch courage.

Yes, I will have that drink. Then I might be able to take the tube.

Golders Green Crematorium is a small town of inter-connecting red-brick chapels that looks like it's been designed to accommodate all-comers. *Any religion or faith, you're welcome here*, it seems to say. The arched windows and towers look like they could be Christian or Jewish; there might even be a touch of the mosque about them. *Bring your dead here*, basically, *we'll sort them out*. The fact that it's on Hoop Lane would make me titter like a schoolgirl, if I didn't have my sombre face on for the funeral. And the word 'Hoop' reminds me of course of Adam, and as I walk along it I wonder if he will be here. I certainly hope he is. But will he speak to me? Will he even acknowledge me? After everything that's happened, I just don't know.

I've overdressed for the weather. It's been so cold lately and I never think of funerals as particularly warm affairs, so I'm wearing my River Island check coat with the faux fur collar. When I bought it I thought it made me look quite moddy and Sixties, but as I catch my reflection in the parked cars I fancy I look more like a baby elephant with a car blanket chucked over it. And a dead cat hanging round its neck.

Not that I'm down on my appearance or anything, at the moment.

Oh God. And the hair. It still surprises me. What was I

thinking? I recently saw an interview with Sharleen Spiteri in the *Sunday Times* and I was quite taken with her cropped, jet-black hair, so I got Nicola at my regular salon to copy it.

I look like a desperate geography teacher. The sort you see in Mail Online who's had a liaison with a Year Eleven girl and the shit's hit the fan. She's dressed up for court, but she's kidding no-one.

Oh well.

I wish I'd worn something lighter. After a succession of freezing cold days the sun has finally deigned to appear, and now the baby elephant is sweating. Especially after the – actually it was an hour and ten, not an hour's walk from Westbourne Park. The faux fur round my neck is wringing wet. Still. I should be grateful for small mercies. At least I'm alive. This makes me snigger. Then I stop and apologize to myself. I do, I actually do that. I do that quite a bit. Think something inappropriate, and then say aloud, 'Sorry.'

A therapist would have a field day.

Actually, a therapist does. And at forty-five quid a pop.

I've heard of feeling sorry for yourself, but apologizing to yourself? No wonder I'm a bloody basket case.

There are a few paparazzi on the gate who look disappointed that I'm not famous. Still, it's better than them thinking I'm 'her off *The Apprentice*'. I was told in a bar by Colin from work's flatmate, 'God, you really look like . . . thingy . . . what's her name?'

'Sharleen Spiteri?' I ventured, hopefully.

He shook his head. Possibly thinking, 'Yeah, right, on steroids maybe.' And then he said, 'Her off *The Apprentice*.'

I don't even know which one he meant. But seeing the cameras does make me worry for a second that someone's going to shout out, 'How's Sir Alan?' As I approach the gates, the cameras go up; then, when they realize I'm really nobody interesting, they're dropped again quick smart.

Some of the women on *The Apprentice* are really quite plain. I can just imagine the sort of woman that guy meant.

Jeez. It was about five years ago. And I still let it irritate me.

Mind you, some of them are quite gorgeous, aren't they? Real dolly bird types. That new breed of businesswoman that looks like a porn star. Well, maybe not a porn star, but the sort of woman who has eighteen different vibrators in her bottom drawer, and no embarrassment about it.

That reminds me of one of the last times I saw Jocelyn. So long ago now. She'd just got back from a trip to Edinburgh, I think she said it was. Anyway, it was somewhere far enough away for her to moan that whoever had paid for the trip hadn't sent her by plane, but on an endless train journey. She had gone to use the loo, but when she'd pressed the button and the door had swung open she had been confronted by the sight of a tiny Chinese woman standing, wearing a Burberry puffa jacket and nothing on her bottom half, her denim skirt abandoned on the floor, staring at a row of four or five dildos in various sizes that she had lined up on the side. What a way to pass a journey.

As I said at the time: she must have forgotten her Maeve Binchy.

The conveyor-belt nature of funerals at crematoriums makes me anxious I'll go into the wrong one and be saying a sad farewell to a complete stranger, too well behaved and worried about what others might think to not stand up again and walk back out of the door. But I locate the West Chapel, and check a framed list on the pillar outside.

14:20. Jocelyn Jones.

The doors are open, and I see that the service has already started. I can't be that late, surely? The small chapel holds about fifty people, and it's almost full. I slip in and take a seat on the back pew. An elderly Irish priest is droning on about how Jocelyn is with her maker, and what a jubilant faith she had.

Now, I'm sorry, but the only faith she had was the album by George Michael.

Quite a few people are fidgeting, and I understand why. Jocelyn did some horrible things during the past few years; she upset a lot of people. Every person who told her to 'just die, bitch' on Twitter has finally got what they want. And here she is, about to be burnt to a crisp. People are feeling uncomfortable with the priest lauding her as something approaching saintly. But I guess that's what happens when someone dies. They rest in peace, safe in the knowledge that they were generous, selfless souls. All tarnishes and blemishes wiped away. Clean slate. Meeting their maker.

The coffin sits raised up between some red drapes, like an odd set for a rather plush puppet show. A photo of Jocelyn rests against it, as if saying 'Just in case you'd forgotten what she looked like, here she is. And yes, she was very photogenic.'

Yes, she was. But there again, she looked amazing in the flesh too. Well, you know what they say. Black don't crack.

And as someone said to me recently, 'Yeah, babe. But fat don't crack either.'

As if that was going to make me feel better about myself. I'm not even fat. I just look like a normal forty-five-year-old, thank you very much.

Well, I try and convince myself that that's the case.

Elephant in a car blanket.

Why do people even have blankets in cars? Why do people

even have cars? Oh, actually, I know why people have cars. It's so they can get from A to B. And drive places.

I really should have studied philosophy.

Maybe I could study philosophy? There's a thought.

Anyway. What was I thinking about? Looks. Black/fat not cracking.

Of course, Jocelyn had help. Honestly. I don't know who this man is I'm sitting next to, but it might very well be her cosmetic surgeon.

But wait. What if it's HIM? I've spent so much time fretting about whether I was going to see Adam, I'd almost forgotten about HIM.

I don't want to see HIM.

I've not seen HIM for nigh on fifteen years. Would I recognize him? Is this HIM? He doesn't appear to have recognized me. But then, we all change in that amount of time.

Oh God. It might be HIM.

It was the millennium. New Year's Eve on the millennium. It was the last time I saw Jocelyn.

So close. And then – fifteen years, gone in a puff of smoke.

Is it HIM? But I can't tell. The thought makes my skin crawl. I try to find Adam instead.

I look around to see if I can see him, but it's hard to tell who's who when all you can see is the backs of heads. And I'll be honest, I'm looking to see if I can spot anyone famous as well. Jocelyn moved in such circles. Though I also wonder whether some famous people might be distancing themselves from her of late.

I wonder if Mark Reynolds is here, the other kid from our school who made it big. I wonder, if he's here and he looks at me, whether he'll think, 'Oh look. A girl from school who just got big.' Even though it's a self-hating attack on my size, I still make myself smile. And then I feel guilty. You shouldn't smile at a funeral. I immediately narrow my eyes as if the crease on my lips is one of pain, remembering something heartfelt from my time with Jocelyn. I then close my eyes, affecting a look of solemn prayer. That's what today's about, solemnity.

People are standing, so I open my eyes and stand too. A recording of an organ is playing. We sing 'The Lord is My Shepherd', and it's then that I see Adam. He's about four rows from the front and he's squeezed in the middle of a pew. It's Adam all right, but he too has put on a bit of weight, and has he started dyeing his hair? I try to see if any of Jocelyn's family are here. There are some black women on the front row, but I don't think any of them are her mum or the twins or Billy. I liked her mum when I was growing up, and I know she despaired at the route Jocelyn's life took. Adam's partner is next to him, I now realize. Me and Jocelyn always found him a bit brash, a bit flash, a bad influence on our Adam.

But he's not our Adam now, is he? Jocelyn's gone. He's not even my Adam any more, we so rarely see each other.

I stare at the coffin, mouthing silent words to the psalm, willing myself to become upset. But instead I just feel numb. I thought I'd be all over the place. They say, don't they, that if you have a difficult relationship with someone, that when they die you might feel worse than, say, someone who got on with them really well. But instead of Jocelyn I just think of all the other people I've lost along the way. That's the worst thing about funerals, the older you get, it's the cumulative effect of grief. I'm not just thinking of Jocelyn now, I'm thinking of everyone else I know who's died. After a while some tears do come, and the man next to me, who may or may not be a plastic surgeon and who may or may not be HIM, hands me a paper tissue.

Which is when I notice his fingernails are filthy, and it makes me pity the people who may or may not be his patients. And confirms to me that it's definitely not HIM. He had impeccable hygiene. In fact, I remember him saying, 'Imperial Leather before penetration!' as he guided me into his en suite.

Or was that his way of saying I was smelly? Jesus! I'm getting offended fifteen years after the event. That must be something of a record, surely?

I calm down.

We listen to the eulogy. It's typical Jocelyn – hardly based at all in reality. Then we listen to a song she recorded in the early nineties. Now *that's* more her: loving the sound of her own voice, and inflicting her God-awful record on people who can't escape. She has the perfect captive audience today, and we have to pretend to be enchanted by its rumbling salsa Eurotrash beat. The lyrics are hideously inappropriate for a funeral. I'm amazed the priest has sanctioned them.

'Do me. Do me. Do me in Ibiza Old Town.'

I see a few people are looking at their phones. I'm tempted to look at my own. Some people at the front, though, I notice are gyrating in time to the music. Others are practically wailing. At first I think, *oh come on, it's not that bad*. But then I realize they're crying because Jocelyn has gone, yet they can hear her voice, and they probably loved her, etc., and I feel chastened.

And then, before I know it, the priest is doing the committal, and the curtains slowly travel to meet each other, and the coffin has vanished from view. Like the flats. Like our flats. And some doors behind the priest are opening and people are heading out into the sunshine. It takes forever to get outside.

I recognize a few people from the telly, but no-one major. A girl from *Hollyoaks* who kept her sunglasses on for the whole service, and that TV chef that Jocelyn had the ill-advised fling with years back. At the back of the chapel is a garden of remembrance, and here the floral tributes to Jocelyn have been laid out along a path like roadkill. We all file past them, looking at them as if they're going to grant us the meaning of life; we try to eke some wisdom out of the words, 'RIP Jocelyn. We'll miss you babe. Love all at Unbeweavable Hair & Beauty Salon.'

I search again for her mum or Billy, or both. Then I feel someone nudging me. I turn. It's Adam. I think he is going to hug me, and I go to hug him, but he's motionless. His eyes are so bright. I don't know if it's just because the sun is so strong, or whether it's because he's been crying. Instead of hugging him, I just awkwardly rub his arms and then step back.

'So sad,' I say.

He nods.

'Such awful circumstances.'

He nods. OK, so he's like a frigging nodding dog. *Help me out here, Adam. Say something.* He doesn't. So I do.

'I went to the old flats before. They've been knocked down.'

He nods.

'Those nights she'd come over to see us, and we'd watch Hollywood movies on video and eat popcorn, and . . . the world was our oyster back then.'

He nods again. But then he does say something. And he says it quite loudly. And I really wish he hadn't.

He says, 'D'you think this has got anything to do with us?'

A cold iron fist grips my heart. I find it hard to breathe.

Liverpool, 1985

'Eat your egg and chips, love. And we'll see whose face pops up.'

Nan had a habit of saying this to me during my evening meal. She had a set of dinner plates and each one featured a famous face from the Bible.

'Can you see yet, love?'

As I wiped up the runny yolk with one of my chips, a scarlet nose with blackened nostril was revealed. I knew these plates too well not to know which one I'd got. 'I think it's Jesus, Nan!'

Nan grinned, lit up a cigarette, and immediately blew smoke lovingly my way. 'Awww. God love the bones of him.'

She said this a lot, my nan, about fellas on the telly, beggars on the street, and our Lord Saviour Jesus Christ. She also said it about Elvis, a framed photograph of whom was hanging over the fireplace like he was a member of our family. I had vague recollections of the day he died. I must've been about seven. It was the summer holidays, and I'd been swimming with Adam at the baths on Picton Road. I'd got back for my tea and found the curtains drawn and Nan crying at the table, a glass of something on ice in her hand. I thought something must've happened to my mum or dad, or one of the neighbours. But then she put 'Love Me Tender' on the record player and told me the world would never be the same again.

'How was school?'

'Yeah, it was all right. Mandy Matthews has had her fella's name done as a tattoo on her thigh and her mum's gone mental.'

'I'm not surprised. She's far too young to be courting.'

Oh, I thought she'd have a problem with the tattoo. I should have known.

'She's fifteen, Nan,' I pointed out. 'Same as me.'

'Exactly. She's still a baby. How are your oven chips?'

'Bit burnt.'

'Sorry about that. I got a phone call, so I had to nip out.'

It was a source of intense frustration for me that I was the only person I knew who didn't have a phone in their house. A neighbour, Sue Overtheroad, took calls for my nan and called her over if it was urgent. The doorbell would go, and you'd hear Sue's voice: 'Nora? Phone!' And off Nan would dash, dropping everything as if she'd been summoned to meet the Pope. And we were Church of England. Cigarettes were left burning in ashtrays, visiting friends were abandoned mid-sentence – and, in this case, oven chips were left to blacken in the Smeg.

That was another source of embarrassment. Nan never called the oven the oven. She called it the Smeg. And round our way, Smeg was a really rude word. I'd not actually any idea what it meant, because it caused such fits of giggles, and I definitely didn't want to appear naive or thick by questioning its definition, so I just laughed along, going, 'I know. Smeg! What's she like?!' And to make matters worse, our oven wasn't even a Smeg oven. They'd've been far too posh for the likes of us, but Nan had heard someone on the telly referring to her oven as her Smeg, and thought it was just a posh word for cooker.

I'd lived with my nan for as long as I could remember. My mum had left when I was only a few months old, supposedly to start a new life in Australia with her 'fancy piece', but I'd never known whether to believe this or not. Maybe she just didn't like the look of me. Or maybe Nan – my dad's mum – interfered too much, and she'd had enough. There was no way I could ever find out. She'd just disappeared into the ether. My dad was away a lot. What we had to say, if anybody asked, was that he was working the oil rigs in the North Sea. But it was common knowledge round our way that in fact he was in and out of prison. I was always spared the details, and Nan would often talk about the perishing icy waters and how he was getting on. But I heard too much talk not to know otherwise. Plus there was always Adam. He knew all the local goss, because his mum ran the sweet shop. And if you worked in the sweet shop, you heard *everything*.

Some nights I lay in bed, screwing my eyes so tight they hurt, trying to conjure up a memory of my mum. Many came, but I knew each one was an invention. A wisp of blonde curls, the smell of a fresh perfume, elegant piano fingers brushing the handle of my pram, all invented. Easier to remember was my dad: the handsome Jack the Lad who only looked like a kid himself. I recalled his dimples, his rockabilly quiff, held tight with shiny Brylcreem – a half-used tub still sat on the window ledge in the bathroom. Hands like baseball gloves. And the gentle rise and fall of his soft Liverpool lilt. I tried to picture him with my mum. I saw nothing.

A new TV programme had recently started called *Surprise Surprise*. (Though Nan called it '*Surprise surprise, Cilla's still got a Liverpool accent*'.) Before it aired, they ran adverts on the telly asking people to come forward if they wanted to trace members of their family they'd lost touch with. Before I could even open my mouth to say, 'Hey, I could try and find my mum!' Nan fixed me with a steely stare and said:

'Don't even think about it, Kathleen. She was a bad 'un, a wrong 'un. She'll bring nothing but pain to your life, believe you me.'

And then she switched over to *All Creatures Great And Small*. And laughed as the ancient vet who we were meant to think was young and swarthy got pulled around by a cow in a field of dung. All over again.

'Have you got any homework tonight, love?'

'English. But I said I'd go round to Adam's to do it.'

She could see I was wolfing the egg and chips down, desperate to get over there.

'You've got yolk on your nose.'

'Oh.' I wiped it away with my sleeve. This often happened. My nose was, let's just say, a bit on the big side. Some of the nastier kids said that when I stood in front of the sun, there was an eclipse. Others shouted, 'Put your torches on, Kathleen's walking down the street!' I just tried to let it wash over me. But it was hard.

'And anyway, you can't go just yet. I've got you a lime mousse for your pudding.'

Sometimes finishing Nan's meals was like finishing a marathon. And by that I didn't mean the chocolate bar.

'Great.'

I scraped up the last blobs of egg yolk with the less burnt chips I'd saved till the last – always save the best till last with food – revealing the familiar painting of Jesus looking quite confused on the cross, as well he might be. I jumped up to wash my dishes.

'I'll do that, love,' Nan said kindly. It always worked. If I wanted her to wash up I just had to start it myself. If I didn't offer, she'd be all, 'Those plates won't wash themselves, Kathleen.'

'Get your lovely lime mousse out of the fridge. I'll get Jesus clean. I got John the Baptist, look.'

She pointed to the draining board, where her now clean plate was drying. It featured a man with a bubble perm coming out of what looked like a municipal swimming pool, but was probably a lake. I was never sure the artwork on Nan's plates was really that good.

I went to the fridge and yanked open the door, bending over to peer in. I saw no mousse. 'There's no mousse in here, Nan.'

'There is. There on the top shelf.'

I looked. On the top shelf sat a plastic holder with a grid on the front and green gunk behind it. I pulled it out. It had 'Glade Homefresh' emblazoned on the back of it.

'Nan, this isn't lime mousse. It's lime-scented air freshener.'

'Is it?'

'Yeah.'

'Oh God. That'll teach me to go shopping without my specs on. I bet the fridge smells nice.'

I sniffed. 'Mm. Dead limey.'

'Sure you can't eat it?'

'Positive, Nan.'

And she made a disappointed sound. A bit like when she thought *Prisoner: Cell Block H* was on, but she'd got the wrong night.

It was safe to say Nan was not the best cook in the world.

Though that's not to say that she never tried to be experimental. She did. I'll never forget the night I came home from school and she announced we'd be having Pisa (she meant pizza): how she took great delight in theatrically drawing the grill pan out of the oven, only to reveal that not only had she grilled the frozen pizzas, but she'd left the plastic wrapping on as well.

Today, however, the upside of not having any pudding meant I could get round to Adam's quicker than I'm imagined. I threw a few school books in a plastic bag, along with my make-up bag, and went out.

The street I grew up in felt like the longest street in the world. Stand at one end of Alderson Road and you could only just make out the other end. On hot days the horizon seemed to bubble away like a mirage. We lived at 357 and we were only halfway down, that'll give you an idea of how long it was. Although the length made it feel, to me at least, extraordinary, it was undeniably very ordinary. Identikit red-brick terrace after red-brick terrace punctuated by religiously named streets, side alleys, the occasional more modern building where a bomb had dropped in the war; it was a street full of colour and noise. Walking along the pavements you could see into everyone's front rooms, and almost touch them – a walk down Alderson Road was a treat for the senses. You smelt a different dinner every four paces, heard a different TV show too. The wallpaper and furniture flashed by like someone flicking a deck of cards, each one more garishly coloured than the last. Front doors were open with kids dashing in and out, phones rang, kettles whistled, voices rowed, voices laughed, babies cried and dogs whined and barked. It was the place that I called home.

Our biggest claim to fame was that a few years previously

Alderson Road had been featured in the TV series *Boys from the Blackstuff*, as they'd filmed an episode in one of the houses. A camera crew had moved in and the family who lived there, rumour had it, had been sent to live in the poshest hotel in Liverpool for a few weeks, the Adelphi. This had caused quite a bit of jealousy on the street. Nan had said, 'Blimey, if they send you to live in the Adelphi they can film what they like in ours.' But then when the series had come out and the episode had shown a family living below the breadline, Nan had claimed, 'No wonder they didn't want to film in our place. We're a cut above.' Even though we weren't.

I couldn't wait to get round to Adam's because he'd been saving for ages and ages and ages and had finally bought himself the Alison Moyet LP that had been in the charts for a looooong time but none of us thus far had been able to afford. We were going to lounge around on bean bags, just the two of us, doodling and chatting, and him giving me advice on my make-up while we listened to *Alf*.

The other thing we were going to do, and he'd told me this earlier that day in Geography while Mrs Maneers was having an asthma attack, was he was going to unveil some Very Important News about this year's nativity play. One thing that we did together, apart from being in the same class at school and being best mates, was we were both members of the local church choir. I know that doesn't sound trendy or cool, and it wasn't something we'd broadcast massively, but we enjoyed ourselves and treated it as one big excuse to have a laugh. We went to the local protestant church, St Thomas's, which had a congregation of about three and a vicar, Mr English, who was on his last legs. If he took too long a pause in his sermon we always had to peer round to the pulpit just to check he hadn't gone and died on us. The church itself was a few streets away from Alderson Road on some wasteland left over from the war – which the council were always trying to buy, but the church remained steadfast in its opposition. Even if the numbers in the choir outnumbered those in the pews. Sometimes I wanted to leave the choir, but I knew I would miss my Sundays spent with Adam. And besides, even though she rarely went to church herself, my nan would never have sanctioned it.

Dorothy's Sweet Shop sat on the corner of Alderson and Cardigan Road. Or as the locals called it, Cardy Road. Although it was called a sweet shop and sold a zillion old-fashioned sweets in row upon row of quaint Victorian jars, it was also a newsagent's, and as such was open all the hours God sent.

I pushed the door open. The shop was empty but for Adam's mum Dorothy sat behind the counter, curlers in, engrossed in a well-thumbed copy of *Flowers in the Attic*, a half-chewed liquorice shoelace hanging from her mouth.

'Hiya Dorothy!' I called as I barged through to the back of the shop and the door that led up to Adam's flat.

'Hi Kathleen. How's your nan?'

'She's great.'

'Oh good.' Dorothy sounded relieved, as if Nan's life had been hanging in the balance, and even though I knew that Nan would, at some point today, have been into the shop to pick up a couple of pints of milk. And Dorothy, although conveying a keen interest in the welfare of my nan, hadn't looked up from her book once. The hand that wasn't holding her book reached up and adjusted her bra strap. She then looked like she'd remembered something important.

'Hey. Kathleen,' she said, like I'd just walked in and this was a new conversation.

'What?'

'Is your dad home again?'

'No. Why?'

'Oh. No reason.'

But she looked like she did have a reason – why else would she say anything so bizarre? How could my dad be back? If he was back, he'd be home with me. And he wasn't.

'Why, Dorothy?'

'Oh, something and nothing.'

'Like what?'

'Someone said they'd seen him on the wasteland the other day. I said it was probably just someone who looked like him.'

I wished I could find someone who looked like my dad. That sounded kind of nice.

'No. He's not back.'

Dorothy nodded. 'Doppelganger, then.'

What was she talking about German sausages for?

'That book any good, Dorothy?' I asked, trying to steer her away from her new-found fresh meat obsession.

She slammed the book on the counter, like she was glad to be back on dry land, talking about something she was an expert on. 'Oh, Kathleen, it's incredible. It's about these four kids locked up in an attic by their wicked grandmother.'

'Realistic, then.' The sarcasm in my voice was obvious.

'Well. Between you, me and the gatepost . . . it's only what they say goes on at 53 Cardy Road.'

'Really?'

'Oh, yeah. No-one's seen the granddad for years. Rumour has it, her with the hatchet face keeps him locked up upstairs coz he's gone doolally.'

'D'you think it's true?'

'I hear moaning of a night sometimes. You know, I sleep

something terrible, Kathleen. And if it's a hot night and I've got the sash up, it's amazing what I can hear in the early hours. Did you know we've got foxes living round here?'

'Really?'

'They cry. In the night. And they sound like dead babies.'

'What do dead babies sound like?'

'Foxes.'

'But don't dead . . . babies . . . or people . . . don't they just . . . not make any noise?' I was confused. As well I might be.

'Well, you'd think, wouldn't you?' Dorothy looked like she was confused now. 'But as I always say, Kathleen . . .'

'Aha?'

'It all goes on round here, I'm telling you.'

And then she picked the book up again, licked her forefinger, flicked a page brusquely and carried on reading. Which I took to be her way of saying this conversation was over.

Nan said Dorothy's gossip was always right. Could Dad really be out of prison? No. No way. Like she said, it was someone who looked like him. But were that family on Cardy Road keeping their granddad locked up in the attic because he'd lost the plot? How would they benefit from this?

Nan often said I was prone to flights of fancy. I struggled, usually, to understand what this meant. But as I left the shop and climbed the narrow staircase to the flat above, I wound myself up into a dramatic frenzy that less than twenty feet away from us, a man was being held hostage against his will. Oh my giddy aunt! What if it was my *dad*?! The thought was too much to bear. By the time I hit the top step I practically kicked the door in and stumbled into the flat, screaming, 'Oh my God I can't breathe I'm so SCARED!'

Only to discover that Adam wasn't on his own.

I really did think that I'd fall into the kitchen and have Adam rush to my rescue, wondering what on earth was wrong. He would hold me up as I staggered to the nearest chair as I gasped for breath and explained that a major international crime was being committed under our very noses. He would mop my fevered brow, pour me a medicinal Vimto and debate with me whether we needed to phone the police or not, or stage a rescue bid, before deciding against it and agreeing that there was probably a very good reason to keep someone locked up in an attic and that, weighing everything up, we probably weren't at risk of being kidnapped by this nameless family and fed to him in bite-size chunks.

But none of this happened, because Adam wasn't alone. He was with Jocelyn.

'Conky! What's the matter?' she gasped, her hands outsplayed on the table as Adam painted her nails a garish shade of green.

I recovered well. I didn't know Jocelyn well enough to be overly dramatic in front of her. I also didn't like her calling me Conky. It was my nickname at school, short for Concorde, because of my stupidly big nose. Adam called me it sometimes, forgetting it hurt me, and she'd picked up on it. I was sure she didn't mean anything nasty by it, but it still stung all the same. I guessed it was one of those nicknames that just tripped off the tongue once you'd said it a few times. Conky. It could sound quite sweet, if you didn't know what it meant.

'Oh . . . nothing,' I said, hoisting myself to my feet by gripping the wall, as if I'd not said my previous sentence. Crisis? What crisis?!

Adam and Jocelyn looked at me, bewildered. Adam cocked his head towards a spare seat at the kitchen table, and I quietly slid into it. I knew I was in for a disappointing night. Ever since Jocelyn had moved to the area, Adam had only had eyes for her.

'Adam's doing my nails,' Jocelyn pointed out, as if I was stupid and had never seen nail varnish applied before.

'Yeah, I can see that.' And I have to admit, I didn't sound that impressed when I said it. But I couldn't help it. Like Nan often said, I always wore my heart on my sleeve. If I sounded surly, it's because that's how Jocelyn made me feel.

Adam and I had been best friends since our first day of nursery together. He'd pushed me off the rocking horse and made me hold his clackers for him while he had a ride. And for some reason, I thought he was great. I followed him round like a doe-eyed fan, and that pattern had pretty much continued to this day. I had high hopes that one day he'd ask me out. He was the perfect boy really, and so unlike all the others in our school. He could dance, he knew all the words to Madonna's *Like a Virgin* album and he was really good at helping you choose accessories to go with your clothes. And, as he was demonstrating tonight, he was really good at applying your make-up and nail varnish for you.

What more could a girl want?

Well. Sex, according to Melinda McCorrigan in our class. She was the most 'experienced' girl in our school because she reckoned she'd done it loads of times in her mum's back bedroom now she was working nights at the petrol station. Whether I actually believed her was another thing, as her descriptions seemed wildly exaggerated. ('When he came it was like Mount Vesuvius erupting. It drenched the back yard coz I'd left the window open. The gnomes looked like they'd had wax poured on them.' And 'It was so big, when I climbed on board my topknot kept hitting the ceiling.')

That kind of thing didn't appeal to me. Firstly, I'd never be able to get away with having a lad back to the house, never mind in my bedroom, or my nan's back bedroom, because if ever anyone came round she would police the visit like a royal bodyguard with sniffer dogs. And secondly, I had decided that I wasn't going to have sex until I was married. I just didn't like the sound of it. I couldn't bear the idea of passing wind in front of a lad, never mind showing him my downstairs doodahs. It filled me with horror. And it's what the Bible preached, according to our vicar, so what was wrong with waiting a wee while?

Another reason Adam seemed like ideal boyfriend material to me was that he had never made any physical advances towards me. All the lads at school would try and have a quick grope in the dinner queue, pretending they were reaching out for a tray or some cutlery, but Adam just wasn't like that. See what I mean? Perfect.

And he had a really high descant voice when he was singing in the choir.

I mean, a lot of the lads at school called him a fruit, and a queg, and a bum bandit and a turd burglar. But I just reckoned they were jealous because he had so many girl friends. He couldn't be any of those things. Why else would he have had posters of a near-naked Madonna all over his bedroom walls?

Some people were so stupid.

If I'm honest, the only reason I really joined the church choir was because he was in it. He loved the drama of it. As the choir was so small he loved being an outspoken, lone male voice in it, and he bossed the vicar about something rotten. I found him very funny, and clever, and he brought me out of my shell more than anyone else did. I could be prone to being quiet, but he inspired in me a confidence to be a bit bolder than I would usually. I thought the world of him, and he did me. That is, until Jocelyn arrived on the scene.

Jocelyn's family had moved to Alderson Road a few months previously from the Wirral, where Jocelyn and her sisters still went to school. Nan instantly took against them, as she remembered Jocelyn's mum from when she'd lived here years back. At first I just put that down to racism: we were a very white street, and people were so scared of anything 'different'. Jocelyn seemed nice, and stylish. She always had the latest fashions, really nice trainers. But Nan scoffed.

'Her mum probably nicked them. Single-parent family, see?' she said one day when we had Adam over for his tea. (Gammon and peas, with a fried egg on top. No chips.)

'But we're a single-parent family,' I argued.

'Your poor mother had a breakdown,' she groaned, like the memory stung her. It was the excuse she rattled out whenever we had company. Even though she must have known that Adam was more than aware of the truth. 'Her slut of a mother couldn't keep a man if she was covered in bastard superglue. Oh, and now she's made me swear. Honestly. You keep away from them. The McKenzies are trouble. And their name's Scotch. Even worse.'

Which made me want to hang out with her even more.

'Her mum works four jobs, you know, Nora,' Adam pointed out. He was the only person under eighteen who could get away with calling my nan by her first name. Honestly, he could charm the birds from the trees.

'Doing what?' I enquired.

'Cleaning a bank before breakfast. Then she's a nurse up the hospital. Then she cleans someone's house of an evening. And then she has a small business on the side.'

'Bloody hell!' I said. 'She's a grafter.'

'She's on the make. And don't swear!' Nan snarled. 'You don't know half the things her mam got up to when she used to live round here. I was glad to see the back of her. No man was safe. Wanting to dip their biscuit in the chocolate pot.'

Adam and I looked quickly to each other, then away, trying hard not to laugh.

Jocelyn was an enigma on the street as she didn't go to the local school like me and Adam, having instead to catch several buses to go over the Mersey to a private school on the Wirral every day, which we thought was the height of sophistication.

'Don't you find that Jocelyn a bit snooty?' Nan continued.

'No, she's dead nice, Nora,' Adam argued. 'It's her adenoids.'

'We've all got adenoids, Adam. It's just some of us like to keep it quiet.'

Nan had a point. Jocelyn did seem to look down her nose at everyone, though Dorothy had suggested this could be an indicator of having an adenoid problem. Apparently if you had one of those you had to hold your head back all the time, which gave the impression that you were standoffish and literally looking down your nose at everyone. None of us had had the nerve to ask Jocelyn if it was true, though she did always sound like she had a cold coming.

Anyway. Here we were: in Adam's kitchen, above the sweet shop. And he was applying varnish to Jocelyn's nails.

'Adam's got some news,' Jocelyn said, lifting one hand to her mouth and blowing on it. I looked to Adam, who wriggled in his seat, beaming with pride.

'About the nativity play?' I said, trying to show off to Jocelyn that I was already kind of in on the goss. Adam nodded, and I felt a pang of jealousy that Jocelyn already seemed to know what the announcement was.

'I've written it. It's amazing. And I showed it to Mr English, and he's greenlit the production.'

'So proud of you, Bubaloo!' cried Jocelyn, in a voice that made her sound like she was in pain. 'High five for Adam!' And they high-fived.

Adam had shown an interest in being literary for a while now. He loved writing essays in English lessons, the more outrageous the better, and he'd won the school poetry competition with his (to my mind incomprehensible) poem about Greenham Common. I knew he'd been working hard for the last few weeks refining his new masterpiece *How Far Is It to Bethlehem?* and I knew he hoped to stage the play during the Christmas service next month. I was also rather hopeful that he'd cast me and him as Mary and Joseph; he'd hinted as much a few weeks ago, during a mooch round the shops in town one Saturday. He'd even suggested asking to borrow the baby from the family who lived next door to him, to play Baby Jesus.

'Who's playing Mary?' I asked, a little too desperately.

'I'm going to hold auditions,' he replied – which wasn't the answer I was expecting.

'That seems fair,' Jocelyn butted in. 'I mean, if you want it to be good, you may as well get the best person for the job. Is it a singing part?'

Adam nodded. 'It's a musical. That's why it's taken me so long to write.'

'Fuck. How long did it take?'

I didn't like it when Jocelyn used the 'f' word. Nan said it was unladylike.

'Three and a half weeks.'

'That's so long!' I gasped.

'I know.'

This was the first time Adam had mentioned he'd written

the nativity as a musical. No wonder it had taken him so long to create. In that moment, my hope disappeared faster than a Wagon Wheel from my nan's biscuit tin.

You see, the thing with Jocelyn was – and everyone agreed on it – she was an exceptionally gifted singer. Well, I say everyone. Her voice was a bit Shakin' Stevens for me. Not that she sounded like him; it's just that whenever she belted it out, she did that shaking thing with her voice. She called it 'vibrato' and said it was an established singing style. I just thought it sounded like she was really straining on the toilet. Adam thought it made her sound like Mahalia Jackson, but I didn't know who that was. (Maybe Michael Jackson's mum?) I also thought it ruined the sound of our modest church choir, as her voice drowned out the rest of us put together. I was fair to middling and could certainly hold a tune, but as Adam often complained, my voice was wafer-thin. And next to Jocelyn, I just looked like I was miming.

'Are there any non-singing parts?' I ventured.

'Yeah.' He sounded enthusiastic. 'Abigail-Jade's mum, and the Archangel Gabriel.'

Jocelyn smiled encouragingly. 'And Kathleen, they've both got really big noses.'

I had that sinking feeling that this was going to be a long night. Why did Jocelyn have to spoil everything?

To cheer myself up, and feel like I was somewhat in the driving seat, I changed the subject: 'So are we going to listen to *Alf*?'

'We listened a bit before you got here,' said Jocelyn, like I was an inconvenience, and that was the end of it. And I wanted to say, 'Oh, really? And tell me, Jocelyn. Has your mum had any odd phone messages recently?'

It was a matter of great excitement that Adam had recently

discovered that Jocelyn's mum had a thing in their house called an answering machine. Basically it meant that if she wasn't in when people phoned up, the machine would answer on her behalf and record any message that someone cared to leave. Then when she got in, she could listen to the messages and act accordingly. Bearing in mind my house didn't even have a phone in it, Adam and I thought this was hilariously space-age. Jocelyn's mum's 'small business on the side' was working as a saleswoman for a teasmade company, which is why she had to have the answering machine while she was out doing her other jobs. But unbeknownst to Jocelyn, Adam and I would often go to the phone box when we knew there was nobody in the house, and call and leave funny messages on the machine.

First up you'd hear Jocelyn's mum's voice saying – in her hilarious Sierra-Leone-meets-Liverpool accent – '*Hello. This is Wavertree Teasmades. We are not here right now. Please leave a short message after the tone.*'

And then she must have been looking for the right button to press, because there was a silence; then you heard her going, '*Where is it?*' And then you heard the beep. And I'd leave messages like:

'*Oh hello, Mrs McKenzie? I'd like to order three million teasmades. Please can you send them to Queen Elizabeth the Second at Buckingham Palace? There's a love.*'

We called them 'anonies', short for anonymous messages. We also left ones like:

'*Does your teasmade make coffee?*'

Or – our particular favourite, even though it had nothing to do with the making of tea:

'*Is Mr Wall there? Mrs Wall? Any Walls? Well, how does your bloody house stand up, then?*'

And each time, we would slam the phone down and wet ourselves with uproarious laughter.

But I couldn't say that to Jocelyn right now. It would betray a secret Adam and I had kept. And I liked that we had secrets from her. It made me feel more special to him than her. Even if at times, like now, I didn't feel I really was.

'Anyway,' Jocelyn continued, 'I wanna hear more about this lad. What was his name? Mark?'

I felt myself blush.

'Mark Reynolds,' says Adam.

WHAT?!?! Why? Why had he told her about Mark? MY Mark?

Oh, but wait. She was taking an interest. He'd told her there was this lad at school that I fancied, and he'd been really sweet about it, and now they were going to be encouraging and lovely, and I'd misjudged her. I smiled, and was about to say, 'Oh, he's a dreamboat,' even though I knew you weren't supposed to use words like dreamboat these days – but before I could even open my mouth, Jocelyn was continuing.

'It's so sweet you fancy him.'

And she said it in such a patronizing way.

'Oh, I know he's really out of my league. And he wouldn't look at me twice.'

'Ah, don't say that, Conky.'

Conky. There it was again.

'Adam says it's quite sweet, the way he talks to you.'

'What, like I don't deserve it?'

'No!' snapped Adam, 'Like he likes you. Like he fancies you. You've gotta start believing that lads'll fancy you.'

'And trust me, Kitty Kat –' if there was one thing that could annoy me more than Jocelyn calling me Conky, it was Jocelyn calling me Kitty Kat – 'some guys like a big conk.'

I felt like hitting her.

I didn't want her talking about Mark. Mark was my business, not hers. My crush, no-one else's. Part of me was annoyed that Adam had been discussing him with her, but another part was flattered that they found me interesting enough to talk about behind my back.

Mark was . . . well, I couldn't think of any other word for it. A complete dreamboat.

I knew that word made me sound like I was about ninety, or that this was the Fifties and I was wearing bobby socks, and not the bang-on-trendy Eighties and my up-to-the-minute leg warmers. OK, they were leg warmers that my nan had knitted me, but they were leg warmers all the same.

And I'd done my hair in a side ponytail like Adam had advised. He said that with that flapping about at the side of my face, it would draw attention away from my nose. I could see the sense in that, though any sudden movements meant I whipped myself with said ponytail.

I said the word again in my head: *dreamboat*. It was a word my nan often used, though admittedly in her case she mostly used it about Elvis Presley. And sometimes Cliff Richard. Or, as she called him, Cliff Richards.

I knew using that word made me sound like a sap. But I liked it, and I could think of none better. And if it sounded slushy, then so be it. That's how Mark Reynolds made me feel.

Mark wasn't in our class, he was in the year above; but I knew his timetable off by heart, and every crossover time between lessons was spent going the long way round to try and catch a glimpse of him on his route between classrooms. That was on a good day. The bad days were when I searched in vain and then discovered that he was off sick, or bunking off. I usually discovered this via my spy in his class, my cousin

Carmelita Isabella, whose mum, my aunty Pam, had a bit of a Spanish theme going on in her life. She'd done up her semi in Wavertree Garden Suburb like a Spanish villa, and had given her kids Spanishy names. As well as Carmelita, she had a son called Paolo. He preferred to be called Paul, but that was lads for you.

Anyway, Carmelita was aware of my obsession and was very quick to whisper, every time she approached, 'He's on his way!' or 'Bad news. He's off sick!', which could bring a black cloud to the rest of my day. Adam was the perfect partner for these 'let's bump into Mark' adventures, and he always seemed to get just as excited as me. Heaven knew why.

Mark might only have been sixteen, but he seemed to be all man. He shaved, he walked with the swagger of a cowboy, and he had LOVE and HATE biro'd on his knuckles, freshly applied each day. He had a dusting of freckles over his nose and cheeks, green eyes and hair the colour of gravy. Ah, Bisto! It was styled in the perfect wedge, that went up and down in length, depending on the time of the month. Oh, it wasn't to do with some sort of male menstrual cycle; it's just he seemed to get it cut near the beginning of each month, which is when his ears would stick out like taxi doors, but as the wedge descended it at first tickled, then more or less covered them, and I loved trying to second-guess when he'd next be going back to the barber's. Carmelita Isabella had found out that he favoured Bracey's Barber's on Smithdown Road, and so I always took a detour if I was anywhere near there of a weekend, but thus far I had never seen him in one of their adjustable chairs.

'There is always the chance that your Carmelita's full of shite,' Adam pointed out, whenever he accompanied me.

There was that. But I didn't quite believe it.

What Mark might ever see in me, I didn't know. In fact, I couldn't in a million years imagine him fancying me. But Adam said it wasn't out of the question, so we needed to keep up our surveillance. So hope beat eternal in this young girl's heart. And some!

Ideally I would have liked a combination boyfriend. The looks of Mark, and the personality of Adam. Because – I had to be honest – I didn't really know what Mark's personality was like. He'd not really spoken to me that much. And even though Carmelita assured me he 'wasn't a knob, like some lads', I hadn't really had experience of that first-hand.

Because he was in fifth form, I knew he'd been at school all the time that I'd been there, but I couldn't remember any bolt-from-the-blue lightning flash happening the first time I saw him. But I'd never forgotten the first time he'd spoken to me.

It was nearly Christmas now, and I'd first spoken to Mark back in April. A lot of the schools in Liverpool had decided to go on strike. I'm not talking the teachers here, I'm talking the students. I didn't really know what the strike was about. Well, I kind of did, but as with my lack of knowledge about Smeg, I didn't want to really show myself up by asking, 'What are we doing this for again?' I knew we were protesting about the cuts to education that Maggie Thatcher had made, and I knew that everyone was fuming about the YTS stuff that you had to do when you left school. The kids who organized the strike and the demo in town said that going on a Youth Training Scheme was just a ruse to keep unemployment figures down, and for businesses to get young kids to work for them as slave labour. But I actually thought going on a YTS might not be that bad actually, especially if you could do it somewhere really interesting like on a movie set in Hollywood, or a theatre, or a nice hairdresser's. Adam said it didn't really apply to us because we were going to London to seek our fame and fortune, but at the same time we didn't want to appear to be scabs and be the only two kids who turned up at school that day, so we treated it as a good excuse to go into town and have a look round the shops. And if we felt like meandering down to the Pier Head at lunchtime to hear some speeches, we always had that option.

So there we were, casually strolling down Bold Street because Adam wanted to look at the bohemian postcards in the Medici Gallery – when suddenly we head the *whoosh* of tyres, and we were nearly cut up by a lad on a BMX bike. He whizzed past us and then jammed his brakes on, so hard he nearly went arse over tit over his handlebars. He looked round, and we saw that it was Mark.

'Are yous going to the demo?' he snarled, like it was an ultimatum.

''Course!' Adam said, in an unusually high voice. It was like he was nervous.

Mark nodded. 'Nice one. I'll walk with yous.'

Oh God. There was no getting out of it now. Although, it had to be said, neither of us seemed to mind. Mark dawdled along at our pace, not getting off his BMX but slowly pushing himself along, feet on the ground as he spouted forth about 'the revolution' and 'Militant know what they're doing' and 'Neil Kinnock needs a good slap' and 'Thatcher's such a knob, lar.' And of course we found ourselves nodding along like the dogs in the back of cars because, it had to be said, there was something quite mesmeric about Mark Reynolds. Adam wouldn't walk past the Medici for just anyone. He certainly had the gift of the gab. There wasn't much need for us to do any talking, as he filled all the airtime and any gaps, but at one point Adam piped up with,

'Yeah I think it's sickening how Thatcher is systematically destroying the working class of this country. And all that.'

Which I was really impressed by, as I'd never heard him speak like that before. Was he trying to impress Mark? And if so, why? He'd never seemed that bothered with any of the other lads in school, preferring to hang out with me all the time.

About fifteen minutes later we arrived at the Pier Head. Usually this place was a dump: a boring space between the ferry terminal and the Liver Buildings, covered in pigeon poop, and smelling of doughnuts from the manky cafe by the ferry ticket office. But today the place was completely transformed. I'd never seen anything like it.

Mark punched the air and screamed, '*Power to the people!*' – which admittedly was a little bit cringeworthy, and me and Adam shot each other a look of mortification, but you could see why he was doing it. The area was absolutely crammed full of teenagers with banners and placards. There must have been thousands of them there. I instinctively wanted to step back. I found that amount of braying kids scary, like being in the biggest school playground in the world. It was as if every school in Liverpool had merged into a massive whole. And I wasn't sure I wanted to be jostled by the throng. Mark seemed to sense that Adam was feeling that way too, and saved our bacon.

'Would you mind my bike for me, while I get nearer the stage?'

''COURSE!' we both screamed with relief.

And that was that. We stayed at the edges of the crowd while everyone listened to the speakers from the council, one after another, treating it like a proper day out. We took turns to ride Mark's bike round in small circles, me particularly savouring sitting on something so personal to him. Adam was hard to get off it too, mind. And Mark was so grateful afterwards, he offered to buy us both chips. Well. It would've been rude to say no.

'So how did you first meet the lovely Mark?'

Sometimes when Jocelyn spoke, I couldn't tell if she was being patronizing or nice. She had had elocution lessons, and didn't care that she sounded a bit posher than us, she seemed to enjoy playing on the fact that she went to a private school. I think it was what attracted Adam to her, how exotic she was, although he always swore blind to me he didn't actually fancy her.

'What, because she's black?' I remember asking.

'No! Because she's . . . oh, you know!'

I didn't know. But I imagined he just meant because she was Jocelyn, different from everyone else on our street.

And so Adam and I took turns in relaying the story of the day of the strike. Jocelyn looked horrified.

'God, I remember that. That was before I moved back here. Our Head swore that if any of us went on the march we'd be completely expelled. And I couldn't do that to my mum. It sounded horrendous, was it?' She actually looked scared.

And so I went on, into a few flights of fancy about how fantastic it had been. I made it sound biblical. I made it sound like it was the Eurovision Song Contest and Live Aid rolled into one. She actually started to look jealous. I got a bit carried away. And when I described how Bruce Springsteen had come on stage and started singing 'Dancing in the Dark' and had pulled me out of the crowd to dance with him like that girl in the video, Jocelyn misread my over-enthusiasm for mickey-taking and went into a sulk. The only way Adam could get her to snap out of it was by getting her to sing for us.

I braced myself. Jocelyn loved the sound of her own warbling voice. I looked around to make sure there weren't any lightweight ornaments on shelves that might bounce off and smash, but before I could do a complete check, Jocelyn broke into a 'soulful' rendition of 'Love on the Rocks', eyes tightly closed, and I tried not to laugh. I looked to Adam, expecting him to be wetting himself. But actually he was transfixed. When she finished we both applauded her, but just then we heard Adam's mum calling up from the shop below.

'What the fuck was that?! You'll scare the friggin' horses!'

After which, a downbeat Jocelyn made her excuses and left.

'You've got to start being nicer to her. She likes you. She's your friend,' Adam said, like he was telling me off. But not in a nasty way – in a disappointed parent sort of way.

'Well, she needs to stop calling me Conky, then.'

'Conky's not that bad.'

'It is to me! How would you like it if I called you . . . called you . . .' I scrabbled around to find a distinguishing feature that might upset him.

And then I remembered: he'd once told me he had a third nipple.

'If I called you Three Tits.'

To which he burst out crying, told me to fuck off, and pushed me unceremoniously out of the door. I nearly fell down the stairs to the shop. Just in time to hear Dorothy turning a page of her book, gasping and muttering, 'The dirty bastards!'

I scarpered.

Jocelyn was coming out of Mr Wong's on the corner of Jesmond Street as I walked home. She was picking at a bag of scraps. I smiled politely, and she offered the bag to me. I turned my nose up at it.

'I don't really like scraps.'

She looked nonplussed then said, 'And why don't you like me, Kathleen?'

Her directness wrong-footed me. But then, that was Jocelyn in a nutshell: she seemed not to care what people thought of her no-nonsense approach. I'd have been too scared of the answers to ask questions like that.

'I do like you. Don't be daft.'

'I hope so,' she said, sounding worried.

And actually, it felt nice. It felt like she wasn't being snobby or patronizing. It didn't feel like she was laughing at me now. It felt like she was being the vulnerable one for a change. And, much as I really wanted to take advantage of this and be a bit arsey back to her, I found I couldn't be.

'I do. I tell you what I don't like, though.'

'What's that?'

'The way you go on about my nose all the time.'

'I don't.'

'You do. You called me Conky tonight when I walked in. And you said I'd be OK playing those parts in the nativity play coz they're meant to have massive noses.'

'God, did I? I don't realize I'm doing it half the time.'

'Right.'

'To be honest with you, Kathleen. I've never noticed your nose being big. It's just . . . Adam said you had a complex about it, so . . .'

'Did he?'

'Yeah. So I was just trying to make you feel better about it.'

I wasn't quite convinced by that argument, but still, she was being civil with me.

'I get called all sorts,' I went on, 'Captain Beaky, The Eagle Has Landed, Pinocchio, Nostrildamus. You name it, I've been called it.' I thought she might laugh, but was impressed when she didn't.

'Well, anyway, I'm a fine one to talk. I've got a real African nose. It's wider than this street, look.' And she held her face at an angle, and giggled. And I dared giggle too.

'I hate it,' she said.

'But it suits you,' I said.

'It's a man's nose,' she said. 'And I've got man's hands, look.' She spread out the hand that wasn't holding the bag from the chippy. 'I could be a goalie,' she said, and again we laughed.

'A goalie with nail varnish!'

'I want to be your friend, Kathleen,' she said solemnly. 'I don't have many friends. All the girls at the posh school live on the Wirral. And everyone else round here won't talk to me coz they think I'm a snob. So I'm caught between the devil and the deep blue sea, really.'

And in that moment, I did finally feel sorry for her. 'Can't be easy,' I said.

She shrugged.

'Walk you home?'

She nodded, and we walked off down the street together.

'What's the posh school like?'

'All right. I'd rather go to yours, though. It's just that Mum says that I have to work twice as hard and be twice as good as white people in order to get on. And I kind of think she has a point.'

'Really?'

'You'll never realize how easy you've got it.'

'Doesn't really feel that easy. At least you've got a mum.'

'Oh yeah. Sorry. Well, at least you're not little orphan Annie.'

'Well, no.'

'I mean, your dad's still alive, isn't he?'

'True. Though where he is, God only knows.'

We'd just stopped outside her house. She stopped eating her scraps and looked at me like there was something she wanted to say. What? Was she going to invite me in? Was she about to take our friendship to the next level? She opened her mouth to speak, but as she did I heard a screech of tyres and turned to see Mark coming along on his bike. I leaned in to Jocelyn.

'Oh my God – don't look now, but that's Mark!'

'You're joking!'

I was hoping he wouldn't see me. I wasn't looking my best, and my nose was feeling particularly humongous after discussing it half the night. My side ponytail had slipped as well. Thank God it was dark.

But he did see me. And he squelched his brakes on and stopped outside Jocelyn's house.

'All right, Kathleen?'

'Oh, hiya, Mark. Didn't see you there.'

Which he could tell was complete tripe.

'Who's your mate?'

'Oh, this is Jocelyn. She goes to the posh place on the Wirral.'

'All right for some. All right, Jocelyn? What makes you travel all the way over there?'

Jocelyn paused for a second, then said one word: 'Oppression.'

Then she turned on her heel and went inside. As the door slammed, I looked at Mark and realized my mouth had dropped open. He was looking at the door. He was looking where she had been. I couldn't tell if he was impressed or offended.

'Is she dead political?' he asked. He sounded completely fascinated, and slightly smitten. Another cause for him to get his teeth into.

I had to nip this one in the bud. I couldn't have Mark, Mr Politics, thinking Jocelyn was more political than me, so I quickly shook my head. 'She's a massive Tory, Mark. I don't know why I hang round with her.'

He looked incredulous. 'You're joking!'

I shook my head. 'No, Mark. It's like knocking about with . . . with . . .' I tried to think of a famous female conservative. My mind went blank.

'Adolf thingy!' I bleated. His eyes widened in horror.

'Hitler?'

'Yeah. Like a cross between him and Mrs Quinlan.'

'The geography teacher?' He looked repulsed. Good.

'I know. Actually, she makes Hitler look all right.'

'Jesus,' he said quietly.

I did this ladylike sigh and put my hand near my neck, like I'd seen posh women do in films when they'd had bad news. I thought it might impress Mark that I was genuinely upset. But he just shook his head sadly, then shoved his foot on one of his pedals and span off into the night.

I grimaced. But at least my little white lie had kept Mark all for myself. And then I found myself smiling, suppressing a laugh. Such a wicked, wicked girl!

London, 2015

I hadn't really wanted to come to the wake, but Adam was insistent. I can't think of anything worse than getting drunk with a load of strangers, but like Adam said, we knew Jocelyn longer than anyone. We should be there.

Should I be here, though? Have I any right to be here? Really? I know I saw her fifteen years ago. She kicked me out of her house.

But what if I've seen her since? What if I've seen her recently? What if I can't remember?

And what sort of person am I, who forgets things so easily?

No. I've not seen her. Of course I'd remember. Duh!

'Still not drinking? How long's that been now?' Adam asks on the way over.

I look at him like he's stupid. 'Oh, I've been back on it for a while now. Only in moderation. I'm in a really different place to where I was back then.'

'Oh, right.'

'No need to worry about me these days,' I say.

'Fine. Yeah. Great.' He sounds surprised, but has the manners to button it.

We're now in a pub a stone's throw from the Crem, and the atmosphere is strained to say the least. It's busy, but subdued by the nature of the party that's here. One concession to the other people propping up the bar is a large plasma-screen television showing some sport with the sound down. We find a table with three stools round it, and make ourselves comfy. It seems to have gone cooler now, thank God, and I'm now quite grateful for my faux fur trim, which has dried out beautifully during the service. Also, keeping my coat on gives the impression that I won't be staying long. Somehow this appeals to me. I rip open a packet of prawn cocktail crisps and plonk them in the middle of the table to share.

'Ooh, prawn cock, my fave,' Adam's boyfriend says in a really camp voice, and I smile politely. Even though he's raved about the flavour, he doesn't take one.

'Have one,' I say, pointing to the bag.

'Carb crash!' he pouts, frowning, so I shove a load more in my mouth. I see his eyes flick up and down my body. What is this? Judgement Day?

'So. What are you doing with yourself these days, Kathleen?' Adam asks, before taking a sip from a pint of Guinness.

Well, at least he's not continuing with the 'Do you think this is our fault?' theme he started at the Crem. I suppose I've got to be grateful for Jason's presence for that. Not the sort of stuff you want your partner to hear, presumably.

Actually, his boyfriend is looking bored out of his skull. Small talk is rarely interesting, particularly if you don't know the person making it.

'Sorry? I was miles away.' I'm busking it.

'What are you up to these days?'

I can't tell him the truth. What would I say? I want him to think everything has stayed fine in Kathleen's World, so I smile and lie and say I'm back at college studying again.

The boyfriend jumps in. 'That's brave!'

'How is it brave?'

'Well, aren't you the same age as Adam?'

'You're never too old to learn, Jason.' I'm impressed by my own belligerence. Especially as I'm speaking such twaddle.

Of course, I shouldn't be drinking this glass of white. This large glass of white. Jem, my therapist, would have a field day. I can just hear her droning on about triggers and self-destruction. But this is about self-medication. My friend has died. This is self-preservation. I didn't want to come to the pub; Adam and Jason press-ganged me. They practically forced this Pinot Grigio down my neck. They may as well have taken a massive funnel to my gob and poured it straight in.

Yes. You keep telling yourself that, Kathleen. Sometimes the tone of Jem's voice is that of a slow handclap.

'And what are you studying?' Jason's asking.

'Counselling,' I lie. 'Well, psychotherapy really,' I add, because that sounds better.

They both look impressed.

'You always were a good listener,' Adam says, as if my life is finally making sense. If only.

Well it's only a partial lie. I did do a little bit of counselling, a while back. Compared to some people – those who know nothing about it – I guess I'm a bit of an expert.

'Kathleen used to be a Samaritan,' Adam boasts to Jason.

'Shermazing,' he says, eyes wide. I can't abide people who say 'shermazing', but I keep that to myself.

I think it's time I left Jem. Things aren't that bad any more. When I don't drink, the anxiety disappears. But she'll never let me go. It's like she wants me to be dependent on her. I think she's brainwashed me into thinking I can't cope without her. Like that time I went to Yorkshire for a fort-night last summer and I informed her I'd have to miss two appointments, and I hoped that was all right. She'd insisted we continue our sessions on the phone each Friday morning. And I bloody agreed to it! Why did I do that? Why? She likes the sound of her own voice, that one.

Well. She likes the sound of her own silence, every now and again encouraging me to talk about my fuck-up of a life.

'Do you think I'm an alcoholic, Jem?' I asked last week.

'Do you?' she threw back at me, without even drawing breath.

What am I paying her money for? Do I have to decide everything for myself? Does she not have an original thought or opinion in her little Dutch head? I don't even know if she is Dutch, because she's one of those annoying therapists who doesn't give you the steam off her soup. The only thing I do know about her is that she's human. Though some might say that was debatable.

'I think I have a drink problem,' I remember I said. 'Inasmuch as drink is a problem for me from time to time.'

And then she gave me this patronizing head-tilt. As if to say, 'See? You're not as stupid as you make out.'

Jem. Is that a Dutch name? Her full name is Jem Pammenter-Fry. I thought she'd be good because she was double-barrelled. More fool me.

Jason is talking, and I realize I've not been concentrating.

'Sorry. I'm so sorry. Miles away again.'

I realize that I've knocked back half of my large wine, and they've only drunk a centimetre of their pints. I stop myself from taking another greedy gulp.

That's it. I'm not an alcoholic. I'm greedy. I must be. Look at the size of me.

'I was asking if you were seeing anyone at the moment?'

Does he know? Is that why he's asking? Does he know what a fuck-up I am, and he's rubbing it in?

'No. No-one at the moment.'

And I think of Harry Monroe. Tears in his eyes in the kitchen. Saying he can't do this any more. Saying I'd changed the rules and not told him. Saying I wasn't the same any more. Me screeching back, 'We all change!'

'Weren't you seeing a curator?' Adam asks.

I nod. 'From the Imperial War Museum.' How apt, I always think, when our relationship became such a war zone. 'But he was more interested in the Battle of the Somme than the battle for my heart.'

The chuckle, the response I was after. You see, I've planned saying this. It sounds so poetic, even if it's not strictly true. I reward my wordsmithery with a gulp of vino.

The first few sips of pub wine always taste like battery acid. After that, it's nectar from the Gods.

'His loss,' says Jason. Like he knows me. Like it could possibly be true. I can almost see Mark laughing in my face. One of those desperate laughs that people don't really do in life, just in movies, where the laugh is hysterical and eventually turns into guttural sobs. The sort of cry-laugh that wins Oscars.

'How did you hear about Jocelyn? Did you see it on the news?'

Adam nods quickly, then gabbles away, 'Anyway, have you heard our news?' he gasps, like everything we've said has been the preamble to this.

'No! What?!' I enthuse back.

He puts both hands on the table in a 'wait till you hear this' fashion. He shoots his other half a look. Jason widens his eyes briefly in a 'Oh go on, you SCREAM, you tell her' fashion. I think he's going to tell me a hilarious anecdote.

Instead he says, 'We've had a baby.'

'A what?!'

'Not a what!' he guffaws, rather irritatingly, 'a baby!'

'Is that humanly possible?'

'Well, he's not a baby,' butts in Jason, and Adam quickly agrees.

'Yeah, no. Not an actual *baby* as such. We've adopted a little boy. He's called Denim.'

'Denim?' I sound incredulous. They look stung.

'We had to keep the name he was given at birth.'

'Denim's a lovely name,' I lie, biting my tongue from adding, 'And a lovely bit of material. I have . . . many items of clothing made . . . of denim.'

Strangely, this appears to appease them. And they start showing me pictures on their phones of a pasty-looking skinny lad with ginger hair and John Lennon glasses, and they start filling me in on some rather inappropriate information about his birth mother and all her problems before moving on to how Denim is now flourishing in their care.

I'm a bad person. I still get a shock when gay people, particularly gay men, have kids. It's like when men describe their partners as their husbands. Again, it makes me a bad person, but it always makes me want to chuckle. It feels like they're showing off. Or wiping it in your face.

Oh God. I sound just like my nan.

'He's adorable,' I say, even though he's not really, but they beam with pride anyway. And then tell me some of his little quirks and foibles, and how he was scared of going upstairs when he first moved in. They make him sound like a puppy.

I'm impressed. They have a place in London with an upstairs. I'm about to ask where it is when I see Adam's eyes light up.

'Did you see Mark Reynolds on the news?' he says, suddenly all gossipy. I prefer him like this. It's like the old Adam, and I slip back into the old Kathleen too.

'I know. Isn't it amazing what's happened?'

'I know! I can't believe it! He's everywhere!'

'Like crabs!' And we giggle. Adam loves it when I'm near the knuckle. In that respect he taught me everything I know.

Jason tries to join in. 'Adam said you were at school with that idiot.'

'We were!' I laugh.

But before we can say anything else, a barmaid has come over to our table with an oval plate of sandwiches and is plonking them down with a curt, 'Can you move them glasses?' We oblige. I've finished the crisps on my own, so I scrunch the packet up and pop it in my pocket. Then, as she walks away, I see someone else advancing towards us. This man is about mine and Adam's age but looks older, due to a completely bald head. But there's something handsome about him, and he is very smartly dressed. He hold his hands out and says in a thin voice, choked with emotion, 'You must be Kathleen and Adam?'

How does he know?

'I'm Ross.'

Ah. The priest said in the eulogy that Ross is Jocelyn's partner. We stand and let him hug us, telling him how sorry we are for his loss.

I don't tell him that hitherto I only knew him as Mr Billericay, as that's how Jocelyn referred to him. Mr Billericay sounds so transient. Like Mr Chelsea and Westminster will be along any moment, just hang tight.

'How did you know what we looked like?' I'm curious to

know. We'd never met, and yet he was on us faster than flies on a buffet.

'She had a photo,' he says, pulling up another stool. 'In the living room. It's still there. So weird, talking about her in the past tense.'

Jocelyn had a picture of me up in her flat? How bizarre. But it makes me feel less guilty about our lack of contact in the intervening years.

'Of course, of course,' Adam says, sounding like Jem. Though she'd rarely be that positive or encouraging.

'Talked about you guys so much.'

Secretly I'm chuffed that the picture must be years old, before the weight gain, and yet he still recognizes me. I allow myself a congratulatory glug of wine for that.

It's then that I remember the phone call. The phone call that night from Jocelyn. The phone call where she mentioned Mr Billericay. Anxiety rises in me. I try to quell it with another sip. More dainty this time. It works. I relax. Jocelyn was always saying stupid things for attention. This man seems delightful.

But maybe everyone seems delightful at a funeral.

Actually, maybe this isn't Mr Billericay. I'd better check.

'Are you from Billericay?'

He nods.

'Yes, she told me. I've never been.' And then I pull a face, because that was such a rubbish thing to say. And he misreads my embarrassment for grief.

'I guess it's hit you hard,' he adds. And we nod. Even Jason nods, and they'd never met. Oh well. What can we say? Maybe he doesn't know all that went on between us. And now doesn't seem the time to tell him. We probably never will.

'If there's anything we can do . . .' Adam says. 'I mean, I'm sure there isn't. And I'm sure you have friends, but . . . well, if there's anything we can do . . .'

'Anything,' I butt in.

'Then do shout.'

'Yes, do. Anything. Shout.'

'There's an echo,' Adam says, joking. But I do find it quite unnecessary. Whose side is he on here? He had as fractious a relationship with Jocelyn as I did.

Ross nods. A humble nod of thanks. As if it's the most amazing thing anyone has ever said to him when, let's be honest, it's only what everyone says when someone has died. So much so that it feels like it doesn't mean anything. So I'm surprised when I hear him say,

'Actually, there might be something.'

'Sure,' says Adam, 'What is it?'

'What is it?' I add. A bit too late. I think I might be a bit drunk. How can that happen after half a glass of wine? Maybe Adam had a point, echo-wise.

'I'm feeling a bit . . . overwhelmed by all the stuff in her flat.'

'You didn't live together?' I'm surprised by that. I thought they did. I assumed they did.

He shakes his head. 'We liked to keep our independence.' He shrugs, like it sounds daft now. 'I could really do with a hand to go through it all.'

I wasn't sure what to say. He obviously thinks we were a lot closer than we were. He misreads my hesitation and Adam's for disinterest. 'I'm sorry. Was that inappropriate?'

'No,' says Adam.

'No!' I echo.

'I'm just thinking. It might be quite . . . cathartic for you to go through it in your own time,' Adam suggests. Which sounds good. Really good. Except, for a second there, I was quite looking forward to rifling through Jocelyn's stuff. Not just in some morbid way of seeing what she owned, but to take a trip down memory lane, reminisce about everything that happened to us over the years.

'What do you think?' Adam is looking at me. And then, by way of explanation to Ross, he adds, 'Kathleen's training to be a psychotherapist. So she'll probably have quite a good handle on this.'

Ross nods, impressed. Nice to know I've still got it. Even if I haven't. I see him thinking, *Jocelyn had such clever friends.*

'And she used to be a Samaritan.'

'I did, actually,' I say quickly, though this kind of implies that Adam's last statement wasn't true.

I really want to say that I will take over. That I will go and root through her stuff. But I know this is a delicate situation and – as per – not all about me. So instead, I am honest.

'Ross . . . we'd all drifted apart, these past few years. I don't know if she told you.'

'I know. I know. But she still talked about you. She missed you.'

'Much as I'd like to help – and I'm happy to help – I think I'd feel like I was imposing.'

'You wouldn't be imposing, I've invited you.'

'Or being voyeuristic.'

'Jocelyn didn't have many friends. But listen, I appreciate it's awkward. I can deal with it. Forget I said anything. Honestly.'

I nod. Adam looks relieved, although he adds, 'I mean, I'm more than happy to help as well, but . . .'

'No, it's fine.' Ross is insistent. 'It's just . . .' His voice trails off.

'What?' asks Jason. Oh, he's joining in now, is he?

'I have to get it all sorted in the next fortnight, as the lease is up on her flat.'

'She rented?' Adam sounds very surprised.

Ross nods. 'And the landlord's a bit of a twat.'

'Well, if it's going to . . . speed things up a bit, I'm more than happy to help.' I sound so kind, so generous, so selfless. I define altruism.

'Me too,' says Adam.

Ross looks grateful. 'I'll take your numbers and . . . talk tomorrow. But can I get you guys a drink?'

'We should get you one,' insists Jason. He has his uses, then. 'What's it to be?'

'Single malt. Thanks.'

Jason looks to me. 'Wine?'

'Er . . .' I look at my phone, as if I have somewhere to be and am weighing up the options. 'Oh, go on then. Large.'

Jason nods and heads to the bar.

'Ross, were any of her family here?' I ask.

'You know they were estranged?'

I nod.

'Well, I did ask them, but . . . they said they'd rather remember her in their own way. Away from the cameras. As it turned out, there were hardly any there. They're very private people. Unlike her!'

Adam smiles.

Ross nods, also smiling. 'I thought they'd change their minds. I knew they were stubborn. But . . . I didn't realize they were quite *that* stubborn. No matter what they thought of her, it would've been nice of them to come and say their goodbyes.'

And then as an afterthought, he added, 'I don't get it. But then . . . a lot of the time, I didn't get Jocelyn.'

Adam and I both nod.

'I guess now I see where she got her stubbornness from.'

We both nod again.

'I know a lot of people hated her. But she was a big softie underneath it all.'

'You don't have to tell us that.' Adam is smiling. And Ross nods. He knows. We get it.

Just then, an avuncular-looking man in his sixties comes up behind Ross and taps him on the shoulder. Ross looks up, and then stands to hug him. As he does, I see his back jerk as he breaks down in tears.

I give Adam a sad smile and he shifts uncomfortably in his seat, playing with something in his coat pocket. He pulls out a packet of cigarettes.

'You don't smoke, do you?' he says.

I shake my head. 'I'll come out with you, though.'

He doesn't need telling twice. He jumps up out of his seat, and I get up to follow him. It reminds me of being a kid again, following him round like his shadow. As we head out he touches Jason's shoulder at the bar and whispers in his ear, then heads to the door. I go where he goes, with a brief smile to Jason. I'd rather be outside passive smoking than stuck on my own with the worse half.

Outside, the fresh air sobers me as Adam lights up. It's like I come to my senses. 'Ross seems all right,' I say tentatively.

Adam doesn't look so sure.

'I don't trust him,' he says quietly, looking away, as if checking no-one can hear. And I wonder just how much he knows.

Liverpool, 1985

'Mary's what?'

'Nan. It's not a big deal.'

'Say it again. She's . . .'

'Jocelyn's playing her.'

'She's black? The Virgin Mary? Mother of our Lord Saviour, Jesus Christ? Who died upon the cross in his little crown of thorns?'

'The vicar says it's fine.' And I wasn't sure the crown was that little, actually.

'That vicar wants his head testing. Did they not know you wanted that part?'

'It's a singing part.'

'So?'

'I'm not as good a singer as Jocelyn.'

'You're in the choir, aren't you?'

'I know.'

'So you're not exactly tone-deaf, Kathleen.'

'Adam says my voice is tinny. Good for harmonies but not for solos.'

'Who the hell does he think he is? Tony Hatch?'

'No!'

'Or Mike Sammes from the Mike Sammes Singers? Coz he's not. He's a fifteen-year-old kid, same as you.'

'But he's directing the play, so . . .'

'And making a pig's ear of it, by the sounds of it. What did the vicar say again?'

'He said, coz Mary and Joseph were from Egypt – or Israel, or wherever Bethlehem is, I forget off the top of my head – that it's feasible they were both a bit . . .'

'A bit what?'

'Duskily skinned.'

'You what?'

'Oh Nan, you heard.'

'So all of a sudden, God's gone coloured?'

'No. I dunno. Nan, it's got nothing to do with me.'

'It's not right, Kathleen.'

'Why are you even bothered? It's not like you go to church, is it?'

'Well, I was gonna come if you were starring in the nativity, love. I'm not completely heartless.'

'Well, you still can!'

'Oh, can I? And witness sacrilege? I think I'll sit in and watch *Howards' Way*, thank you.'

'Suit yourself.'

'I don't think I like your tone, Kathleen.'

'I'm still playing Abigail-Jade. And the Archangel Gabriel.'

'I dunno what they're teaching you up that church of yours, Kathleen. But I certainly don't recall an Abigail-Jade in the Bible.'

'She's the main character.'

'Oh, is she now? So much for Jesus. The world's on its head. The world. Is on. Its head.'

She turned her back to me, and continued frying an egg.

'Pass us Mary Magdalene down from that shelf, love. Me nerves are in shreds.'

She always pronounced it Mary Magda-leeney. Usually I'd correct her, but tonight I couldn't be bothered. There was no winning with her. As I reached for the plate I heard her mutter, 'Abigail-Jade? Who the frig is Abigail-Jade when she's at home?'

Adam's version of the nativity opened with a teenage girl from Liverpool, Abigail-Jade, all excited on Christmas Eve and kind of kicking off at her mum – Jean from the choir, who was proving really rubbish at learning her lines – that she wanted to open one of her presents, and she wanted to open it *now*. And Abigail-Jade's mum giving her hell because it was quite clear she had forgotten the true meaning of Christmas. And so she sat Abigail-Jade down and started to tell her the Christmas story from this massive book that had CHRISTMAS STORY written on the cover (made by Adam, who was not only writing, directing and starring as Joseph, but was also designer and props maker). And that was when, to quote Adam, 'the magic happened'.

As I sat by the Christmas tree between the choir stalls in a smelly dressing gown left over from some previous nativity play, the congregation would hear singing at the back of the church and look round to see Mary and Joseph coming down the aisle singing a two-part harmony version of the title song, 'How Far Is It to Bethlehem?', with Mary sat on a donkey. And then the Christmas story would happen around us, with the innkeeper and shepherds and wise men and everything. Well, I say wise men; it was Tonya, Tamana and Tamara, the trip-lets, with cotton-wool beards on.

Jocelyn was of course playing Mary, and her shaky

rendition of the song filled every corner of the church when we rehearsed. The older members of the choir were on Nan's side, and got into quite a heated debate about the fact that Mary was black. Adam and I sided with the casting, but you could tell they weren't happy, by the way they rolled their eyes and checked their watches every time she opened her mouth.

Adam was really lording it over everyone during the nativity play rehearsals. He'd had to rope in everyone from the choir to play a part as he'd written such a big piece, and there weren't really enough people to share the load. It was also impossible to find a real-life donkey, so Jocelyn was pretending to ride one of those horse's heads on a stick with wheels on the bottom. She thought it looked lousy, but Adam was insistent that the magic of theatre would see them through. The other problem was that I, as Abigail-Jade, was meant to be hearing the Christmas story first-hand and, according to Adam, drinking in its sights and sounds.

'Drink it in more! MORE! I need to see it in your FACE!' he'd yell at me. 'Face face face face FACE!' And then he'd hit the ground with the cane he'd taken to bringing to rehearsals. He didn't need a cane to help him walk, he just felt it made him look more imposing, like the woman who taught the dancing in *Fame*.

However, in the middle of drinking in all the sights and sounds of Jesus's birthday, I also had to leg it up to the pulpit to double up as the angel. Adam said he'd come up with a solution for this that would be a 'coup de théâtre'. Whatever that meant.

Not everyone was entranced by the play. A new lad who'd joined not so long ago had taken to inspecting his nails and rolling his eyes heavenwards every time Adam opened his mouth. Paul, they called him, and he must only have been

about eleven, but he claimed to have been in a semi-pro production of *The Sound of Music* at the Empire and so 'couldn't
believe the level of unprofessionalism' in rehearsals. Adam
couldn't stand 'Sound of Music Paul' and insisted to me that
he was just after his job.

We rehearsed twice a week after choir practice in the
church, and the most exciting thing was that the vicar had
entrusted a set of church keys to Adam so that he could lock
up once we'd finished. One night me, Adam and Jocelyn
decided to hang around after rehearsals and have a 'church
party'. This involved us bringing a few bottles of Lambrini
and some packets of Wotsits and sitting in the choir stalls,
gabbing away like we were in a wine bar. I didn't really like the
taste of the alcohol, so just pretended I was more tipsy than I
was. Then, after the Wotsits were all gone, Adam said he had
something to show us. He led us over to the organ behind the
choir stalls. Encased in oak panelling, it was a very handsome
beast. Anyway, he leaned in and tapped one of the panels, and
it miraculously opened up. It was a secret door.

'It's the organ loft. Come on.'

And he disappeared inside, and we followed him in.

I was getting on a lot better with Jocelyn these days, especially after our little chat outside Mr Wong's. She seemed
to have calmed down since being cast as Mary, like she had
nothing to prove now, and she was turning out to be quite
sweet.

Once inside the panelling we climbed a sturdy wooden
ladder that led to a tiny space, about the size of my nan's box
room, nestled behind the organ pipes. We sat there for what
felt like ages, marvelling at our own secret den. It was so warm
and cosy in there. Life felt good in that moment. Or maybe
it was just the effect of half a beaker of warm Lambrini. The

floor was dusty, and we were surrounded by cardboard boxes and plastic bags that appeared to have Christmas decorations spilling out of them.

'Your play's amazing,' said Jocelyn, looking through one of the boxes, and Adam smiled.

'I came up with the concept ages back. It came to me in a dream,' he said.

Blimey. Pretentious or what?

'I think the storybook book ending really works,' Jocelyn added.

'Except when I have to leave the living room and stick me angel wings on and then go in the pulpit and be the angel,' I pointed out. All that glistens . . .

'We've covered that with the new line from Abigail-Jade, Kathleen. I need to go to the loo, I'm bursting.' Adam was getting ratty.

'D'you think you'll be a writer one day, Adam?' Jocelyn asked. She had pulled out a bauble from the box and was studying it, transfixed. I was starting to feel I'd not had as much Lambrini as these two.

'I am a writer. I am writing,' he said, like a sigh.

'Professional,' Jocelyn corrected herself.

'It's my dream,' Adam cooed. 'What's yours?'

'I want to be a top recording star.'

Adam sighed deliciously. 'I can see that happening. You've got an amazing instrument.'

Instrument? She played an instrument? This was news to me.

'Thanks, Adam.'

'What instrument d'you play, Jocelyn?'

'He means my voice.'

'Oh.'

'What about you, Kathleen? What do you want to be?'

Jocelyn was looking at me with such keenness, I didn't want to let either of them down. At the same time I didn't want to lie and say I wanted to be a dancer, or an actress, or a prostitute, just to keep them sweet and make them think that I too had showbiz aspirations when I didn't. And, oh, I don't know, maybe it was the Lambrini talking, but I answered honestly.

'I wanna be an embalmer.'

They both looked at me like I was completely crazy.

'A what?' Adam gasped.

'An embalmer. They drain the blood out of a dead person and replace it with embalming fluid. I think that'd be a really interesting job. And it's a dying art, coz no-one can be arsed getting embalmed these days so embalmers are dying out.' And then I added, for dramatic effect, 'To coin a phrase.'

I smiled. I thought that little joke was quite good. However, it was met with stony silence. And, I'm not being funny, but I'm sure I heard some tumbleweed drift across the organ loft right at that moment.

I immediately realized it was the wrong thing to say, because they both looked at each other and Adam asked Jocelyn what sort of singer she wanted to be.

I zoned out. I'd been honest. And they weren't interested. Fine. I didn't have to be interested in their ridiculous dreams.

For years now, I'd thought I'd love to work with the dead. Dead bodies didn't scare me because Nan had dragged me round to the houses of everyone and anyone she knew who'd died since I was knee high to a coffin. I understood the need for grieving relatives to be able to say, proudly, he/she looks so at peace. And I could imagine myself saying, 'Then my work here is done.'

Everybody dies. Not everybody becomes a professional writer or recording artist. My plan seemed infinitely more practical and achievable.

I zoned back into Jocelyn's monologue about how she saw her recording career panning out. It sounded very much like she was just describing what had happened to Madonna. I tried to stifle a yawn.

Suddenly Adam kneeled up. 'I just wanna say . . .' Oh God. I suspected a Lambrini Love-In was about to be upon us. 'I love yous two SO much.'

I was correct.

'And us three sat here. It's like our own little club. The Loft Club. All for one and one for all.'

'The Loft Club's a rubbish name,' I pointed out.

He shot me an Exocet glance. 'Well, what would you rather I called it?'

'I don't know. The Breakfast Club?'

'But we don't have breakfast here,' Jocelyn pointed out, sounding as equally peeved as Adam.

'I know but it's a great movie,' I said.

Jocelyn rolled her eyes. 'That ginger girl is SO ugly.'

I knew it was pointless to argue. Even though I disagreed with her.

'I feel so close to you all,' Adam continued. I could see Jocelyn nodding in Lambrini-infused agreement. 'Let's always be there for each other, and never let one another down.'

Jocelyn held her hand up. Adam matched it. Slowly, I raised mine.

'The Loft Club,' Jocelyn said, like it was the best name in the world. And far superior to the Breakfast Club.

'The LOFT CLUB!' Adam and I joined in. me sounding more enthusiastic about it than I really felt.

'I feel like we're in a movie or something,' Adam added, then took a sip of his Lambrini. Some spilt down his top.

'Like *The Breakfast Club*,' I said, 'only not in the morning. And in a church loft.'

I didn't have to look at Jocelyn. I knew she'd be rolling her eyes.

'It's like we're the figures in this bauble,' Jocelyn said and we both looked over. She passed the bauble around for us to have a butcher's. It was more delicate than I'd anticipated, close up. And in the glass were three tiny men.

'But they're all men,' I said. 'They're like . . . the Three Wise Men.'

'I'm being poetic,' she explained and Adam nodded as if this were life-changing. 'The three of us. Here. Now. Trapped in glass forever.'

'You're making me feel claustrophobic,' I said, and Jocelyn snatched the bauble back and stared at it some more herself.

Just then we heard a noise in the main body of the church. A bang. It reverberated round the building, echoing for what felt like minutes. We all froze. Had the vicar come back? Were we about to be found out for having our church party?

We all knelt up and crawled across to the organ pipes. Peering in between them, we could see the main body of the church. Someone was standing near the front row of pews. They were bending over. They were picking something up and putting it back.

'He's knocked over a hymn book,' whispered Adam.

Well, it wasn't the vicar. This was a young lad.

'Who is it?' whispered Jocelyn.

And then the lad faced the front.

And, oh my days, it was like the Star of Bethlehem had shone down upon us and a heavenly choir had burst into song. Standing there in the church, looking up at the altar was none other than Mark Reynolds.

'What the fuck's he doing here?!' Adam yelped, a little too loudly.

Mark looked up, hearing this. I could see panic in his face.

I could also see he had a black eye.

'Mark, are you all right?!' I called. And then he looked really confused.

'I think he thinks it's the voice of God,' Jocelyn said with a grimace.

'Mark, wait there! We're coming down!' I called again.

And now he was looking like someone who was reasoning that maybe God didn't have a strong Liverpool accent.

Once we were down on ground level, it was clear something was wrong. Mark had a black eye, and cuts to his face. The sleeve of his tracksuit top was ripped.

'What's happened?' Adam asked.

Mark shook his head, bravado rising. 'Nothing.'

'Have you been in a fight?' I asked.

He shook his head.

'Who did this to you?' Jocelyn asked. Her voice sounded so wholesome. But he didn't reply.

'Was it your dad?' Adam asked. I looked at him. It sounded like he had inside information. But then, his mum did find out a lot behind that sweet-shop counter.

Mark, again, didn't answer. But he did say, 'I was just looking for somewhere to put me head down for the night.'

'Come and stay at ours. If you want,' Adam suggested.

Mark shook his head. 'I wasn't sure where I was gonna go. Then I seen the door open here. I was gonna get me head down on one of the benches.'

Adam looked to the open organ loft door. 'I can go one better than that.'

Mark looked across to the door too, none the wiser. But he was about to find out.

Five minutes later, Mark was snugly ensconced in his new home.

'I could bring you a sleeping bag from home!' Jocelyn said, all excited.

'I can bring my spare pillow!' Adam chipped in.

What could I bring? What? It reminded me of those lyrics from the Christmas carol – what can I give him, poor as I am? Then I struck on it.

'I could bring a plate with a picture of Moses on it!'

Three faces looked at me like I was mad.

'It's like that film, isn't it?' Adam said during dinner break one day.

'I know,' I said, without thinking. Then realized I had no idea what he was talking about. 'Which one?'

'*Whistle Down the Wind*. You seen it?'

I hadn't. 'I've seen *The Breakfast Club*,' I said, like that was some kind of help. Like all films had the same story.

'There's this escaped convict on the run and Hayley Mills hides him out in her barn coz she thinks he's Jesus.'

'Why would she think that?'

'I forget. But it was really good. Even if it was in black and white.'

'What? It didn't even change to colour halfway through, like *The Wizard of Oz*?'

Adam threw his head back and laughed. I liked it when I made him do that.

We'd been hiding Mark in the organ loft for a whole three

days now, using Adam's key to get in and out to bring him drinks and food that we'd squirrelled away from our family larders. Sometimes we'd be in a rush, on our way to school, so couldn't stop.

Last night we'd stayed and chatted to him for ages, and he'd opened up about the rows he had with his dad. I found it an eye-opener. There was me thinking that everyone else had the perfect life, and that it was just me who had the lousy time . . . Dad away 'on the rigs', Mum done a runner. But scratch the surface of anyone's life, and it seemed that pain and misery weren't far beneath. Mark hadn't cried again, but the closeness I'd felt last night had stirred something in me, cementing all the feelings I'd had for him over the past few months. The angry young man on the demo had been replaced by a sensitive lad with a lot on his plate – a plate with Moses on, no less. I'd been true to my word. He seemed at once mortified that we knew his secret, but relieved that he was no longer suffering alone. Jocelyn had come with us last night and she'd offered to sing for him. I'd had to bite my tongue to stop myself from laughing, but imagine my surprise when Mark had said yes, he'd love to hear her. Jocelyn had then closed her eyes. I thought, oh here we go, hope none of the windows break. But when she opened her mouth and sang, she made the most beautiful sound I'd ever heard.

The song she sang was called 'The Troubles of the World'. It was like an old Negro spiritual (and I wasn't being racist calling it that, as that's how she actually described it), and it was really deep and slow and . . . well, spiritual. By the time she finished, I realized that I was crying. I saw that Adam was, too. And Mark was just sat with his eyes shut. It was like we'd all shared something. The song had made me think about my dad, and how I hardly knew him. I'd even conjured up a picture of my mum, on Australia's Gold Coast, digging sand castles with her new family, the one she loved. (I didn't even know if she was on the Gold Coast. I'd just heard about it, on the telly.)

It made me think, too, about my nan. I was usually such a typical teenager with her – infuriated by her and her smoking and her plates and her cooking and her constant endless gabbling – that I never stopped to think about everything she had done for me since I was little. She'd done more for me than anyone on this planet, and I was rarely grateful. It made me want to go home and give her a hug.

Which, about an hour later, I did.

'I just want to say thank you,' I said.

She looked at me cautiously.

'For what?'

'For everything you do for me. Everything you've done. I'm a surly cow, I know. But I do appreciate it.'

She looked as stunned as if I'd come in with a severed head and swung it around, getting blood all up her beloved Artexing.

'Have you been drinking?' she whispered.

I shook my head. Though, truth be told, we had shared a bottle of Lambrini in the organ loft.

'Drugs?'

'No!' I scoffed. Chance'd be a fine thing.

'I know a lot o'kids your age don't half experiment with that Mary-Joannie.'

'It's marijuana, Nan.'

'I don't mind you pronouncing it, as long as you don't inject it.'

'You smoke it, Nan.'

'Or that.'

And then she looked back at the telly, and turned the volume up. But I didn't care. At least, for once in my life, I'd said how I felt. She looked back suddenly.

'What's in the Kwik Save bag?'

'Ingredients.'

'For what?'

'A cake?'

She looked incredulous. 'You're making a cake?'

I nodded. 'It's Jocelyn's birthday tomorrow. Me and Adam are gonna surprise her.'

Nan appeared to mull this over. Then she jumped up, invigorated.

'I've got a Noah's Ark cake decoration transfer somewhere. You get mixing and I'll find it.'

My heart sank.

Jocelyn was fifteen the next day. The cake could have been stunning, if I'd been left to my own devices. It was a chocolate cake with a buttercream filling – so far, so good – but the top was a bit of a mish-mash of styles. As well as me icing HAPPY BIRTHDAY on it, Nan had insisted I use the Noah's Ark transfer, so that was unattractively squashed underneath the lettering.

'What's the boat to do with?' Adam asked when I showed it to him in the sweet shop that morning.

'Oh, that's . . .'

Dorothy peered over. 'Is it the Love Boat?'

'No, it's Noah's Ark.'

'Oh.' Dorothy sounded surprised. 'Is she into the Old Testament?'

'Not really. I just . . . thought it was unusual,' I lied.

'Well, it's a bit late to take it off now,' Adam sighed as he clipped the lid back on the cake tin. We had planned to go over to Jocelyn's house really early before she set off for school on the Wirral and surprise her with it, before heading on over to see Mark with some provisions for the day. We set off, but just as we were stepping foot out of the door Dorothy called my name. I looked back. Adam huffed, wanting to get off.

'It's just . . .'

'Mother, hurry up!' Adam hissed. Gosh, he could be rude sometimes.

'Well, Enid Dunn said she seen your dad. Getting a take-out at the Bridge.'

The Bridge was a nearby pub, situated, appropriately, on the bridge into town.

'It must be that lookalike again, Dorothy.'

She nodded, but looked unconvinced. 'Just thought I'd say.'

'Come on, Kathleen.' Adam dragged me out of the door.

'Did you get Mark anything?' he asked as we strolled along.

'A bag of cheese and onion crisps and an Um Bongo. From my packed lunch. How about you?'

'Some liquorice torpedoes and a tin of Spam.'

'Is there an opener for the tin?'

'It's all-inclusive. Oh, and a Tunnock's teacake.'

'Oh, I love them.'

'I know. He's living the life of Riley. Here we are.'

When we knocked on Jocelyn's front door we could hear her mum in the hall on the phone. We could hear the words, 'Yes, our teasmades are of the highest calibre, Madame', spoken in Jocelyn's mum's thick Sierra Leonean accent. It always made us chuckle. Then we heard her stop talking and approach the door, calling, 'You have got a bloody nerve, young lady!'

And then she opened it. And looked quite surprised to see us standing there.

'Hello, Mrs McKenzie. Is Jocelyn in, please?' Adam said, all sweetness and light. Like we were overzealous Jehovah's Witnesses.

I held my cake tin up. 'We've brought her a cake for her birthday.'

Jocelyn's mum looked like a rabbit in headlights. She looked back into the hall and we heard a door slam loudly. Was Jocelyn there? Why wasn't she coming to the door? Jocelyn's mum looked back to us, and smiled thinly.

'It is her birthday, isn't it?' I bleated.

'Well, yes, but . . .'

'Is everything OK, Mrs McKenzie?' Adam reached out and touched her arm.

She coughed and spluttered a bit, then said, 'Jocelyn did not stay here last night. We had a bit of a row. She went to stay at her cousin's in Toxteth.' Only the way she said it sounded like Tox-DEATH.

I found it unnerving. And I immediately smelt a rat.

Was she lying? Why did I get the feeling Jocelyn was there? Someone was there that she didn't want us to know about. But why would she make up the story about Toxteth?

'But I will take your cake, and give it to her later. You are good people.'

'Thank you, Mrs McKenzie,' I said, handing it over.

'If only she was more like you. So thoughtful. So kind.' She stroked Adam's arm. 'You are like my albino son.'

'Ah, thanks, Mrs McKenzie.'

I waited for her to bestow a heartfelt compliment on me. But she just gave me a bored smile, then stepped back and shut the door.

Adam and I looked at each other, and as we did we heard some sort of row going on inside the house. Jocelyn's mum was arguing with a man. Which was odd in itself, as no men lived in that house. Was that why Jocelyn wasn't there? Did her mum have a new boyfriend, and Jocelyn didn't approve? Jocelyn could be such a snob.

'I don't believe a word of that,' I said to him.

'I know. Me neither.'

'Who's that fella she's rowing with?'

Adam shrugged.

'Like your nan said. She was a bit of a goer in her day.'

And we chuckled and hurried away from the doorstep.

As we walked round to the church, I had an increasing sense of foreboding. Adam chirruped merrily away about not realizing how big Jocelyn's family were, and second-guessing what the row might have been about. As we turned the corner and hit the wasteland on which the church sat mournfully in the corner, I began to feel I didn't want to go inside. But Adam was bounding ahead. And I always followed, even if this time I did so reluctantly.

'What do you think?'

'About what?'

'About this row! What d'you think they were arguing about?'

'I reckon she's got a new fancy piece, and snobby Jocelyn was slagging him off,' I proffered. Adam shrieked with laughter, loving the scandal of it all.

And then I saw it. Up ahead at the church.

A side window, a vestry window opened. And Jocelyn climbed out.

'Adam, look.'

I nodded towards the church. He turned and looked. She didn't see us. She was stood with her back to us, and she started straightening her clothing. She even seemed to readjust her knickers.

'What's she doing?' asked Adam. His voice was monotone. Like he already knew the answer.

And then she leaned in to the window, and Mark leaned slightly out of it. And they stood there for what felt like eternity, hugging.

'Something tells me,' said Adam, 'she never stayed in Toxteth last night.'

London, 2015

I wake up in a bed I don't recognize, in a room I don't recognize. My head hurts. But this feeling is familiar. The sore throat, the repugnant taste in my mouth. I am fully clothed. My coat lies on the floor. I panic. Sit up. My bag is nearby. I climb out of bed and look inside. My purse and keys are there. My phone – where's my phone? I see that it is charging near the window. Did I do that? Someone else must have. Who?

This is a nice room. In other circumstances, I'd enjoy it. I just don't know whose room it is. I try to remember where I was the night before. I have no recollection of going to bed.

Then it hits me. Jocelyn's funeral.

Oh God, did I cop off? Have I had sex? They say that death and sex go together, the ultimate celebration. But I am fully clothed. Thank God for that.

I climb out of bed. No obvious injuries to legs, I feel no pain there, so hopefully I didn't fall over.

I open the white curtains. This room is upstairs. Below me I see a tiny but picture-perfect garden, and some decking. A shed at the bottom of a path. A rainbow flag in the window of the shed.

So far, so gay.

And a child's bike, and . . . oh, of COURSE!

I must be at Adam and Jason's. That's something of a relief. But.

Oh God. Oh God, I must have got hammered, and they brought me home because I couldn't explain where I lived enough for them to put me in a taxi.

This whole room is white. Thank God I wasn't sick all over it. I notice a half-drunk glass of red on the bedside cabinet, red rings surrounding it where it's been moved. And an ashtray with two cigarettes in it. Eurgh. Someone's been smoking inside. In my room. Disgusting. Then I recognize the taste in my mouth. It must have been *me* smoking. Even more disgusting.

I check my phone to make sure I've not called or texted anyone while drunk. It's half nine in the morning. I've not made a call since yesterday morning, or sent a text. I do have a text from the cab company, though, from six yesterday evening, saying the taxi was outside the pub.

I check Twitter and Facebook. I've not drunkenly ranted on either, so that's good too. This could be a lot, lot worse.

Except that Adam has seen the state I get into.

That is less good.

Oh fuck.

I bet he and Jason had a massive row about it. I bet Jason was all, 'Your mate's pissed, I'm going to bed.' Hopefully Adam defended me. Hopefully my 'grieving' was enough to excuse it. Hopefully they'll assume it was a one-off. . . .

Panic grips my throat. I can't leave the room. I sit on the bed instead, which is when I notice the bottle of Evian under the bedside table. I grab it, unscrew the top and glug it back.

That's better. At least I didn't reach for the glass of red.

My tongue feels too big for my mouth. My mouth feels too

big for my face. My brain feels too big for my head. I am an ogre. Everything is too big.

I wonder what I was saying to Adam last night. This is the problem when you have no recollection. I like to think I'm a nice drunk, a happy drunk. I hope I didn't say too much about Jocelyn. I hope it was one of those drunkennesses that result in me going catatonic, unable to speak. I hope it didn't make me garrulous and gossipy, eager to spill any beans. I hope all beans were safely kept in their tin.

But Adam always did like a gossip. I put it down to growing up in a sweet shop, where every visitor brought fresh news.

I see Mark suddenly, disgusted with me. 'You're slurring your words; go to bed, woman. You can't speak. Fuck's sake.'

I push the memory away. It wasn't last night, was it? This isn't his new place? No. That's an old memory. An ancient one. I've had a few sleeps since then.

This is a really lovely room. It's so much nicer than my own. For a second I fantasize about moving in with Adam and Jason. And then I realize I don't actually know for sure this is Adam and Jason's place. This could be anyone's – anyone who'd have a rainbow flag in their garden shed. And a kid's bike and a mini trampoline. It has to be theirs. It has to.

Someone taps on the door.

'Hello?' I call out.

The door opens, and Adam comes in. He's dressed in a dressing gown and is looking sheepish.

'How's the head?' he says, and comes and joins me on the bed.

'Shocking, I can't believe how pissed I got last night.'

'Join the club.'

'I don't remember going to bed.'

'Neither do I.'

And all of a sudden I feel relief. Like a boil has been lanced. It rises through me like euphoria. We both got in a state and that's OK, because Adam can't be an alcoholic. He can't be. The law of averages decree that. Oh, this is wonderful news.

'Jason says we were dancing round the living room to Kajagoogoo.'

'Oh God.'

'He went to bed and left us up chatting.'

'What was I saying?'

'I've no idea! There's the remnants of a Chinese on the coffee table. I don't even remember ordering it.'

'Where is Jason? Is he cross?'

'Nah. Gone to work. Oh God, Kathleen, I feel so much better that you slept in your clothes and don't remember going to bed.'

'I know. What are we like?! Oh God.' I suddenly realize something.

'What, babe?'

'We didn't wake Denim, did we?'

'No, the nanny had him back to hers last night.'

'God love the nanny,' I gasp. Even though usually I am quite critical of anyone who has a nanny. Especially if you've adopted. Why have a dog and get someone else to bark for it?

God, my analogies are shit today.

'Looks like we'll both have to go to rehab next time!' he chuckles, and I smile tightly. I wondered when he'd bring that up.

Adam's house turns out to be in Kentish Town, in a twee little side street of workman's cottages that they bought for a song ten years ago but is now probably worth about two million. We make bacon sandwiches and take them into the garden to eat. Two big mugs of builder's tea, a few Beroccas and some amazing moisturizer he'd found in America later, and I am starting to feel almost human again. Almost.

'Oh well,' he says, sounding sleepy as he screws his eyes up against the sunlight, 'does you good to have a blowout every now and again.'

'Exactly!' I say, as if this is rarer than a blue moon for me.

We sit in silence for a while. Then he suddenly says, 'Hey. Kathleen.'

'What?'

'Kajagoogoo.'

And we both fall about in hysterics.

'Have you got things to do today?' he asks, as if a plan is forming.

'No.' Well, at least for once I'm being honest. 'Why?'

'How d'you fancy a walk up on the Heath? Get some fresh air.'

As always. Adam leads, I follow.

I have a luxurious long hot soak in his bath before putting on yesterday's clothes and we walk arm in arm away from Kentish Town up towards Hampstead Heath. We pass an entrance to an underground wine bar that Adam informs me used to be 'a very busy cottage'. Maybe my brain's on a go-slow today but I have to get him to remind me what a cottage is. I blush when he tells me and he pokes me – 'You're still wet behind the bloody gills, Kathleen!' – and we laugh, though I am embarrassed. I want him to think I'm a woman of the world now. I've seen so much more of life than when we used to hang out. I'd like to think I'm unshockable now. But I guess, in his eyes at least, the die is cast.

When eventually we hit the greenery of the Heath we take the path to the top of Parliament Hill and look out over the breakfast bowl of London.

'I suppose once upon a time we'd've been able to see Harmony Heights from here. You can see everything else,' I say, and he nods.

'It would've been over there. By Trellick Tower.'

'That's where Jocelyn lived,' I say.

'Poor cow.'

'Did you ever go?'

And he pulls this face that most certainly doesn't answer the question. It can be read as 'I couldn't be arsed.' It could also be read as 'I did, but I don't want to talk about it.'

'Did you?' he asks.

I do a similar grimace, which he accepts. God knows what he thinks.

There's so much I want to say, but I don't know if I should. Stuff I know that would show I'm anything but the naive little schoolgirl still; but for some reason, I hold back. Some secrets are best kept that way. And they don't all show me in the best light. Not when I think of everything I've kept hidden.

But surely I should be able to be honest with Adam. He's one of the few people I know who I've been close to for a long time. Everyone else in my life comes in and out like the figures on a cuckoo clock. But although he's standing near me, I fear there's a chasm between us. I don't want to leap across it. Not yet. Not till I know it's safe.

We move to an empty bench and sit down.

'Why d'you think she became so angry?' he asks.

I shake my head. It's a tough question, and there are so many answers. My hangover hasn't quite subsided enough to go into too much emotional territory. So I just reply, 'Maybe we all get angrier with age.'

'We're looking fifty in the face, kid,' he says, pulling a face.

'Oh please. It's five years off. Let's just pretend we're early forties for now.'

'Forty-fabulous,' he says, and I smile. Then he corrects himself, 'Forty-fierce.' And he holds up his hand to high-five me. I oblige.

I hate high-fiving. It feels so American, so teenage. And it makes me feel like I definitely am staring fifty in the face. Or down the barrel of a gun.

'D'you think Ross was serious about us helping him sort out her stuff?'

I shrug. 'Probably. I thought it was a good idea yesterday.'

'And now?'

'Not so sure. It's easy to feel closer to someone when you've just been to their funeral. But I think the more time that passes, the more the distance will set in again. And it'll just feel weird.'

'I know what you mean.'

We sit in silence for a while, drinking in the view. I don't want to be here. I don't want to leave, but I also don't want to move. It's the oddest feeling. An inertia. An antipathy. I want Adam to leave, but at the same time I don't want him to go. Maybe I'm going mad.

'I feel so numb,' he says after a while. And maybe that sums it up. Maybe he feels the same way as me. I don't expect him to want to be my best friend, or want me to hang around; I'm sure it's appealing to spend time with the past, but equally appealing to push it away.

'I'm not sure whether I should head home,' I say. And I mean it. My honesty today has surprised even myself.

Adam considers this, then tilts his head to one side. 'Fancy a Bloody Mary first?'

We walk down to the Magdala Pub, where Adam seems

to know the bar staff. Once we're ensconced in a booth, he informs me that this is the pub where Ruth Ellis shot her lover.

'Who?'

'Ruth Ellis. The last woman to be hanged in this country. You can see the bullet holes in the wall somewhere.'

'She was shot?'

'No, she shot him. She was hanged.'

'God, my brain's not in gear today.'

'They made a film about it. *Dance with a Stranger*.'

'I got confused, sorry. I thought Ruth Ellis was that swot who went to Cambridge when she was about nine.'

'Oh, that was Ruth Lawrence.'

'Wasn't she in *Starlight Express*?'

'No, that was Stephanie Lawrence. She died.'

'Really? How?'

'I think she drank.'

'Oh God. Don't say that.'

I lift my Bloody Mary up, and we clink glasses ironically. 'Cheers!' I'm slowly starting to feel human again.

'Such a sad story.'

'*Starlight Express*?' I mean it as a joke, and he chuckles.

'Ruth Ellis. Hanged. Then her dad hangs himself. And her son. And her daughter. Years later, mind.'

'Really?'

'Suicide. The ultimate taboo.'

I nod.

'Did you see how the word was never even mentioned yesterday?'

I nod again.

'Just . . . the euphemisms. A tragic accident. A terrible accident. An incident. I suppose people aren't ready yet.'

This conversation is making me nauseous.

'Why d'you think she did it, Kath?'

I sigh. 'I really don't know.'

'Maybe she did have a conscience after all. Maybe it caught up with her and . . . did you hear, the police said she had a phone call from someone ten minutes before she died? From a phone box in Liverpool. Near the Wavertree Technology Park.'

'That's right by where we grew up.'

'I wonder who it was?'

'Maybe it was her mum.'

'Why would she use a phone box, though?'

'I don't know.'

'Who else d'you think it could've been?'

I really don't want to go there. Not now. Saved by the bell, Adam's mobile rings. He pulls it from his pocket, pulls a face to show he doesn't know who's calling, and answers.

'Hello?'

I like this Bloody Mary. It feels like a meal. It's so warming and filling, and they've even put a stick of celery in it. Surely with the tomato juice, this is two of my five a day.

Adam is nudging me. He mouths the word 'Ross' to me. I take more of an interest. He's nodding a lot, making a few 'aha' noises. Everything is in the affirmative.

'Sure. Of course. No, of course we will, that's no problem. When do you go?'

Go? Where is Ross going?

'Yeah, no problem. I can come over Friday. Pick the keys up. OK, Ross. No, honestly, it's fine. Absolutely fine. Don't you worry about a thing.'

When he eventually hangs up, he stares at his phone.

'What? Where's Ross going?'

'Fucking Dubai.'

'Blimey.'

'He's going over to Jocelyn's on Friday to take away all the stuff he wants. Wants us to meet him there.'

'What, do it all in a day?'

He shakes his head.

'He wants us to go through the rest of her stuff while he's away.'

'On our own?'

He nods again. 'Talk about reneging on responsibility. He just wants us to do his dirty work.'

I take this in. Me and Adam. On our own in Jocelyn's flat. I'm not sure what to make of that really.

'Same again?'

Well, it would be rude to say no. 'Can I have two sticks of celery this time? Then it's like we're having lunch.'

He laughs and heads to the bar.

Liverpool, 1985

'I thought you were going to school?'

'I don't feel well.'

'You only left the house twenty minutes ago. Did you give Jocelyn her cake?'

'Yes. No. I dunno. We gave it to her mam.'

I was walking like I'd strained something. I had. My heart.

'Well, what's the matter?'

'I don't feel well. I'm going back to bed.'

'But I've got to go to work.'

'I'm sure I'm not gonna die.'

I sloped off up the stairs as Nan stood, incredulous, hands on hips, watching me go. I stood in my bedroom and kicked off my shoes, then dived onto the bed. Actually, the last thing I'd said might not have been true. What was true was that I did actually want to die.

I'd never wanted to die more in my entire life.

Jocelyn and Mark. Mark and Jocelyn.

My mind raced. Was I overreacting? Had she just dropped by the church to say hello? No. She was hugging him. I bet he was kissing her. I'd wager there were actual tongues involved. She was climbing out of the vestry window. She had pulled her skirt down and done something to her knickers. Whether they had actually had sex or not, it didn't matter. Well, it did – but they had clearly been up close and personal, and . . . well, her mum said she hadn't stayed at their place last night, so it made sense that Jocelyn had spent the night, *all* the night, with Mark in the organ loft. And I bet he wasn't just showing her the pipes.

A brick of pain pushed its way up through me, and I thought I was going to be sick. I wasn't. But I did burst out crying. I tried to swallow the tears but that was impossible, their force was too strong, so I tried to muffle them into my pillow. That seemed to work. And once I heard the front door go, and I knew that Nan had gone to work, I came up for air and lay gasping for breath on the bed. It was like I'd been winded, had a punch to the stomach. I never knew it was possible to feel this bereft.

She knew I liked him. I'd told her. Adam had told her. She knew. And yet she went and did that.

So much for the Loft Club.

I kept seeing images of them at it in the loft. He was on top of her, rolling about. I didn't really know what sex looked like; I'd seen bits on the telly and in dirty magazines that me and Adam had found down the back alleys – but that seemed to be dolly birds with loose elastic and even looser morals, spreading their legs and hiding their vaginas behind empty goldfish bowls. Still, my imagination didn't let me down, though I wish it had. It was all slippery lips and hands kneading flesh like dough, it was Jocelyn looking to the ceiling and gasping 'Oh Mark!' in a Minnie Mouse voice. A voice she probably didn't even have. It was him being a dirty bastard and not being able to say no. It was black on white. They liked exploring their difference, and . . .

How did it happen? How did it start? Had it been going on for ages? I'd told him she was a Tory, for God's sake! How could he?

I knew he was sixteen, but if they'd done it last night, she'd only have been fourteen. She was so loose, and I'd had no idea! I had assumed she was like me, saving herself for marriage. Her mum was so strict! Stricter than my nan! She'd told her she'd have to work twice as hard as a white girl to prove herself. I felt like going round to her mum right now and telling her what her precious daughter had been up to last night. And this morning. And to think, me and Adam helped make it happen. We'd made the organ loft like a second bedroom, Mark's second home.

I felt like going round to his dad's and telling him where his runaway son was. Not that he'd seemed to be that bothered. There were hardly missing persons posters up everywhere. The whole thing stank. Of him and her. And the smell made me sick.

I felt words bubbling up inside me. They wanted to spill out. I had to tell someone what had happened. I wanted revenge, pure and simple. I wanted to climb on my high horse, enjoy the view, then expose Jocelyn and Mark for what they were.

But what were they?

They might have been two people in love. I'd not stopped to consider that.

But they'd only known each other five minutes. Jesus, did he jump into bed with every girl who sang a song that was vaguely in tune for him?

Maybe I should tell the vicar just what was going on above the organ in that sacred place. Vile, vile, vile.

I heard the front door go. Why was Nan back? Had she

returned to check I was OK? Oh God, was she bunking off work because I had told her I was poorly? I'd have to keep it up. She'd be losing money for this inconvenience.

Still, I'd not asked her to miss work.

I still needed to talk.

Stuff it. I didn't care. I was upset, I was in shock. I would go downstairs and tell her everything that had happened. She'd be angry with me for hiding a fugitive . . . God, listen to me, treating him like he was on the run, like in that movie . . . but she would be furious when she heard what had gone on. She always said Jocelyn's family were trouble. I should've listened to her in the first place. Nan was so often right.

I hauled myself off the bed. I would go down there and tell her what was what. And it'd be good. Because she'd make me swear never to go near Jocelyn McKenzie again. And a good job it would be, too. I'd get Adam round tonight and she could tell him as well. He'd do it if she told him to. He respected her. Oh, this was going to be good, this was going to be perfect. Finally, he'd see Jocelyn for what she was. He'd kick her out of the nativity, install me in the lead role, get some other sap to play Abigail-Jade and the Archangel Gabriel, and stardom would be mine. Nan was right, I could hold a tune: why couldn't I be Mary? And then I'd have Adam back all to myself.

I stomped down the stairs.

'Nan?!'

I walked into the back room, and nearly jumped out of my skin. A huge mountain of a man was stood in the doorway between the back room and the kitchen. He had Nan's biscuit barrel in his hand and was sloppily eating a Rich Tea. Didn't he know it was rude to eat with his mouth open? His sleeves were rolled up and he had an odd circular tattoo on his lego'-lamb arms that didn't seem to mean anything. I looked up to his eyes. Who was it?!

'All right, Princess?'

It was my dad.

We sat drinking tea by the electric fire. He looked different from my memory of him. The Rockabilly quiff had gone, and his hair was shaved all over like an American conscript or Action Man. His hands were still massive and they clasped his mug, dwarfing it, making it look like he was sipping from a thimble. His once-cute dimples were hidden by a week or so's growth of beard. He looked older. Not so much Jack the Lad as Jack the Dad. Only I'm not sure he was that paternal. He'd not even asked why I wasn't in school. That's what dads were meant to be concerned about, wasn't it? That, and the football. And no lads ever going anywhere near you. But then, unlike most dads, he had been locked away from society, so maybe he didn't know what the Dad Protocol was.

'How was it?' I asked tentatively.

'What?' His voice was still gentle, like I remembered it.

'Where you were?'

'Where did your nan say I was?'

'The North Sea.'

He nodded, taking this in, a smile crossed his face like he was impressed.

'On the oil rigs,' I continued.

He sighed and took a sip from his mug. Like a giant at a tea party. I felt tiny and vulnerable in his presence. I took in his nose, almost for the first time. Why wasn't it big like mine? How come he got a flat one and I had one that could shield a glacier? Did my mum have a big one? Is that where I got it from? And then I realized that the reason his was so flat was that it had been broken, on more than one occasion maybe, over the years.

Maybe I should've got into more fights.

'You don't sound like you believe her,' he said.

I shrugged. I didn't want to get into an argument. But from what I remembered about this man, he very rarely raised his voice.

'Where were you?' I asked, sounding for all my life like Jocelyn. Direct, to the point. As Adam had taken to saying recently, in an American accent no less: *Don't fuck with me, fellas. This ain't my first time at the rodeo!* I had no idea why he said it, but every time he did it made us wet ourselves with laughter.

'You know where I was, Princess. I was inside.'

'For what?'

'All sorts. List as long as your arm. Moonlighting when I was signing on, taking and driving away, armed robbery.'

'Armed robbery?!' I gasped, sounding almost impressed. That was Big Time. Yikes!

'Oh, don't worry. I'm not a very good armed robber. That's why I got three years.'

I was so glad Nan wasn't here. I was so glad I'd chosen to bunk off today. In a way I was even glad that Jocelyn had slept with Mark and it had upset me so much, because for once someone was being honest with me, being a grown-up. And it felt comforting. I knew that Nan only ever lied to try and make me feel better. But that counted on me never discovering the truth, and round here that was impossible to avoid.

I remembered Nan telling a story about growing up in the war. How she and her brothers and sisters had seen the May Blitz. How all over Liverpool bombs were going off and buildings blazed, lighting the sky up a million different colours. Her sister had asked her what was going on. And Nan had replied, 'Don't worry, Lily. They're just fireworks.'

And that's what Nan had done to me. Tried to make me less scared by saying the bombs were only fireworks.

'How long you back for?'

'As long as me mam'll have me.' And then, as an afterthought, he added, 'And you.'

'You can stay as long as you want as far as I'm concerned.'

Well, at least he wasn't back-stabbing me. Unlike some.

I stared again at the tattoo on his arm. Only now did I realize it was in fact a bruise. And it looked angry. It looked new. It looked like someone had been grabbing onto his arm. Maybe he'd been helping an old dear across the street and she'd fallen? Though it was more than likely he'd got into a fight. Typical Dad, getting into trouble so soon after getting out. He saw me looking, and he quietly rolled down his shirt sleeve to cover it.

'You've been in the wars,' I said.

'I bruise easily,' he said. 'It's nothing.'

That's how I felt, come to think of it. I bruised easily too.

He went for a bath, and there was a knock at the door. Adam was stood on the doorstep, arms folded and steam coming out of his ears, practically.

'Well, I phoned the vicar. Told him he had squatters. He's fuming!'

And he barged his way in. He was so wrapped up in what had gone on that he didn't notice Dad's bag or coat strewn across the couch.

'He's gone round there, mob-handed.'

'Mob-handed? He's about ninety!'

'Yeah, well, he's taken backup.'

'Backup?!' What did he think this was? *Cagney and Lacey*? 'Who's he taken?'

'Jean who irons the surplices, and Peggy who does his cleaning. I told him he may as well call the police. I also impressed upon him the fact that this had to sound like an anony.'

'Anony?' I knew that Adam called anonymous phone calls 'anonies' – but what was he on about now?

'Anonymous tip-off.'

He paced the room, arms still folded. He was so on edge. This had really got to him.

'Why's it got to you so much, Adam?'

'We gave that lad a home. A home, Kathleen! And look how that gobshite REPAID us!'

And as he said 'repaid', he really banged the table. The noise shocked even him. He fell onto a hard-backed chair. He couldn't look at me. I could tell he was crying, eyes transfixed on the window.

Time for some truth-telling.

'Adam?'

He didn't answer.

'Do you fancy Jocelyn?'

He swung round.

'Oh for fuck's sake, Kathleen! Are you thick?'

'No, I'm not!'

'Then open your frigging eyes!'

'I don't get it!'

'I fancy fucking Mark!'

He looked away, back out of the window, and we both sat there in silence. Well, I say silence; he kept making little whimpering noises, like a puppy wanting to be let out for a wee. Eventually he spoke.

'And I'll tell you something else.'

Oh God. The penny dropped.

'Are you gay, Adam?'

He gave me a look as if to say, 'ha ha, very funny' –
although actually I was being deadly serious. 'That Jocelyn
. . . is a fucking slut. I wash my hands of her. And I'll tell
you something else.'

'You're not gay?' I was so confused.

'If she thinks she's playing Mary after this – the VIRGIN
Mary – she can go and fucking swivel. Virgin, my hoop. She's
had more pricks than KerPlunk by the looks of it.'

Dad came down from his bath shortly after. He was wearing a damp towel and an old T-shirt. I immediately became
embarrassed. Not only was it alien to have such an inescap-
ably male presence in the house, at once casual but at the same
time all-pervading, but I worried that the display of male leg
might be intoxicating for the newly gay Adam. Well, newly
gay to me. Dad announced he was going to go into town for a
look around, and did I want to come? I jumped at the chance.
He was the lifebuoy to which I was able to cling after the
stormy events of the morning. Adam declined, saying he was
going to seek solace in the sweet shop. But he told me to mark
his words, he had decided to wash his hands completely of
that church, that nativity play, the whole shebang. Too many
painful memories. I thought this was a bit of an overreaction,
and didn't really believe he'd see it through.

How wrong I was.

Adam and I resigned from the choir and the production,
which caused consternation amidst the flock. Who would
play Joseph now? Adam said he had to leave because of
artistic differences. He just never said who those differences
were with, or what they were.

We washed our hands of Jocelyn. We heard on the grapevine that Mark was back at home. We broke up for Christmas and saw nothing of Jocelyn. She didn't come knocking. I thought she might, particularly at Adam's door. She didn't know that we'd seen her climbing out of the window. But maybe she'd twigged. But then I remembered that as Adam and I had backed away from the wasteland that day, he had shouted SLUT very loudly, and then we'd run. It was more than feasible that she'd heard this.

We knew it wasn't an ongoing thing; we soon heard that Mark was dating a girl from Kirkby who was a member of the Young Socialists and had had three lines in *Brookside*.

We heard that Jocelyn was a smash hit in the role of Mary, and lots of people had commented how refreshing it was to see Mary being Sierra Leonean.

We also heard that Paul from *The Sound of Music* made quite the impression as Joseph. And his younger sister Pauline, not from *The Sound of Music*, was dull as crud as Abigail-Jade and the Archangel Gabriel – and she was in such a rush to do the quick costume change from one to the other that she tripped down the pulpit steps and gashed her forehead open, and an ambulance had to be called. She was blue-lighted away, still with her angel wings on. Unable to continue with the performance, Jocelyn decided to entertain the congregation with a soulful medley of Christmas carols.

Adam said he thought this sounded ghastly. I added that I wondered whether any of the stained glass windows had shattered and had to be replaced afterwards.

Nan knew that something had gone down between me and Jocelyn, but she was too busy fussing over the new member of the household to be that upset or that punitive about me stopping going to church. She talked a lot about 'the rigs' and 'that perishing North Sea', so much so that Dad eventually silenced her one day with, 'Mam, she knows. Stop digging a fucking hole.'

And Nan had looked alarmed. And then embarrassed. And then carried on as if she'd never invented a cover story at all. She still never mentioned prison, though. It was as if Dad had just been on a really long holiday – as uninteresting as it was long, since none of us particularly wanted to talk about it, never mind see any pictures.

Jocelyn continued to ignore us if we ever saw her in the street. I'd see her every now and then, waiting at the bus stop to go into town to catch the train to school. Or coming out of the chippy with a bag of scraps.

Then I discovered that Adam had put a note through Jocelyn's door saying he couldn't be her friend any more because we knew that she'd slept with Mark, and how hurtful he thought this was to me. I was a bit cross when he told me. He was as angry as I was, and I didn't see why I should have to take all the blame. But, me being me, I just went along with it. Besides, I had my dad back now. And I had Adam all to myself. Things were definitely looking up.

Liverpool, 1986

It was a new year. There was new life on the street. Some of the houses had a fresh lick of paint. The weedy trees on the wasteland, struggling to grow between abandoned petrol cans and rocks, bore flowers if they were lucky. Ice-cream vans called after school every evening. People stood outside the pub instead of sitting in. Soon we'd be going back to school after the long summer break.

The rumours were that Jocelyn had moved away. I didn't know how they'd started, but it was Nan that first told me, and I told Adam.

We walked past her house a lot, just to see if we could glean anything. One evening during the summer holidays we saw a woman in a nurse's uniform sitting smoking on the step. She was white. We stopped.

'Does Jocelyn not live here any more?' Adam asked her.

The woman shook her head. 'They went away. They'll be back, like.'

'Where did they go?' I chipped in.

'Llandrindod Wells,' she said, like it was the most natural place to go to in the world. Like she was going to add, *Where else, love?*

'Why's she gone there?' said Adam.

The nurse shrugged. 'Her mam was a bit off-colour. The air's better for her there.'

And then she stubbed out her ciggie by wiping it against the brickwork next to the front door, and scuttled inside. The conversation was over. Adam shouted after her, 'How long have they gone for?!' She just scowled back and shut the door like she hadn't heard him – but we knew she had.

As time went on, the strength of our feelings about Jocelyn dwindled. I guessed it was because the crushes Adam and I had had on the hitherto saintly Mark had waned, and therefore the fact that Jocelyn had 'gone there' felt increasingly less painful or important. In fact, one night while Adam and I were out for a walk around the local streets, he even went so far as to say he missed her.

'Why?' I asked. Although to be honest, part of me kind of missed having one more person to speak to, other than Adam.

'I dunno. I guess I'd just like to ask her what he was like.'

'In bed?'

'How big it was. That kind of thing.'

And we both fell about in hysterics. The way we did.

'How long ago was it now?' he asked.

I shrugged. 'Well, it was December, wasn't it? Ages ago.'

He nodded.

We turned off Smithdown Road, back into Alderson Road, when we saw a car pulling up outside Jocelyn's house. We instinctively slowed down to get a good look. Maybe it was the odd nursey one, back from a shift at the hospital. Maybe she'd killed someone today. She looked the sort.

It was dark. It had been raining earlier, and there were puddles everywhere. As the car pulled up it sprayed the pavement outside Jocelyn's with water. The engine went off, the lights died and whoever was inside took forever to get out. The passenger door opened and Jocelyn's little sisters got out. I always forgot she had any. They ran up to the front door, which was opened by someone inside, and she went in. Then Jocelyn climbed out. She was all wrapped up in a massive coat, the sort that looked like a duvet. She looked tired and drawn, not her usual fabulous self. Her hair was tatty and had no style to it, and she looked seriously knackered. She was standing on the pavement looking into the car, which is when her mum got out. She appeared to be carrying a basket. While Jocelyn went and opened the boot and started hauling suitcases out, the streetlamp by their house lit up what was in her mum's basket.

I gasped.

Jocelyn's mum had a baby in there.

We walked on. Her mum saw us coming, and faltered for a second. She looked to the boot of the car, where Jocelyn was getting the last of their luggage out.

'Jocelyn,' she said quietly, alerting her daughter to the fact that we were approaching. Jocelyn took the hint and looked round.

'All right, Jocelyn?' Adam chirruped.

Jocelyn nodded, and looked embarrassed to have been seen.

'How was Llandrindod Wells then?' Adam continued.

Jocelyn looked to her mum as if she didn't know how to respond.

Her mum smiled. 'I thought I wasn't well. And then I had this little bundle of joy.'

'Mum had a baby,' added Jocelyn. You know, just in case we hadn't worked out what that small human being was doing in a carrycot.

'Congratulations, Mrs McKenzie,' I said.

'Yeah. Congratulations,' Adam echoed.

'I better get him inside.' And with that, she vanished into the house.

'Nice to see you again, Jocelyn,' Adam said, still cheery.

'Yeah,' I agreed. 'It's been too long.'

Jocelyn was acting all mortified. And she picked up some suitcases and said, 'I've got to get in.'

And get in she did.

Adam and I walked on.

'Fancy her mum not knowing she was pregnant,' I said, eventually. But I could see Adam was thinking.

'She hasn't got a boyfriend, though. So who's the dad?' he said.

I shrugged.

'That baby was very light-skinned. Did you see?'

I nodded. Adam looked at me, paling by the minute. 'When did the Mark thing happen again?'

'December. Just before the nativity.'

'And where are we now? What month?' He was saying all this like he was my teacher at school and I needed to be extra clever to work out the answers, but once I did, I would feel very proud of myself.

'September,' I said.

'And how many months is that, since Jocelyn slept with Mark?'

I counted it out on my fingers. 'Nine.'

'Nine.'

We carried on walking. Adam linked me. 'No way is that baby hers. It's Jocelyn's.'

'Really?!'

'She's been in the family way. They've been away. Come

back with a cover story so that her daughter doesn't look like a slag.'

I had a feeling that Adam was right.

'It's as clear as the nose on your face.'

My nose, again!

'That baby's Jocelyn's. Bet you any money.'

BILLY

London, 2015

Dear God,

I know I don't speak to you very often and I know I should try more. I know I've stopped saying my prayers but you know that I start each day by saying to you, 'Help me get through this,' and that I finish each day as my head hits the pillow saying, 'Thank you for getting me through.' I know it's not enough though, even if it feels sometimes like it should be.

I went back to the flats today. The mud was dry and jagged with cuts. Like someone slashed it with a knife. But you'd never know she'd been there. There's some African shops built in the bottom of it. I go and buy a can of Lilt and then sit on a wall and think, staring at the spot. I thought there might be a circle on the ground the colour of aubergine. But that would be just too poetic. Someone has cleaned it all up.

Gone.

The Lilt was warm. I think their fridge mustn't have been working.

As I sat there I seen *her* turn up. She was with some fella. He really looked familiar. Eventually they went into the flats. She saw me. She looked at me. But she didn't register me. I was nothing to her.

Sounds familiar, right? No change there.
I'm upset. I shouldn't take it out on you. I'll go.
Amen.

ADAM

London, 2015

Whenever I tell people what I do for a living they always think it's really strange. Picture the scene. A crowded bar. No! A table with strangers at some ghastly wedding. Someone leaning in. Wearing a fascinator. A lady, probably. Or a quirkily dressed man. Jeez, what kind of wedding is this?

'You do WHAT?'

'I'm a hairdresser's agent.'

'A hairdresser's WHAT?'

'I'm an agent. And I look after a hairdresser.'

'You're an agent and you look after a hairdresser?'

'Yes, that's what I . . .'

'A hairdresser needs an AGENT?'

'This one does.'

'To do what?'

'Sort out their deals. Book their flights. Manager their haircare range, their franchise. You know, their chain of . . .'

'I don't really understand all that.'

So why bloody ask? But I can't be rude.

'Well, it's a lot to take in.'

'Who is she?'

'It's a bloke.'

'Sorry?'

'I said it's a bloke.'

'A BLOKE?'

'Yes, some men cut hair, it's not all women.'

'An actual BLOKE?'

'That's what I said.'

'Is it Nicky Clarke?'

'No.'

'I can't stand Nicky Clarke.'

'It's not him.'

'He looks like Myra Hindley.'

'It's not Nicky Clarke.'

'Who is it?'

'You wouldn't know them.'

'Who is it?'

'It doesn't matter.'

'I might've heard of them.'

'It's Jay-Jay Velazquez.'

'Sorry?'

'Jay-Jay Velazquez.'

'Beg pardon?'

And so it goes on.

At wedding dos the questioner usually turns to their partner/mother/insouciant donkey and shouts, 'He's a hairdresser's agent.' Pause. 'No fucking clue either, love.' And then they both turn to look at me, the donkey in particular giving me decidedly intense evils. They then both tuck into their bread rolls as 'the soup's taking forever'.

Hey. Don't get me wrong. I never wanted to be a hairdresser's agent. I didn't grow up on the mean streets of Liverpool – well, actually, they weren't that mean, I lived above a sweet shop, it was hardly *Goodfellas* – thinking, 'If only I could become a hairdresser's agent. My life would be MADE and I could escape this bunch of clowns.' I, like the average person I previously outlined, wouldn't have had a clue what one was. To me, hairdressers were just something that my mum went to every now and again if there was something fancy to get ready for. Most of the time she dabbled with home perming, or a mate would come round and shove a perforated swimming cap on her head and hook wisps of hair through to tint. I used to love watching the theatre of it, front-row seats. Trips to the hairdresser's were rare occasions to be cherished, especially after the seventies when Mum decided that wigs were a vital part of her going-out wardrobe.

I remember one time she'd agreed to babysit for someone up the road and she wore a dazzling new red curly wig. At the time I thought it made her look like the funny one from *The Liver Birds* who now pulls pints in *Emmerdale*. Looking back, she looked more like Ronald bloody McDonald. So anyway, she goes to babysit the same kid again the next week, only she forgets and puts on a different wig. Her Lesley Judd bob wig, to be precise (I never forget a wig). Well. She only comes back half an hour later saying the lad took one look at her and burst out crying, refusing to believe he'd ever met her before. She was fuming. She swapped wigs, legged it back, and we didn't see her again till midnight. Mission accomplished!

Back then I was a kid full of a million multi-coloured feelings, but my strongest desire was to perform. To write. To do anything showbizzy. I wanted to be a theatrical, basically, to lounge around in Soho on a chaise longue in a smoking jacket casting my pearls of wisdom before the glamorous swine. I had my brief time in the sun, eventually; but these days I'm very happy working out of the limelight and behind the scenes.

I've done a shedload of different jobs in my time, but about fifteen years ago I took a temping job with a big hairdresser's agency in London. Jocelyn sorted it for me, as she was then seeing the guy who ran the agency, Leon. Leon liked the cut of my jib and after a few months promoted me to being a booker, and before I knew it, I had my own client list. But after a dozen or so years I got sick of the day-to-day grind with hairdressers I couldn't stand, or hairdressers who were rude, or vile, or both. But I did hit it off with Jay-Jay.

Then about a year ago I decided to retire – controversial at 44, but fuck it, by now I had a rich boyfriend and a small child – and Jay-Jay went nuts and somehow persuaded me to go it alone, work from home and just look after him. He earns a shitload of money to my shedload and I take 20 per cent, so I'm comfortable, and quite like the fact that I can make my high-powered business calls from the comfort of my own couch, often in my Deputy Dawg pyjama bottoms.

Jay-Jay Velazquez's real name is Jason Vaughan. He came to the agency as a naive twenty-year-old, just a few years younger than me, with some hairdressing prizes under his belt and a rather forced cheeky-chappy demeanour; but I caught more than a whiff of eau de bitchy queen in his cutting asides to know that I defo fancied a night out with this fella. Not coz I fancied him, but because I knew we would have a scream. Which we did. And for some reason, possibly after about eighteen vodkas, I started referring to him as Jay-Jay instead of Jason. And because of his Hispanic dark looks, that turned into Jay-Jay Velazquez about eighteen more vodkas later. And Jason, being a narcissist, loved it. And kept screaming it round the club.

'I'm Jay-Jay Velazquez! I'm Jay-Jay Ve-fucking-lazquez! What's my name?!'
JAY-JAY VELAZQUEZ!

From that moment on, I was his favourite person at the agency. If he needed something sorting he'd phone me instead of Leon, and within a few weeks Leon got over himself and deigned to let me be Jay-Jay's agent full time. Especially when he threatened to leave the agency if Leon didn't allow it. He had him over a barrel. Leon hated it. I, of course, LOVED it. I'd gone from reception to the main table in under six months, unheard of at that place, and all because I'd shown Jason Vaughan I could have a laugh with him. And also possibly because I was the only person at that agency who could understand a word he said. He'd gab away in his thick Glaswegian accent and you'd see the other agents nodding away, clearly not understanding a word he was saying, eyes flitting to me to see if I was frowning or smiling. If I laughed, they followed suit. Then when he'd left they'd be all, 'What did he say? WHAT DID HE SAY?'

Or 'God, wasn't he funny? He's such a hoot. I was literally PISSING myself.'

'He was telling us his mum's died.'

'Was he? Poor love. He seemed in bits. I did wonder.'

I like to think it added to his intrigue.

Also, he wasn't daft. When a Hollywood film star was paying him ten grand to fly round the world and cut her hair for the Golden Globes, he made sure she got every word he said. You don't wanna go into Lady Gaga's suite before the Oscars and have her going 'WHAT ARE YOU SAYING? CAN YOU WRITE IT DOWN? HERE, WRITE IT WITH THE BLOOD FROM THIS RAW STEAK I'M USING AS A PILLOW.'

Basically that's how he continues to be the star he is today. He's all sorts to all people. He can fit in with people from any walk of life – if he so desires. And, of course, he's a fucking good hairdresser. Well, I would say that, I'm his agent. But he is. Take my word for it. Unless you're a hairdresser, you'll know that as fact.

My fella refers to him as the Diva. But that's another story.

I've been lucky really, what with this week being Jocelyn's funeral and me and Kathleen suddenly hanging out together like old times, because Jay-Jay is away this week, so I have a tiny bit of breathing space to mingle. And it's been so good to see old Kath. Thank God she's put on weight. I thought it was just me who got to forty-five and turned into Giant Haystacks. My weight's got even worse since I don't have to go into work every day in an office. Now when I do venture out to meet-ings and see people I've not seen for a few months, I see them looking me up and down, and then I get the inevitable:

Oh, you look well.

You suit a bit of weight.

See, I didn't like you when your face was thin.

You look healthy. Good for you.

And believe me. None of these are compliments in the circles I move in. That's why I wanted to leave the business. Bitch Central. The people I deal with make RuPaul look like Pam Ayres.

The phone goes. It's Jay-Jay. He's back from wherever and wants to meet for lunch, coz he has something important to tell me.

'Can't you tell me now? You've got me worried, Jay-Jay.'

'No.' He sounds solemn. 'This deserves face to face.'

I immediately go into panic mode. It's what every agent does when a client says they can only meet face to face and they need to talk. It can only mean bad news. He wants to leave me. He wants to go in a different direction. He doesn't think I'm doing enough for him. He wants me to take a lower per cent of his income. He thinks I'm too fat for him. But all roads lead to the first one.

He wants to bloody leave me!

I quickly phone Jason as I'm picking out clothes from the wardrobe.

(I know. It's confusing. The two men in my life having such similar names.)

'Jason, he wants to leave me. Jay-Jay wants to . . .'

'Bollocks. He thinks the sun shines out of your arse.'

'He thinks the sun shines out of his dog's arse, doesn't mean he'd want fucking Pauline to be his agent.' Pauline is Jay-Jay's bull mastiff.

'You're overreacting.'

'I'm not! What's so bad that it has to be done face to face? It'd be OK if I had a client list as long as my arm, but I haven't. It's just him. If he goes, I've got nothing left!'

'Adam . . .'

'Oh, shit, who's going to look after Denim?!'

'Denim's at school, darling. And we have a nanny.'

Right. Yes. Of course we do. Of course he is.

'Now calm down, Adam. You know what Jay-Jay's like. He's a coward. If he wanted to leave you, he'd be too scared of saying it to your face. He'd ping you an email.'

Actually, that rings true. My heart rate starts to slow.

'Look, I've got to go. But let me know how you get on.'

'Tar.' And I fling my phone on the bed, pissed off with myself for being unable to pick out a simple outfit, and head to the shower.

An hour later, I'm sitting in my private members' club in Soho looking like something Graham Norton threw up in the Nineties. Why did I choose this stupid spangly jacket? And the dayglo yellow leopard-print pants? If he comes here undecided, this garish ensemble will make the decision for him. Not so much *it's not you, it's me*, but *it's not you, it's your clothes*. And who could blame him, eh?

Why am I doing this so much lately? Why am I making such poor choices? Jason says it's the shock of Jocelyn dying. It's made me forgetful and I keep getting confused. The other day I couldn't for the life of me remember where Jay-Jay had gone to, and I had to go to my laptop and check his diary to confirm. When I lie in bed at night I worry I've got early-onset Alzheimer's and I keep thinking of *Still Alice* and how sad that scene was when Julianne Moore's in bed panicking, and it's enough to send me into a panic, but when I wake Jason like Julianne wakes Alec Baldwin, Jason's not half as accommodating or supportive as him and growls at me to get to fucking sleep.

He thinks I'm a drama queen.

If the cap fits.

A waiter approaches with a garish cocktail.

'Here you go, sir.'

'Is that a porn-star martini?'

I recognize the lychee.

'Yes, sir.'

But I don't remember ordering it. I feel panic rise in my chest. Oh God. It's started. Jay-Jay will walk in and I won't recognize him, and I'll think he's my nephew or something and I'll offer him a toffee. I have early-onset Alzheimer's and it'll kill me quickly coz I don't go running like Julianne Moore.

But then I see the waiter's eyes flitting across to the other side of the bar, then he bites his bottom lip. And he says,

'I'm so sorry, sir. This isn't yours, is it? I got the wrong table. I do apologize.' And he whisks it away.

And I relax. I'm not going mad, and I'm not losing my memory.

Bloody hell, I should sue this place for giving me palpitations.

But then I think, *Was it a lychee? Or was it a slice of passion fruit?*

Damn. I can't remember the ingredients for a porn-star martini. And I can't remember the names of simple fruits.

Mind you. Lychees and passion fruits. They're hardly oranges and lemons.

See?! I can remember oranges and lemons! Things are looking up.

Or is there a fruit-based spectrum for the diagnosis of dementia? Exotic fruits are at the lower end. When you get to everyday fruit – well. Basically, you're fucked.

Just then, Jay-Jay arrives. He can't look me in the eye as he orders a Diet Coke. He's been in AA for years and tells me all the alkies drink Diet Coke.

'Jay-Jay, about the outfit . . .' I start to say, when he swings round in his seat and looks me straight in the eye.

'I got you here today, Adz, because . . .'

He looks like a deflated football. Like there's no oxygen inside him to help him form any words. I feel a catch in my throat. He is. He's going to leave me. Shit on me from a great height. Why didn't I at least wear a hat?

'I feel so bad about this. And I was just going to send you an email, but . . . I discussed it in the rooms last night, and everyone agreed I owed it to you to see you and say it to your face.'

Oh, shite.

Mind you, what are *rooms*? Oh yes, that's what he calls AA.

'You want new representation?'

He looks genuinely bewildered by that. Sort of throws his neck back in a jolt so his head does a weird whiplash thing.

'What?'

'You've got a new agent? Is it Lindsey at Premier? I know she looks after Sam.'

'Oh fuck off, Adz. The thing I want to say is this.'

He leans on the table. And again can't look me in the eye. He carries on.

'A few weeks ago, I put this thing on Twitter.'

'A tweet. It's called a tweet.'

'Aye, a tweet. And in it, I said that I wished that cunt Jocelyn Jones would hurry up and die.'

WHAT?

Is that what this is about?

'And then she did. And I forgot she was your pal. And I was like "Fucking great news aye", and I was really slagging her off and posting Vines of her being vile. And . . . see, I didn't like her. But I keep forgetting she was your pal.'

I've given up policing Jay-Jay's tweets. I had no idea he'd been doing this.

'And I just want to say how sorry I am. Coz someone told me you had the funeral the other day. When I was in Miami.'

I'm so relieved he's not leaving me, I break into a smile. An agent's job with any client is to make them feel good at all times. In case they leave you and you lose their commission. And as he's my only client, it is imperative he stays. So even though part of me wants to argue a little and point out there was a nice side to Jocelyn, I don't.

'Oh, Jay-Jay, please. There's no need. Yeah, she was my mate, but even I was horrified about what she said about . . . so many things. She liked a reaction. She'd've probably loved you posting Vines after she'd died.'

He looks so relieved now. 'Really?'

'Aye,' I say, mimicking his Scottish accent, which is my way of signalling that everything is all right. He takes my hand quickly. I wonder what he's going to say next.

'I'd never wanna hurt you, Adz. You're my rock. You get me?'

'I get you, Jay-Jay. Now come on. Man up. And tell me all about Miami. How was Kate Winslet? Did she behave herself?'

He does a head toss and a grunt as if to say ask a silly question. 'See that girl, Adz? I fucking love her. She's my rock.'

OK. So everyone is clearly his rock at the moment, and he loves them. I let him witter on for ten minutes, then order some soft-shell crab. I ponder on how much I've changed recently. I don't mean the 'I think I've got Alzheimer's' stuff. More . . . when I wanted to leave the agency, I never wanted to look after a hairdresser again. And Jay-Jay convinced me to keep him on and work for him, and a huge part of me didn't want to, but I thought I owed it to him and the situation wouldn't be too manic. Now, a few years later, I realize I must enjoy my job and the kudos it brings and the job satisfaction, if I'm going to panic so much about him leaving me.

Which he isn't.

And I feel utter relief.

And that makes me feel good. I must be enjoying my life.

My food arrives. As I'm tucking into my first claw, Jay-Jay brings the conversation back to Jocelyn.

'So. She killed herself.'

'Yeah.'

'I'm trying to be sympathetic, but . . .'

Here we go. How many people have said this to me lately?

'. . . well, I guess at least it shows she had a conscience. About all that bile she was always spouting.'

'I guess.' Though I don't necessarily know that's true.

'I guess when you live your life through soundbites, there's a hole in your soul.'

'Erm . . .'

'That was a good song, wasn't it?'

'Abba?'

'Yeah. I mean, I can't remember it, but I remember the title. So how was the funeral?'

'Oh, you know . . .'

What can I say? What can you say when someone's killed themselves, and they weren't that popular, and no-one really seems to care?

'Suicide was the elephant in the room. It was nice hooking up with friends I'd not seen for ages, though. I saw my best mate from when I was a kid. Kathleen. Me, her and Jocelyn used to hang out together all the time.'

He laughs. 'She knows where the bodies are buried!'

Which makes me laugh, too. 'Yeah. Something like that!'

'Adz?' He's sounding tentative. I don't like it when he sounds tentative.

'Aha?'

'She did commit suicide, didn't she?'

And the tone of his voice shows he's inferring something else. Or that he wants reassurance. He often wants reassurance, and it's my job as his agent to give it to him.

'Yeah. Sure. Why?'

'Nothing.'

'No, what? Tell me, Jay-Jay!'

'Well d'you remember that day? Months back. And she'd

112

written that piece in the paper and we were both raging. The piece . . .'

'I remember that piece.'

How could I forget?

'Well, d'you remember what we talked about afterwards?'

I shake my head. It's true, I can't. Can I?

'We went for a walk. Up to the Heath. Och, it doesn't matter.'

And he grins as if to say it's nothing, and he's making a mountain out of a molehill.

And then I start to feel weird, as certain memories flood back. And then I remember. I know what we discussed; I just didn't associate it with that particular day.

I change the subject and talk about some of the options that have come in for him while he's been in Miami. A TVC for Pantene, shooting in New York, and the upcoming shows in London, Paris and Milan.

But he glazes over and says, 'So you hadn't seen this girl since you were a kid?'

'Kind of.'

'So how many years is that?'

'I don't know. Well, no, I knew her well into my twenties. We moved to London together, but then we eventually lost touch. Well, we fell out. All three of us. Big time.'

'God, that sounds like my life. What did yous fall out over?'

'Oh, I . . .' Of course I can remember. How could I ever forget? 'It was so long ago. It was probably dead trivial, but back then it felt so huge.'

And I steer the conversation back to Pantene.

After a while he asks after Denim. I tell him Denim is fine.

'Awwww, my little godson. Give him a big sloppy one from me tonight.'

I know. I asked Jay-Jay to be Denim's godfather, and he accepted. It was a business move more than anything. As Jay-Jay is so loaded I knew Denim would never be short of a decent present on birthdays and Christmas. Shallow? I hold my hands up.

'And how's that nanny thing?' He sounds less keen now. Jay-Jay doesn't like the nanny.

'Jay-Jay, I've told you . . .'

'That boy needs a nice gay boy for a nanny,' he spits.

'In order to get the adoption passed we had to prove that Denim would have a female influence in his life, other than our mothers. And so we said we'd have a nanny who was a woman.'

'Was a woman?' Suddenly he's interested. 'Is she transitioning?'

'Get you with all the jargon. No, she's not. She's cis.'

He nods. And then I realize. He just thinks I'm abbreviating her name. Our nanny is called Cissy.

'No. Cis. It means you're born with . . .' And then even I can't remember the proper definition. 'Well, it's short for cisgender anyway. And you identify with the gender you were born with. Or something.'

And then I'm saved by the bell. Or the buzz. I feel my phone pulse in my pocket. I whip it out and check what's occurring.

A text from Kathleen.

Still on for tomorrow?

I reply, *You betcha.*

And Jay-Jay's words ring in my ears.

She knows where the bodies are buried.

London, 1990

The air was thick with the sound of Sinead O'Connor emoting the frig out of her never-ending number one song, 'Nothing Compares 2 U'. Some days I liked it. Some days it made me want to peel all my skin off and jump in a vat of salt.

'It's so pretentious,' I said to Kathleen over a cheeky Coke in the Pullman carriage. 'Fancy spelling it "2 U" rather than spelling it out properly.'

'Lazy bitch,' she agreed. 'Oh, change the subject Adam, I'm sick of thinking about her. She's everywhere.'

'She's ubiquitous,' I said, showing off that I knew the word and what it meant.

I could tell Kathleen wasn't so sure.

'In fact, that should be the name of her next album.'

'Change the subject,' Kathleen repeated.

What could I say? Oh yes. Gossip.

'Paula Yates was in with her kids again this morning.'

Kathleen rolled her eyes. 'Christ, have they nicked anything?'

'No, they were just creating merry hell.'

'Huh, what's new?'

'They better not've spilt cherry Vimto over any of the frocks again.'

Kathleen rolled her eyes again, this time more dramatically. 'Jesus, Sinead, will you just GIVE . . . OVER?!!'

As she boomed the last few words, a figure loomed large over us. A six-foot woman with a severe orange bob, dressed in a hot-pink geisha dress complete with wooden shoes that were a cross between a clog and a flip-flop. Our boss, Wendy.

'Adam? Kathleen? Why's the concession closed?'

Shit. She wasn't meant to be coming in today.

'Oh, we were just taking a break, Wendy,' I said, as if we'd both just run a marathon and were staggering round in tin-foil blankets drinking orange squash. Actually, I thought it sounded quite good, so I added a pathetic whimper on the end.

Wendy was unimpressed. 'Together?'

'Well . . .'

'When the concession's closed, I'm not making money.'

'Sorry, Wendy. It's my fault,' Kathleen said. 'My granddad just died.'

Wendy's nostrils flared. 'Again? That's the third time. Get back to fucking work.'

I liked how cheeky Kathleen had got lately. I just wished she'd remember which lies she'd used before. Wendy was heading away from the train and back onto the shop floor.

Kathleen and I were working at Hyper Hyper, an alternative fashion emporium on Kensington High Street. Yes, in that there London. It was an incredibly eclectic, cacophonous place on two floors, crammed with stands that sold clothes from up-and-coming designers. We worked in the basement for Wendy Wan (pronounced *one*), for her label Wendy1. The Pullman carriage was the shop cafe and was the carriage of a train that you went into to sit down and have a cup of tea in. To our minds it was the quirkiest, trendiest thing on the planet. Even if it did appear to play Sinead O'Connor on a loop. Every time I heard it I pictured her in the video, that solitary tear running down the valley between her nose and cheek. Only they played it so much in here that in my imagination there'd been so many tears, the place was drowning in her pretentious pain.

Wendy Wan had not long graduated from Central Saint Martins and had created quite a buzz with her futuristic, clubby clothes. They were really cool, but at twenty-five quid a T-shirt, me and Kathleen thought they were a complete rip-off. Especially as that was currently what we each earned in a week here. Wendy had recently married a Chinese bloke, hence the surname, and expected all her staff to dress in Chinese clothes. When I say all her staff, I basically mean me and Kathleen. She'd interviewed us the day she set up stall here and liked that we came as a double act, could be quite funny and had Liverpool accents. She said it made her enterprise very 'global'. Scousers in Chinese dress selling weird shit: that, to Wendy, was the essence of global. Whatever global meant – I didn't really get it. But it paid me my wages, so who was I to argue?

We hurried back to the concession, though it was tricky for Kathleen and Wendy in their tight Chinese dresses. They shuffled. It was easier for me in my Chinese pyjamas and trainers, so I got there first.

'I did ask Zoe from Ghost to keep an eye on the stall, Wendy,' I heard Kathleen saying.

'She doesn't have a vested interest. You do.'

Once back I saw that Zoe from Ghost, the stall next to ours, was flicking through a copy of *Jurassic Park*. She called out, in her thick-as-treacle Dublin accent, 'Wait till you read this. You'll DIE.'

'What's it about, Zo?'

'Feckin' DINOSAURS.'

'Jeez. Like that's gonna catch on!'

She seemed stung. 'It's actually complete gas!'

'Yeah, right!'

Just then Wendy and Kathleen shuffled back.

'Don't talk to Ghost.' Wendy snapped. Fraternizing with the enemy was frowned on by our boss.

Zoe gave her daggers and called, 'I shifted one o' them weird cubist T-shirts for you. Money's in the till.'

'Thanks, Zo!' I called back. And Wendy allowed a tight smile before checking that everything was hanging on the rails just the way she liked it.

The cubist T-shirts were these oversized T-shirts that had rubber cubes hanging off them. The Pet Shop Boys had worn them in a photoshoot in *i-D* recently and now everyone was going mad for them, even if when you wore them out it was hard not to knock people's drinks over, or have people ask why you were wearing a Christmas tree dressed by Picasso. Wendy busied herself for five minutes, running her finger along the till desk to check it wasn't dusty, counting money in said till, flattening down lumps in the wicker-style flooring mats with her wooden soles, before she decreed that she was happy with the place; and then she buggered off to meet Yuki, her fella, at Quaglino's for lunch. Though it has to be said, with all that shuffling it took her a good twenty minutes to get across the basement and slowly limp up the stairs to the ground floor, where she not-so-promptly disappeared from view.

On the whole working at Hyper Hyper was great craic, to coin an Irish phrase. Most of the time we treated it like one big playground. Nicking mannequins from other people's stalls and hiding them in the loos was one of our favourite pastimes, as was taking money out of the till and nipping across to Marks and Spencer's and buying some champagne to help speed up the hours before closing. Now, I wasn't saying that everyone who worked there was operating some sort of scam, but . . .

Or maybe I was.

Well, maybe not everybody.

OK, quite a few were.

Some days there could be a real party atmosphere, particularly on a Saturday when the management paid for a DJ to play all afternoon. Other days, we made a party of our own.

Today, though, was about making money.

Once the coast was clear and Wendy had definitely left the building, Kathleen dragged a sports bag out from under the till desk and pulled an old checked shirt of hers from it. She then took a needle and thread out from the desk drawer, and sat down to get to work.

Kathleen and I had moved to London the previous year to follow our dream of making it big in showbiz. Well, that was my dream; I wasn't really sure what Kathleen's was, but she seemed more than happy to float along on my coat-tails. And she did have her uses. It turned out that her nan's cousin had a daughter called Lou who was London-based and cleaned for various people in South London. Lou – or Loo Cleaner, as me and Kathleen called her – cleaned for a posh woman called Delia who lived in West Norwood, and she was off travelling and wanted someone to house-sit for her. Me and Kathleen got the gig.

West Norwood wasn't that amazing, but it was London and so it had an inbuilt feeling of glamour, even if it wasn't exactly Primrose Hill. The house itself was a lovely place, all stripped wood floors and rickety staircases. Every wall seemed to be covered in books. Really good books, the sort no-one would ever dream of reading. Things hung from ceilings – old bike wheels, puppets of eagles – it was like hanging out in Aladdin's cave. And it was ours, rent-free, for six months. We didn't know we were born. All we had to do was keep an eye on the place and walk her smelly Dalmatian, Kinnock, twice a day, that was the deal. Kinnock was a lovely dog, despite the smell. But he did have a tendency to fart quite a bit. And he showed no shame.

My favourite thing in the house was Delia's electric type-writer. When Lou had explained that I had aspirations to be a writer, she said I could use it as much as I wanted. So I decided that during our six-month residency I would use my time wisely and make sure I wrote a play. I had it all worked out in my head. It was going to be a masterpiece. A master-piece called *Supper with Sam*. I know. Genius title.

We got the jobs in Hyper Hyper quite quickly; there seemed to be loads of shop work going in central London. In the evenings I would work on *Supper with Sam* and Kath-leen would do her night job, selling cigarettes at a trendy bar called the Atlantic round the back of Piccadilly. She had to walk round like a cinema usherette with a tray of all kinds of ciggies. Those were the days.

She'd recently started experimenting with different looks, and her current one was a severe bob like our boss Wendy. Everyone agreed it really suited her, and it made a feature of her massive nose, rather than trying to distract from it. Now her nose appeared to poke proudly from her heavy fringe, and suddenly became magnificent rather than monstrous. It was like she was finally falling in love with it.

So while she was out showing her nose off and selling tobacco to the cocaine-snorting ne'er-do-wells from the city each night, I would sit in the upstairs bay window, looking out over the rooftops of West Norwood, dreaming and writing my life away.

I knew I was a good writer. I'd never told Kathleen this, but I'd bunked in to the back of church all those years ago and watched my first piece, *How Far Is It to Bethlehem? (Not Very Far)*, and aside from some ad-libbing from that cheeky twat who reckoned he'd been in *The Sound of Music* – which was doubtful, he'd been far too tall for a Kurt – the script held together well. And apart from a few old dears who fell asleep, it was received very well. Jocelyn had got a round of applause every time she'd finished a song. And even though I say it myself, it had been a genius idea to rewrite 'Ain't No Mountain High Enough' as 'Ain't No Manger'. During the final bows I'd slipped out again, unseen.

I mean, it was a shame half the play was missing because of that silly cow Paul's sister tripping up and having to be carted off in an ambulance. And basically the play turned into Jocelyn singing her favourite carols a capella. But the bits of the play that we did see – well, they really had legs.

So I was pretty damn confident writing *Supper with Sam*. The words poured out of me. And as a famous playwright once said, *if you're unsure what to write about, write about what you know*. I think it was that Chekhov. So I did.

'How's the play coming along?' Kathleen asked as she studiously unpicked the label from the checked shirt.

I looked around the shop floor, affecting an air of nonchalance, not that I really understood what nonchalance was, and said, 'Yeah, really well actually. I'm past the second interval and into the denouement now.'

'It's got two intervals?' gasped Kathleen, sounding mightily impressed.

'Well, it's a massive big work of art, Kathleen,' I said with a shrug. 'I was toying with three, but . . .'

She pulled a face at that. 'I hate long plays, Adam.'

The cheek of it. The bare-faced *cheek* of it!

'Er, Kathleen. The extent of your theatrical experience is seeing Cilla Black jump out of a bag o' washing and singing "Surprise, Surprise" in Widow Twankey's laundry bag, in thingy at the Empire when we went with the school . . .'

'*Aladdin.*'

'So don't tell me how long plays should be. Have yer ever seen any Shakespeare?'

'No. Have you?'

'Course not! I'm too busy writing me own masterpiece! But take my word for it. They all last a lifetime, *comprendez*?'

'Sorry, Adam.'

'You don't even mean that!'

'I do!'

'Oh, you're doing me head in, Kathleen. I'm going for a walk.'

And off I went in what could only be described as a huff. God, Kathleen could be annoying sometimes. She was so whiney! And moany. Most of the time she was fine, a hoot, a scream, but some of the time she made me really miss Jocelyn.

I thought about Jocelyn a lot. And as time went on I'd forgiven her for sleeping with the love of my life, Mark.

OK, so 'love of my life' was a bit of an exaggeration. But he was the first bloke I'd met who'd awoken that side of me. Don't get me wrong, I'd always been camp, I'd come out of the womb wearing tap shoes and belting out the bridge from 'From New York to LA', but even though since time immemorial I'd been called a queer at school, I'd never been sure whether it was true. Because I'd never actually fancied any lads.

Till Mark. I guess my life thus far was divided into two categories: BM (Before Mark) and AM (After Mark). Mark, with his wedge and his swagger and his tight trousers that left bugger all to the imagination, and his freckly skin and his hazel eyes and his perfect white teeth. Mark who actually gave me the time of day instead of punching my arm, shouting FUCK OFF QUEER, then legging it or doing a piley-on. Mark who it was easy to follow round everywhere coz it was common knowledge that Kathleen was obsessed with him. I egged her on to swoon over him as it gave me a good excuse to follow him round everywhere too, feigning support.

And then it had happened.

We'd seen Jocelyn climbing out of the church window that day, stepping out of the vestry – no longer a virgin, now a proper woman. And she'd made that journey with him. And even though I knew that day would arrive sooner or later, I just didn't expect it to arrive with her.

The great thing about writing *Supper with Sam* was that it had been cathartic for me. I hadn't told Kathleen yet but it was all based on our teenage years and, put it this way, was set in the organ loft of a fictional church in Liverpool, St Samuel's. There was a character based on me (a hopeless romantic with a pocketful of dreams, literary leanings and a yearning to move to the Smoke), a character based on Kathleen (bit nerdy, big nose, hanger-on), and then of course the bitchy black one based on Jocelyn, and the hunky one based on Mark. The great thing with the play was that I could rewrite history. So just before the second interval, my character and the Marky one copped off together. Which made him getting off with and having a baby by Jocelyn at the end even more tragic for all concerned. It was going to be amazing. I could just feel it in my waters. Every time I read it back to myself it moved me to tears and made me laugh out loud. I couldn't think of anything else I'd ever seen that was like it. It was unique.

Well, it would be, whenever I got around to finishing it. I was nearing the end of it, but at the same time didn't want the writing process to end. I loved retreating into this semifictional world in my head – it made more sense and gave me greater pleasure than anything that was happening in the real world. So I was aware that lately I was really taking my time with every new line of dialogue, because I wanted to drag that warm sensation out for as long as possible.

The liberating thing about the process was that because I'd had to put myself in the shoes of all the various characters, I'd come to a point where I felt a degree of forgiveness towards Jocelyn. I'd had to imagine how she was feeling. I kind of got her now. I'd at no point said to her, 'Please don't sleep with Mark, I fancy him.' She'd not been breaking a pact any of us had made to 'not go there' for the sake of the others. She'd obviously fancied him as much as me and Kathleen and, when the time had come, she'd gone for it.

Basically, she was one lucky bitch.

And now that I'd had to put myself in her shoes to write a character 'sort of' based on her, I discovered an empathy for her I'd hitherto lacked.

She was only doing what I would have done given the opportunity, so why should I be angry about that?

What's worse, she'd ended up having a baby. And because we'd all fallen out in such a stupid way, it meant she had to go through all that on her own. And because we weren't there we'd had to buy into the lie that the baby was really her mum's, and wasn't she lucky having a baby later in life, and there was nothing wrong with it, and . . . and all that shit.

I'd actually tried calling her a while back. I'd phoned her

mum's place in Alderson Road, only to be told by a voice I didn't recognize that Jocelyn had moved away. And when I'd asked where to, they'd replied, *Who gives a damn?* Which I felt was very Hollywood circa 1955.

I'd actually wanted to reply in a breathy American accent: *Me, Goddamit! I do! I give a damn!*

But I hadn't. And I'd hung up.

Maybe she'd run away, like me and Kathleen had.

OK, that's a bit dramatic. We'd told everyone where we were going, and they didn't try to stop us, as they saw the sense in us having a place rent-free for six months in exchange for walking a dog twice a day. But running away sounded so dramatic. Like pretending I was an orphan – another thing I liked to do occasionally. It went down really well in Hyper Hyper. But where would Jocelyn have run to, I wondered? Where did you go when you wanted to break into the music business like she did – presuming she still wanted to do that? London was the obvious choice, but maybe she'd gone somewhere closer to home, like Manchester.

Or maybe she'd won Mark back and they were living together with the baby.

Perish the thought. Anyway, I knew that wasn't true, or else my mum would have told me. My mum knew all the local gossip. So I'd called her immediately.

'No, love. I thought they'd all moved away, to be honest with you, coz I've certainly not seen that mother of hers in months. How's that Kathleen getting on?'

Mother. Always gossiping. Then the one time you actually needed something from her she was next to useless. Family, eh? Can't live with them, can't get gossip from them when really necessary.

The baby would be four by now. He would probably be a

lovely coffee colour and be completely gorgeous because with Jocelyn and Mark's genes . . . well, he'd have to be, right? His name was William, that much we did know from living on Alderson Road. But whether people called him that, or Will, or Billy, was anyone's guess.

He was probably still living with his grandma. Thinking she was his mum. His sister long gone from their lives, unable to cope with seeing her child brought up by someone else, yet so close to home. Or maybe she'd buggered off because . . . well . . . she actually just didn't give a damn. Like the person on the phone. Maybe that person had been her mum, putting a voice on. The possibilities were endless.

Some nights when Kathleen was out at work and I was meant to be tapping away on my typewriter, I would take a break and amuse myself by phoning a gay chatline. It was a premium rate number, which meant that it must've been costing me a zillion pounds a minute, but it was worth it. Despite my confidence at work, or my confidence about my writing, one thing I still got nervous about was going into gay bars or clubs and chatting to blokes. What I felt more at home doing was ringing the chat rooms. Apart from anything else, I could reinvent myself on the phone. Turn the Scouse accent on a bit, lower the voice and emit an aura of 'just in from football training', and soon all the guys in the chat room wanted to go into a private conflab for me. It worked every time. Sometimes I said my name was Mark. Somehow I managed to make out I was the straight-acting guy of their dreams, when actually I was just acting. And, let's be honest, there was nothing too straight-acting about sleeping with a fella.

Mark. Maybe by pretending to be him, I could at last feel close to him.

Some nights I just entertained myself by creating a bonkers character and chatting to whoever on the phone. Other nights, I bit the bullet and went to meet whoever I was chatting to. When I did, I would leave a little note on my bed telling Kathleen where I had gone and who I had gone to meet, just in case they turned out to be a mad axeman. And every time, even though I wasn't the big macho lout the guys thought they were getting, none of them ever complained.

Maybe I was a better actor than I thought.

None of them ever screamed, 'OH MY GOD, YOU'RE CAMP! I WAS EXPECTING BARRY FROM *BROOKSIDE*!' I suppose, like me, they were glad to find some comfort, any old port in a storm.

Usually I could have my fun and games and be home well before Kathleen got back from the Atlantic. She was none the wiser. As far as she was concerned I lived the life of a play-writing monk.

I turned a corner to head back to the Pullman cafe when a figure dressed head to toe in black and with what could best be described as a two-foot conical black dunce's cap on her head came hurtling towards me, sniffing. Floor manager Kiki Daniels. I knew what the sniff meant: it meant she'd just come from the staff toilets, and had had a little 'livener'.

'Everything OK?' she barked at me as she sped past.

'Yes, thanks, Kiki,' I offered. 'You?'

'Getting there!' she barked, and disappeared from view as she turned a corner. Then I heard her shouting it again: 'Geddinthere!'

There was nobody very interesting in the cafe, so I pootled back to the stall, where Kathleen was now sewing a 'Wendy1' label into her old checked shirt. She then hung it up on the rack.

'How much are we charging for that?' I asked, trying to sound like I'd forgiven her, even though possibly there was nothing to forgive.

'Thirty?' she asked perkily, as if nothing had happened. She could be great sometimes, could Kathleen.

'Good work, old thing,' I said in a cod posh accent. And then we both fell about hysterically.

After we'd settled down, Kathleen nudged me and nodded. I looked to where she was indicating. A young French designer was walking past. His name was Michel, and despite his incredible sense of taste there was no concealing the fact that he was a walking skeleton. After he'd passed, Kathleen sighed.

'God love him. D'you reckon it's the AIDS?'

'Gotta be.'

She looked to me.

'Adam?'

'What?'

'I just want you to know.'

'What?'

'If you ever get the AIDS I'll give up work and nurse you.'

I wasn't quite sure how I felt about that. It was incredibly touching and flattering to have someone offer to do so much for you, if need be. But at the same time it felt so very reductive – that just because I was gay, I might somehow end up like this designer.

'Oh, I wouldn't worry about that, Kath.'

'No?'

'Nah. I hardly ever do it, anyway. And when I do I'm really safe.'

Well, that wasn't a lie. Truth be told, I'd've been more than happy to have every sexual encounter of mine take place with me sporting a balaclava and rubber body stocking.

'I know but . . . well, if you do . . . get the AIDS.'

'Kathleen, will you stop calling it that?'

'Calling it what?'

'Calling it "the AIDS"!'

'Well, what am I meant to be calling it?'

'Just AIDS. Like the Asda isn't really "the Asda", AIDS is just AIDS. Not "the AIDS".'

'What's AIDS got to do with Asda?'

'We're changing the subject of this conversation now. OK?'

She silently fumed. We both sat there in silence for a bit. Tough. She had to learn. After a while I softened.

'D'you want to talk about Morrissey?' I ventured.

She wrinkled her nose and shook her head.

'D'you want to talk about that lad you fancy off *Why Don't You*?'

She looked horrified. 'That was about ten years ago! He's a friggin' kid!'

I laughed. She laughed. I'd caught her out. The ice had thawed.

'What d'you wanna talk about?' I ventured.

She sighed, and said, 'Cynthia.'

For a few weeks now she had become a bit obsessed with the woman who lived next door to us in West Norwood. She was a striking woman who was often to be seen with her hair in a chignon, dragging a pull-along suitcase behind her, dressed head to toe in red, white and blue. We thought she was always going away on holiday till another neighbour let it slip to Kathleen – she spoke to all the neighbours, I avoided them at all costs – that Cynthia was in fact a trolley dolly. Next time Kathleen had seen her, they'd struck up a rapport.

And now she had become Kathleen's favourite topic of conversation.

'I seen her last night, just getting back from a long haul to Berlin.'

I didn't know what long haul meant, but Kathleen let the words hang in the air, waiting for me to ask what it was. I didn't give her the satisfaction.

'Long haul, in case you were wondering, is when the flight goes overseas. If she was going, say, London to Manchester, that would be short haul. I think. Actually, I'm not sure.'

I stifled a yawn. She laughed.

'Cynthia has such a hoot with the other trolley dollies. They just go to these foreign climes for a day or two, hang out in some swanky hotel, get wrecked in the bar, then sober up and do a flight back.'

'Go'way,' I said, rapidly losing interest in Cynthia. She sounded like a great lush.

'Cynthia says she's always being asked out by rich business-men. Cynthia says without the uniform she's always been a bit of a plain Jane. But stick the pencil skirt on and bun up your hair, and they're throwing themselves at you.'

'Go'way,' I repeated. Which she took as a sign to carry on.

'If she's flying somewhere miles away like Sydney. When she has a break. Guess where she sleeps?'

'No idea.'

'In the tail of the plane. There's a stepladder they climb up and then they sleep in these bunk beds in the tail of the plane. She says it's the most unglamorous thing. Bras everywhere, honky breath. Then they wake up and three seconds later it's, "Chicken or fish?"'

'Chicken or fish?'

'They're the main meals they serve on a flight.'

I nodded my head. 'But what if you're a vegetarian?'

Clearly Kathleen didn't know this and hadn't thought to

ask her new best friend. I could tell she was lying when she replied, 'I think they rustle you up some cheese on toast in a special grill, out the back with all the bags.'

I let silence fall. And as it was clear she was improvising. And she was no Mike Leigh, as she'd've probably agreed.

Five minutes later some French tourists came in and were very animated, rifling through the rows of quirky clothes. Then they alighted on Kathleen's hideous old lesbian-style lumberjack shirt and went into raptures. I couldn't understand what they were saying, but their tone was almost orgasmic. Minutes later they left the shop with their new 'trendy' purchase, our old shirt. And we were thirty quid up. Result!

We had just stopped jumping up and down to celebrate our profit when Cherish from the Burlesque basque stall came running past doing a bizarre shouting-whisper thing, hissing *RAID!* to us.

All over the shop we heard tills slamming shut, shutters going down and a stampede of feet legging it to the Pullman. This could mean only one thing. Social security were doing one of their regular raids.

Kathleen and I were quite quaint for Hyper Hyper. As we were living rent-free and earning twenty-five quid a week, plus our extras on top, we had no need to sign on. But many people did, and then took the work there cash in hand. And when the DSS came a-calling, they ran to the cafe and pretended they were just in on a casual day's shopping. As we never wanted to look weird, or spoilt, or not cutting-edge, we would join them in the cafe doing lots of scared 'hope they don't catch me, Tory bastards' acting. It was huge fun. And gave us an extra half hour's break. It must have been very odd for those DSS snoopers. They must've wondered how the store managed to stay open, as every time they popped their heads in the place was like a ghost town. Though the cafe was always suspiciously crammed to the rafters.

As we sat there this time in the overstuffed train carriage, Zoe from Ghost introduced us to her pal who had just popped in. This was Tim. Ordinary name, extraordinary-looking guy. Punky, almost trying too hard to overcome his suburban name. But then he explained he spelled it with two T's. And then it made sense. Turned out Ttim was talent-spotting for a new pop video. This was always happening. Because Hyper Hyper was seen as the epicentre for all that was trendy in London, talent scouts were always coming looking for people to populate the latest video for some famous or never-heard-of-before (or after) band. Ttim was casting dancers for a new video by Ecstasy Jake, a new two-piece electronic dance band: 'You probably know them from the Madchester scene,' he said. And me and Kathleen found ourselves nodding. When Zoe said we could probably wear some zany Wendy1 outfits, Ttim begged us to be in the video. We'd get twenty quid each. Promising him we were amazing dancers, we sealed the deal with an Appletiser and an Orangina. We had to get to the Windmill Theatre near Piccadilly Circus the following Saturday. We couldn't wait. Me and Kathleen – practically pop stars!

The following Friday it was our day off, and I finished the play. As I typed the stage directions –

```
Off, we hear a baby cry. Sam and Whitney look
to the door. The sun sets through the stained-
glass window. Blackout.
THE END
```

– I actually cried. Tears fell on the paper and blotted some of the words. So I had to type it out again.

I pulled the paper from the typewriter and put it face down on the pile of others, turned the pile the right way round and left it on the side, like an exhibit in a museum or art gallery: Play.

It looked so beautiful.

It looked like an achievement.

It looked like the phone book.

Then a panic set in. What to do with it now?

'In a Hollywood movie you'd get on a bus . . .' Kathleen started saying, wafting about in a kaftan she'd found in Delia's wardrobe. 'And you'd meet some amazing theatrical agent, and you'd drop the script and she'd pick it up, and then she'd sign you up on the spot.'

'We're in London, it'd be the tube,' I countered.

'Suppose.'

But we both knew this wasn't going to happen.

'So what do I do?' I asked.

And then Kathleen had a brainwave. 'Let's ask at the library.'

The librarian at the local library guided me to a book called the *Writers' and Artists' Yearbook* when I told her of my quest for theatrical world or West End domination. It was in the reference section, and there in its pages were lists of all the literary agents who looked after playwrights such as myself. But as I was flicking through, I found another section. It was called NEW WRITING THEATRE COMPANIES. It was basically a list of all the London-based theatres – and there were a page and a half – who accepted unsolicited scripts from unperformed writers like myself.

I did a bad thing: I nicked the book. I was in a rush. I didn't have time to join. And anyway, it was in the reference section.

Besides, I'd bring it back once I'd finished with it. Honest I would. If there was time, once I'd been snapped up by all these amazing new writing companies. I couldn't wait. Bring it on. The world, and theatreland, was my oyster.

But first, Kathleen and I had the serious business of becoming pop video stars for the day.

We'd been up front with Wendy as to why we couldn't come in that Saturday, and we'd sold it to her from a PR perspective, saying that Ecstasy Jake were the coolest thing ever and so it would be good for them to have some backing dancers who were wearing her clothes. She saw the sense in this. Everything was exposure. But what we'd not really figured was 'the journey'. We had the clothes, we had the attitude. But we also had to get from West Norwood to Piccadilly Circus dressed like two cubist Christmas trees. We toyed with packing our clothes in cumbersome holdalls and travelling in our normal clothes via public transport, but as we'd never been in a pop video before, we weren't sure of the lay of the land once we got there. And the last thing we wanted was to be turned away at the door by Ttim for not looking cool enough. What if there was nowhere to change? What if we had to immediately start dancing? No. We'd have to travel looking completely bonkers. The fashions lately had all been very ravey and hippy, baggy jeans and tops and long hair and floppy hats. Wendy's stuff was linear, fitted and futuristic; and so Kathleen and I did look like complete freaks as we wandered down the high street to the bus stop. Shopkeepers stared, cars slowed down, even blind people seemed to freak out a bit.

What? I felt like saying. *Never seen two people in Lycra catsuits with various planets hanging off them before?*

Well. I don't suppose they would have.

Wendy had even made us some special hats, in the shape of flying saucers.

'We look like twats,' said Kathleen. And Kathleen very rarely swore. However, this time she was right, and justified.

'Yeah, but we're fierce twats.'

She didn't look so sure.

'We've just got to get into town, and then no-one'll bat an eyelid.'

Again, she didn't look so sure.

For some reason we had decided that the best way to get to Piccadilly that day would be to get the bus, then a tube to Charing Cross station, and then walk across town. We must have been mad.

Once we got on the bus, I think the driver actually thought we were aliens. Then Kathleen said something I'd not previously considered.

'Oh, it's that big demo today. About the Poll Tax.'

I had known about this, but in my excitement at finishing the play and then the excitement about filming a pop video, I had completely forgotten. I felt a pang of guilt that I hadn't gone on the march myself. It seemed to be the most unpopular issue, right across the board, no matter what your politics were. Thatcher had brought in a tax to take the place of domestic rates, calling it the Community Charge, and it was a flat rate, no matter how rich or poor you were. And even rich people thought that was unfair. Basically, if you were on the electoral register, you had to cough up. And loads of people couldn't. Oh well. Maybe we'd see a bit of the march and walk alongside them as we made our way across town. But then I remembered what we were wearing. Maybe I should make a banner? Even aliens say NO TO THE POLL TAX.

We were in for quite a shock when we got off the tube at Charing Cross. Instantly we were aware that something was wrong: the foyer of the station was awash with people, some milling about, some desperate to get out. Up ahead we could hear sirens and shouting, the unmistakable sound effects of something amiss. Instinct said we should have turned back and returned the way we'd come. The drama queen in both of us made us dart for the exit.

Up on the streets it was carnage. Charing Cross Road was a thick throng of people trying to make their way left, towards Trafalgar Square. The air was thick with the smell of burning, and plumes of smoke licked the sky above us. I wasn't sure where they were coming from, but it seemed to be near. We could hear sirens and cars being driven at speed – someone was putting their foot down, screaming.

We pushed our way through to the square to get a better look at what was going on, which was when we saw the lines of riot police with blue helmets and shields like satellite discs. Some were lashing out at the crowd, who seemed to be trying to escape them; then there it was again, the sound of a car being driven at speed. That's when we saw a police car zooming into the crowd. People screamed, and dived out of the way. Some poor bugger got dragged along by it for a good twenty feet. Now it was our turn to scream. Kathleen grabbed my hand and shouted, 'We've got to get across the square!'

'Sod that, Kath, let's get back to the tube!'

'We can't, look!'

I looked back, and now the route we'd taken was blocked by a row of police. What fresh hell had we stepped into so willingly? And what the hell was this hell, for God's sake?

'Look! Even the fucking aliens are protesting!' a woman in a donkey jacket called out as she passed us, blood pouring down her face.

'We've got to get out of here,' I gasped to Kathleen. And we tried to wind our way across the square to get to the bottom of the Haymarket, so we could walk up the hill to Piccadilly Circus. It felt like we were salmon, swimming against the tide. Every step we took, we had to duck to avoid missiles being hurled. Admittedly, these were mostly placards being thrown at the police. But who could blame these people when the police seemed to be on the attack? Did the coppers love the Poll Tax that much they had to attack everyone who was against it? They might be fighting an awfully long time if that was the case.

'I wonder if Mark's here?' gasped Kathleen as we passed one of the lions that guarded Nelson's column. Anarchists were dancing in the fountains around the statues. Well, I assumed they were anarchists. They weren't particularly well dressed, if not. But as we crossed Trafalgar Square it became increasingly obvious that the people on this demo were, on the whole, just normal people who looked like they'd come for a day out and got the shock of their lives.

As we left the square at the north side, we looked back and surveyed what looked like Armageddon. I could see where the fire was coming from now. On the south side of the square some of the buildings were covered in scaffolding, and above the scaffolding were some builders' huts, which were ablaze. I could see people trying to escape the huts, others climbing to safety to avoid passing riot vans, scaffolding poles being ripped out and thrown onto the braying crowd beneath.

We thought we'd escaped the worst by getting into a side street, but heading up towards Piccadilly was no better. Every-where we turned we saw people smashing shop windows, looting – it was madness. For the first time since moving to London, I didn't feel safe. Particularly as we were surreally running through this landscape dressed as if from the future. Like we were installation art. Like this had all been laid on to set off our look. But I also knew that the last thing you wanted to do when the police were being so antsy was to stick out like a sore thumb. So I realized I was lifting my arms aloft. Sometimes. Like I was waving a white flag: *I am not guilty. I come in peace.*

'I bet he was there,' Kathleen was saying, rather out of breath by now. This had to be the most exercise either of us had had in years. 'It's exactly the sort of thing he'd be into. Ah, it's a shame we never seen him.'

'Kathleen, there must have been about two hundred thousand people there. Of course we didn't see him.'

'What was all that about, then?' Kathleen sounded genuinely confused.

I looked at her afresh.

'Are you taking the piss?'

'Eh?'

'Kathleen . . . you said yourself there was a Poll Tax demo going on.'

'Yeah, I know, but . . .'

'Why d'you think all them people had placards saying PAY NO POLL TAX?'

Now it was her turn to lose her temper. 'I know that, knobhead! I just wondered how it went from a demo to . . . World War Three.'

She had a point. I'd not seen anything so scary first-hand in my whole life. All the people. All the noise. The fear. The anger on the coppers' faces. What had the demonstrators done to piss them off so much?

'Anyway, come on. Or we'll be late for the bloody video.'

The looting continued all the way up to Piccadilly Circus, and even though up here we felt we'd escaped the danger zone, there was still evidence of it everywhere. Bins crammed with placards, the odd scaffolding pole lying in the gutter, shell-shocked people wandering round like the walking wounded. The atmosphere was eerie, to say the least.

The Windmill Theatre was on Great Windmill Street, just off Shaftesbury Avenue where it splits off from the Circus. We'd looked it up many times in our *A to Z* and memorized the route, so we found it quickly and with a certain pride.

'Well, here we are!' I said, trying to brighten up after the events of the past half-hour.

We looked up at the unimposing black building. It looked tiny, its name written in unlit neon tubes above the entrance – the entrance which looked decidedly closed. I tried the door: locked. A voice behind us called out, 'Are you here for the video?'

We turned. A pretty black woman stood before us dressed in a silver shift dress and silver pumps. Oh, and a Lisa-Stansfield-style silver cap with mirror badges on it.

'Only it's cancelled coz of the disturbance at Trafalgar . . .'

She didn't finish the sentence.

She recognized us.

And we recognized her.

It was Jocelyn.

London, 2015

My mobile rings. It's Cissy.

'Adam? I've just had the school on the phone. Denim's feeling off-colour so I'm going to pick him up.'

I feel a stab of painful paternal empathy. *I* should be going to pick him up, not the nanny.

'Right,' I say, feeling immediately awkward and pissed off that I've agreed to do what I've agreed to do today. 'What exactly's the matter with him? D'you think he's being bullied? For having two gay dads? Or . . . or he's got a phobia of one of the teachers?'

'Adam, I think he's just a bit off-colour. Relax.'

'OK.'

But when I hang up, the last thing I want to do is go and sort through Jocelyn's old bits and pieces. I want to go home and look after my little boy. I want to put daytime telly on and snuggle up with him on the couch, falling asleep to *Doctors*.

Doctors.

Oh God.

Actually, I'd rather be out of the house.

It's a sunny day, so I decide to have a mooch round Portobello Road before heading to meet Ross and Kathleen at

Jocelyn's flat. It's been a while since I've spent any considerable time in Notting Hill, and I'm struck by just how gentrified the area has become since we lived nearby all those years ago. The chocolate-box cottages painted every colour under the pastel rainbow, or the rows of white stucco facades, look more higgledy-piggledy than I remember. But the noisy old market still exudes the aura of the underdog, rather than the back-drop for some movie where Hugh Grant spills orange juice on a Hollywood star. The other thing I'm struck by is that wherever I turn, it's there, looming large on the horizon, like a scary monster from a kids' story: Jocelyn's block of flats. It's a Sixties tower block, the sort of thing Prince Charles would once have described as a carbuncle, but that these days we seem to be just plain used to; and it dominates the sky wher-ever I look up, staring down, foreboding. What secrets does it keep, I wonder?

And the more oppressive it becomes – literally every turning I take, there it is, glaring ominously – it feels more and more like it's Jocelyn herself. A giant Jocelyn, perish the thought. Watching over her kingdom, watching over me.

Go on. I dare you. Tell the world my secrets.

I hurry on, ignoring the voice in my head.

What's the matter, Adam? Cat got your tongue?

Yeah, maybe. Got a problem with that?

Tell them you were there, Adam. And tell them why.

I hurry into a rather garish juice bar and order a 'Green Goddess, large' from the laminated menu on the wall, then try to calm myself as the woman behind the counter, who for some reason is wearing a Grotbags fright wig, pushes wheatgrass, limes, kale, spinach, you name it, if it's green she's attacking it, pummelling it through some sort of electric mangle thing to provide me with a thick, radioactively neon-green gunge of a drink. Once she's put a straw in it – it stands bolt upright, as the 'liquid' is so thick – she charges me the best part of a tenner, but I grab it gratefully like she's given me a cure for cancer. I feel so honoured to have been in her shop, and received a health drink from a Notting Hillbilly. I still don't get the wig, though. Maybe she's got the wrong weekend for Carnival.

Why did I say I'd do this? Why did I say I'd go to Jocelyn's flat and go through all her stuff to save her bloody partner a job? I know why: because Kathleen was so gung-ho about it. And, OK, in the heat and the emotion of the funereal moment, I thought it was a good idea for me and her to hang out a bit more and do that catching-up thing. But I'm not sure I want to now. If I really wanted to be friends with her, would I not have found some way of contacting her during these intervening years? Blimey. I've seen more of Jocelyn than I have of Kathleen.

And Jocelyn's told me . . . stuff. Stuff I can never tell Kathleen.

Or could I tell Kathleen?

No. I don't even know if she was telling the truth. And I don't think Jocelyn would want me to, somehow.

No, I can't. If you do something against a dead person's wishes you probably get struck by lightning, or turn into a pillar of salt. And let's face it. No-one's got *time* to be a pillar of salt these days, right? Oh yeah, I can really see Jay-Jay Velazquez LOVING being represented by a pillar of frigging salt.

'Hi, guys. This is Adz, my agent.'

'He's quite . . .'

'Salty? I know.'

I'm babbling, mentally. I must stop this.

I return to the street and take a slurp of my green goo before looking up at the sky again. I feel less afraid now. I've made a decision. I must never tell Kathleen what Jocelyn said. And now I've made that decision, I feel less afraid.

I walk on. I'm just doing a grown-up thing. Going to my old mate's and doing her old man a favour at a really difficult time. Others have dealt with far worse. Get over yourself, Adam.

It's weird. If I turned and walked the other way, in about ten minutes or so I'd be by our old flats, Harmony Heights. Long gone, of course, since the homes-for-votes scandal of the nineties, and the clear evidence of asbestos that we're lucky didn't kill us all. But to think that that's where we spent so much time together, and Jocelyn ended up only a stone's throw away. And in a block of flats. The only difference being, this block is now a Grade 2 listed building, while ours collapsed like . . . like . . . well, like a pillar of salt. I know this about its listing because I Googled it last night. I know so much about Trellick Tower now. And the thing I love most about it is that the Hungarian architect who designed it was called Goldfinger. So apt; Jocelyn loved that song, and would often sing it in the style of La Bassey at parties. You know, for the lolz, as kids today say. Or the shits 'n' giggles. Back then, we just did things for the plain and simple old laugh.

In the end, even though the tower looks close enough to touch, it seems that no matter how far I walk I'm getting no closer to it. So I take a cab. Kathleen is sitting on some steps outside the block, reading something on her phone.

'Is Ross not here?' I ask, as I pay the driver and wait for my change. Kathleen puts her phone away and jumps up.

'I dunno. I was waiting for you to ring the bell. Didn't want to do it on my own.'

As the cab drives off, I'm left wondering yet again why I agreed to do this.

In the space of our short exchange, I've become infuriated beyond measure. Kathleen is a sap. The follower, never the leader. The sheep. She may as well not talk. She may as well just go BAAAH!

And I'm going to be stuck with her for the rest of the day.

'Can you remember what number it is?' I ask, looking at the keyboard next to the door where you punch in numbers for the flats.

'Er . . .' Kathleen is staring at them too now, as if they will suddenly light up with our answer.

I check the address on my phone as if A TODDLER COULD BE DOING THIS and soon enough I have it. I punch it in, and Ross buzzes us in.

Before I head inside, I look out at the street in front of the flats and remember what I saw that night.

'Where d'you think she landed?' asks Kathleen, seeing me looking.

'How should I know?' I say, sounding quite convincing.

'Maybe there.' Kathleen says, pointing next to the block. 'Or there.' She points further away. 'Maybe she landed on one of those cars. Though that's the sort of thing that would make Twitter.'

'What is this, Kathleen? The ghoulish guided tour?'

'Sorry.' But then she continues. 'If someone landed on your car like that, would they bounce off? I guess you'd have to go to a garage to get the indentation taken out of the roof.'

'I really wouldn't know, dear.'

'Or a Polish car wash place thingy, and have the blood power-jetted off. It'd be very artistic if she'd landed in the trees.'

She seems nervous. And catches me glaring at her.

'But as you say. We'll never know.'

I nod.

I'd be crap at killing myself. I'm too much of a coward. Some people say suicide is a coward's way out, but not in my book. The older I get, the more scared I get about everything. When I was a kid I'd've thought nothing of going on the tallest big dipper in the world. These days, I'd stand at the bottom and mind the coats. I watch videos online of young people bungee jumping, and my legs turn to jelly. Is that what it was like for Jocelyn? This building is so high. To throw yourself off takes courage. To know that it's such a long way down, to know that there'd be a good twenty seconds (at least) to go before hitting the ground. What must that feel like?

My legs once more turn to jelly. I don't wish to think about that right now.

And I certainly shouldn't be thinking about that night. It's not good for my blood pressure.

I head inside. Kathleen follows. Of course she does!

If you stand back from Trellick Tower, it looks like a very busy office block where they still let people smoke; but architecturally what makes it stand out is that it looks also, to me anyway, like an old woman leaning on her walking stick. You have the block itself, and then another tower which houses the lift shaft. And that's linked to the flats by a series of walkways. Originally it was built this way so that the noise of the lifts didn't get on everyone's tits when they were indoors. It makes me think, what would happen if the lift shaft collapsed and fell down, breaking away from the main body of the flats? Would everyone have to be airlifted to safety?

My mind works overtime sometimes. I have a very noisy brain. Sometimes I should learn to do the brain-activity version of shutting the fuck up.

The lift brings memories flooding back of the old flats; even though I've never been in this lift before, it feels familiar. And small. A claustrophobe's nightmare, as it's one of the narrowest lifts I've been in. Any more than me and Kathleen, and you'd be stuffed. Or the lift would be. It's like standing in a metal coffin.

Apt.

But it's worth it by the time we hit the twentieth floor, because the first thing you notice about the place when the lift doors open is the light. Light, light and more bloody light. You really are walking through a pavement in the sky. And then again, when we step into Jocelyn's flat, it's like we're exposed to the elements, it's so light.

Her flat is rather beautiful. And Ross is rather stressed. He's on a call and tells us to make ourselves at home while he 'wraps it up with Dubai'. Whatever that means. We go for a nosey around. It's bigger than I thought, and on two levels. It's like a proper house in a block of flats. How novel. And the light floods in from both sides of the flat. The floors and walls are white. There are mirrors everywhere. It feels luxurious and floaty and . . .

'Isn't it gorgeous?' gasps Kathleen.

I nod.

'I didn't think she'd have such good taste.'

I shake my head, though I'm not sure why.

'Mind you. She did shag Mark Reynolds.' And with that, Kathleen snorts really unattractively.

There are two balconies. One off the living room, another off the bedroom, and I wonder which one she did it from.

As if reading my mind, Kathleen motions to the one off the living room and whispers, 'Bet it was this one.'

We open the door and step onto the balcony. It's only three feet or so wide, but it's long. I hold onto the low wall that's there to protect, and realize how easy it would be to hop over. Looking down, I see rows and rows of tall terraced houses backing onto the canal near Paddington. The Westway fingering its way across the horizon, other tower blocks; and in the distance, the nose of Canary Wharf jutting above the sprawl, the London Eye, the Shard. How different from our own view of yesteryear, when London hadn't got so damn tall. In our day she wore court shoes; now she's in skyscraper heels.

Peering right over, we see the entrance where we came in to our right, wasteland below. Is that what Jocelyn landed on?

Breaking the moment, Kathleen mutters, 'Can we not tell the landlord she didn't die, and I'll live here? It's amazing.'

'It's a very overused word, amazing,' I say without thinking. It's something Jay-Jay says and I agree with. It's the go-to response for so many people these days, and it stinks.

How was your lasagne? *Amazing.*

What do you think of Peter Andre? *Amazing.*

My whole family have been wiped out in a nuclear disaster. *Amazing.*

But I realize once I've said it that this has come across as rude. Which it is. Kathleen looks to me, stung.

'But you're right,' I say, totally rescuing myself, 'it's fucking amazing.'

And Kathleen smiles. And I realize I have some sort of power over her, to make her feel like shit. Or to make her feel great.

Again, I remind myself: *don't tell her what Jocelyn told you. Don't tell her anything.*

Concentrate on making her feel great. That's always better than making someone miserable.

As my old mother used to say, 'If you can't say anything nice about someone, say nothing at all.' Which is a bit like this. Why make someone fed up when you can put a smirky smile on their face?

Mind you, when my mum used to say that she often followed it up with some major gossip about you-know-who from God knows where being caught getting up to all sorts with her from number whatever, and oh my days, would you believe it?! She talked an inordinate amount of shite, my mum.

I don't half miss her.

I should get back to Liverpool more, hang out with her. She's seventy-five now, she won't be around forever. I'm luckier than Kathleen, her nan died years ago. But then, she was getting on. I've not yet dared ask her if she's in contact with her dad. Well, that's not true. After the funeral I did say, 'Oh, I was so sorry to hear about your nan.' To which she'd replied that it was all right etc., and then I'd added, 'How's your dad?' and she'd said yeah, he was great, or something, and then changed the subject. Which led me to believe that she didn't really know. But I could be wrong. And I'm a coward for not asking her.

Kathleen has gone back into the living room.

'Ooh, look at this!' she's calling. I follow her back in. She's running her hands up the door from the living room to the lounge, a boring-looking wooden door, with a glass panel above, quite typical of Sixties and Seventies social housing. Except Kathleen is pointing to something. 'Look! The light switch is in the door!'

And she's absolutely right. Instead of the usual light switch on the wall, the flat appeared to house its switches in all the door frames.

'Clearly designed by someone with too much time on their hands,' chuckles Kathleen. She switches it on, and electric lights zap on. She switches them off again, and I say:

'What's your dad up to these days?'

And she says very quickly, 'Oh yeah, he's great. Really great. How's your mum?'

'Yeah, she's cool. Bit creaky, but . . .'

'Aww, give her my love.'

'Yeah, I will.'

'Hey, have you noticed . . .'

'What?'

'At the funeral, Ross said he recognized us, because she had a photo of us in her living room.'

'Oh yeah.' I look around, but can't see it. 'Maybe he took it down.'

'But he'd give it to us, surely?'

I nod. She has a point.

'Unless he's lying,' she continues. Blimey. She's being a bit suspicious of old Ross here, isn't she?

'But why would he lie about . . .'

'Oh, I don't know. Just being daft.'

But it is a bit odd. Ross said there was a photo of us in here, and now there isn't. Maybe he's taken it down to give to us later. He was so keen to have us over to help him. And now we're here and the odd but predictable thing is . . . there is no proof here of Jocelyn's former life. There is nothing to say she was once friends with us. But is that so strange? There is nothing in my house currently that depicts my friendship with Kathleen and Jocelyn. And why should there be? They haven't been a big part of my life for so long. Do I have to have a memento of every bloody friendship I've had, writ large in knick-knacks on the mantelpiece? And if it's OK for me not to have that evidence on display, why should I expect different from Jocelyn?

Just because I've agreed to sort her flat out, doesn't mean I should have had the fondest of places in Jocelyn's heart. She probably never gave me and Kathleen that much thought in recent days. And that's OK. We cannot be all things to all people. She probably went for days and weeks without even remembering we were friends. And that's fine too.

Kathleen sees me staring in a daze, and offers a meek smile. She doesn't want to tell me what her dad is up to. Again, it makes me think that she plain doesn't know. She might be suspicious of Ross – well, I can be suspicious of her. I am about to challenge her on this when Ross returns, rubbing his hands.

'Boy, am I glad to see you. Who fancies a coffee?'

The moment has passed.

He picks his phone up and makes a call, and ten minutes later a skinny young blonde girl appears with Costa coffees for us. He introduces her as his PA, Finty. Finty is so young she has the look of an embryo, but I can't help but have a pang of suspicion about her. I am convinced she and Ross are shagging. I look to Kathleen, and I can just tell she thinks the same. Finty slinks off to the living room as Ross talks us through the plan of action in the kitchen. Apparently he and Finty have been through a few things and grabbed some stuff for sentimental and nostalgic reasons, but they have a meeting at twelve and need to leave us to it for a bit. What he wants us to do is to go through all Jocelyn's stuff and put it into three piles. Bin, charity shop, of interest. These basically meant:

Bin: crap that won't be valuable to anyone and can therefore go in the bin.

Charity shop: clothes, knick-knacks that might be of interest to the local charity shop, raising money for the Terrence Higgins Trust.

Of interest: anything we think Ross might want to look at on his return from his trip abroad. Any personal papers, bank stuff, letters from people, stuff that might be too exposing to show people who didn't know Jocelyn.

It's then that Ross explains he will give me a key, and we can come and go as we please for the next two weeks. He won't be here. He and Finty are off to Dubai. (I bet they are.) They'll be back in a week, and hopefully by then we will have 'broken the back of it'.

I love how he assumes we can just drop everything and work on this full-time. But neither of us argues with him. The idea of going through all Jocelyn's stuff is quite tantalizing. Minutes later they're going out the door, and Finty's cooing to us, 'Ciao, pussycats!'

As soon as the door shuts, we both burst out laughing and impersonate her – not only her voice, but we prance around like she had in her tiny mini-skirt, all pouting and preening.

'Seems a bit soon, doesn't it?' Kathleen says with a grimace.

'What? For him to be shagging someone else?'

Kathleen nods.

'You don't think . . .' Kathleen is chewing her bottom lip.

'What, Conky?'

She gasps and throws her bag at me. It misses, but the drama is superb. 'You BASTARD!'

And we both howl with laughter. Then we settle down; we

are meant to be here to go through our dead friend's stuff. We should have a sense of decorum.

'You don't think she killed herself coz she'd found out about Ross and Finty?'

It's certainly worth considering.

'I mean, think about it,' Kathleen continued, 'She passes judgement on people for a living, she's well known for it. She's always slut-shaming and . . .'

'Was . . .' I correct her.

'Saying women need to be better in bed to stop their fellas straying, and then he goes and trades her in for a younger model. Maybe it was about to come out in the papers and . . . she shat herself and . . .'

I don't like it when Kathleen swears. It doesn't suit her. She never used to swear when we were kids. It makes me feel like life has tainted her and makes me wonder what she's seen. Even if, right now, she might have a point. She sees me mulling it over and her face lights up, thrilled that I can see the validity of it.

And it does indeed make sense.

'Well, there's only one thing for it,' I say.

'What's that?' she says.

'Let's go through her shit!'

I offer my hand up for a high five, she slaps it, and boy – she packs a mean punch!

Finty has left rolls of bin bags on the table in the kitchen. We rip some off and wonder where to start. We plump for the bedroom. Surely everyone's juiciest secrets are in their bedroom? Before heading there, Kathleen has a look in the fridge and pulls out a bottle of wine. She offers it to me with a shrug as if to say, shall we?

'It's not ours.'

'We're helping him out.'

'It's ten in the morning.'

'Twenty past!'

She chuckles, and seems to blush, and replaces it in the fridge door. I then realize she was just winding me up. I think.

Kathleen practically dives for the bedside cabinet. 'I bet she's got a MASSIVE dildo in here!' she says, ripping the door open. Again, I'm not sure I like this older potty-mouthed Kathleen. She wasn't like this the other night. Maybe she gets more ladylike the more she's had to drink.

She lets out a disappointed groan.

'What?'

'It's tiny. It's one of them bullet things you can get in Sainsbury's.'

And she holds what looks like a large silver bullet aloft. I feel myself blushing now. It's embarrassing, hearing meek and mild Kathleen spouting forth about vibrator size.

'They're really shit,' she says.

'Please stop now, Kathleen.'

'Doesn't touch the sides,' she adds as an aside. I feel a bit sick in my mouth. Suddenly she's swanning out of the room, saying she needs to 'piss like a racehorse'.

And I wonder . . . is she tipsy? She's being very . . . forward.

I decide to give her the benefit of the doubt. Maybe she's feeling a bit emotional. It is all a lot to take in. Our friend is gone, and here we are, about to rifle through her possessions like we were as close as we were when we were kids. I open the other bedside cabinet. There's little of interest in there: a couple of pairs of what look like reading glasses, some used earplugs, some coconut body butter. I stick it all in the rubbish bag. As I'm doing that I hear Kathleen calling me.

'Adam! Quick! Come here! Look what I've found!'

I rush to where her voice is coming from. She's in a little room that just houses a toilet and a sink. She is standing staring at the wall.

What's she found? What's she seen? Has she found IT – the reason why Jocelyn killed herself?

She points to the wall. 'Look.'

On one of the walls is a framed gold disc for Jocelyn's record. 'That's got to be a piss-take, surely,' I say, unimpressed. The song had done so badly.

'No, not that, *that*!' She points elsewhere, guiding my eyes away from the framed disc.

Above the sink is a framed poster for *Supper with Sam*.

My voice catches in my throat as I do an audible gasp. Immediately tears prick my eyes, and I have to bite my top lip to stop myself from crying. What a wuss I am.

See? She hadn't really. She hadn't forgotten me.

'She didn't forget me, then,' I say in a stagey whisper.

Kathleen shakes her head. 'Every time she took a shit, she thought of you.'

I look at her, expecting her to be grinning, trying to gross me out. But she is transfixed by the poster. She was being genuine.

I look back to the poster. Blimey. *Supper with Sam*. That's a blast from the past.

'Oh my God, Adam, look at this!'

Kathleen is pointing up. I look to the ceiling to see a Christmas bauble suspended next to a skylight. It's purple glass with gold decorations on it, and it hangs from a gold ribbon. I know what's inside it without even having to stare further.

'The three wise men,' I say.

'The loft club,' Kathleen says. 'Blimey, she's had it all these years.'

And suddenly I feel very sad.

London, 1990

Amazingly, *Supper with Sam* was snapped up very quickly by a 'new writing venue' (posh theatre speak for a theatre that puts on new plays by unheard-of writers) in Shepherd's Bush called the Boiler Room. The artistic director, Anthea, who was very fond of wearing those dayglo hippy pants that wouldn't look out of place on a beach in Goa, described the play in the initial letter she wrote to me as 'garrulous, visceral, an exploration of the pain of the Troubles as seen through the eyes of four disaffected youth'.

The Troubles. Oh yes, I should explain. When I sent the play to the various theatres I panicked and worried that people might think it was autobiographical. So at the last minute, to give it some distance, I wrote on the title page:

The play is set in the fictional town of Ballymcknock in Northern Ireland, present day.

When I first met Anthea – she had leathery flip-flops and each toenail painted a different colour, which I found impossibly theatrical – I could see she was disappointed that I didn't have a thick Belfast accent. But after a period of adjustment you could tell she thought I was a genius to have written a coruscating account of Northern Ireland despite never having stepped foot in the country.

'You might not have an Irish passport, but you have an Irish soul,' she was fond of saying.

The Boiler Room was so called because they'd decided that by putting on new plays in a small room above a pub with the sound of traffic rattling around Shepherd's Bush Green, they were stoking the fires of important TV drama or the bigger London theatres. 'Come see our stuff today. You'll see this writer's work on a bigger scale tomorrow,' etc. The idea of which, of course, I loved. Today the Boiler Room and Anthea's cheesecloth waistcoats; tomorrow the RSC, Channel 4 – who knew?!

Maybe they should have called themselves The Deli, as Anthea was quite fond of saying. 'The plays we put on are like broccoli in 1982. You could only get it in delis. Eight years later you can get it in Kwik Save.'

I wasn't sure what that really meant, but it sounded good. She was one of those posh birds with the gift of the gab.

One thing I was less keen on was Anthea's assertion that my play was, and I quote, 'far too fucking long, darling'. I'd argued the punters would be getting value for money. She slapped her desk – causing her tobacco tin to jump a few centimetres in the air – and said 'No. I know theatre. I am theatre. All decent plays are two hours, including an interval.'

'Try telling Shakespeare that,' I'd countered.

She'd practically snorted. 'I'd've told him the same. Over-rated, over-produced SCHMUK. Roll on the moratorium.'

'Is that his latest play?'

She'd pointed to me without even cracking a smile and said, flatly, 'You're funny. Funny sells. Put more jokes in this.' At which she'd jabbed her finger at my script.

So . . . what? Let me get this straight: I had to cut an hour out of my play (according to Anthea) *and* add more jokes. Make your mind up, Anthea, girl!

But I didn't say anything. I just nodded. And panicked. But I made the changes. I wasn't going to risk not having the play put on because of artistic differences.

Anthea decreed she was going to direct the play. 'I get Ireland. I am Irish.'

'Where are you from?'

'Tunbridge Wells. But my grandma was Falls Road through and through. Well, she had a cleaning lady who was.'

The Boiler Room didn't pay its writers or actors when they put a play on. Anthea assured me this was completely normal. The arrangement was something called a profit share. Basically everyone did the show for free, and then when the play made money at the box office they would split the profit between everyone involved.

'Does that mean you and everyone in the office work for free, Anthea?' I'd asked.

She shook her head. 'No, we're on a wage. Peanuts, basically, but we have charitable status.'

Breadline Bohemians, I called them in my head. She had a way of dismissing me quite regally with a flick of the wrist, so I found it easier to just shut my mouth when she said stuff like this and nod in agreement. Pointless pissing off the woman who had the power to make or break my career.

Needless to say, I found the whole experience of putting on *Supper with Sam* incredibly exciting. Choosing the poster design, the designer, casting the actors. I couldn't make all the meetings as I couldn't afford to just jack in my job at Hyper Hyper, but every second I spent at the Boiler Room I soaked up and recalled to myself in bed later that night in vivid technicolour. I knew I wanted to treasure these memories for the rest of my life. What if I never had a play on again? Everyone was saying (well, Anthea was) I was the new theatrical voice of my generation, but even geniuses are wrong sometimes. If this never happened again, I needed to remember everything in vivid detail.

Kathleen was desperate to read the play, but I lied and told her it was illegal, that the theatre had told me I wasn't allowed to let anyone see it until it was on. And Kathleen believed me. But all she did, all day long, was ask me questions about how it was coming along.

'What's it about, Adam?' she'd whine over the futuristic outfits at work.

'It's a coruscating look at disaffected youth in Northern Ireland.'

'My God, it sounds so deep.'

'It is. It's like a garrulous and coruscating swimming pool.'

'Wow. And have you heard any more about that coloured girl from thingy?'

'Showbiz Comp? We're still waiting to hear. And we don't say coloured in London. We say black.'

'Black? Right. Sorry.'

'It's all right, Kathleen. But you do need to work on your racism if you're not gonna show me up on opening night.'

'Sorry, Adam.'

'It's OK.'

'D'you think . . . and say no if it's gonna be a ballache. D'you think I could invite Cynthia to opening night? She loves the theatre. I was telling her about the play.'

'Yeah. Feel free to bring your girlfriend,' I said, sounding a bit more cutting than I meant to.

'Don't be like that, Adam. You're always so busy with your writing and rehearsals, I've got to have other friends.'

'I'm only joking, Kathleen.'

'And she was dead excited to hear about thingy off the telly.'

'She's only human, babe.'

In the end, we did manage to get that girl off the telly. I was OVER. THE. MOON. God, the cast was so fantastic. I was particularly excited by this casting of Harriet Newland, who was almost a household name thanks to starring in the children's TV show *Showbiz Comp* for eight years. She was now twenty, and wanting to recreate herself as a serious actress of the theatre. She had hit the headlines briefly in the tail end of the eighties for being found with cocaine on her in a nightclub. But, like she said at the audition, 'I've grown up a lot since then. Just like the kids do in this incredible piece.'

Blimey. Harriet Newland thought my play was incredible!

And then she'd done this amazing Northern Irish accent, bellowing TO BE SURE, TO BE SURE, FURRR PLAY TO YE in a really deep, gruff voice. She sounded like Jim McDonald from *Corrie*.

Anthea later said they'd need to find a cheap voice coach.

The lad who was playing the character based on Mark was currently in an advert on the telly for cider. Every time it came on, me and Kathleen would shout THERE HE IS! And we'd watch the advert, then coo over how fantastic he was in it, even though he didn't have any lines and he just sort of giggled at his 'mate', who was the main character in the advert and really liked the cider, and how much more of a man it made him when he drank it. The actor's name was Tom Hangs. Which was always a bit embarrassing because when I'd tell people I had Tom Hangs in the play they'd look incredulous, gasp and be like . . . *You have Tom Hanks in your play? That's amazing! He was so good in* Big. And then I'd have to say, 'Well, no. This is Tom Hangs. With a G. He's really good, though. He's in that cider advert. Laughing.' People seemed less interested then.

The girl playing the character based on Kathleen was a girl with a massive nose called Suki. She was from New Zealand and so her Northern Irish accent wasn't brilliant, but Anthea had worked with her a few times and said she was 'magical' on stage.

'She's lambent, Adam. Wait till you see her. And that nose!'

'Yes, it is pretty big.'

'Big? It's got its own postcode. Biggest schnozzle in *Spotlight*.'

And then, of course, there was the guy who was playing the character based on me. Anthea said she'd (yet again) cast a fantastic young actor who she thought epitomized the character really well. I couldn't wait to meet him. When eventually we met for warm white wine and crudités at Anthea's Bayswater flat, I got quite a shock. He was SO effeminate. He kept SCREAMING literally. And everything he said he said so LOUDLY and laughed his HEAD OFF. I was really put out. I took Anthea to one side.

'He's going to tone that down, isn't he?'

She did a side-eye thing. 'Why?'

'Well, he's . . . so . . .'

'Camp?'

I nodded.

'The character is camp, Adam. He's like you. He doesn't give a shit what people think. Audiences will adore him. Just like people adore you, Adam.'

Ouch. That stung. I wasn't that camp, was I? Was she saying I was really similar to him? His name was Joshua Moonlight (I mean, that had to be made up, right?) and I really took against him. I've never felt like that about many people. Margaret Thatcher, Julie Andrews, and him. Joshua Moonlight. Or Joshua Fucking Moonlight, as I usually called him. Behind his back, of course. Face to face, I was too scared of him.

The designer was an Israeli woman called Irit who had been an award-winning theatre designer in Jerusalem, but had recently moved to London. Oh. And she had recently become registered blind. I had a pang of doubt when I found out that the woman who was going to be responsible for the look of the play couldn't see anything, but Anthea put my mind at rest.

'She's partially sighted. She can still see things. And design isn't always about having a good eye, it's about having a good imagination. It's about feeling the play. Irit feels things deeply. But don't judge her too much. Her English is appalling.'

Fuck me. If her English was bad, how was her Northern Irish?

Following the crudités and wine at Anthea's, the actors did an informal read-through of the play in her lounge, sitting on beanbags and scatter cushions.

Irit sat cross-legged, playing with some worry beads and nodding astutely at times, and looking completely baffled at other times. Anthea veered between closing her eyes and looking close to orgasm, to staring out of the window looking like she wanted to throw herself out of it. I just sat there feeling confused.

Their Northern Irish accents were awful. In that moment I realized it probably would have been a good idea to cast some actors from the actual place. As the play ended, round about the time I had expected the room to be in floods of tears, I looked at Irit and realized she had fallen asleep. Anthea poked her with her bare foot as she stood up and announced that the read-through had been 'eye-opening' and 'delicious' and given her lots of 'food for thought'. Harriet then ran to the loo and locked herself in, crying her eyes out really loudly, screaming that everyone hated her and that she was the worst actress in the world. Cue everybody else standing at the door, tapping it and telling her how amazing she was and how she was one of the most gifted performers they'd all ever had the privilege to work with. Eventually the sobbing died down, the lock flicked and Harriet came out, dabbing her eyes with some toilet paper and thanking them quietly, between sniffs.

Later I went to meet Jocelyn and Kathleen for a post-mortem.

'Have you heard?' Kathleen gabbled excitedly over a pint of lager top in a pub up a back street in Covent Garden. 'Harriet Thingy's doing Adam's play.'

'Newland!' I bleated, sounding a bit desperate. Desperate to show off.

Jocelyn looked nonplussed. 'Is that supposed to mean something?'

'She's that amazing coloured girl from *Showbiz Comp*.'

'Black.' That was me.

'You know! The one who set fire to the mixing desk after the caretaker put his hand up her skort.'

'Skirt.' That was Jocelyn.

'No, it was a skort,' I agreed. 'It's a sportsy thing. Cross between a skirt and shorts.'

Jocelyn looked like she was stopping herself from rolling her eyes. 'That's great news,' she said, flatly. 'What's it about?'

Fortunately Kathleen jumped in. 'It's a coruscating look at the troubles in Northern Ireland as seen through the eyes of four disaffected youth.'

Jocelyn nodded. 'Northern Ireland?'

'Yeah, it's just something that really interests me,' I lied. Jocelyn took this in and did a grimace with her lips that could've been interpreted as sarcasm, but that I took to be a kind of sign language for, 'Wow, that's completely impressive.'

'What interests you about Northern Ireland?' she asked, before licking a prawn cocktail crisp.

'Oh, you know . . .' I said. 'The Troubles and all that.'

She nodded, then said, clearly bored with the conversation already, 'Shall we go into town and do an E?'

Jocelyn was into going out and doing ecstasy. Me and Kathleen pretended we were, so that we didn't sound uncool, but secretly we'd never tried it. We'd been knocking about with Jocelyn pretty regularly since bumping into her at the abandoned pop video filming a few months before. It had, of course, been such an incredible surprise to see her. She was the last person we'd have expected to bump into after our riot-strewn sojourn through central London. She'd been doing some running work for the production company that were making the video and it had been left to her to tell anyone turning up that it was cancelled. It was only part-time voluntary work, so she didn't feel that loyal to the company, which is why she soon abandoned her post and retired to a local pub with us. And ever since then we'd met up each week to paint the town red. Or pink, if we headed off to the gay club Heaven.

Jocelyn was now working in some boring office job for Westminster Council, in the housing department. Kathleen and I were amazed. The girl who once dreamed of being a superstar, reduced to working a menial office job? I could tell that, no matter how briefly, Kathleen revelled in this information, feeling even she had a funkier, trendier, sexier job than allegedly cool, hip Jocelyn. It turned out Jocelyn had flunked her exams at school and left home after one too many arguments, then run away to London.

OK, so she had won that one. We'd told people we'd run away, when we hadn't really. Jocelyn apparently really had. She claimed she'd not spoken to anyone in her family for 'aeons' and had no intention of ever speaking to them again. She'd had to put her music career 'on hold' while she earned enough money to pay her way in the Big Smoke. And we all agreed it was a very expensive city to live in. She'd lied on her CV, applied for a few office jobs and, remarkably, got the one in the council.

'You're like Deirdre Barlow!' Kathleen had said.

Jocelyn looked horrified by this. 'Why?'

'Well, she sometimes works in the housing department at the council. Folk are always asking her to pull strings.'

Kathleen had started watching as many soaps as possible with something approaching religious fervour. Her two main favourites were *Coronation Street* and *Brookside*. It was as if now that she was cast adrift from living in the North, she had to cling on to some romanticized version of it to make her feel secure and give her a sense of identity. Those shows held little interest for me; I had bigger fish to fry. I was going to be a world-class, world-famous, world-dominating playwright.

She'd also taken to videoing every soap and stockpiling them whenever her bezzy mate Cynthia was away on a long-haul flight, and then she'd go over when she was back and they'd watch them together, talking all things trolley dolly.

The way things were going at the moment I thought Kathleen was going to suddenly say, 'Chicken or fish?'

Every time I thought of the play opening, I got a slight panic on. Kathleen and Jocelyn were bound to come and see it. What would they think? They would know within the first few lines that it was based on what went on in the organ loft all those years ago.

And then I tried to calm myself. They would love it. Imitation was the highest form of flattery, surely.

The other thing I would panic about was my depiction of Jocelyn in the play. Hard-faced. Opinionated. Brutally selfish. And shagging the Mark-style character. And having the baby by him. And pissing her mates off. How was she going to take to that? It hardly painted her in a glowing light.

Especially as . . . and this was amazing . . . whenever we asked Jocelyn to tell us the truth about what had happened in the organ loft, and getting pregnant, and having the baby, she stuck to the party line. Why was she doing this, when she no longer had contact with her mother? Why was she letting her win like this? It was hurtful, if I'm honest, to have her continue to lie to me, to us; it just didn't make any sense. Her version of events was steadfast – no matter what angle we came at it from, her story remained the same. Well, I'll tell you what, she was a bloody good and consistent liar.

Her versions of events was this: she'd spent the night in the organ loft with Mark, but nothing had happened between them. She had gone there because she'd argued with her mum over something as trivial as what time she was allowed to go to bed, and it had escalated. She'd walked out and, upset, hadn't known where to go. So she went to the church and took solace with Mark. Mark talked to her and they fell asleep, and when she was leaving – climbing out of the window, as seen by us – he had hugged her and told her everything was going to be all right. She didn't fancy him, he wasn't her type, and she couldn't understand why me and Kathleen just suddenly stopped speaking to her, cutting her dead in the street. Her mum then fell pregnant by a boyfriend and the pregnancy was very difficult so they had gone away for a month in the summer holidays for her to take the air at Llandrindod Wells. Her mum gave birth to a little boy, and they returned to Liverpool. And our wrath. As far as she was concerned, this is what had happened, and nothing else. So there.

'You know, you can tell us,' I'd say sadly, disappointed that she couldn't be honest with us.

'Tell you what?' she'd say, chippily.

'That you had a baby by Mark, and your mum passed it off as hers.'

'Oh, fuck off, Adam.'

And she meant it.

'I've done nothing wrong. I've got nothing to be ashamed of.'

'I just wish you'd be honest with us,' echoed Kathleen. 'You know we wouldn't judge you. We don't judge you. How is he?'

'Who?'

'William. Your son.'

'My brother. And he's fine.'

'How d'you know?'

'Because I phone my aunty in Toxteth sometimes. I'm not completely heartless. He's doing well. Thriving, they say.'

'Why did you fall out with your mum? It can't just've been about stuff to do with bedtimes.'

'I'm going.'

And she always did. If we asked too many questions, she would just pick up her bag and walk out. No matter where we were. Off into the night full of fury and incredulity, incredulity that we had the audacity to challenge her.

'D'you know what she doesn't like?' Kathleen would coo.

'What?'

'That she's not your number one girl any more.'

And with that, Kathleen would slip her arm into mine and simper like the cat who got the queeny cream.

When I first saw the poster and flyer for *Supper with Sam*, I panicked afresh. It showed a picture of a stained-glass window, and in that glass was a picture of a black Virgin Mary cradling a mixed-race child. And the wording said, 'SUPPER WITH SAM . . . this was no virgin birth!'

The blurb on the flyer read:

> Belfast. Today. In the organ loft of a run-down
> church in Ballymcknock, three teenagers edge
> warily towards adulthood in their makeshift den.
> When fugitive Sam hides out in the loft, a bomb is
> dropped that will change their lives . . . forever.
>
> Starring Harriet Newland as Whitney
> (*Showbiz Comp, Crossroads*) Tom Hangs as Sam
> (*Caucasian Chalk Circle* on tour, Copperhead Cider
> advert) Suki Fielding as Conky (*I Sniffed Terry
> Christian's Armpit*) and Joshua Moonlight
> as Alan (*You Rang, M'Lord?*).

It's weird. I had no idea that camp Joshua had been in *You Rang, M'Lord?*, and I'd seen every single episode. I also had no idea that Harriet had been in *Crossroads*. And I dreaded to think what *I Sniffed Terry Christian's Armpit* was all about.

'Oh, it's my one-woman show I won a Fringe First for,' Suki was happy to tell me. 'It's about raving, Madchester, flares.'

I came home one evening to find Kathleen in a funny mood. She was picking at a chicken salad in the living room, the telly on, avoiding eye contact.

'What's up?' I asked, though it pained me to say it. I felt she was being a bit of a drama queen.

She did a big intake of breath, then let it out slowly. Then went down the side of the sofa and pulled out . . . a flyer for the play.

'Oh,' I said, sitting next to her. Slightly mortified, but at the same time elated that the flyers were clearly out there.

'There were a pile in the library,' she sniffed. And looked at me. Dear God, she looked like she might cry. She was furious. She was furious, surely, because I'd picked at the bones of our lives and made . . . a really great stock from it, actually. This show was going to be life-changing. I just had to convince her of that.

'How could you?'

'It's such a good story, Kathleen.'

'How could you call me Conky?'

And then the tears really did flow. And she lunged at me and threw her arms round me and cried for what felt like seven years.

So it transpired she wasn't that fussed that I'd based a play on our teenage years. She was upset because of the big nose thing.

'But Kath . . . Conky isn't you.'

'Isn't she?' She sounded a bit disappointed by this.

'No. Wait till you see it. You have this amazing speech . . .'

'I thought it wasn't me.'

'Sorry. Conky has this amazing speech about bullying and . . . name-calling and . . . everyone who's read it says it's one of the highlights of the play.'

She seemed encouraged by that, almost placated.

'Of which there are many,' I added quickly, 'Of course. And Conky's so likeable. She's really empowering to women and stuff. Everyone likes her. And Suki's incredible, she really takes you on a journey. Wait till you see how fantastic she is, you'll be over the moon.'

'So it isn't me?'

'It's a fictionalized character.'

'Does she live with her grandma?'

'Yes.'

'Are her mum and dad still together?'

I shook my head.

'Is her dad in prison?'

I nodded my head.

'And she has a big nose?'

I nodded.

'So it is me.'

'It's inspired by you. Kathleen, you're my muse. All great artists have muses. You're mine.'

And for the first time, she smiled. Then the smile froze on her face as she looked at the picture on the flyer again.

'Jocelyn's going to kill you.'

'You might be right there.'

'Do you want some chicken salad? Or maybe some fish.'

It had begun.

'No, I grabbed a homity pie from Cranks. Ate it on the train.'

But all of a sudden I felt very sick. She was right. Jocelyn was going to kill me.

And this was bad news, because recently Jocelyn had promised to help us find somewhere to live once we lost the use of the place in West Norwood. Meeting her couldn't have come at a better time. She was going to use her contacts in the housing department and make sure we had a roof over our heads. She wasn't yet sure what shape this would take, but we were pretty much dead certs for a council flat or a housing association flat in Westminster somewhere. And Westminster was dead posh! So we had to keep in her good books. And her finding out there was a play based on something she'd rather forget, to the extent that she preferred to lie about it, make out it hadn't even happened . . . surely we were in for some kind of nuclear reaction!

Before I knew it, First Night was upon us. When I got to the pub/theatre there were flowers and champagne waiting for me from Anthea. She, however, seemed to have turned into a nervous wreck. She was chain-smoking roll-ups and running to the loo every five minutes. If I'd been nervous before getting there, she was making me feel worse. And I'd still not told Jocelyn what the play was about, but she had insisted on coming to my big opening and was even getting her hair done for the occasion.

The dressing room was full of actors disrobing and getting into their school uniform costumes, and the air was ripe with nervous farts and panstick. All of them seemed to be saying various phrases in their cod-Belfast accents, trying to get them just right for the big event. Harriet kept announcing she was going to be sick, then running off to the loo, then coming back, seemingly disappointed that no-one had followed her in there to check she was OK. Suki was banging on about her agent being useless and really using this job as a 'shop front for her wares'. Joshua Moonlight was uncharacteristically quiet, but would then smack his lips repeatedly, all part of his 'warm-up'. Tom Hangs just hung out looking handsome. One day I hoped I'd be able to do that. Just hang round being awesome, and nobody worrying whether you said much, because you were just so cool. One day!

When I went downstairs to the pub the place was heaving with the first-night audience. Jocelyn was in a corner with

Kathleen, and they were both standing in front of a massive poster of the black Virgin Mary in the stained glass.

'Where's Cynthia?' I asked, excited. I was quite looking forward to showing off to the one neighbour I knew.

'Oh, she had to suddenly go on standby. She's in bits.'

'Right.'

'But I've been thinking,' Kathleen continued, 'I might retrain.'

'You're not trained in anything,' I pointed out, trying to point out that this evening wasn't about her. For once, it was actually about me.

'True.'

'Retrain as what?' Jocelyn asked.

'An air stewardess.'

I rolled my eyes.

'Jocelyn, tell her,' I said.

'Tell her what?'

'You can't be an air stewardess, Kathleen. You go on the runway, they'll think you're Concorde.'

Kathleen looked hurt. As well she might. And then she laughed it off. 'Oh, I was only joking.'

And then I felt bad. I was bad. Oh God.

'Anyway. Jocelyn's got some great news!' said Kathleen, trying to sound brighter than she probably was.

What? Was she not going to pass comment on the poster? Did she not understand the significance of this? It was a black VIRGIN MARY. It was HER.

Jocelyn pulled a set of keys from her coat pocket. 'I've got you a new flat.'

'WHAT?'

'It's in a tower block in Paddington. It's empty. You'll be squatting at first. But once you've been there for a few weeks you'll have rights, and the housing association that owns it will have to rehouse you. Especially if we say Kathleen's brutal ex-boyfriend is trying to beat her up all the time. You might have to record a few answerphone messages pretending to be him.'

'That's incredible, Jocelyn.'

'What are friends for? Now we've got a major show-biz opening to get through. Do all these people know these characters are based on us?'

I looked around the room. She was taking this very well. How did she know? I'd told her so little about its content, fortunately because she hadn't asked too much.

'You know?' I asked, in a tiny voice.

'The poster's a bit of a fucking giveaway, Adam. Well. If they don't know now, they will do soon. I'm going to buy some champagne.'

Of course. Of course they were going to enjoy their moment of glory. The show was going to be a huge success and they felt they were part of it, had inspired it. And so they became the most embarrassing members of an audience ever. Jocelyn and Kathleen both laughed a little too loudly and long at all the jokes. They cried really loudly and did lots of sniffing in the sad bits. And they did lots of cries of, 'God, I actually said that, remember?' in between lines, or 'I can't believe this is based on me,' or 'That actually happened!' and so on. So that by the end of the play everybody knew that the girl with the big nose and the black girl were eerily similar to the girl with the big nose and the black girl in the play. And when Suki did that amazing speech:

CONKY: Call me what you like. I don't care.
Your words can't cut me any more, so they

can't. I've heard them all. Too many times.
Captain Beaky, The Eagle has Landed,
Pinocchio, Nostrildamus. You name it, I've
been called it. Well, it stops right here and
it stops right now. My name is not Conky. It's
Fionnula-Jayde. And from now on that's what
yous'll be calling me, you got that? Fionnula-
Jayde. Say it. Say it loud. I want everyone
to hear. Shout it from the rooftops if ye
have to.

FIONNULA-JAYDE!

Kathleen punched the air. The audience was rapturous at
the end. Jocelyn jumped to her feet and started a standing
ovation. Kathleen and her were drinking in the applause as
if it was for them. And . . . was I imagining it, or was Jocelyn
putting on a soft Belfast accent in the bar afterwards? I saw
her throwing her head back and doing a lot of screechy
laughing. And I also heard her saying, 'Oh he's so naughty.
His imagination is incredible. Of course I didn't have a
baby!'

Oh Lordy. I had got away with it. I'd nicked the story of
my life, of our lives, and made a piece of art out of it, and
my friends didn't care. In fact, they were pleased. They were
proud. What amazing friends they were. I dragged them
both away from the first-night party and took them upstairs
to the theatre again. I opened a bottle of champagne and
we drank it on the set. In the make-believe set of the place
we'd actually been in all those years ago, toasting ourselves,
toasting each other, toasting the play. It felt good. I had them
back again, back onside. The future was crammed with possibilities. Anything was possible. The world was my oyster. I

felt giddy with anticipation – for what, I wasn't sure. But thus far it hadn't turned out too badly. Life was pretty fucking good, OK?

'This set's so beautiful,' said Kathleen. 'You'd never know the designer was blind.'

'She's partially sighted,' I corrected her. 'She feels things, she senses things. And she has a very willing assistant who she tells what she wants.'

'It's like we're back there,' Jocelyn said wistfully. And it felt like again we might ask what really happened that night back in the church. But we didn't. Because we already knew. It remained, for now, this time, unspoken between us.

'Anyway,' she added, 'we'd better get back to the party. I'm sure that one who played Mark was giving me the eye.'

We all giggled. Imagine if she now got off with Tom Hangs. Talk about life imitating art imitating life.

'Is that one Suki a lesbian?' Kathleen asked. 'She keeps staring at me. It's embarrassing.'

'She's just jealous your nose is smaller than hers.'

And we all giggled again. This champagne was going to my head.

'Hey. Guess what I did today?' Jocelyn said, eyes widening, which meant there was MAJOR gossip coming.

'What?! WHAT?!'

'I went and did some test shots for a Page Three spread.'

We must have looked horrified. The smile froze on her face.

'I could make a lot of money from that, kids,' she said.

But before we could respond, someone else appeared in the theatre. It was Anthea. She was looking sheepish in the doorway leading to the stairs down to the pub. I jumped from my beanbag to my feet.

'What is it, Anthea? Are the reviews out? WHAT DID THEY SAY?'

'No. Blimey, the play only finished an hour ago, keep your hair on. No, there's . . . someone downstairs. Says he knows you. He's a bit pissed.'

'Who is it?'

'He says he's Kathleen's dad.'

I looked quickly to Kathleen, who was biting her bottom lip.

'What's he doing here?' I was bewildered.

'Oh God. I spoke to him this morning. Told him what I was doing tonight. Think I might have mentioned a free bar. He's drinking heavily at the moment. It's quite sad.'

'I didn't even know you were in touch with him.'

'Only every now and again. He phoned me at the house. I don't know how he got the number. I'll get rid of him. I'm so sorry.'

She hurried to the doorway and disappeared down the stairs. I looked to Jocelyn. She was looking petrified.

'Are you OK?'

She nodded, but didn't say anything.

'Word on the street is the reviewers loved it,' Anthea said with a smile, then followed Kathleen down.

Something was wrong with Jocelyn, I could just tell. She'd gone from deliriously giggly and excitable to frowny and troubled in the space of seconds. Maybe it was the champagne.

'Are you feeling pissed?'

She thought about it a second, then looked relieved. 'Yep. That's it. Actually, Adam, I'm going to go home. I don't feel too good. But, you know, congratulations on the play.'

'You're not going to stay for the party?'

She shook her head.

'You were fine a few minutes ago.'

'I've had too much to drink.'

'Well, I'll walk you down. I'll walk you to the tube.'

'No, you go and have fun. I'll wait here for a bit till I feel better.'

'I don't want to leave you, if you're not feeling well.'

'I'll be fine, Adam. Please.'

She sounded forceful. I knew better than to argue with her.

'But Tom Hangs was giving you the eye. You said.'

She shook her head. So I left her and went down to the party. I couldn't see Kathleen or her dad anywhere. The place was still packed. I got lots of congratulatory slaps on the back and hugs from people I didn't know. Harriet introduced me to her agent and for twenty minutes I went onto autopilot, showering in the praise, letting it wash over me; but all the time I kept thinking about Jocelyn's abrupt volte-face. Then I saw her peering out from the doorway that led to the theatre, looking about. I watched her hurry through the crowd to the exit, head down, ignoring everyone. At the door she snatched a full bottle of beer from a table, and then disappeared into the night.

If she was so poorly, why did she need a lager for the journey home?

I tried to ignore all this, forget it, and enjoy the night. I turned to the people I didn't know who were telling me how much they loved the play, and how fascinating it was that I'd never even been to Northern Ireland.

'It's like *Whistle Down the Wind* in an uplift bra,' this woman was saying. And I nodded, even though I thought it was a bit reductive.

Jocelyn had gone, and I didn't know where Kathleen was. I was the toast of the room, but I suddenly felt incredibly alone.

Maybe I'd go home and phone my chatline.

BILLY

London, 2015

Dear God,

Someone has set up a Twitter account pretending to be Mum's ghost. She rants on in the style that whoever is writing it thinks that Mum would use, if she was still alive. It's actually pretty accurate but it upsets me when I look at it. And I can't stop looking at it. But then other times it brings me comfort. Like she hasn't gone at all, like she's there somewhere, taking everything in and earning a buck being horrendous about it all.

It's also nice, but weird, to think that someone else is thinking about her so much. Who is it? Sitting in their living room, typing away, thinking what would Mum say?

Mum would want a cut of the royalties. Not that you get royalties on Twitter. But she'd want something. Or she'd sue, if only for the publicity.

Why are you pretending to be me, cretin? You're not as beautiful or as perfect as me.

I miss her.

Amen.

JOCELYN

London, 2015

I always get a buzz doing live TV. Even when, like right now, the audience boos like a herd of irritated cows when I come on. I secretly like Joanne and Joolz, the two madcap presenters of *Lunchbreak*. Though I'm usually averse to anything one could describe as madcap. I could almost hate them for making me conjure up that word.

They originally appeared on *Britain's Got Talent* as a pretty abysmal singing duo before moving into kids' TV and now this, their own lunchtime show for grown-ups, shop-fronting Z-list guests like me. I am weaved, plucked, primped and preened to within an inch of my life. I am wearing a stiff figure-hugging silver sequinned number that will be returned to the designer as soon as I get home. I have more make-up on than a drag queen on the back of a float at Mardi Gras, and as for the heels . . . let's just say if I ever need to retrain as a circus performer, I'll have no trouble mastering the stilts.

'Stop booing her, guys!' Joanne (or is it Joolz?) is braying at the audience. 'She's here to give her side of the story!'

'She's a human being too!' chirrups Joolz (or is it Joanne?), but she does a sarcastic shrug as if to add 'Or is she?' so I laugh it off as I join them at their dinner table and insist, 'Oh, I'm used to it, don't worry about me. I'm a tough old broad.'

'YOUR ARSE IS BROAD!' someone calls from the audience, and I give a repulsed look. After all. That is a downright LIE.

'You'll be hearing from my lawyers!' I call back, which gets a laugh.

The idea about *Lunchbreak* is that the whole thing takes place over everyone's lunchbreak. I'm meant to be eating the plate of sushi before me, though I don't, and the audience all sit with packed lunches on their knees, tucking in. It's a ridiculous sight and puts me in mind of feeding time at the zoo.

The zoo for ugly people, that is.

After a bit of preamble from the two Js about my dress, my nails and isn't it a gorgeous day? (I imagine that's so they can convince the audience at home that this is actually live telly) I hear one of the two presenters saying . . .

'Soooo . . . How do you feel about being called the black Katie Hopkins?'

I do my customary eye roll. 'Oh, please. I'm nothing like her.'

'You're outspoken, brutal . . .'

'RENTAGOB!' someone shouts from the audience, which garners a round of applause.

'Yes, but I have this,' I interrupt, and point to my face, as if that explains everything.

'Well, yes, you're very beautiful.'

I do a sideways tilt of the head, body language for 'that much is true'.

'SHE'S UGLY!' someone shouts from the audience. To which I quickly rejoinder, 'Er – eye test?!'

'INSIDE AND OUT!'

And then the two Js continue rabbiting on about my latest

misdemeanour. All I said in my column this week was that there were too many ugly women on telly, and something needed to give.

'Would you say you were vain, Jocelyn?' one of them asks.

I shake my head. 'Just honest. I tell it how it is. And this . . .' I point to my face and look to the audience. 'Is pretty fucking special.'

I then pick up my chopsticks and grab a piece of sushi, as if I've done nothing out of the ordinary.

It works. They go into overdrive, apologizing into camera as the audience boos, guffaws and gasps, almost in tears over my use of bad language before the watershed. Packed lunch boxes tumble to the floor as agitated ugly people jump up to wave their fists at me. Perfect. I look unrepentant. I am unrepentant. I know I have secured my YouTube moment. I look into the audience and see Ross skulking at the back. He winks. Job done.

You see, this is why they hire me, these two-bit chat shows. This is why they pay me between five grand and ten grand a pop for turning up. They want controversy. They want people at water coolers up and down the country to be talking about their crappy little shows and saying, 'Oh, what? You didn't see her? That vile bitch Jocelyn was on and she swore. Oh, it was so funny. You should've seen Joanne and Joolz's faces. They were a picture. Have a look on YouTube. I think *Lunchbreak* might've tweeted the clip actually.' And then they get more traffic to their website, and somewhere in their tiny minds they hope that more people will tune in next time just in case it happens again. They claim not to like me, these television producers, but the truth is, they need me. Sometimes I am their only hope to get a mention in *Heat* magazine. I know my value in the world, and it's four simple words:

I give good headline.

The interview continues for another five minutes, but I don't bother saying anything controversial again – that ship has passed. I babble on, reasonably intelligently, about how television is a visual medium and that is why we want to be visually appeased, and not see a load of fat boilers with faces like bags of spanners talking to us from the corner of our living rooms. We get enough of that in real life, thank you very much. It's the same reason we want to see clothes looking good in the fashion world by hanging them on walking pencils. We see enough normal-sized women squeezed like toothpaste tubes into narrow garments in the real world. And there's nothing wrong with that. But television isn't the real world.

Joanne and Joolz start doing this sort of homeboy thing with their hands and going on about keeping it real and soon it's time to go to a commercial break. They know I've given good value and shake my hand effusively before a runner whisks me off set as the audience – gosh, it's getting tedious now – boos me. I slip them the finger and then head off set.

The runner hurries me back down a brightly lit corridor to the green room, where the other guests are waiting to go on – someone from *Doctors* and a 'zany' chef – neither of them can look me in the eye. I grab my coat and turn to go without acknowledging them. What is their problem? Do they hate me? Or is the real reason they can't lower themselves to smile that they realize I have stolen their thunder? No-one will be talking about their appearances on this tawdry little show, only mine. As I head into the corridor, I hear a runner screaming at them, 'WHICH ONE OF YOU WANTED COUSCOUS?!'

I'm pleased to see Ross is here, and he takes me by the arm.

'I'll take over from here,' he snaps at a woman with a clipboard and walkie-talkie, and we head to the exit.

'Good work, Princess. Good work,' he hums in my ear, like a mantra, 'Number one trending topic in the country as of this minute? The General Election? No. Jocelyn fucking Jones. Back o' the net!'

I say nothing, just smile. As I said. Job done.

The walls are covered with massive, brightly coloured photos of daytime television stars past and present. Every single one of them looks like a parody of themselves.

Oh, how apt!

'And now,' coos Ross, 'curtain up for . . . the second act.'

I nod. I know what's coming. I feel a mixture of nerves and excitement, but cover them well. A security guard opens a door for us, and as we head into the sunlight a wall of noise hits me. My car is waiting and Ross opens the door for me, but I stop to give a wave to the braying crowd beyond it.

'EVIL BITCH!' someone shouts.

'FUCKING SNOB!' calls another.

'CUNT!'

To which I call back, 'Your mother would be proud!'

And as I do, an egg flies out from the crowd and hits me square in the face. Before I can show any signs of a reaction, Ross shoves me onto the back seat of the car. As the door shuts and the car pulls away, I hear a huge cheer going up. Ross passes me a hand mirror and some wet wipes. I see the driver eyeing me suspiciously through the rear-view mirror.

'Hazard of the job,' I smile to him, as if I am always getting egged.

I check my face in the mirror and am furious to see that I have egg yolk in my weave. I do what I can with the wet wipes and see that Ross is punching his fingers on the screen of his phone.

'What am I saying?' I ask. Ross writes a lot of my tweets for me. It's all about protecting the brand.

He clears his throat. 'First tweet: "Whoever egged me just then. Good aim. #militaryprecision".'

I nod.

'Second tweet: "and thank you. Egg is so kind to the skin. #freefacepack".'

I nod again.

As we sail through central London, I wonder if my family back in Liverpool might have seen the show. I wonder what they'd make of me now. All my mother ever wanted was for me to be a cut above. She sent me to elocution lessons, for God's sake. Well, there's not a hint of Scouse in my voice now. I have erased my accent, just as I have erased the past. And it was all so easy to do! I am cool, calm, collected. Public school if ever you saw it. A black woman with privilege? Now that's what I call reinvention!

The driver has the car radio on. The Lib Dems have been annihilated in the General Election and Labour have more egg on their face than me. Voice after voice fills the car, bleating on about how amazing or catastrophic this landslide is. As we hit the Westway, Mark Reynolds comes on, self-appointed mouthpiece for the Labour Party.

'The way I see it,' he says, 'the Labour party and Ed Miliband in particular need to be taking a long, hard look at themselves in the mirror today.'

In a heartbeat I'm back there. In the organ loft. Lying in Mark's arms. As emotions I've long since buried bubble up inside me, I try to quash them.

'Excuse me, could we have the radio off please? Thank you.'

The driver dutifully snaps the radio off. Ross looks at me. I look out of the window. Ross returns to jabbing at his phone.

By the time the car arrives at Trellick Tower, a video of me being egged has gone viral and I've been retweeted 1,457 times. Ross is already fielding calls for offers to appear on more shows tomorrow. Result.

All in a day's work. Although I do say to Ross in the lift, 'Next time, tell Finty not to get it in my weave.'

When we get in I squeeze out of my borrowed dress and hand it to Ross to return to his contact. It's clear that he wants sex. He's always like this when I've gone viral, but today I send him away with a flea in his boxers as I have a weave to rescue. He leaves cursing Finty's poor aim, huffing and puffing under his breath about what trouble that girl is in. I enjoy how fickle he can be; he's been singing her praises most of the way home about what a good little girl she is. And considering I'm convinced he fancies the pants off her, I find it curious that a grown man can describe the object of his lust as a 'girl'. He says he's going to the designer's, but warns me he'll be back in an hour. With 'her'. He's got a pitch for me.

'It was Finty's idea, actually. It's a cracker.'

Oh, is it? Really!

I put my mini kimono on and head to the bathroom, where I spritz my weave with some cold water then finger-comb the tiniest splodge of shampoo through. I then turn the shower on and lean backwards so I just wet the hair, then run my fingers through it to clean it off any leftover egg. Shower off, I finger comb some conditioner through it and repeat the process. I then cover my head with a towel and squeeze dry the hair, saying all the time my favourite mantra: *A weave . . . you squeeze. You squeeze . . . your weave.*

The thing you must never do with a weave is rub your scalp

as if it were your own hair, and by squeezing into a towel and not rubbing vigorously, you hopefully avoid getting the weave tangled. I'm lucky, I can afford proper hair. I joke that it's made from virgin nuns in Guatemala, but actually the truth is probably just as bizarre. I leave the towel on for a while and go and sit in the living room. On a sunny day like this, it's like sitting in a greenhouse.

I put the TV on for a while, but again, he's there. Mark Reynolds. He's not even an MP, and yet they wheel him out as a political commentator all the time. He's been on *Newsnight* that often, they've given him his own swivel chair. He's aged well. Men don't, as a rule. But he's slightly built, and that's a bonus for any man. I don't know if he dyes his hair, but he hasn't got a grey hair on his head. He doesn't strike me as vain enough to dye his hair. And his clothes say Morrissey fan, not Jeremy Paxman wannabe.

I switch the TV off. Too many memories, and they should remain buried.

An hour or so later, Ross is back with Finty. They sit side by side on one of my sofas as I look lazily out of the window. I think it never pays to look too excited or nervous. Make them impress me. Make them work for their bloody money. Finty burbles a few apologies about getting egg in my weave. I ignore her at first, so she carries on. I enjoy the power I have over her. I turn to tell her it's OK, but don't do it again, but I can tell Ross is bored, as he butts in.

'So . . . here's the pitch.'

'Anyway, sorry about the egg thing, Jossy,' coos Finty, one last time.

'Shut up.' Ross snaps. He's in full-on manager mode.

'Soz.'

Finty has an annoying habit of abbreviating everything like

she's texting you and not speaking to you. I hate it when she calls me Jossy. I know she's only shortening Jocelyn but it feels like she's taking the piss, making a joke out of everything. I just ignore her.

'So. We have quite a quiet May.'

'We do,' I say nonchalantly, as if this is none of my fault, which of course it isn't. I stare at a pigeon wrestling with a bit of bread on the roof of the low-rise block beneath me. How the bread got up there is anyone's guess.

'So. Here's the thing.'

I keep looking out of the window. Is everything about my life a performance these days?

'In May, the press reveal . . . that I have left you for Finty.'

I swing round and look at the pair of them. I must be looking furious, as they both seem to cower.

'Sorry?' And that is so unlike me, I rarely apologize.

'I mean, he hasn't,' Finty says. 'It's just a story we put out there.'

'You get some sympathy, some hatred. Acres of press about how the mighty have fallen, how you had it coming, you're defiant, columns columns columns, and then . . . the *pièce de résistance*. You take me back.'

I look back out of the window.

'Imagine the headlines, Jocelyn.'

And I do. I can see them. The I-told-you-sos, the she's-past-its. But they have a point. It would keep me in the press. I'd just have to work out what to say without looking too stupid or – heaven forfend – undesirable! The thought makes me burst out laughing. Quickly I stop. I need to take myself more seriously, not show Finty that mostly this is a performance.

'It could really fit into your Women Beware Women thing, we thought,' Finty says salaciously.

And she's right, of course. My manager-stroke-boyfriend running off with the PA is my equivalent of hubby going off with the nanny.

I've already written a lot about that.

It's rich territory.

I like it.

I like it a lot, actually.

And it might even engender some sympathy for me.

I look back at them. Smile imperiously.

'Good work, guys.'

Then I stand up and excuse myself.

I walk into my bedroom and shut the door.

I slump on the bed and consider my appearance in the full-length mirror on the wall.

I hate myself.

As this wave of self-loathing washes over me, I do what I always do to distract myself.

I open my laptop. It springs into life.

I log into Facebook. I have created a false profile. I am a white teenage girl with hair extensions called Jamie-Lee Davenport. I don't have many friends on there.

But I have him.

I click on his name.

I see his profile picture smiling back at me. The bronzed skin. The small dreadlocks. The green eyes. So handsome. That gap-toothed smile. I know without looking that he has three large freckles on his neck. But I look anyway.

He's thirty now. Thirty. But I don't mind that that makes me feel old.

I smile. I feel better. But that feeling passes too, and the wave comes again.

I close the laptop.

Why would that make me feel better?

I look in the mirror. Does he look like me?

I look away. Can't even bear to see myself today.

I wait for the wave to pass.

It often takes a while.

My phone buzzes. I know that buzz. It means someone has sent Jamie-Lee a message on Facebook. How weird. No-one ever sends Jamie-Lee a message on there.

I grab the phone. Open the Facebook app. I do indeed have a message. Well. Jamie-Lee does. Maybe it's some spotty teenager saying I FANCY YOU N TING. That has happened before.

I see the message has come from someone called Darius D'Eath.

It immediately makes me think of that God-awful Darius from *Popstars* all those years ago. Was that his name? Then I remember: it was Darius Danesh.

I open the message. It's a picture message. Of a baseball bat with nails hammered into the end of it. It's a chilling image. The text accompanying the picture reads:

Jocelyn I know this is you and this is what I am going to shove up you you vile whore.

The picture is shaking.

And then I realize.

The picture isn't shaking.

My hand is.

London, 1995

It was a nice feeling, knowing no-one could hurt you. You could feel protected, that no-one could ever, ever get to you, no matter how hard they tried. But it was a hard-won feeling, one that had taken years of practice to perfect. I was proud that I'd finally achieved it, but it hadn't always been easy. I'd look around at other people, I'd see people crying in the street, people rowing and think . . . why? Why should they care? There was another way. My way.

It had all started when I was a teenager, when bad things had happened to me, when I felt there was no control in my life, pushed pillar to post by a mother who wanted me more than anything to achieve, ACHIEVE, goddammit, to fill a hollow in her life, do the things she could never do. The academic version of the pushy showbiz mum. Not so much *Sing out, Louise!* as *Work hard, Jocelyn!* Moving me from the Wirral to Liverpool on her next big whim, or little whim, rather; teasmade company here, cleaning empire there. All of them doomed to failure. And all the time I knew. I knew that each time she let a new boyfriend through the door, I was destined for better than that. It was not the life I wanted.

Maybe it's because my mum always taught me that at school, and in life, if I wanted to get on I had to be twice as good as the white girls. I never quite believed I was. But Mum seemed to have that belief intrinsically, so we had to be. No say in the matter, we HAD TO BE. And so maybe it rubbed off. And as bad things happened, so it became easier, in fact somewhat necessary possibly, to close myself off and stop myself from being hurt by the world. And it was possible. Look at me now. And that's where it started. With my mum. She pushed me so hard that it felt like she'd pushed me away, somewhere where normal people didn't exist. In a hinterland that had stood me in good stead for now. Apart from the world, not part of it. An observer rather than a participant.

There was something rather delicious about lying in a bed, stretching out your legs and arms as far as they would go, really pointing your toes out, and still feeling the bed just went on forever. Not so much a bed, but a country. And God, these sheets were clean. Even though I'd spent a night in them, getting up to all sorts with Mr Love, they still smelt Lenor summer meadows fresh.

The other good thing about this particular bed was the view. OK, so looking up at the ceiling was like looking at any other ceiling, but if I crooked my head down and stared out beyond the rise in the duvet where my feet were . . . that view. That VIEW!

Mr Love's apartment was on Park Lane, and on the other side of my feet were the tops of the trees in Hyde Park. If I lifted my feet, they vanished. They were erased, gone. They didn't exist.

When I was a young girl, one of my favourite things in the whole wide world was this daft little eraser that sat at the top of my pencil. It was pink and looked like the end of a finger. You could buy them loose from Woolworth's, and then attach them to the end of any pencil. It wasn't so much the eraser

I liked, it was what you could do with it. Make any mistake on the page and you could just upturn your pencil and, in a couple of strokes, completely obliterate where you had gone wrong. A perfectionist like me took great pleasure in every long, slow swipe of that rubber.

Lying here, in Mr Love's crisp bed, it was as if I had done that with my life. It was as if every morning I could wake up and pretend that nothing had ever happened in the past. Fresh start. Blank page. Tabula rasa.

It was as if I had been born fully formed this morning. Slap bang in the middle of the nineties. Slap bang in the middle of 1995, in fact. As if the only music I had ever heard was this burgeoning Britpop they kept talking about on the radio. Lennon and McCartney? Who the hell were they? I only knew the Gallagher brothers and the girly-looking Mr Albarn. They'd been fighting it out for the top spot in the album charts, didn't you know? And cheeky suburban Albarn had pipped the naughty minstrels La Famille Gallagher to the top spot. The working-class Mancunians had been beaten by the middle-of-the-road nice boys singing about having a house in the country. Exactly. Said all you needed to know about Britain today.

'Baby girl?'

I turned to see Mr Love had popped his head round the door. His hair was wet and his bangs were clinging to his forehead; clearly he'd just stepped out of the shower.

I loved the word bangs. Everyone else described this latest haircut as curtains. I'd heard an American on TV call them bangs. So I did too. I thought it marked me out as exotic.

Nevertheless, my hackles rose – as much as they could while lying in a lap-of-luxury bed. He only usually called me *baby girl* when there was a problem, or he wanted something.

'Mr Love?' I replied coolly, showing I was aware a problem might be hovering overhead.

'You about tonight? Something I want to talk to you about.'

Interesting.

'Sure. We could . . . rent a video or . . . something.'

That seemed to throw him. We never rented videos. I didn't even know why I'd suggested it. Mr Love worked for a film company, and as such often brought the new releases back on video for us to watch anyway.

'Erm . . . sure . . . or I could get Bolshy to cook.'

Bolshy was his housekeeper. I knew this was an old family nickname, because she had been rather left-wing in her youth.

'Sure. That'd be great.'

'See you tonight.'

What on earth did he want to talk to me about?

I slipped out of the bed and into a kimono he kept on the back of the bedroom door.

'Is Bolshy here today?' I asked breezily as he mooched about his galley kitchen. These apartments may well have had views to kill for, but some of the rooms were tiny.

'Yah, she'll be over to clean and whatnot.'

Whatnot. Forgetting for once that this was the first day of the rest of my life, I compared Mr Love to all the guys I'd known back in Liverpool, or when I'd been on the glamour modelling circuit. Not a single one of them would have utilized the word *whatnot*. And possibly with good reason. It made him appear at once effete and effeminate.

Still, that was one of the many surprises about Mr Love. For ages I'd thought he was a gay Sloane, when actually he was one of the most rampant red-blooded males I'd ever met. Although describing him as red-blooded felt more like a red herring than anything else. His blood definitely had hues of blue, related as he was – although somewhat distantly – to the Royal Family themselves. In fact, one of his first jaunts abroad as a child had been holidaying with Princess Margaret in Mustique.

Funnily enough, I had met Mr Love for the first time five years previously. I had been to that tiny theatre in Shepherd's Bush to see Adam's terrible play based upon our teenage years. Had I not been averse even back then to wrapping myself up in a protective blanket so that no-one could hurt me, I would have been affronted by what he presented as entertainment. His take on the teenage years of myself, him and poor Kathleen. But I found his outrageousness appealing. The effrontery of portraying us like that, his brass neck, his impudence. I'd found Kathleen crying in the toilets at the interval.

'Why?' she said. 'Why does he have to do this?'

And as the words left my mouth I decided to use my 'off the top of my head wisdom' as my own sage advice too.

'It's a play,' I said, trying to sound as emboldened and unfazed as I could. 'The clue's in the name.'

'*Supper with Sam*?'

'No.' Gosh, she could be dense. 'The word is *play*. They're playing. And this game is nothing to do with us.'

But then something had happened. Something that had shaken me, momentarily. And later I made my excuses and left. And as I walked off into the night, I thought many things. But I thought . . . *I am not the girl I was back then, the girl Adam thinks this play is about. And yet again, I find I have a choice in my life. Only my choice right now is not like the one I made all those years ago.*

The old me could so easily have cried, stumbled onto

Shepherd's Bush Green with my pashmina around my shoulders and my dignity somewhere near my ankles. And I didn't want to be that girl.

So I stopped myself from crying. I held my head high. And I walked away from the theatre feeling, shakily, invincible.

I thought, what would a strong, determined woman do right now?

Ahead I saw the hazy lights of a wine bar, glowing from a corner of the green. I headed towards it.

The Albertine was a cosy, ramshackle wooden affair full of men and women hunched over too-small tables, talking and drinking wine by candlelight. Some were eating. Lots were laughing. The room reeked of bonhomie. I pushed my way to the bar and surveyed the blackboard behind it. Back then I was new enough to London, and new enough to places like this, to not know my way through a wine list. And so I did what one should always do when one feels out of one's depth. I leaned in to the couple next to me and said,

'I'm so sorry to interrupt you. But might you be able to recommend me a decent rosé?'

It was Mr Love. And his pal Percy. And the rest, as they say, was history.

And indeed that particular night, as they also say, out of bad came good.

That night, my life changed.

'I wonder what it is he wants?!' I giggled excitedly to Adam, over lunch at Quaglino's.

Adam put his knife and fork down, casting aside his tricolore salad. 'I've got it. Oh my God. I'm gonna need a new hat!'

'WHAT?!' Even though I knew what was coming.

'He's gonna propose!'

We both giggled like the school girls we weren't, and Adam demanded we have a glass of champagne to celebrate. When I demurred – I didn't want to become squiffy ahead of any potential proposal tonight – he overruled me and ordered two glasses from a passing waiter.

'Now, remind me why you call him Mr Love?'

'Oh it's silly, really. His first name's St John and I just couldn't bring myself to say that on a daily basis.'

'Oh God, yes, I remember now.'

'And when I told him that, he told me that when he was a baby his nanny used to call him Mr Love-a-Lot as he was always smiling.'

'His nanny. Fucking hell, Jocelyn, what are you like?'

'And I kind of ended up abbreviating it to Mr Love.'

'And even more embarrassingly, it stuck!' laughed Adam as two icy glasses of bubbles appeared at our table.

'Cheers, Jocelyn.'

'Cheers, baby.' As we clinked glasses, I suddenly gasped, 'Oh Christ, you said you had gossip about Kathleen. Come on. Spill!'

'Not before you've shown me your new toy!'

'Oh God. It's in my handbag. Two secs.'

I had recently invested in my new pride and joy. I pulled it out of my handbag and passed it over for him to fawn.

'Oh my God, it's incredible. Will it work in here?'

'I don't know. You might have to pull the aerial up, but we're underground, so probably not. But isn't it gorgeous?'

'And it works?'

'Sure.'

'You can actually phone people on it?'

'I called you on it before.'

'I know, but I wasn't sure whether to believe you. Oh, can I make a call on it after lunch?'

'Sure.'

'Knocks spots off my pager.'

'It's my pride and joy.'

I loved saying that. I'd only had my new mobile phone a couple of days and had, I'm sure, racked up a whole lot of cash on its bill by phoning people non-stop on it as it was such a novelty. I'd phoned Mr Love so much at the office that he'd actually asked me to stop calling. Spoilsport. And I'd already managed to scratch its tiny, beautiful screen with over-enthusiastic yanking of it out of my handbag all the time to check no-one had called me on it. Thus far, they hadn't. But someone would one day, I was sure of it.

Adam was unable to get a signal in this subterranean eatery, but that didn't stop him pretending to punch in numbers and talk loudly to various imagined friends, which caused quite a few of the other customers to look over, unimpressed or beguiled.

'What does it sound like when it rings?' he asked.

'No idea. But I bet it's a beautiful sound. Like a magical, heavenly dawn chorus!' And again we laughed.

Adam was such good fun. I'd always thought that when his writing didn't take off after the dire reviews for his second play – I couldn't for the life of me remember the title right now, but it was something to do with Standing on the Brink of something or other. Anyway, whatever it was, it was an INCREDIBLY pretentious title, considering it was about a woman who worked in a sweet shop. Clearly based on his mum – I'd always thought that he'd slump into a depression. Thus far, he hadn't.

'Anyway. Come on. Gossip about Kathleen. Shoot.'

It amazed me that he and Kathleen had remained such good friends. I knew on one level he loved her, but fuck me, he loved to slag her off.

'I'm not speaking to her.'

'Why not?!'

'She's having a nose job.'

I clutched the table, threw my head back and howled.

Oh, that was too much. That was too funny. Kathleen? Sheepish little Kathleen was having PLASTIC SURGERY?

'But why aren't you speaking to her? That's a genius idea! Our little Kath? Going all Hollywood?'

'Well, exactly, it's just bloody ridiculous. Who does she think she is? Miss Ellen?'

'But if she hates the one she's got . . .' And we all knew she hated the one she had.

'I've told her. It lends her character.'

'She needs it,' I added, with more bitchiness than I'd intended. Must've been the champagne.

'It's the most interesting thing about her,' he agreed.

'God, you're outrageous.'

'I know. Oh. And she's applied to become a fucking trolley dolly. She's got ideas above her airport, that one.'

'Stop making me laugh!'

'Comes with the turf, kid,' he said, pretending to rearrange his bust, sounding for all the world like Bet Lynch from *Coronation Street*.

The turf he was talking about was his new role in life. He had recently ditched any pretensions about wanting to have another play on because, he had decided, 'I now realize I was destined to be centre stage. Not at the back taking notes.' Adam was now a fully fledged drag queen, performing several nights a week at a variety of gay bars, pubs and clubs, calling himself Josie Jumpsuit. I thought that was a dreadful name but he, of course, was convinced it was genius. Kathleen and I had been to see him perform a few times and, although he was a bit rough around the edges, he had actually made me laugh. He lip-synched very well to several singers and cracked a few off-colour jokes in his Liverpool brogue, often picking on various members of the audience. He had once pointed me out and said I was 'the least convincing tranny he'd seen in years'. It had got a massive laugh from the 'crowd' – there were about twenty old men in a sticky carpeted pub in Putney – so fair play to him. Who was I to deny him his moment of glory?

Now he seemed to spend his days scouring second-hand shops for different jumpsuits to wear at night, often taking them home and getting the ever-ready-to-please Kathleen to customize them so that they were a bit more sequinny and glamorous. I imagined her sat in their Harmony Heights flat, hunched over that sewing machine like she was in a sweat-shop. Since the closure of Hyper Hyper both Adam and Kathleen had tried their hands at various things, between periods on the dole. Kathleen had tried to be a fashion designer, with zero luck. Now she worked several jobs; the latest was, she screen-printed sets of white bed linen with various patterns and sold them at Greenwich market. She was doing OK for herself, apparently. Amazing what people could do when they put their minds to it.

But trolley dollying? Our little Kath? I couldn't see it myself. Nothing about her reeked of the jet set.

'Everything OK with the flat?' I asked.

Adam nodded. 'Great, thanks, you're a star.'

After finding a squat for us to live in a few years ago, I had eventually managed to get their names on the list for a housing association flat, of which they were now proud tenants. The deal was that since I had helped them get it, I could stay there whenever I wanted. It was a roomy two-bedroomed place in Paddington, and the lounge was big enough for me to treat the sofa bed as my pied-à-terre whenever I needed it. Not that I'd needed it that much recently, what with me practically living with Mr Love.

I had become rather reliant on Mr Love, as recently it had become apparent that at the grand old age of twenty-five I was somewhat past it. With his blessing I had done some glamour modelling, and for about a year I had been popular on the pages of certain tabloids with my top off, lip gloss on my nipples and a faraway look in my eyes. I was flavour of the month for all of about a month, as I was seen as exotic and different in that tits-out world on account of my skin colour. But my heart had never been in it, and when I'd had the chance to record a record, I'd jumped at it. 'Do Me in Ibiza Old Town' had bombed. And who had been my manager through these ill-advised journeys? Mr Love.

I had enjoyed, briefly, the attention of getting my top off, after years of wondering if I was as good as white girls and believing from my mother that I had to work twice as hard as them to prove my worth. Well, in the glamour world, that just wasn't true. Just by taking my top off and revealing my (hitherto in my eyes) cumbersome breasts, I discovered a welcome power over men. And that power was pretty intoxicating.

However, my mother proved to be right, ultimately. I had no longevity as this kind of model, because on the whole it seemed the largely white *Sun*-buying public preferred their girls Caucasian. And unless I wanted to venture into porn, which I most certainly didn't, then there just didn't seem to be any sort of future in it for me.

Mr Love didn't seem to mind. He didn't seem to mind what I did. He had actually appeared to enjoy the idea of other men ogling my semi-naked form. Mind you, he'd been convinced I was the next Madonna as well. He got me my record deal, for what it was worth. And, as he kept pointing out, Samantha Fox had done it – why shouldn't I?

Well. Possibly because I hadn't had the talent in the first place.

I knew my limitations, and I had rapidly discovered that it's one thing being the best singer in your church choir; it's another to compete with experienced recording artists in the cut-throat world of the music business.

I had enjoyed my brief flirtation with fame. But no-one wanted their thirteen-year-old buying 'that dirty lady's' record once they found out what my previous career had been.

It was during my glamour days that my mother stopped speaking to me altogether.

And now I was in a bit of a pickle. I'd been out of the normal workplace for too long. If I applied for a job in an office now, what would I put on my CV? Two years getting my baps out for magazines and newspapers? A number 83 hit record with a Europop beat? That wasn't going to convince anyone I was any good at photocopying.

I occasionally got recognized. But it was mostly men in un-appealing raincoats. The sort with stains on. And I doubted they were in any position to find me work.

Well, there was one job offer I'd had lately. But I CER-TAINLY wasn't going to be taking that one up. I almost told Adam about it, but pulled back, doing one of those lousy 'Guess what? Oh . . . nothing . . .' exchanges so often heard in soap operas.

There was no need for me to tell him about Black Orchid.

When the bill came he offered to pay it, citing as his reason that 'Josie's quite flush this week', so I let him. And as I trudged off into the daylight, the prospect of Mr Love proposing to me made my heart soar.

But why should it soar? I'd never told him I loved him, despite him telling me several times. And – if I was honest with myself – this was because I didn't love him. I loved the life he gave me, but could I honestly describe my feelings for him? What I loved was that he was my meal ticket. And right now, with so few other options on the table, that was something I was prepared to suck up.

Besides, I was careless. I was fearless. I was bold and invincible. Nothing could hurt me – I had reinvented myself as an ice queen.

Who needed feelings, when Mr Love had cold, hard cash?

I realized I sounded very much like a prostitute.

Mr Love was already home by the time I got back, remarkably early for someone who constantly claimed to be at the cut and thrust of the international movie business, even though in all our years together he'd had two tiny credits on some straight-to-video movies. 'Runner' on one and 'additional material by' on the other. But then he always said movie development was a long, laborious process with constant disappointment and rejection. I could hear him rattling pots and pans in the kitchen so I called a quick 'Only me!' as I walked through the apartment.

The evidence was everywhere that Bolshy had been, things we'd left lying around neatly put into piles on various surfaces, something that didn't bother me but I knew drove Mr Love mad. *Why won't she put THINGS AWAY?!* I nipped into the bedroom to throw my jacket on the bed, which was when I saw another pile. A pile of all my clothes on the bed, next to an open suitcase.

'Blimey!' I said, 'Bolshy's taken this pile malarkey a bit far, hasn't she?'

Which is when I sensed him behind me. I swung round. He was looking sheepish in the doorway.

'Shit. I wanted to get to you before you saw that.'

And in that moment, I knew that this pile was less to do with Bolshy and more to do with him.

And there was only one reason a man put his girlfriend's stuff out in a pile next to an empty suitcase.

It meant he was dumping her.

Mr Love was dumping me.

'What's going on?' I asked with an imperious tone, the implication being that I knew and heartily disapproved.

'Come into the kitchen.'

So I did. I followed him in and saw a bubbling shepherd's pie on the side.

'I want you to have this.'

Mr Love grabbed a bulging envelope from the tiny table at the end of the kitchen and handed it to me. It felt heavier than it looked, and when I looked inside I saw it was full of twenty-pound notes.

'I don't understand.'

'There's a thousand in there. Look on it as severance pay.'

'You're dumping me?'

He looked like he didn't like the sound of that. He was looking very pale. He usually looked red and flustered in the kitchen, even if he was just reheating something bland that his former nanny had cooked four hours earlier.

'This was never really going to work, was it?' he said, and

even though I knew on paper it would look like a question, I knew that this was very much his statement of fact.

'I don't know, St John. You fucking tell me.' Ooh, his pet hate, women swearing!

'Well, look at you.'

'What about me?'

'A second-rate Page Three stunner?'

'Oh, please!'

'A pop-star wannabe who even Song for Europe wouldn't touch?'

'That was a misunderstanding.'

'Are you really the sort of girl that Mummy and Daddy are going to approve of? I think not, Jocelyn. Definitely not.'

'Why don't you chuck the other thing in, while you're at it?' I practically spat. 'I'm black as well.'

'That's unfair!' he bleated. 'I have many black friends, as well you know.'

'Just a shame I've never met them.' Which was a lie. I didn't find it a shame at all.

'Well, I had two black friends at Eton,' he said rather pompously.

'What's brought this on?'

'Nothing.' But any idiot could see he was lying. Something had.

'Have you met someone?'

'NO!' He said it with such force it felt like the shepherd's pie would bounce off the side.

'Methinks the Hooray doth protest too much!' I cackled, with just the right amount of glee.

Mr Love folded his arms. 'Well, it's not my fault, is it?'

'What's not?'

'It's Mummy and Daddy.'

'What about them?'

'They think it's high time I settled down. And maybe they have a point.'

'Ah, so they've introduced you to someone.'

'No. Yes. Well, I met her years ago, if you must know. And yes, we're to be betrothed.'

'What's her name?'

'Jemima.'

I suddenly felt nauseous. It took all my willpower not to vomit over him right there and then.

'And what's the thousand pounds for?'

'To help you . . . start a new life.'

'Right.'

I pushed past him and headed for the bedroom, where I started shoving all my clothes into the case. I thought he'd follow me in and change his mind, or apologize, or . . . God knows what . . . but instead I heard him getting plates and cutlery out.

'You going to stay for some pie, baby girl?'

'WHAT AM I? TWELVE?' I roared, creating a noise that surprised even me.

I yanked the zip round with such force that the end of it came off in my hand. I double-checked I had the envelope of money. And without even a backward glance I walked out of his apartment, and out of his life.

Out on the street, I wondered where I could go. I took out my mobile phone and called Adam's number. But of course there was nobody in, and they clearly hadn't decided to invest in an answering machine, so I eventually hung up. Kathleen would be working her evening job and Adam might by now be on his way to performing in some seedy dive bar.

I had a key to their place. I could just go and let myself in, bed myself down.

But part of me didn't want them to be able to tell me, 'I told you so.' Even if they hadn't told me so. I didn't want to see that look in their eyes. That look that said, *See? You're just like us. You didn't deserve that life. And here you are. Back in the gutter. Back to square one.*

Still. A thousand pounds was a lot of money. I could get the deposit on my own place with it. But if I was going to get my own place, I would need to find a way to fund my lifestyle. I had developed rather expensive tastes since living with Mr Love. I didn't feel ready to give them up now.

I furtled in my handbag till I found what I was looking for.

A business card. Black with swirly silver writing. The outline of a shiny red rose. A name.

Tina di Antonio

And the name of her business.

Black Orchid

No explanation of what the business was. Just a number.

I returned to my mobile phone. Dialled the number, heard it ring out, then a very sexy voice answered, almost purring down the line.

'Hello? Black Orchid?'

'Tina? It's Jocelyn Jones.'

'Jocelyn. Darling! To what do I owe the pleasure?'

'I'd like to come and talk to you.'

'Superb.'

She gave me the address of a house in West Kensington. I hailed a cab.

Looked like I was going to become a Black Orchid girl after all.

London, 2015

The deal with Finty is off. Her girlfriend is dead set against it. It was news to me that she was even a lesbian, if I'm honest. She's one of that new breed where you can't tell. The sort of girl Sue Perkins would go out with.

'It's about the most interesting thing about her,' I commented coolly to Ross when he told me. Before adding, 'She doesn't go out with Sue Perkins, does she?'

And he said he didn't think so, and very much doubted it.

I'd tend to agree.

When he told me the deal was off, it was like it was the worst news in the world. It was like a scene from a World War II movie where someone rushes into the parlour and says, 'It's happened. We're at war. Bally Hitler.' Only this time as we sat drinking tea we didn't hear any air-raid sirens or bombs dropping. Actually, it's hard to hear anything happening outside when you live this high up.

The Finty situation is incredibly annoying. It's back-to-the-drawing-board time. Ross paces the flat, cursing Finty's girlfriend.

'Finty's up for it. Course she's up for it, she's ambitious as fuck.'

'So why don't we do it?'

'Girlfriend's a loose cannon. All it'd take would be for her to go to the press saying this is a sham for publicity purposes, and your career would be over. OVER.'

'There's no need to say it twice.'

'They'd never believe another word you said.'

'Yes, I'm not stupid, Ross.'

'They'd be like . . . you can't trust a thing she says, or . . .'

'OK, Ross, I get the fucking picture!'

That shuts him up. But only temporarily. He turns on me, like some cheap villain in a Sunday-afternoon Western.

'Are you on your blob?'

'Oh piss off, Ross.'

'Just remember, you. The only reason you're one of the most hated women in Britain, the only reason you keep a roof over your head and a shitty little weave on your skull's coz of me. It's this brain that gets you the column inches, as well as yours.' And he does a dramatic tap on his head.

I have to stop myself from saying, 'Oh, is that where a brain is?' but I know to just ignore him when he's in one of his angry, belligerent moods. The superior ice-queen mode won't cut it now. I know what will.

'So. What are we going to do?'

It's a great ploy of mine. In just a few words I appeal to his vanity by acknowledging I would be nothing without him. He laps it up. Nods his head a lot.

Men, so often, are like dogs. When they turn vicious, chuck them a biscuit, it soon calms them down.

'I'm not sure,' he says, 'but I'll think of something. In the meantime . . . write your column.'

And he heads for the door, no doubt into the throbbing metropolis to gather his genius thoughts together and form a plan of action that will keep me talked about around water coolers up and down the country – and, more importantly, his mortgage paid.

I actually wrote my column early this morning, but I hoick open my laptop to read through my musings and see if I can still stick by what I said.

BABY ON BOARD? BABES I'M BORED!

I know a lot of you will find this hard to believe, but I do actually take public transport quite a bit. And by that I'm not counting taxis. I was on the tube yesterday and I had just hunkered down in my seat to read someone else's leftover newspaper – kindly wedged 'twixt cushions – when a woman got on at the next station with one of those ghastly BABY ON BOARD badges on. All our seats were taken, and she just stood there, eyeing us all shiftily till one of us, a man of course, did the chivalrous thing and stood up for her. And she sat. And the porcine (look it up) pregnant princess didn't even say thank you. The cheek!

Well excuse . . . me!

She wasn't even that pregnant. It was five o'clock. I bet she'd not put a full day's work in like the guys I was sitting amongst. And yet, just because she had un-protected sex a few months ago, we're in less need of a bally chair than she is?

I'm sorry, but in my book the only people we should stand up for on tubes are the elderly or infirm. And being pregnant is not an illness. It's not an affliction. It just makes you selfish.

Stand up.

And keep your legs together next time, lady! I got me some serious sitting to do!

Toodle pip!

Jocelyn x

I sigh, admiring my own daring. This will be LOATHED. And then I attach it to an email and ping it over to Ross with the subject line: QUITE PLEASED WITH THIS.

Five minutes later he replies:

I love you Queen Genius. Xx

That'll do for now.

I take a stroll down to Portobello. With my shades on and my hair hidden away in a dayglo headscarf, I feel like an extra in an Almodóvar movie. I also know I won't get recognized. I go to a little cafe I've been going to for years, which is tucked away on a side street, overlooked by the fancier parts of the market, almost hidden in its skirts. It is a kooky little place run by a wizened old Polish woman called Eva, who, no matter what time of the day or night, greets her regulars with a snifter of vodka. Even if you were in AA, she would be offended if you turned her offer down. Friends old and new have to take a shot of her vodka before ordering anything else.

Today is no different. As I whip off my sunglasses and beam a smile at her, she's already unscrewing the lid of the bottle.

'She is here, Alfred. Your girlfriend, she is here.'

I turn to see a smiley old man in the corner.

'Hi Alfred!' I call, and he smiles some more.

I hear a shot glass hit the counter and turn to see Eva indicating that I should drink it. I oblige, and feel a shoot of heat travelling rapidly down my chest. I return the empty glass to the counter and order a coffee.

'You go sit with Alfred. The coffee I will bring over.'

I am never sure if Alfred is his real name – he's a Polish man, and Alfred doesn't strike me as terribly Polish. I guess he's one of those earlier immigrants whose names sounded odd to parochial English ears and so they anglicized them. All I know is, Alfred is in his early nineties and came over to this country as a result of the Second World War. He worked as a miner in Nottinghamshire till the pit closed, and when his daughter moved to London he moved too, to be nearer her. But she then moved to Australia, and Alfred found himself marooned in West London with very few friends to his name. Which was when he discovered Eva's cafe, and he built himself a group of friends from her regulars.

The others joke that I am his girlfriend and that he has a twinkle in his eye for me, but really I look upon him as the granddad I never had. I have no contact whatsoever with my own family, and Alfred has taken their place. He is a man of few words, though he is as sharp as a tack. When I sit, we always play a kind of 'I Spy' game where he picks a letter and I have to guess the word he is contemplating today. It kills the first five minutes and he enjoys the fact that I pick the most ridiculous words. Eventually he will crack and say, 'No, you are incorrect. The word I am contemplating today that begins with C is contradiction.'

The other thing to know about Alfred is that he is blind. I don't know how long he has been blind – presumably he wasn't blind when he was down the pits – but he certainly is now, and one of the joys of this is that, although he is quite up to speed with modern culture, he does not recognize me as a vitriolic tabloid queen. He just knows me as the nice lady who comes into the cafe most days. And the freedom to leave the professional Jocelyn at the door is a truly welcome and wonderful thing.

He asks what I have been doing today and what my plans are for the rest of the day, and I enjoy the lies I weave as I create the persona of a wholesome girl who does her vegetable shopping at the market and then goes home and cooks it fresh, and has an early night listening to Radio 4.

I never stay long with Alfred. After fifteen minutes he always says, 'Go. I must be boring you. I am old man.' And I argue and say he could never bore me. But after twenty minutes I always leave, pay for his coffee, and slip away. When I stand outside the cafe I look back. And even though he can't see me, he is always giving me a little wave.

That bit gets me. It makes me quite emotional. A man, with no sight, trying to place me and send me on my way. Thinking he might be seen, even though he cannot see. I turn, trying not to let a single tear fall behind my newly reinstated shades, and walk off into the market. All I need is a white stick and I'd look more blind than Alfred.

When I am in London, I always try to see Alfred if I can. If I don't get to see him I can feel quite rudderless and distracted, even if I don't have deep, meaningful discussions with him. I guess he is an escape from all the crap.

And there's plenty of that when I get back to the flat.

'I got rid of Finty coz my new idea's quite . . . sensitive.'

He's been watching *Loose Women*. Sherrie Hewson is laughing so hard she looks like she might keel over. She is clutching the woman next to her and squealing. Ross switches it off and Sherrie vanishes from the corner of the room.

'We're going to reunite you with the son you gave up for adoption.'

I want to see Sherrie Hewson again. I want to see anything other than have to listen to him.

'I didn't give anyone up for adoption, Ross.'

Why? Why did I think it was a good idea to tell him? He who would sell his own mother if he thought it'd buy him a new towel rail for his en-suite.

'You know what I mean.'

'I had a baby, and my mum passed him off as her own. That's not the same.'

'Exactly – you had less of a say in it.'

'This isn't fair, Ross.'

'It's genius. You could probably get a book deal. Everyone will want to interview you. Look how big those *Long Lost Family* shows are. Everyone loves an abandoned child. And you were a child at the time. Folks are gonna go batshit crazy for it.'

'No, they're not.'

'They are.'

'It'll just be another excuse for people to hate me.'

'They won't hate you, they'll feel sorry for you!'

'Even worse!'

'And then of course there's the *pièce de résistance*.'

'Don't even go there.'

'The dad.'

'Ross, don't.'

'Everyone knows who Mark Reynolds is these days.'

'Yes, a gobby Scouser who thinks he knows about politics.'

'Left-wing rent-a-gob to mirror your right-wing one.'

'I don't want him involved.'

'We'll get acres of press.'

'I don't want him involved, Ross.'

'Imagine the articles about your cruel mother taking the baby from you. How you had to run away to London coz you couldn't face the pain. Then we get Mark's reaction when he finds out he's a father. The reunion of father and son. The reunion of mother and son. The possibilities are endless!'

'Ross, I think you're forgetting something.'

'*Ker-ching!*'

'What about bloody Billy?'

214

'Billy?'

'Exactly. You don't know anything.'

'Ah. Billy's your son.'

I falter. 'He . . . he doesn't know any of this.'

OK, so that's a lie, but Ross isn't to know that.

'Well, it's about time he found out.'

'Why?'

'Well . . .'

'Because you have a mortgage to pay?'

'Well . . .'

'That how it works, is it? When you turn someone's life upside down.'

'You don't think he deserves to know?'

'I don't want to be his mother. It's too late. This is doing it all arse about face. Why the fuck did I tell you?'

'Because deep down, I don't think you really mean that.'

'Mean what?'

'That you don't want to be his mother.'

'What?! You think I look like the maternal type?!'

'I think you've closed yourself off over the years, to the point where you're too scared to even think about being his mum.'

'This conversation finishes right here, right now.'

'You heard what I said, though. Acres of press, Jocelyn. Acres.'

'Well, maybe I don't want acres of press.'

'That's like saying none of us needs oxygen.'

'Well, maybe I don't want acres of press about *this*.'

'Think about it though, babe. Mark Reynolds. Yeah, you and me might think he's a bit of a tosser. But he's a left-wing pin-up. Girls fancy the pants off of him.'

'Girls? He's forty-five! More, probably!'

'You know what I mean. He's a cheeky chappy. He's seen as really cool. He goes on *Mock The Week*.'

'So?'

'So, this could be really good for you. As if she couldn't surprise us any more – we go and find out she shagged Mark Reynolds, and they had a bloody KID.'

'Yes. I get the picture. I just won't let it happen, so you better start coming up with some other clever ideas. Preferably ones that don't involve my family, or Tony Benn wannabes.'

'But it could make you millions.'

'The day you sell that story, Ross, we'll see a litter of pigs flying across Trellick Tower.'

'But . . .' He was sounding desperate now.

'No buts, Ross! It ain't gonna happen!'

And with that I flounced into the bedroom and threw myself on the bed, kicking the door shut.

To be honest I was amazed the floor was still supporting the bed. Thinking about the past, and Billy, and what happened back then on Alderson Road, he's right, Ross is right. I do try to wipe it out and usually I can do that but when he confronts me with it, like now, well. It's like someone has very quickly pulled the floor out from this flat and I fall, spinning out of control, to the ground at a speed of about a hundred miles an hour. Freefall, I go into freefall. And when you hurtle towards the ground that fast, you're going to get hurt. I imagine falling and as I hit the ground the pain is like an actual kick in the guts. I double over, on my side, in agony, gasping silent cries into the duvet.

I can't do this. I can't be under the same roof as Ross. He might come into the bedroom intent on continuing the conversation, and I don't want to think about it now. I don't want to think about it ever. But his words seem stuck to the walls in here and they bounce off and I hear them over and over again until I want to scream.

I scramble up off the bed. I run from the flat. I have to get out. I have to get away from Ross and the words on the walls.

I'm not completely stupid. I fear that tears may be imminent and though I don't take anything substantial with me, I do think to take my headscarf and sunglasses.

The lift doesn't descend as quickly as I'd like it to, and although it goes quite slowly I throw myself to one of its walls and hold on for dear life, as if I'm getting G-force, as if I am just dropping down a hole.

Once outside, I run.

I run and run with no thought to where I'm going or where I want to be; I just want to be away from Ross and the thoughts. But, like the route is blueprinted into my DNA, I find that within ten minutes or so I am getting my breath back just round the corner from the Polish cafe.

As I stand there gasping for air I see Alfred turning onto Portobello Road, arms linked with a portly woman with a red face, who is wittering on incessantly. I immediately feel for him – he seems to hate small talk. I imagine he has seen so much in his life, and so much in the war, that the banal chit-chat of this kindly woman is of little interest to him. He's probably seen people in concentration camps, people hanging from trees, and what is this woman bleating on about now? Her bunions? For the lack of anything better to do, I follow them. They walk slowly, but that's fine for me right now. I have nowhere else to go, nothing else to pass my time. Along the market the woman stops, and seems to be describing things to Alfred. Oh well, at least she's making the journey reasonably interesting for him.

For all I know, this could be a new girlfriend of his. Although he's only ever mentioned a deceased wife, that's not to say that he's kept this woman from me. I've kept plenty from him, why shouldn't he keep something from me? She has an intimacy with him I've never seen anyone have before, but then, my encounters with him have been limited to the corner table of the cafe. I can't say, hand on heart, I've ever even seen him stand before. But this could just be the intimacy of the carer.

They stop at a cashpoint. He gets a card from his wallet and she goes into mother mode, taking it from him and . . . well, I can't hear what she's saying as I pretend to admire the guava fruit on one of the street stalls . . . I can tell by her body language that she knows best, and he better leave it up to her. He looks resigned as she inserts the card into the machine and taps in the number she already knows. I see she is laughing. Nervously? Eventually a pile of cash comes out. She places some of it in his wallet, which she returns to him. As he is placing that carefully in his inside pocket, she is sticking the rest of the money into her handbag.

Does he know she is doing that?

I want to run up and intervene.

But maybe she is his carer, and if she is, maybe she needs paying.

I should not be so suspicious.

They walk off down the street and I can't help but feel that she now, suddenly, seems to be in a very good mood.

I don't know if I've just witnessed a crime.

Surely I haven't. Surely people aren't that cruel.

But then, my columns are cruel. I am the mistress of cruel.

No. No, I couldn't possibly have just witnessed something bad happening. Not to him, not to Alfred.

They eventually turn off down a side street, and I instinctively know where they're heading. All the houses round here are inordinately expensive. It costs about a million pounds to buy a garage, if you'll believe the *Daily Mail*, but peppered around the area, usually where the gorgeous white stuccoed houses were bombed in the war, you'll find little blocks of council housing. And I am convinced that's where Alfred and his fat lady are heading. So confident am I that I quicken my pace and walk past them. I become quite paranoid as I pass them, as I suddenly fear Alfred might have a finely tuned sense of smell due to his inability to see, and that he'll smell my Michael Kors perfume and cry out 'Jocelyn? Is that you?' and my cover will be blown. But then, even if that was to happen, does it really matter? There's no law about walking down the same street as someone you drink coffee with. Though admittedly there is something intrinsically weird about following someone around without their knowing.

Someone recently posted a video of me online. It was silent footage, taken on a phone. In it I leave the flats, walk to the shops, return home with a bag of shopping. All the time, the person filming it was about ten paces behind me. And I had no idea. It completely unnerved me. And I am reminded of it now. I'm doing a version of the same, and yet when it was done to me I felt violated. Me, who is happy to pawn off or sell anything about myself . . . come, look, make the most of me and react . . . unhappy that someone had documented a single, silent trip to the shops without my knowledge or consent.

But what if it was Darius D'Eath?

I try to push that thought from my head.

I stop at a corner, as I know they will not make it this far. I look back and see that yes, they're heading into the low-rise council block. I stand and watch. I don't know why I am doing this, but something about the mental exercise or the concentration is appealing; it distracts, it completely takes my mind off anything else I could be thinking about. A minute or so later I see Alfred and his friend walking along a walkway on the first floor – clearly they took a lift, as Alfred couldn't have walked up that quickly. The friend waits patiently while Alfred fiddles about in his pocket for a key, then slowly slips it into the lock on one of the front doors. I hear her cackle quite loudly, a vulgar, cracking laugh. And then he heads into his flat and she walks away, instantly making a call on her phone.

I instinctively feel she's ordering some drugs, to be paid for by the money she stole from Alfred.

Of course, I could be wrong.

Mind you, can drug addicts really be that fat?

Now that I'm not being distracted by Alfred – now that I can no longer see the money-grabbing porky piece – I am alone with my feelings, my memories, and I don't like it. I feel a rising panic. I see a phone box, and instinctively run to it and go inside. I haven't been in one for years; they seem so redundant. It smells, as they always did, of urine. Clearly they're still being used as public toilets, and with the rising cost of using a loo in London – fifty pence at Victoria Station, thank you – I can't say I'm surprised. A few panes of glass are missing, but I still feel protected from the world. I pull out my mobile and stare at it, trying to control my breath. As I do, I mentally file away the state of the phone box and the cost of public lavatories for a future column.

And then I do it. I jab in the number so familiar it's almost part of my DNA – but a number I have not called for years.

I hear the phone at the other end ring.

I think it's going to ring out.

And then she answers.

I hear her voice. Crystal-clear, as if she's huddled in the phone box with me.

'Hello? Wavertree Printing and Photoshop?'

Ah. So that's the business she has today.

I say nothing. I can't. I can't think what to say.

She waits. And then I hear her say, 'Jocelyn? Is that you?'

I can't even bring myself to say yes.

'Jocelyn?'

Why? Why can't I answer her?

'Jocelyn. If that is you. I am so, so sorry.'

I quickly hang up. Those are words I never expected her to say. I am dizzy with shock.

She's sorry.

I should have stayed on the line. I should have said.

Which bit are you sorry about, Mum?

My phone buzzes. Another message for Jamie-Lee.

A picture of a hangman's noose.

MAKE YOURSELF COMFORTABLE, BABES.

Paris, 1999

It was snowing as I stepped outside the airport and despite my humongous fun-fur coat, I was freezing. Mind you, I was wearing very little underneath. As well as shivering, I was starting to panic. This evening was not panning out as intended. I was meant to get off the plane, come out of departures and immediately see a sign that read 'Miss Smith' – then be whisked away to my secret destination. Well, my pretend secret destination. The client wanted to think I had no idea where I was going, but of course Tina had told me everything. Now I had to decide: did I make my own way to meet the client, or hang on and see if this bloody limo turned up?

I scoured the carriageways outside Arrivals to check there were no limos waiting or errant signs with 'Miss Smith' on them and, satisfied there weren't, headed back into the warmth for a cigarette. Once I'd located the cosy indoor smoking area I settled down, lit my cigarette, then took out my beautiful mobile phone and called the office.

'Hello, Black Orchid?'

'Tina, it's Jocelyn.'

'Ah. Miss Smith!' she said, then giggled, as it was of course a *nom de plume*. Very apt, seeing as how I was in Paris. 'Everything OK?'

'No. Bloody car hasn't turned up.'

'Oh. Shit. Maybe it's the traffic. OK, give me five minutes. I'll call you back.' And without saying goodbye, she hung up.

I was just sitting there minding my own business when I saw a woman walking towards me. I assumed she was heading to use the cordoned-off smoking zone, so I looked the other way and took a nonchalant drag on my cigarette. But then I heard her calling, 'Jocelyn? Is that you? Jocelyn!'

The voice was familiar. I swung round to look, but couldn't for the life of me place who this demented creature was. She was practically jumping up and down with excitement that she recognized me.

Oh God. A crazed fan. Someone who had bought my record. Just what I needed when I was about to start work.

'Don't you recognize me?' she said, suddenly deflated.

I shook my head and responded icily, 'So sorry. I meet a lot of people.'

To which she threw her head back, and shrieked with laughter. I really willed my phone to ring and for Tina to save the day and get me out of here, but then the woman said,

'It's coz of my nose job. Jocelyn, it's me. It's Kathleen!'

Well, right here, right now, you could have knocked me over with a feather. She looked incredible. She looked so different.

I jumped up and hugged her, mortified and delighted.

'Oh my God, Kathleen, you look amazing! God, I didn't recognize you!'

'Shit, was I that ugly before? We can't all be dusky Page Three stunners like you, you know!' And she threw her head back and roared. Again.

Dusky? I could have hit her.

'Anyway, what are you doing in gay Paree?' She laughed again, as if she was the first person in the world to come up with that pronunciation.

'Oh . . .' I blustered, 'I'm here for a job interview.'

'Blimey! For what?'

'Oh, to . . . present a TV programme on some kind of Eurotrash channel.'

'Are they looking for someone who dresses like a high-class hooker?' This time she poked me and looked me up and down. Then did her hilarious high-pitched shriek thing again.

And this time I joined in, as if I found it incredibly funny. But actually all I kept thinking was, *Shit. Do I really look the part?*

My phone was ringing.

'What are you up to now?' she was asking.

'One sec, I've just got to get this.'

'Oh my God, you've got a mobile phone! That is so funksy spunksy!'

Funsky spunksy? I'm SORRY?

It was at this point that I realized Kathleen was a little bit tipsy. Actually, she might have been more than a little tipsy. I backed away from her to answer the call.

'Babe, hi, it's Tina. Car's outside. Sorry for the confusion, silly prick had gone to the wrong terminal. All sorted now. Phone if there are any more problems. Good luck.'

'Thank you.'

I hung up and saw that Kathleen was laughing at some unheard joke.

'Kathleen, I have to go now. Are you OK?'

'Am I what?'

'Being here on your own. Are you OK?'

'Need to get back to my thingy.'

'Your what?'

'Hotel. I just came here to see my pal off.'

'You're on holiday?'

'No, I fucking live here. Duh! Course I'm on holiday. I brought my new nose on holiday. We're having a great time!' And again, shrieks of laughter.

'And will you be all right getting back?'

'To where?'

'To your hotel.'

'Are you coming to my hotel? Fuck, are you staying in the same place?'

'No. I have to go somewhere else, and I need to go immediately. I'm just wondering if I can drop you somewhere.'

'Oh, wonderful, are you driving?'

'No, I've got a car. Well, a driver. D'you know where it is you're staying?'

'Jocelyn, I'm not completely fucking stupid. Come on.'

And she was marching out of the arrivals hall, out into the snow. I followed her out, worrying how I was going to square it with the driver. What if he reported back to Tina that two of us had got in the car? Maybe I could just explain I was giving a lift to a friend in need who was stranded at the airport. Well, it was sort of the truth, though it wouldn't look good.

By now a man was walking towards the entrance with a sign reading 'Mis Smith'. The misspelling reminded me he probably spoke no English, so I launched into my best French accent, explaining,

'Ah oui. Je suis Miss Smith et malheureusement je dois prendre mon amie a son hôtel, merci beaucoup.'

'My God, Jocelyn! You're really good! Bonjour!' She was actually waving at the driver. He looked Sudanese to me, skin as black as mine, though under the panoply of stars and falling snow it looked almost blue-black. And he was tall, athletically so, and he looked completely unimpressed.

I linked Kathleen's arm, as she was looking perilously close to swaying so much that she'd fall over, and I followed the disgruntled driver to an awaiting blacked-out limo.

Why? Why did I have to bump into her tonight, of all nights?

Once in the car, we set off, and it was at this point that Kathleen decided she couldn't remember the name of her hotel.

'You must remember it.'

'Beg pardon?'

'I said, you must remember it.'

'Remember what?'

'The name of your hotel.'

'Do you?'

'No, I don't, I'm asking you. D'you know what arrondissement it's in?'

'Le week-end.'

'Do you know where it's near?'

'Are we near?'

'Oh for God's sake, Kathleen!' I'd never seen her like this before.

And then she started pretending she did remember what it was called. But she kept making up French words, as if by sounding French, it would be an actual name of a Parisian hotel. She kept saying stuff like, 'Vrababababab haw hee haw heee haw vravra vra vra oui oui nonnnn'.

The driver was looking at me through the rear-view mirror now as if to say, in French, 'What the six-foot baguette do we do with this crazy chick now?'

And unfortunately, I had no answer to that.

'That's not a word,' I pointed out.

She leaned in to me. 'Do you like my nose?'

I couldn't help but roll my eyes. Normally I'd entertain such pleasantries, but tonight I really wasn't in the mood. I had a job to get to. I pawed at her coat and tried to pull some evidence from the pockets. A room key. A map of Paris with 'this is my hotel' written on it. Anything.

She seemed to find the rifling through her pockets routine highly amusing and, thankfully, didn't stop me, even when I – BINGO – managed to pull out her purse. I tore through it, looking for evidence of where she was staying. I found nothing. I sighed. This was ridiculous. What did I do now? Why had I been so kind? Why had I offered to take care of her, to get her home?

This would teach me to be altruistic. What lesson had life taught me thus far? Look after number one. Always look after yourself.

I checked my watch. It was nearly eight in the evening. I knew from my itinerary that my client was expecting me round about now. I was sure that Tina would have called him to explain the nature of my late arrival, but that was to do with my car being stuck in traffic, not because I'd picked up some new-nosed nightmare I used to know.

Damn, what was I going to do now?

I could hardly take her with me to the job. Even if she was half cut and would probably fall asleep in the corner. It just wasn't the done thing. Not when so much money was changing hands. Fingers crossed.

I had to take decisive action that would get rid of Kathleen, but also make sure she was all right.

I snapped. 'Kathleen. I need to know which hotel you're staying at because I can't take you to my job interview.'

She started scratching at her stomach. Oh God, that was

all I needed. She had scabies. Or worse, crabs. Keep her away from me! KEEP HER AWAY FROM ME!

'*Kathleen, I'm being serious!*'

But then I saw, as her coat opened, that she was wearing a bumbag round her waist. She unzipped it and pulled out a large triangle of green plastic. Hanging off it was a key.

'I told you,' she said, 'The haw hee haw hee haw hee croissant oui oui.'

I grabbed it off her and thrust it under the nose of the driver.

'Vous savez où est cet hôtel, monsieur?'

And he nodded. And I felt a stab of relief so strong I could have wept.

'GOD, YOU ONLY HAD TO SAY,' Kathleen said really sarcastically, like she was shouting out of the window. And then she threw herself on me, hugging me. 'God, I love you, Jocelyn!'

I shoved her off me and told the driver to put his foot down and go to her hotel first. But by now I knew I was so befuddled my French had deteriorated, and I had probably told him to put his shoes on and go quickly to the supermarket.

Oh well – he seemed to get the picture. And we didn't go to the supermarket, not that there would have been many open at this time in the evening. We went to her hotel. As soon as I saw the neon light flickering its name like a nightclub lighthouse I leaned across her to open her door and practically shoved her onto the pavement before the driver had applied the brakes. She fell onto her arse as I told the driver to take me to the assigned address. I didn't even say goodbye. I didn't even look back to check that she was OK. Blimey. I'd got her to her hotel. What more did she want?

At least I'd never have to see her again while I was in Paris.

I'd been in some very weird and wonderful situations since working for Black Orchid, and tonight was no exception. The client's name was Mal Kerrigan and, despite having an apartment in central Paris, a stone's throw from the Sacré-Coeur, he actually came from Basildon. All Tina had said ahead of my visit was he was an 'NCG' – a no-contact guy, my favourite type of clients as they were happy for you not to touch them – and that he was into role play, and I would have to pretend to ride around his apartment on a horse, shouting 'Clip clop!'

Despite the bizarreness of this request, Mr Kerrigan treated the start of the evening like a date. He showed me in to the apartment with a flourish of the hand, asking if I'd like the grand tour. I agreed willingly, always interested in posh places like this, and he took me on an endless guided tour of black-walled rooms, chrome tables, mirrored doors and floor-to-ceiling windows. At one point he took my coat from me, the fur slid down my skin and he looked impressed by the leather pencil skirt and matching leather bra I was wearing. Well, those and my fuck-off Dior heels. He practically licked his lips, possibly wishing he hadn't stipulated no contact. And then . . . back to the tour!

'Look at this!' he'd splutter, then press a button and a net curtain would cover the window, purring along slowly like a modesty blanket train.

'Oh! You must think me so rude. I haven't offered you a drink!' he said as we made our way into the stainless-steel kitchen. Standing on a butcher's block in the centre of the room were two ready-made Manhattans. Much as they were crying out to be drunk, I demurred.

'Actually, might I have a gin and tonic? Sorry.'

You never knew when a guy might try and drug you. Better

to be safe than sorry. Of course, Mal was insistent this was fine, and went about fixing me a drink before my eyes. No drugs in that, thank you. We clinked glasses.

'Here's to a very successful evening!' He smiled.

'Indeed!'

I was always a bit surprised when people who had a particular fetish seemed normal and down-to-earth and polite, and treated the evening like a first date. It was quite sweet, really. And he seemed sweet. He suggested we go and relax in the lounge. As we settled into his mile-long leather settee, staring out over a view of Paris, he kicked off his loafers. I thought I heard him trying not to sneeze, but when I looked to him, he was in fact crying.

Believe it or not, this was quite common. Some men were so relieved to finally be able to act out their deepest, darkest, weirdest fantasies with someone that the relief they felt made them emotional. They didn't feel alone, strange, weird; finally someone got them, and it was OK to be whoever they wanted to be. I let him sniffle on for a while and took a sip of my drink. But when it felt like the crying might never stop, I said softly, 'It's OK, Mal. It's all OK.'

To which he clenched his fists and his face and said, 'Thanks, Shirley-Rose. Thank you so much.'

Please don't ask why I had called myself Shirley-Rose. Tina was of course well aware of my real name and she said that some clients would recognize me from my days on Page Three or in the lower rungs of the pop charts, but she also claimed this work was smoke and mirrors. The fantasy was more important than the reality. If I said my name was Jocelyn, that was it. They were paying money to spend time with me, that was it. But the more confusing notion of, 'Could it be her? Wait, no, her name is Shirley-Rose, it can't be. And yet it looks like her. It really does, would apparently add to the excitement, even though I hadn't at the time quite understood that.

I did now. Oh boy, did I get it now.

I didn't like to use the word 'prostitute' for what I did. Maybe I was in denial, but on nights like this I certainly didn't feel like one. I didn't fit the image of the street-corner crack whore out to get her fix, or to give money to some violent pimp. I didn't fit the image of the matronly neighbour in a local brothel with no-nonsense carpets and a makeshift jacuzzi. I did, however, fit the image of the high-class hooker who travelled the world and earned a fortune doing very little. Particularly if, like tonight, it was an NCG.

I knew better than to ask Mal why he was crying. He was the boss, he could do whatever he wanted. He was paying five thousand pounds an hour for the privilege. He'd paid for my first-class flights over and back. He'd put me up in the George V hotel for the night, the best the city had to offer. What were a few tears compared to that?

Eventually he calmed down. 'I'm so sorry.'

'It's fine. Must be an emotional evening.'

He nodded. Then he started crying again. 'It's my girl-friend.'

The fact that he had a girlfriend came as no surprise. Often the NCGs were partnered. Even though they were spending a fortune for your company, it felt like if they didn't actually sleep with you, it wasn't infidelity. Fair play.

'Well, my ex-girlfriend.'

Oh, OK, so they'd split up. Still, my rationale still stood.

'I feel so bad I split up with her. I wanna put that right to-night.' And he looked at me, pleadingly.

'And is that where I come in?' I asked coquettishly, licking the rim of my glass and then taking a dainty sip. I leaned my head back and swallowed the G&T in the most pornographic way I could muster. I knew he'd appreciate it. He then talked me through what he wanted me to do. It was simple enough. He directed me to the other side of the room, and I readied myself to perform the little sketch he had in mind.

It was one of the most ridiculous things I had ever had to do in my life. But I could not laugh. I could not go, *Are you for real?* I could not refuse to do it.

Also, another part of me was fascinated to see how he reacted to the scenario.

Basically, Mal Kerrigan wanted me to dump him. I had to pretend to be his girlfriend and finish with him, so that he would no longer feel guilty about having finished with her.

I know. Go figure.

I stood at the other end of the room to him.

'Tell me when you're ready!' I called.

'Hang on!' he replied. And with that, he quickly slipped out of his chinos and folded them neatly on the back of the settee. He then did the same with his underpants, revealing an erect penis that jutted out angrily in front of him in a strange boomerang shape. He then laid back on the settee, the monstrous appendage swaying in the non-breeze like one of those golden cats you got in Chinese restaurants, with the waggly paws. OK, so it was his waggly paw.

He pointed to an empty space next to him and said, 'That's my phone.'

I nodded.

I saw him gather himself in, focus, get ready. He closed his eyes meditatively for a second or two.

When his eyes snapped back open again, he smiled over. 'I'm ready.'

I did a thumbs up gesture. And then got ready to roll.

I did exactly as he'd asked me to do.

I paced the room a bit, murmuring to myself. 'God, I really need to finish with Mal. God, he's such a wimp.'

I could tell that behind me he was masturbating. He was loving this. So I went off script a bit.

'What a loser. The sooner I finish with him, I'll no longer have to look at that boomerang of a tentpole ever again.'

I heard his rhythm getting faster. He liked my improvisation.

'Think I'll call him.'

I then mimed lifting up a phone. I pretended to dial a number, and then I made a ringing noise.

I heard him say, 'Oh, that's my phone ringing. Wonder who it could be?' And I watched as he mimed picking up a phone.

'Hello?'

'Hi, is that Mal?'

'Yeah. Bridget?'

'Sure. Look, Mal. We need to talk.'

'What about?'

'I can't do it over the phone. I'll come over.'

'How are you going to get here?'

'I'm going to ski.'

'OK. See you in a bit.'

'See you in a bit.'

We both mimed putting our respective phones down.

I then mimed pretending to ski across the floor, dragging my feet and waggling my arms a bit.

I could hear him wanking again. Whatever I was doing, I was hitting the spot.

I then stopped in front of the settee. Mimed dismounting

from my skis. And as I turned to him and said, 'Mal. I'm going to have to finish with you,' he came all over my leather skirt.

I stood there.

So much for no contact.

He closed his eyes, let out a massive sigh, and smiled. When he opened his eyes again he said, 'Thank you so much.'

'My pleasure.'

'Let me get you a cloth. Then I can call your driver.'

Ker-ching. And five grand in the bank to one Miss Jocelyn Jones.

I had changed my surname to Jones when I'd embarked on my glamour modelling career. I saw it as an astute move now, for one so young. I'd made it at the time so that I couldn't be linked back to my folk in Liverpool, nor they me. The last thing they'd ever have wanted for their go-getting high-flyer would be to be found doing semi-pornographic shots in a ra-ra skirt for glossy magazines.

The same driver who had done the round-the-world trip with myself and Kathleen earlier drove me to the George V. It had to be one of the most sumptuous hotels in the world. And something I could very easily get used to. Staying there was like staying on the set of a movie. A rom-com in which the heroine sips champagne on her balcony and the camera picks out the Eiffel Tower in the background. However, although there was some com in my current situation, there wasn't much rom as I stood on my balcony in my fur and sipped on a glass of bubbly. I was more *Pretty Woman* than *When Harry Met Sally*, but there was no Richard Gere to sweep me off my feet and tell me that working girls were OK and that he loved me, and why didn't he give me a makeover?

I retreated into my room and slipped out of my working

clothes and into the fluffy white robe that lay invitingly on the bed, along with some white slippers with the hotel crest monogrammed across the toes. I ran myself a bath, finished my drink in the bath, then put on something more modest and headed down to eat in the restaurant. As I crossed the vast circular lobby, all white and pale-gold marble, I caught the eye of a man in his late thirties who quite, quite took my breath away. He was with a woman, possibly his wife; but our eyes met, and he knew instantly that I was trouble.

There was something about being in Paris, doing the job I'd just done, knowing there was money heading into my bank account, staying in this expensive hotel, that just made me feel very, very naughty. And a little bit sexy. Which was strange, as sex was something I just wasn't interested in.

I suppose most people would assume that working girls are obsessed with sex and can't get enough of it. I, however, think it was my relative lack of interest in penetration that made me perfect for the gig. I wasn't bothered about my own gratification. Sometimes it was as interesting as pegging out washing. A repetitive task that I could do over and over, up and down, up and down, but who cared? I was being paid for it. Sometimes it was arousing, sometimes it was fun. But oftentimes it required the icy detachment I had perfected since my teens. I mean, the last thing Mal Kerrigan would have needed was for me to squeal at the end of our session, 'Now . . . now . . . now you bring me off! Please?' I'm sure there were women like that who worked for Tina. But not this pussycat, no sirree.

I was a cat – I could step back, appraise, watch, and seem completely disinterested – but it wasn't a mouse I was after. It was cold, hard cash.

I had once heard Tina describing me over the phone. 'One

of our very special bookings is the breathtaking Shirley-Rose. As black as the ace of spades, she walks like she has diamonds at the top of her thighs and when she talks . . . well . . . it's like hot honey dribbling down a gangplank.'

She sounded like a cross between Maya Angelou and Barry White.

'Do I really walk like that?' I remember asking her when she hung up.

'Fuck off do you. I read it in a book. Anyway, we're selling the fantasy. Shut up and be grateful I'll have you, you rotten old whore.'

Which had made both of us laugh. A lot. She was one of the few people on this planet that I would allow to be so rude to me.

I ordered oysters for dinner, followed by lobster and salad. I had two glasses of wine, and throughout the whole meal the sexy man from the lobby stared at me. Oh, occasionally he'd look at his wife, give her the time of day. But he'd positioned himself so that she had her back to me, and he was looking directly at me.

I liked it. It turned me on. I rarely felt that so I enjoyed it. Besides, it was going nowhere. He was with his wife. It wasn't like he was going to follow me to my room and then knock. Was it?

No, it wasn't. Once dinner was over I retired to my room, half expecting to see him join me in the lift, or hear footsteps following me down the lushly carpeted corridor. None of this happened. I sat on my bed, staring at the door.

Of course. He was a gentleman. He was married. Not all guys wanted the services of Black Orchid.

Like me, he never came that night.

*

Returning home, there was no need for me to don the fur-coat-and-no-knickers look. Even though I was sitting in the nose of the plane – the poshest place on board – I dressed down in some Muji sweatpants and hoody. My message to the world was, 'I do this all the time. I don't need to dress to impress.' And it was partly true.

I flicked through the in-flight magazine as we readied for take-off. I could hear a stewardess moving between my fellow first-class passengers offering them a shopping list of pampering massages, complimentary drinks – you name it, with this airline they did it. I was trying to decide which film to watch. A bit of *Shakespeare in Love*? *Life is Beautiful*? Or maybe even *Gods and Monsters*? They had the latest offerings. Well, it's what we paid for. Well, it's what Mr Kerrigan had paid Black Orchid for.

And what had he had in return? My good self, clip-clopping round his room making imaginary phone calls.

Good work, Jones!

As I turned the page to inspect the TV offerings, I could hear a man slipping into the seat on the opposite side of the aisle. I could tell instinctively that he was a man; I knew by now the smell of most men's aftershaves. And this man was wearing the very woody Rochas Man Rochas scent, which hadn't long been on the market. God, I loved that smell. A proper man's smell. I didn't look over. For all I knew he'd be a sixty-stone businessman in loafers, and why give him the gift of my interest? I just listened as the stewardess fawned over him.

'Can I give you a hand with your attaché case, sir?'

'Can I fetch you a complimentary glass of bubbles, sir?'

'Would you like me to ease down your slacks and nosh you off, sir?'

OK, so she might not have gone that far, but she may as well have done. After a while she was offering him the massage, the wine list, but he shushed her with a very abrupt,

'I'll just have two litres of Evian and some lightly steamed asparagus.'

I nearly spat out my tongue.

I suppose by now I should be used to this 'New Man' thing – despite smelling like woody, proper men, doing unmanly things – but still that working-class part of my DNA lingered. You could take the girl from Liverpool, but you couldn't take Liverpool from the girl, they said. And right now I had to try not to laugh. Men where I came from would have asked for beer and a kebab at the Last Supper. And here was a man who was asking for . . . run that by me again?! . . . two litres of Evian and some lightly steamed asparagus?!

I had to see him. I turned to see him.

Oh, shit. I saw him.

It was the sexy man from the lobby from the night before. He saw me looking as he settled back in his seat, and the smallest smile sharpened his lips.

My eyes flitted to the seat behind him. Where was his wife? Looked like he was travelling alone.

Instinctively I went to say, 'I love asparagus.' God knows why. But I couldn't even get that out, because the air stewardess was blocking our eyeline; my vision was completely blocked by an aubergine coloured suit-skirt. And then, instead of offering me a bewildering bevy of amazing in-flight treats, she was instead saying:

'Oh my God! Fancy seeing you here!'

I looked up.

Oh my God, indeed. The stewardess was none other than Kathleen.

'What a wonderful surprise!' she gasped, 'What have you been doing in Paris?!'

What? Sorry? She knew what I'd been doing in Paris. I'd told her last night.

'Job interview.'

'Wow. Amazing. What was it for? How did it go?'

The penny dropped. She had no recollection of last night.

Give her her due, she looked to be in amazingly robust health for someone who, thirteen hours previously, had been thirty-three sheets to the wind.

What should I say? Embarrass her?

Kathleen. I saw you last night. I spent about an hour travelling round Paris with you, trying to find your hotel.

Maybe she'd appreciate me telling her. Maybe she'd have woken with the horrors this morning wondering what she'd done the night before, and wondering how she'd found her way back to her hotel.

Or maybe she was just rewriting history.

Yes. I know you saw me pissed last night. But I'm at work now. The last thing I need is you mouthing off about how bladdered I was when I'm working in First Class.

Maybe that was it.

I suddenly realized she was literally humming with Anaïs Anaïs. Or Anus-Anus, as I called it. I couldn't stand the smell. There must have been Christmas stockings full of the stuff up and down the country last year, because every woman you met seemed to be wearing it. Including Kathleen.

As I mumbled some incoherent claptrap about the job not working out and how I didn't really want it, she leaned in to me.

'What d'you think of my new nose?'

'It's gorgeous!' I replied.

So she had no recollection of last night. Either that or she was a very good, and bizarre, liar. She grabbed my wrist.

'I'm gonna get you a bottle of champagne. Make this a flight to remember.'

'No, Kathleen. I don't drink on planes.'

She looked at me oddly, but it was true. Flying to me wasn't the once-a-year treat it was for most people. I'd done enough high flying to know that it just didn't suit me. The notion of rolling off the plane and heading home tipsy and dehydrated wasn't one I cared to recreate. With the sort of work I found myself doing I had to try and keep a clear head at all times, so I wouldn't be out of control and in danger. Like Kathleen had been last night.

Eventually Kathleen had to go as we prepared for take-off. I looked across at Mr Lobby. He appeared transfixed by a book that nestled in his lap. He'd put on some glasses to read and, for reasons of the 'I find you attractive' variety, I found this impossibly cute. He was quite a bit older than me. I was nearly thirty. He was forty plus, I'd have said. His hair was cut close at the sides where it had gone grey, and slightly less cropped on top, where it had more of a sandy brown colour. He had cheekbones Paul Newman would have been proud of, and his eyes were a startling green. His nose, on which those frameless reading specs were perched, was not that strong, and not that dissimilar to Kathleen's new one. But to me, every inch of him was perfect.

As if he could feel me looking, he glanced up, away from the book and at me. I held his gaze. He'd held mine enough the night before at dinner. And I immediately felt that familiar stirring, between my legs, but deep inside me. He smiled. I smiled. Then he returned to his book.

I knew what would come next.

Five minutes later, after we'd taken off and once the lights came on indicating we could move around the plane, he unclipped his seat belt, left his book on his seat, and walked to the back of First Class. I gave it a few minutes, then unclipped mine. I looked to his seat and saw that he was reading *Girl with a Pearl Earring*.

A classy bloke, then. I liked to think. Well, at least he wasn't reading something smutty like *The Girl with the Pearl Necklace*. That was a book of a whole other nature.

I found him sitting at the small circular bar that sat between First and Business. It was a free bar, so you could help yourself, and it was unmanned most of the time. He had a glass of champagne in front of him and the same next to him. I sat down.

'I heard you don't like drinking on planes,' he said. Well, in his case I was prepared to make an exception. 'So I got you a ginger beer. That way I can at least pretend you're having a good time.'

I took a sip. 'I'm sure there'll be no need to pretend. Where's your wife?'

'Wife?' He sounded taken aback. 'I'm not married.'

That old chestnut.

'So who was the woman you were with at the hotel last night? Your sister? You were giving her a lot of attention if she was.'

He let out a soft chuckle. 'Would you believe me if I said she was my mother?'

'Not at all. She was younger than you. Unless she has a particularly good surgeon.'

'Good. Because of course she wasn't. She was Karen Paterson.'

'Karen Paterson? Is that meant to mean something to me?'

'Not necessarily. She's a make-up artist of mine.'

OK. That threw me.

'You need to wear make-up?'

'No. At least, I hope not.'

I shook my head.

'I'm a hair and make-up artists' agent.'

'OK.'

'Karen is a world-famous make-up artist. Now lives in Paris.'

'Right.'

'Step up from when she was a data inputter from Hamilton.'

'Sorry?'

'When I first met her. That's what she did.'

'Sorry. You're her agent?'

He nodded. I knew he could tell from my tone that I had no idea what this involved; but it intrigued me that someone in that sort of job could earn sufficiently good money to need an agent. He told me all about his job, and I was enraptured. Mind you, he could have been a bin man and in that moment I'd have been enraptured by that too.

The more he told me about his clients, the more unsettled I became. I honestly thought that working for Black Orchid was one of the most lucrative jobs in the world. And yet his clients were demanding astronomical figures and were flown round the world to do the hair and make-up of front-cover, red-carpet celebrities. It was fascinating. And I was a little bit jealous. Jealous that they earned their money from a talent they'd spent years perfecting. And, OK, jealous that they got to spend time with this heavenly man beside me.

Kathleen passed with a large bottle of Evian water.

'Ah. Sir. I was just bringing this to your seat.'

She glanced at me with a look of, what was that? Jealousy? Did she have her eye on Mr Lobby too?

'I've changed my mind on the water front.'

'I love that film!' Kathleen chirruped. '*On the Waterfront*.'

Oh, do shut up, Kathleen, I thought.

Turning to look at me, he continued, 'I think I've got everything I need right here.'

That cast a warm glow, I had to say. Kathleen bristled. 'I see you've changed your mind about drinking,' she said to me through pursed lips, and then did a little giggle as if she'd meant it as a cheeky joke.

'It's ginger beer,' he said. 'Now if you don't mind, we were in the middle of something.'

'Of course. So sorry. So is that a no to the lightly steamed asparagus, too?'

'No, you can still bring that. And some hollandaise. We can share.'

Kathleen looked befuddled. She was definitely jealous.

'Hollandaise is a sauce,' I said, pretending I'd misread her fury for confusion.

'Yes, I know.' She was sounding crotchety now. Another stewardess passed, and heard her tone of voice.

'Kathleen, could I have a word, please?' this older woman said. I saw Kathleen push her tongue against the underneath of her bottom lip.

'Yes, Candice,' she said, and then followed her colleague, who looked like her superior, behind a curtain and out of view.

It was time for our second drink. This time I asked for champagne.

His name was Leon McKenzie. Which made me laugh. He wondered why, so I explained that my surname had been

McKenzie too, till I'd changed it. And of course he wanted to know why I'd changed my name.

And I told him.

I kind of told him everything.

I told him how I'd changed my name by deed poll as I'd wanted to make a break from my past. How I felt that that way, I wouldn't be bringing shame on my family. Or, if I was honest, be linked to them.

I told him about my son. I didn't go into any detail about his conception; I was still too ashamed. And I told him about the glamour modelling. And the singing. And Mr Love. And Black Orchid. I even told him how I'd met Kathleen the night before and she hadn't remembered. I told him about Adam, and all the dreams I'd had as a kid. And how although I was earning more money than I'd ever dreamed of, my life felt hollow. For the first time in a long time I was honest with someone and it felt incredible, literally as if a weight had been lifted from my shoulders. I just felt safe with him. There was no need to pretend. I told him it all, one seemingly unending monologue. And when I eventually did finish – by which time a few more people had joined us at the bar, though none of them were particularly listening in, mouth and martini deep in their own conversations – Leon took my hand. He took my hand and he said softly, 'I'm honoured you've told me.'

Just then the curtain behind us swished, and Kathleen was upon us with a lightly steaming plate of asparagus.

'For the lovebirds,' she said with a wink. I couldn't tell whether her tone was loaded or encouraging.

Four champagnes in, and the plane started to shudder.

Kathleen was back again then – any excuse to butt in.

'OK, guys, we're running into some turbulence now, so if I could ask you all to return to your seats?'

Slowly everyone got up.

'Just got to go to the loo,' I whispered to Leon, and he nodded. Though as I turned to nip to the loo, I didn't see him turn the other way to return to his seat.

I went into the cubicle. This being first class, it was replete with posh products and a fresh rose in a vase that was attached to the wall. I didn't take long to wee, but by the time I'd finished and was washing my hands, there was a light flashing above the sink saying RETURN TO YOUR SEAT. I unlocked the door and the plane juddered. The door swung open and Leon fell into the cubicle, pushing me back against the sink. I let out a shriek and then, before I knew what was happening, his tongue was in my mouth. And mine in his, and then I was aware of him kicking the door shut behind him. We were locked in. Me, Leon, and so much turbulence it felt like we were standing up on a roller coaster. His hands were all over me, and mine him, but we also couldn't stop laughing, as it was near-impossible to stand properly without falling.

But almost as soon as he'd fallen into the cubicle and on top of me, there was an urgent banging on the door.

'Back to your seats, please! I know what you're up to! Out of there at once!'

Giggling like schoolkids we jaggedly fumbled at the door. Then we realized that whoever was out there was opening it from the outside.

The door opened, crushing into us. Outside I could see Kathleen's supervisor, and another woman with a camera. She quickly took our photograph, then returned to her seat.

'Who the fuck was that?'

'Seats! Now!' the supervisor was shouting.

As we juddered towards our seats I caught a glimpse of

Kathleen, with a smirk on her face, peering out from behind a curtain at the other side of the bar.

Once the turbulence subsided, Leon called Kathleen to his seat.

'I want to know who the woman was who took our picture.'

'I didn't see anyone take your picture, sir, sorry.'

'When we were in the toilet.'

'Sorry?'

'We were in the toilet together.'

'That's not really allowed, sir.'

'I know. But we were. And someone took our picture, then ran back into Business. Can you find out who she was, please?'

'What did she look like, sir?'

'Well, she had a bloody camera in front of her face, how should I know?'

Suddenly the supervisor was upon them. 'We don't accept foul language to members of cabin crew, sir.'

'He only said bloody. And he's upset,' I jumped in.

'Candice, it's fine. Like Jocelyn said. He's upset. Someone took his picture. And I'm going to find out who it was.'

The supervisor rolled her eyes, and retreated. I could now see that Leon thought the sun shone out of Kathleen's backside.

'What colour hair did she have?'

'Sort of . . . ash blonde.'

'That's very specific.'

'He's a hair and make-up agent,' I butted in. Kathleen frowned.

'What does that mean?'

'Tell you what,' Leon said. 'You find the bird who was taking our picture. And then I'll tell you.'

Kathleen nodded, and headed to Business.

Ten minutes later she came back, looking upset.

'Couldn't find anyone. And I've been asking around. You know, did anyone see someone with a camera out during the turbulence. Out of their seat. I really felt like Jessica Fletcher, actually.'

'She usually solved the crime.' Leon sounded hurt.

Kathleen gave us a patronizing smile. She put one hand out to the armrest for my chair, one onto his, and knelt in the aisle.

'What say I get you a complimentary glass of champagne?'

'We're in First Class. Everything's complimentary.' Leon now sounded annoyed.

Kathleen shrugged. 'I know, it's just they tell us to say that.' She made to head for the bar. But before she went, she leaned into me and giggled.

'You never change, do you? What are you like?!'

And then she went to fetch us our drinks.

After the plane landed at Heathrow and they started letting passengers off, the supervisor came and asked myself and Leon to remain in our seats. I saw Kathleen hovering behind her.

'I'm so sorry,' she stage-whispered.

And then we saw four policemen coming into the cabin. And I knew what was going to happen.

The headlines in the papers the next day said EX POP STAR IN MILE HIGH CLUB ROW. It claimed we'd been arrested for indecent behaviour, after being caught by 'horrified passengers, having intercourse in the first-class cabin'.

Actually, we'd received a caution after sweet-talking the policeman back on terra firma.

I assumed I'd never see Leon again. He must have been so

embarrassed. I could imagine the mick-taking he would be getting at work.

So I was very surprised when, that night, I got a text message from him. I wondered what the sound on the phone was at first – hardly anybody ever texted me. It usually meant they had a fine-fangled phone. I was impressed.

I have a rather roomy bathroom. And no bitch outside ready to knock. Fancy a rematch?

Turned out nice again.

It was the eve of the new millennium.

Would the Millennium Bug actually happen? Would planes fall out of the sky? Would every computer in the world crash? Was it the end of the universe as we knew it?

As I walked the Soho streets, the excitement was tangible. Most people seemed to be heading towards the river to watch the fireworks later that night. I was sober as a QC, but everyone around me seemed to be bang on it, in the middle of the biggest hen or stag do EVER.

But I had reason to be sober. I wanted to savour every moment of tonight.

I would have thought the 'toilet incident' would spell misery and doom for me, despite it kick-starting my relationship with Himself. But bizarrely, it seemed to have been the making of me. Well, maybe not the making of me, but the making of my career. On the back of it I was offered a monthly column in *BAPS* magazine, the non-thinking man's *Loaded*. Each month there'd be the latest soap star sticking her finger in her mouth, wearing little but a smile on the cover, and inside I would offer sex advice to whoever had written in. I got quite the name for myself, with my frank and bitchy advice. It took five minutes to write, and put me back in the public eye.

Two months into the job, I'd had a letter forwarded to me from the magazine. I got quite a bit of fan mail now so I opened it as I did the others, bored, slightly interested, but assuming it was going to be asking for a picture with my tits out, or demanding I do a topless shoot for the magazine. LET'S MAKE THIS HAPPEN!

But when I saw the name at the top of address, my heart sank to my boots.

It had happened.

Billy McKenzie
45B Josephine Avenue
SW2

Dear Jocelyn,

I've wanted to contact you for a long time now but didn't know how to go about it.

Ah well. Now you're giving your sex advice to strangers, I can find you.

His written English was impressive. Even if the content was predictably accusatory.

I've known for ages you are my mum. And yet you don't want to know me. Why is that? I know Mum (your mum. I should call her Nan but that's the name I was brought up knowing her by) wanted to cover it up. But I'm not daft and tongues wag and of course she told me the truth when I asked. Call her what you like, she didn't lie in the end.

I don't know what you went through when you had me. I'm sure it was pretty tough, and times were a bit different back then. But I would love to meet up with you and talk to you about it. If you're game?

Game. I wasn't just game. I'd been on the game. Oh shit.

> I've always felt a bit lost. And would love to at least make sense of how I came to be in this world. Maybe that would help me.
> Hope you can get back to me.
> > Your son
> > > Billy

No kisses.

My God, he was living in Brixton. That was SW2. There was a phone number scribbled at the bottom of the page. I dialled it instantly.

Which is how I came to be making my way to a restaurant in Covent Garden to meet the son I'd not seen for ten years.

Why was he living in London at such a young age? Who was he living with? How would I feel seeing him? What would I say? What would he think of me?

What must he think of me?

His mother. The girl who gave him up, and what had she done with her life?

He didn't know anything about Black Orchid; no-one but Leon did.

But what was the evidence for how I'd behaved since relinquishing him?

I'd done glamour modelling. I'd sung a shit song in the charts. I'd been caught having sex on a plane, and as a result I now gave relationship advice in a soft-porn magazine.

Well done, Jocelyn. You've really excelled yourself. You thought it didn't matter what you did with your life. You thought you could hurt no-one but yourself.

How wrong you were.

Kettner's was a down-at-heel pizza restaurant in the heart of Soho. The fact that he'd asked to meet me there was at once intriguing and thrilling. The fact that a thirteen-year-old knew it existed and found it quite trendy was appealing, and made me stupidly proud as I wandered through the bustling streets to find it. And him. I'd been to the restaurant before. I knew where it was. And as I wound through the streets it was as if the sky was lit up by it, a Soho lighthouse, flashing away for everyone to see.

Come to me. Come to me.

This was the moment. This was the moment I'd been waiting for, for the past ten years. I was finally going to meet my son. But what did I feel more than anything as I walked to see him? What I had always felt. Shame.

It was a horrible feeling, and one I'd always tried to run from by pretending to myself that it hadn't happened, that it hadn't been my fault, that I'd been young, naive. But since the arrival of the letter, denial had been an awkward island to get to. The sea was choppy, and the boat was leaking. And my shame threatened to drown me.

I remembered so little about him now, so adept had I been at washing away the memories, the pain. But I remembered certain things. I remembered the pain of the fourteen-hour labour, the bloodied, shitty sheets on that cast-iron bed in Llandrindod Wells. Mother mopping my brow like she was a farmer and I was an insolent sow, so few niceties were needed. Nothing to see here, just a kid giving birth in a strange bed, not knowing if the rusting smell was from the bedstead or the blood between my legs. The primal screams, the tears, her reprimanding me for swearing. The disgusted tutting when I told her to fuck off. The kindly midwife telling her to leave the room, but she didn't. The final push, and he was out. And

I suddenly felt more empty than I'd ever felt before, or since. Holding him. Smelling him. He was a grey-purple colour. The unmistakable nose. He was my son, all right. And then Mother taking him, almost like a yank, ripping a turnip from the soil and wrapping him in white cotton. The blood from him seeped through, and then she finally deigned to leave the room. And after that, he was hers and not mine.

And the longer I spent in her company, their company, the more unhappy I became and the more I hated that bitch for what she had done. And the hatred festered in me till it threatened to consume me, to poison me, which is why I had to get out, run away, run anywhere where I didn't have to look at my son and look at my mother and look at them together, pretending everything was all right. It was far from all right.

And now, tonight was hopefully going to make it all all right. Wasn't it? God, I hoped so, with every fibre of my being.

Leon had originally wanted to come with me.

Leon. My saviour. My guiding light. Just as I had once run from Billy, so when I met Leon, I had run straight to him. He was home.

As soon as we'd got together I had kissed Black Orchid goodbye. I now made my living as Jocelyn Jones, agony aunt and columnist. Of course, the dosh was nowhere near as good as escort work, but it was enough. And anyway, my boyfriend was loaded.

I know – what a shame I was to the female race. But then, this was nothing new to me. And of course, feminists ahoy, swings and roundabouts, I might have been reliant on a man but at least I wasn't selling my body to strangers. Or anyone. Any more.

When I told Leon I didn't want him to come with me, he

was all for hanging around outside the restaurant to check I was OK after our meet. But I knew I had to do this on my own tonight.

'What am I meant to do? It's the fucking millennium. Why did he want to meet tonight of all nights? He's like you. A drama queen.'

I had no idea what he meant. Drama queen? Moi?

'He's thirteen, Leon.'

'My argument still stands.'

'What are you going to do?' I'd asked.

He'd seemed really put out that I'd not wanted to spend the new millennium eve with him. But, clearly, when my long-lost son said *jump* . . . I said, *how high?*

We'd only spoken briefly on the phone. Billy wanted to 'keep it all for the meet'.

He'd sounded softly spoken. He'd sounded well spoken. Little trace of any Liverpool accent and, call me a snob, I was proud. He sounded kind, and caring. And so mature. Thirteen, and he'd booked the table at the restaurant himself!

'What are you doing in London?' I'd asked.

'I've lived here for most of this year,' he said. And the more he spoke, the more I detected a soft London accent.

'With who?'

'Aunty Gina.'

I felt crushed. I didn't even know who Gina was.

I would ask. I would ask tonight, as part of my 'million questions for your son the first time you meet him as an adolescent'.

What would he look like now? The last I'd seen him was the night I'd left Liverpool to head to London that one final time. I'd packed a bag. Everyone else was in bed. I'd peered into the box room where he lay in his cot. I'd leaned over him. Kissed my hand, placed it gently on his forehead. Then quietly crept out of the room.

As I arrived at the restaurant, I started to panic. This was like going on the worst date in the world. The one you'd looked forward to for forever, but then the moment it was upon you, the stage fright arrived and you really couldn't face it at all. The thing you'd most wanted in the whole wide world suddenly became the thing you most feared.

I stood outside the doorway, and then found myself stepping back.

I now found I couldn't go through with it.

OK. I would walk around the block.

I quickened my pace, and hot-footed it as fast as I could away from the restaurant. Relief flooded me, and I realized I'd become a lot more anxious than I'd admitted to myself. But I also found that the further I moved away from the main door, the more fretful I became. I didn't want to go in, but I didn't *not* want to go in more. I stopped. I turned round. I went in.

As I stepped into the warmth I saw my mother, back in Alderson Road, standing in front of the electric fire.

'You are having this baby, Jocelyn, whether you like it or not. Abortion is murder, and I will not sanction it. You will have the baby and I will say he is mine.'

'You can't take my baby from me! You dried-up old prune!' And then she'd hit me.

Back in the room, Jocelyn, back in the room. This is a restaurant. You're not back in Liverpool now.

In my head, it'd be like something in a movie. A speakeasy. I'd make my way through the cool sounds of jazz. People would part and then I'd see him in a corner, sat nonchalantly nursing a Coke, staring into the middle distance. I'd cough, he'd look over . . . it would be like I'd never been away, never left his side.

It was, of course, nothing like that.

'Hi, I'm meeting Billy McKenzie for dinner,' I said to the maitre d' in the small entrance hall. He checked through his list of bookings and made a mark with a pen.

'Yes, if you'd like to follow me, the rest of the party's already here.'

Rest of the party? Bit of a grand way of saying that Billy had arrived before me. As we wound our way through the raucous restaurant I clocked Billy sitting in a corner. He was so tall, so grown-up. He looked more like twenty than thirteen. And then I saw that he wasn't alone.

He was sitting with a man.

A white man, about my age.

He was sitting with Mark Reynolds.

The sight of the two of them together, chatting, stopped me dead in my tracks.

Billy looked round as the maitre d' pulled out a chair for me to sit on.

On autopilot, I slid into it. It was like the world was suddenly running in slow motion. I saw Mark register shock that I was here. Confusion. Then he looked to Billy.

The world jolted back into normal time.

'Hi, Mum,' said Billy, a provocative smile on his face. Almost a smirk.

'What's going on, Billy?' Mark looked back to me. 'Hi, Jocelyn. Long time no see.'

I nodded. I was speechless. After looking forward for so long to seeing my boy for the first time, I now felt only fear. What was he doing? What was he playing at? Why had he got us both here?

He was so beautiful, though. Just look at him! The tone of his skin. Still has my nose, poor bugger.

'Billy's your son?' Mark was sounding so shocked.

I nodded again.

'What the fuck's this all about?'

Oh, nice. He was swearing in front of my son. He was swearing *at* my son.

'I just thought it'd be a nice family outing,' Billy said.

'How do you two know each other?' My voice sounded faint. Like I'd spent a lifetime shouting.

'I don't believe this. Billy?' Mark was sounding angry now.

'How do you two know each other?' I was sounding more assertive now. Finally finding my voice.

'I'm sorry,' Billy was saying to Mark. 'It was the only way I could get to meet you. And easier than saying, "I think you're my dad."'

'Your what?!'

'I know you are.'

'Can one of you answer me, please? How do you two know each other?'

'He wrote to me. Said he wanted to get into politics.' Mark was looking white as a sheet now. 'I've become a sort of mentor to him. Working-class, mixed-race lad from Brixton? We need more of them in politics.'

'Why are you spending time with him on New Year's Eve, though? That's weird. He's a thirteen-year-old boy. He's only just turned thirteen.'

'Thirteen?' Mark said to Billy, paling.

Billy shrugged. 'So I lied to get on the course, so what?'

'He said his mum was coming. Quick pizza, that was it. He told me his mum hadn't been well.'

'I know you're my dad,' Billy said again, quietly.

'He said she had cancer. I just felt so bad for him,' Mark continued. 'He's been on my Introduction to British Politics course at the City Lit.'

'Who told you that?' I asked Billy, 'Who told you Mark was your dad?'

'Kathleen.'

What. The. Fuck?

'How come you've been talking to Kathleen?'

'Last time I went back to Liverpool, we went to the funeral of an old lady. Kathleen was her granddaughter. And I met her.'

Silence fell around the table. Billy broke it. 'She'd had a few drinks and . . .'

'Mark's not your dad.'

'She said you'd be like this.'

'Why did you lie to me, Billy?' Mark was sounding angry. As well he might.

'I just wanted to hang out with you.'

'So why didn't you just tell me the truth?'

'I am interested in politics.'

'Mark's not your dad,' I said again. I was making a habit of that tonight, repeating myself.

'Why would you think I was your dad?'

'Kathleen told me. You don't have to lie to me.'

'We're not lying.'

Mark was looking genuinely perplexed. 'Why would Kathleen think I was his dad? When did you have him? I didn't even know you had a kid.'

'Will you two stop pretending?'

'Mark's not your dad. I've never slept with Mark.' And this, of course, was the truth.

I could see tears were pricking Billy's eyes.

'Mate, if I had a kid, I'd defo step up to the plate,' Mark was saying, and Billy appeared to believe him.

'Who's my dad, then?'

But of course I couldn't tell him.

'Just . . . someone I met at a party.'

He looked back to Mark. The hurt in both their faces, that something wasn't right. I could see Mark was hurt that he'd been lied to – oh principled one as he was! And I could see the devastation, that Billy really wanted this man to be his father. But he wasn't.

Mark stood up. 'I'm gonna go. I don't need this. Not on the fucking millennium. It's messing with me head. See you.'

And off he went. Which left me and Billy on our own. Much better.

I picked up my menu and tried to gee him up, by picking out interesting-sounding ingredients.

'Come on. Choose what you want. This is on me.'

But he didn't pick his menu up.

'So my dad was just someone you met at a party?'

I nodded.

'So you don't even know who he is?'

I thought about it. What to tell him? Then I shook my head.

'How old were you again?'

'Billy.'

'Fourteen?'

'Well . . .'

'Almost the same as me now.'

Billy stood up.

'Where you going?'

'You think I wanna spend time with you?'

God, he was cocky for thirteen. He put me in mind of that Neneh Cherry song 'Manchild'. He had the outer trappings of a proper bloke. But his emotional state showed he was just a child.

He leaned down and whispered in my ear.

'Slut.'

And then walked out of the restaurant. Walking like a boy who owned the world. Old beyond his years. I could feel myself starting to cry, and stopped myself by biting my lip.

The maitre d' swished up.

'Everything all right, madam? Your table looks a tad depleted.'

I nodded. 'I'm so sorry. We shan't be needing it any more.'

I handed him my menu, and stood up to leave. I could see he was giving me daggers. They'd probably turned away so much custom tonight and here we were, walking out without so much as ordering a glass of tap. I pushed past him and headed for the exit.

I tried to call Leon a few times, but his phone kept ringing out, then going to voicemail. No doubt he was in some bar somewhere, celebrating the new millennium with some hair-styling pals. He'd done a lot of foreign travel lately and I couldn't keep up with the names of all the people from the Paris office or the Milan office, and it was some of those guys he was meant to be seeing tonight.

I checked my watch. It was only a quarter to eight. I would head home, run a bath and pour myself a glass of wine.

As I walked, I just felt empty. The crushing disappointment that the evening hadn't panned out as I'd hoped was almost too much.

What the fuck had Kathleen been mouthing off at Billy for?

I wanted to slap her. I felt my hand clenching itself into a ball.

I wanted to hurt her.

I tried to bury my anger, but it wasn't working.

In a doorway on Soho Square, a homeless woman sitting on some cardboard in raggedy clothes asked if I had any spare change. I didn't. She then asked if I had a spare cigarette. I didn't smoke. But suddenly that sounded like the best idea in the world.

'Hang on,' I said, and I hurried to the nearby late-night newsagent's and bought twenty Silk Cut. I returned to the woman. I took one out and she lit it for me, then I handed her the pack. Without asking to be invited or seeking permission I sat next to her in the doorway and tried to quell the anger I felt at Kathleen. The homeless woman said nothing, just sat there smoking and looking up at the sky. Eventually I finished my cigarette. It wasn't my first ever one, and it probably wouldn't be my last, but it seemed to have calmed me. I stood. And the homeless woman said,

'You're a very kind person.'

I smiled. Shook my head. 'I'm not, I'm a cunt,' I replied.

She smiled. 'We're all cunts, darlin.'

I nodded, and headed to find a taxi.

Home these days was Leon's place on Elgin Avenue in Maida Vale. One of those pretty white stucco houses with the pillars. A glossy red front door. And a brass knocker in the shape of a lion's head. The lights were on as I stepped out of my taxi. Maybe he'd not gone out yet. I slid my key in the door, and gently pushed it open.

A handbag sat on the hall floor.

A handbag that wasn't mine.

It was a bright red handbag, and it looked amazing contrasted with the black and white floor tiles it sat on.

In the kitchen I heard gentle giggling. And then a woman gasp like something was hurting.

Slowly, and as quietly as I could, I walked towards the kitchen door. It was open, and I could see Leon. He had bent a woman over the kitchen table, and he was fucking her.

It was as if all breath evaporated from my body. My legs went to jelly.

He was really going for it. He was about to come.

'You dirty bitch!' he said, and slapped her arse.

Yep. Any second now.

'WHAT THE FUCK D'YOU THINK YOU'RE DOING?!' I suddenly roared.

His eyes widened in shock as he stumbled backwards, his pathetic erection slipping out of his slut and waggling about angrily.

And the woman screamed, and stood up.

And when I saw who it was, I ran forward and slapped her. Hard.

'Jocelyn!'

'Get out of my house, Kathleen!'

Her face was red with lust, shame and from that pretty good slap. She stood there, frozen.

'I won't say it again, Kathleen!'

She sort of squealed, and ran from the house. I turned and looked at Leon. He was like a stupid, quivering wreck. A stupid, quivering wreck with his cock out.

'Put that away.'

He quickly tucked it back into his jeans.

I went to the fridge to get a bottle of wine. 'Happy fucking millennium,' I said flatly.

Kathleen. She really did get everywhere.

'Babe. I can explain.'

'Cliché!' I said, holding my hand up in a Jerry-Springer-guest sort of way.

'She's been hounding me for ages. Whenever I see her on the flights she's all over me like a rash.'

'Don't tell me,' I said, pouring the wine. 'She practically raped you.'

I saw his eyes light up at that suggestion. 'Yeah. Yeah, it was a bit like that, actually.'

'You can't rape the willing, love.' I took a glug of wine, but it just tasted bitter. Maybe I had too much bile in me right now. I looked at the glass. And then, with a sudden sharp movement, I chucked it in Leon's face.

How very *EastEnders* of me.

I put the glass on the table. The table on which he had, mere moments ago, been fucking my childhood friend.

The childhood friend who had fucked him, and fucked everything up with my son.

Thank you, Kathleen.

I took a deep breath.

And then I went upstairs to run my bath. As the water ran my mobile rang. I half expected it to be Billy, calling to apologize, calling to explain, calling to . . . what? Why should he? I checked the caller ID. I immediately picked up.

'Hi, Adam.'

'Jocelyn! Just ringing to wish you a happy new millennium! Just before the madness starts.'

The madness. It had already started here.

'Thank you, honey. You too.'

And I didn't know what it was that triggered it – maybe it was the familiarity of a voice I'd known for so long, its reassuring tones – I mean Christ, I hardly ever saw the guy. I couldn't remember the last time I'd seen him. But I couldn't pretend with him, suddenly, and I burst out crying.

'Jocelyn! Jocelyn, what's the matter, babe?'

'Oh, nothing. I'll be all right.'

'No, Joss. Come on, tell me.'

'I'm fine.'

'Tell me.' His voice was more insistent.

'I just found Leon and Kathleen. Together.'

Silence. Then . . .

'Jocelyn, where are you? I'm coming over.'

BILLY

London, 2015

The room is light. Well appointed, as an estate agent might say. Though I don't really know. To my knowledge, I've never met an estate agent in my life. Or maybe it's like paedophiles. We've probably all met many, it's just that in social situations they don't let on.

She is wearing a browny-green trouser-suit thing and has a dusting of dyed-pink hair. She looks like an elongated olive, bashed by a brick. I imagine her rolling out of bed in the morning, plump and oily, and her husband taking a massive rolling pin and rolling her out till she is long and thin.

The image amuses me. She doesn't seem to like it when I smile, and she scolds me with a frown.

'How are you getting on with keeping a diary?'

She's asked me to jot down notes about how I'm feeling each day. As homework goes, it's not exactly brain surgery.

'Fine,' I reply, 'I do it in the form of letters to God.'

Ha!

I see her visibly twitch. People often twitch when I mention the big man himself. Especially people with degrees. Ruby always warned me. People who go to higher education often lose their faith. That is, if they had any faith to start with.

'Last time we met, we were discussing the time you arranged to meet your birth mother for the first time.'

'Jocelyn,' I prompt her, in case she has forgotten.

'Jocelyn,' she concurs, with the air of someone who already knew. 'And you concocted the meeting with her and the man you believed to be your father.'

'Mark,' I prompt her.

She nods. What a memory. It's almost like I pay her to listen to me rambling on. Though she has left out the bit about me practically grooming him for months by becoming his student at night school.

'And of course, that didn't go quite as you had imagined it would.'

'Is correct.'

And I was just starting to tell you this when you informed me that our fifty minutes was up, I want to add, but am far too polite to. Instead, I give her one of my tight little smiles. And feel myself pinching the inside of my right hand, to stop myself from getting angry. Smile through the anger. Smile through the anger. *It's OK, Billy. Now is your moment. You can tell her now how that felt.*

'Talk me through what that was like for you,' she says, and I release the grasp on my skin, relief flooding me like warm milk on a cold night.

'Well, it was a long time ago. I behaved very differently then.'

I'm not quite sure why I have responded in this way. Seconds ago I wanted to tell her how it had felt. Seconds before, I was angry that I'd been denied the chance to tell her how it had felt. And now she's asked me, and I'm shielding that information from her. It's a childish reaction, especially as the main purpose of therapy seems to be to rake over the coals of the past to see why the smoke in the present is making you cough.

I quite like that image. It pleases me. Sometimes I do fancy myself as a bit of an urban poet.

But then I question myself. Is it really that good an analogy? If the coals exist in the past, then how can they be creating smoke today?

OK. Fine. I am no urban poet. Not today, anyway. The muse must not be upon me.

She is saying nothing. Just staring, head cocked to one side, knowing that eventually I will crumble or crack. Or both.

Well, just as long as I don't crack up.

Or maybe it's too late for that.

Then crumble I do.

'I felt stupid. I felt winded. I felt . . .'

I want to say angry, but I don't want her to think I'm an angry person.

'Yes?'

Oh well. In for a penny, in for a pound.

'Angry.'

She nods.

'I felt stupid that I'd believed what that woman had told me. At the funeral. Kathleen.' I almost spit her name.

'You were very young. It's not surprising that you believed her.'

'I know, but looking back . . .'

'I think you need to cut yourself some slack, Billy.'

'Maybe. I'd spent so much time planning that moment, and it was all for nothing.'

'It was certainly very industrious, what you had done. Some might say mercurial.'

I have no idea what mercurial means.

'Manipulative?'

'Well, you certainly manipulated the situation and the people involved. You went out of your way to befriend and flatter the man who you assumed was your father, without telling him your reasons, and . . .'

'Yes, I see now that was a complete waste of time, and I'm glad he wasn't my father. He was so vain, so easily flattered. So open to it.'

'Or maybe he just saw in you a good cause.'

'Because I'm black?'

I half expect her to contradict me with *You're not black, you're mixed race* – she loves getting one up on me – but instead she says,

'A disenfranchised youth to whom he could open a gateway. Anyway. We're not here to talk about him. Though we can, of course, explore your feelings about him.'

I zone out, and she thinks I'm self-analysing. I'm not. I'm just thinking. I'm just wondering how she manages to sit there, and I manage to sit here. What happens in someone's life that means I'm the one that's seeking help, and she's the one that gives it?

She is white. She has privilege. In fact, she reeks of it. She may come across all bleeding-heart, but it wouldn't surprise me if that blood ran blue. I picture her in a nursery. I picture her as the little girl in *Mary Poppins*. Edwardian parents and a flying nanny. What a happy childhood she must have had. And then I remember mine. And Ruby. The heavy footsteps on the stairs. The fat legs. The dry skin in her elbows. The nylon housecoats. The ever-present Bible. The priest dropping by, treated like royalty, treated like family should have been treated. Cherished, loved. She showed him more respect than she ever showed me. The slippers. How could I forget the slippers?

And the constant knowledge that something wasn't right.

And the big sister who ran away, when she wasn't really my sister at all.

Ruby was strict and ran our house with a rod of iron, sometimes literally. I remember her once taking the poker from the fire and striking Jocelyn with it when she back-chatted her. Thank God the fire wasn't lit, and the iron was cold. It wasn't long after that that Jocelyn moved out.

I can picture her being hit with the poker. Clear as day. The way Jocelyn shrank away, hands raised to her head to protect herself.

And then sometimes I have to remind myself that I was too young to remember. And it's possible I wasn't even there. But maybe I did see it. Or maybe, and it's more than likely, I just have a very vivid imagination.

I was brought up in a terraced house on Alderson Road, but left not long after my twelfth birthday. I was a measured, quiet, diligent child who wouldn't have been out of place in a Dickens novel. Oh, not your ragamuffin delinquent, sleeping rough and picking a pocket or two. No, your well-behaved swot, sent away to the country for his health. If I'd seen a goose I wouldn't have said boo to it. I was the model child.

Maybe, looking back, what I actually was was scared.

Ruby always expected the best of her children – Jocelyn, the twins Princess and Daphne, and me. She expected us to achieve, to become something, even if all she had become was worn out. But she wanted better for all of us. Me and the twins seemed destined to do well. Jocelyn, on the other hand, was a different kettle of fish. She was the sly one, the fly one, the one whose soul was dancing. Behind her eyes, her mischief crackled through like flames behind a fire-guard.

Again, this is what my sisters told me.

Trouble, that's what she was. It was a confident cock of the head, a raise of the palm, a saunter from a room once a bomb had been dropped. She wasn't going to be told what to do, she'd been told enough and wouldn't take any more. Ruby used to say she had the devil in her.

Sometimes Ruby hit the devil out of her. Sometimes she said she was going to 'smack the black' out of her. Though much as she'd try, she never succeeded.

I only know all this because of the twins. I was a toddler when Jocelyn left. But I felt her absence keenly. She had brought colour to the house, warmth. And I missed that when it vanished overnight. But the stories they told me, I cherished them. Here was someone who had found a way out of this freezing cold landscape.

I learned to get by on my own, be self-sufficient, rely on myself for company, live in my head, my dreams. When austerity surrounds you, it's very easy to retreat.

Ruby had many beliefs and convictions that she clung to and drummed into us at any given opportunity. These included:

Jesus was our friend, our father and saw everything, even when we were on the toilet 'doing dirties'. (Though the twins were always quick to point out that she'd only really 'found God' after Jocelyn had left.)

Sierra Leone was the most beautiful country in the world, and it was our duty to be great ambassadors for it at every given moment.

Freetown, the capital of Sierra Leone, was one of the most beautiful cities in the world.

Although we lived in a four-bedroom house, one of the bedrooms was always taken up with 'stuff for home'. This basically meant that Ruby stockpiled things that she would pack into suitcases and take back with her on her twice-yearly trips to the motherland. These bits could be anything from pairs of tights to multipacks of crisps. She claimed she walked around the poorer parts of Freetown, handing them out to the poverty-stricken.

(It was our belief that she actually went home and sold the articles for the highest price she could get. She always returned home and rigged herself out in all the latest fashions, as befitted a Sierra Leonean living in Liverpool.)

Egg custard was the work of the devil, and wasn't allowed in the house.

Rustie Lee's laugh brought shame on all black people, and if she appeared on the television it had to be switched off.

Television was occasionally the work of the devil. Except for *Blankety Blank*, which she loved. And *Songs of Praise*, though to her mind the hymns were not catchy enough most of the time.

Hymns should be sung at full throttle, so that the knick-knacks rattled.

Heating in a house was a waste of money. If you were cold, wrap up.

White working-class people – who we were surrounded by, of course – were common. We were a cut above. Exceptions could be made for God-fearing white working-class people. White middle-class people could be given the benefit of the doubt.

Actually, the list was pretty much endless.

Ours was a quiet house. Just the ticking of the grandfather clock and the hum of some sample teasmades. And every now and then, an explosion of noise when Ruby lost her temper.

Of course, I did not call her Ruby back then. Oh no! Mother or Mummy. She never liked Mum, she felt it vulgar. But the twins said Jocelyn often pointed out that the number of gentlemen callers she had from the church was vulgar. But Ruby claimed they were just friends, and she should wash her mouth out with carbolic. I was only really interested in what the twins had to say when they were talking about our errant older one. The one that got away.

But as I grew up, I began to realize that maybe Ruby was right.

I will never forget the time I went in to school and a boy in my class thrust a copy of the *Sun* in front of me. It was open at Page Three, and there was a woman with her breasts out. We would never have anything as common as the *Sun* in our house, so this racy concept was new to me. Plus I was only about seven.

'That's your sister!' he screeched. 'With her fucking tits out!'

'Dirty bitch!' shouted another lad.

'Your sister's got massive knockers!' yelled another.

And that was how I found out my sister had become a glamour model – or, as Ruby called it, 'a dirty, dirty lady'. Though her pronunciation was more like 'dutty, dutty ledder'.

Was Ruby right? Did Jocelyn have the devil in her? All I knew was it was wrong, and horrible, to see your big sister naked as the day she was born.

I remember reading the words underneath.

Juicy Jocelyn from London loves nothing
more than rock-climbing and walks in the fresh air.
And boy, does she have a spring in her buxom step.
Hitch 'em high, Jocelyn! That's quite some valley!

The 'hitch 'em high' bit must have been about the braces that were partly hidden by her breasts and holding her hiking shorts up. She was posing next to some stones. I think it was meant to look like she was on a nature trek, but I was pretty sure the background of cloudy sky looked a bit painted. And why had they said she was from London? She was from Liverpool.

Still, at least I had learned one thing about her. She was very much into rambling and hiking.

What a sap I was.

And then there was her singing career, which seemed to end just as soon as it began. I remember huddling round the twins' boogie box in their bedroom when Ruby was out, and listening to the song.

'She sounds poorly,' I said, because she did. She seemed to be gasping for breath, like she had run 400 metres. I always got out of breath when I ran 400 metres. 'Is she asthmatic?'

I knew all about asthmatics. A teacher at school was one. She was always sticking an inhaler in her mouth. It fascinated me.

'She's pretending to have sex, you idiot,' said a twin. I forget which one.

'Sex?' I was horrified. 'No. Maybe she's out of breath because she's been out on one of her big hikes,' I suggested, and the twins folded their arms in unison and shot me the most patronizing look possible. They were good at those.

Ruby definitely was right. Our big sister had the devil in her. I didn't really like the sound of Jocelyn.

It put me off hiking for life.

I was glad she had left to explore the countryside and long walks in the fresh air. She could do her dirty stuff elsewhere, and leave us to get on with it. Whatever it was. Things pretty much stayed on an even keel then, for the rest of my days at Alderson Road.

But little did I know they were going to be short-lived. Ah, the naivety of youth!

Looking back, I suppose the day I learned that Ruby was not my mother was the day it all started to go wrong for me. It's pretty big news to get. And it's pretty big news to get in your local sweet shop.

There was a sweet shop, round the corner from us, just off Alderson Road, where it met Cardy Road. It was a really old-fashioned place, seemingly untouched by the twenty-first century. Dark wooden shelves bursting with glass jars of sweets in every colour of the rainbow, and although it was a popular shop and the jars were in constant use – Dorothy, the owner, had a set of matching wooden stairs that rolled around the shop on castors – every jar seemed to be coated in cobwebs.

Or maybe that's just how I remember it now.

I had got a job there as a paper boy as a present for my twelfth birthday. Yes, you heard that right. Ruby was so in-fused with a Protestant work ethic, that hard work made you closer to Godliness, that my twelfth birthday present was her announcing to me, 'I have secured you a paper round. You will now be earning your own money.' Only Ruby could think this was generosity wrapped up in a shiny bow. Of course, I earned peanuts, but when I told Ruby this she said, in her braying Sierra Leonean accent, 'Peanuts are better than no nuts. Think of all the things you can buy.'

Oh yes, like one of your beautiful teasmades, Ruby.

The twins argued with her that I was too young for a paper round, that legally I had to wait till I was thirteen. Ruby pointed out that the law had never bothered them before, so why should it bother them now? And anyway, the only law that really mattered was God's law. And he said this was a wonderful idea.

Again, Ruby, like one of your teasmades.

I don't remember the time Ruby first told me that I was to call her Mother. But I wish I could time-travel back to those days in my crib and see her looking down and telling me. Just to see if there was any doubt in her eyes, any sign of guilt about the lie she was telling me.

Come to Mummy!
Where's your mummy?
Mummy loves you.
I am Mummy.
Mummy is me.

I actually enjoyed being a paper boy. My route took me all the way from St Brigit's church on Lawrence Road to the east, and as far as the Bridge pub to the west. In between was a grid of streets that I pushed my way through each morning from half six till half seven. And my new boss said I was so speedy, I could 'be in the Olympics for running, just like those other lovely coons'.

But I forgave her. Ruby said I had to. Sometimes I did; she certainly didn't say it with hatred. Other times, I'd take a fiver from the till when she wasn't looking. Tough titty, Dorothy.

Dorothy the sweet shop lady was actually very nice most of the time, but boy, was she one for the gossip. Every action she did, every scoop she made into those dusty jars was accompanied by a high-pitched piccolo flourish of garrulous Gosh-wait-till-you-hear-thises and You'll-never-guess-whats that held little interest for me, but seemed to keep the women of the parish entertained. As I loaded my bag with the papers of the day she would witter on to anyone who'd listen about the latest salacious scandal she'd heard, usually involving someone not scrubbing their step, or scrubbing their step so much it could mean one thing and one thing only – the woman was having an affair. How she could jump to such conclusions was beyond me, even then; but jump to them she did, and at the time, I have to say, the connections she threaded together out of thin air made complete sense.

When the shop was empty, she would pick up the phone and continue her monologue to anyone who'd listen. I used to wonder if she just picked up that receiver and jabbed in any old numbers at random and took pot luck; she hit the buttons so hard and so quickly, without even looking, and seemingly didn't wait for the other person to pick up before getting a head start and launching into a rapid: 'Wait till you hear what I've got to tell you, you'll DIE. DIE.'

One morning I was returning with my empty bag after delivering my round. As I came into the shop she was half whispering into the receiver, 'And she said it hurt, and I said, "Well I'm not surprised. It's not natural. We all know what that was designed for, and you're talking a lot of it."'

At which she chuckled. A really dirty chuckle, and I wondered what it could be that hurt so much. But then she saw me, and paused, smiling awkwardly as I returned my bag to the shelf where they lived behind the counter.

'Thank you, William,' she said as I made my way out of the shop. 'One sec,' she said down the phone. She was clearly waiting for me to exit. I opened the shop door and the bell rang in the usual way, and as soon as it did she continued with her gossiping. Only, as she did, a magazine on one of the shelves by the door caught my eye. Princess Diana had not long died, and lots of the magazines had her picture on the cover. One of them had a picture of her and alongside it a picture of an

Asian man with the headline HER SECRET LOVER. It was always exciting to see a black or brown face associated with anything to do with the establishment, so I lingered to have a look. But with the ringing of the bell, Dorothy obviously assumed I had left the building.

Which was when I heard her say, 'Sorry, it was my paper boy. The one I told you about. That family. The coons.'

Which made me seethe.

'No, it's not their surname, you stupid cow, that's what they are. I've told you about them. Grandma's bringing him up as her own.'

And that's all it took. Seven words. Said so quickly. And yet they changed my life.

Grandma's bringing him up as her own.

But as that stand-up comic used to say, *hey. But wait. There's more.*

'So he thinks his mum's his sister. I know. Very complicated. No, he's no idea. Yeah, she was a sweet girl really, used to hang around with our Adam, before she beggared off to the Smoke and got her tits out for five pieces of silver. He's a good paper boy, though, so the old girl's obviously doing something right.'

As the world seemed to stop turning and everything went a little bit hazy, I felt like my knees were buckling and I was about to fall backwards. I steadied myself as she continued to warble on about this and that, but if I'm honest, it just became like white noise.

White noise from a white woman.

Grandma's bringing him up as her own.

He thinks his mum's his sister.

Sweet girl really, used to hang around with our Adam.

Five pieces of silver.

I grabbed the shelf behind me as I felt my heartbeat

quicken, and the blood in my ears swished round so noisily I thought it could be heard from three streets away. Around my whole paper round.

They say that, don't they? When someone looks older than their years. *Have a tough paper round, did you, lad?*

How was I going to get out? How was I going to get out of here without her realizing I'd heard what she'd said? As soon as I opened the door, she would hear me, and know I'd heard what she'd said.

I said a prayer to Jesus.

And Jesus saved me.

As if by magic, a shadow appeared in the doorway and some kids came in on their stop-off to get sweets for the walk to school. As the bell rang and they came in, I slipped out behind them and into the blinding daylight of the street.

I had a desire to run.

I didn't want to think about what she'd said.

I wanted big open space. I wanted space. I wanted to be in space. I wanted to fly.

So I ran. I ran so fast, in the hope that I might take off and soar into the sky. I ran into the street. Which is when I felt metal hit my leg and side, and the ground somersaulted over me.

I had run into the path of a car.

The next thing I knew, I was waking up in hospital. A kindly nurse who looked like an angel was smiling down at me.

'Hello, William. Look. Your mother's here.' She stepped back. Ruby was sitting there, with a tear-sodden face.

Crocodile tears?

Guilty tears?

Who knew?

But all I remember is, I said, 'She's not my mother. She's my grandmother.'

And that's when I knew. The rot had set in.

That was the year, as Ruby would put it, I went off the rails. She would never be drawn on the nature of my maternity if I continued to question her about it, claiming that 'that bump to the head has sent you funny'.

Jocelyn had, of course, moved years before, and none of us knew where she was. Well, I knew the newspaper had said she was in London, but every time I told Ruby I wanted to get in touch with her, I was brick-walled with the usual, 'No-one knows where she is and no-one needs to. She has the devil in her.' In the end, I learned to just shut up and not ask.

Another of Ruby's rules: Don't rock the boat.

I let it lie, though obviously my resentment towards her and the situation was festering, and now I certainly did go off the rails.

Because imagine how that feels. Imagine how that feels, when you learn that it wasn't your sister who got her tits out for a living and simulated sex on records in the charts – it was your mother. The woman who gave you life. And that was a lot to play with when you'd been brought up to fear God, keep your trap shut and follow as straight a path as possible.

All I could keep thinking was, I'd found out my mother was a slut. A dutty, dutty lady.

That was no lady. That was my mum!

No wonder I went off the rails.

I used to imagine her in my head. Imagine meeting her. It was the same every time. I travelled down to London on my own on the coach, sometimes the train – I knew I could do this, as I say, I was so self-sufficient, I could do more than most twelve-year-olds – and I somehow had her address, and

I would go and visit her. She'd not been expecting me, so she would be caught unawares, and that's when I'd discover she was nothing like the naughty pictures or the record made her appear to be. She was lovely. She was always dressed in white. A big white smock thing, and she was in her garden picking blackberries from the bushes. She'd put them into a flat basket she'd have slung over her spare arm, and she'd turn and look at me. At first she'd be scared, because she didn't know me.

I remember I liked that. I liked seeing her scared.

Sometimes I imagined she wet herself, she was that scared. A little puddle. Middle of her smock. Poor little lamb, all embarrassed. Gosh, how humiliating for her. Glorious.

'Don't be scared,' I'd say, 'for I am William.'

I know. How very Old Testament.

'William?'

'But they call me Billy now. It's me, Mum. Your son.'

And she'd let the basket tumble to the floor, then hurry inside, upset. I'd follow. She'd sit at her kitchen table, crying.

I liked seeing her cry.

'Please. Please forgive me, Billy. I've been such a poor role model. I've done things I'm so ashamed of, just to make ends meet. I'm a good girl, I am.'

I know. How very *My Fair Lady*.

'I was kidnapped. By these men. They kept me captive and made me do these . . . things! I'm so sorry, for those things must have caused you deep distress. I'm sorry. But I didn't choose to do them. They were forced upon me. I hated every second of every photo shoot. I hated pretending to be copulating when I was singing that awful song. I'm sorry if you were bullied off the back of it. Please. Please say you'll forgive me.'

And every time, I'd step forward.

And her eyes would light up as if she knew I was going to offer my forgiveness.

And instead, I'd go up to her and slap her round the face, leaving an angry red welt across her cheek and one of her eyes.

I liked that.

But that was only in my head.

I could never be that brave.

In the real world, the first thing I did that was out of character for me was that I asked a girl out to the school disco. Her name was Briony Adlington, and she was the most beautiful girl in school. At first she said yes, but then she must have got a better offer, because a week or so before the disco I heard a rumour that she had agreed to go with the vice-captain of the Year 8 football team. I went up to her between lessons and asked if it was true, and with a nonchalant shrug of the shoulders she confirmed that it was, and offered a meek apology.

I was not best pleased.

I was not pleased at all.

But what to do?

I'm not keen on the word 'revenge'.

I much prefer words like 'karma'. Or 'just deserts'.

In the cobbled alleyway behind our house, there was a lot of dog shit. I took some and wrapped it in clingfilm and slipped it into one of Ruby's Jiffy bags, and took a bus into town and posted it to Briony at the main post office in the city centre. I did this once a week until my anger subsided. That took about three months. It gave me so much pleasure. It was balm to my soul. The idea of her receiving these parcels. And the smell. Oh, it was glorious. I used a different post office each time, just in case her family had made some sort of complaint. Meanwhile, every time I saw her in school I gave her the broadest smile, as if her actions hadn't hurt me, hoping that would put her off the scent, the scent of dried-up old dog shit, and it seemed to do the trick.

A few weeks into the 'shitstorm', I saw that Briony's photograph had appeared in the school magazine. She'd won a poetry prize.

I wondered how the poem went.

I wondered if it was . . .

I'm Such A Twat
By Briony Adlington, Year 8

I'm such a twat,
There's no doubt about that
I should've taken Billy to the disco
He is far superior to that idiot I ended up going with
But hey
That's what happens
When you're a twat.

OK, so my structure might've needed work.

Gosh, she looked so full of herself, standing there beaming into the camera looking all holier-than-thou. When actually, the rumour was that after the school disco she'd had sex with the so-called footballer round the back of the gym block. What a hypocrite. And she wasn't yet thirteen!

Brazen.

Not unlike my mother. And we all know what happened to her.

This similarity to Jocelyn made my blood fizz even more. But what to do with all this pent-up energy?

Oh yes!

I carefully cut out Briony's picture from the magazine, and set to work. I wasn't particularly artistic, in so much as I was pretty useless at drawing, but when I put my mind to it I was capable of creating a masterpiece. As I did now. Each night for a week, when I was supposed to be doing my homework, I painstakingly put together a flyer using Ruby's newly purchased computer. Fancy lettering. And then, using Ruby's photocopier, I copied it. Thank heavens Ruby liked to run a business or two and had all the latest gadgetry. It took a bit of readjusting with the size of the lettering and getting the angle of her photograph just so, but eventually the flyer was ready. And I put it in twenty different phone boxes around Liverpool. What I had created was a mock-up of a prostitute's calling card, with Briony's home phone number on. 'Busty Teen Babe Briony For Hire'. The idea of her holier-than-thou act being shattered in the privacy of her own home gave me great pleasure.

Really, when I think about it now, this is the sort of thing that these days would win the Turner Prize. It could be called *Just Deserts*. And to think, I was only twelve. If it's not too big-headed of me to say so, this sort of karma was bordering on genius for one so young. I was like Mozart with a photocopier and Pritt Stick.

And so the time had come for me to plan the third prong of my three-pronged attack. I was going to give her a scare somehow. I had watched enough horror movies to know it was easy to do, especially around Halloween. I was toying with hanging out in the alleyway behind her house, climbing into her back yard, and then somehow getting to her bedroom window and giving her the shock of her life; I just had to work out how best to achieve that. I was not a natural climber. I would need a stepladder, but how on earth was I going to get that over a brick wall and into her back yard?

And then something magical happened: I discovered what Briony's father did for a living. He was a window cleaner.

Window cleaners had ladders to ply their trade. Window cleaners probably left their ladders . . . indoors? No. In their back yards? More than likely.

Now you have to remember, this was quite some time ago. These days the back alleys of Liverpool are cordoned off with wrought-iron fences and gates, and the yards are safe havens where bikes are never stolen, nor hanging baskets, nor knickers from the line. They are well-lit – with low-energy bulbs, no doubt – places where only bins skulk, in every colour of the rainbow. But back then you could wend your way across the city and hardly have to cross a road. So it was very easy to walk up behind Briony's house and stand in the entry and look up.

After a few visits, I had worked out which was her bedroom. The back bedroom overlooking the yard. Result!

The more difficult thing to do was this. No matter what sort of disguise I was wearing, it was going to be hard to climb up a ladder and knock on her window without her opening her curtains, screaming, and drawing the attention of everyone else in the house. So how did I then climb down the ladder and run off before someone else in her family made it downstairs and out into the yard to apprehend me? Or beat the living daylights out of me? It was going to need some more thought.

There was a chink of light at the end of this particular tunnel, as I also discovered that both of Briony's parents were deaf. If she called to them to chase me, they wouldn't hear. But I didn't know if she had some secret panic buttons in her room that lit up round the house saying GIVE CHASE.

Maybe my mind was working overtime.

American horror movies were so misleading. On that side of the pond there seemed to be no notion of terraced housing and alleyways and the like. They all seemed to live in sweeping cul-de-sacs in sprawling Seventies bungalows and mansions with nothing between them but trees and litterless drives and wide streets. Kids went trick-or-treating. Bikes were ridden, there was little traffic. It was perfect for giving the girl who'd betrayed you the shock of her life. Although admittedly, no-one did to Jamie Lee Curtis what I had in store.

And then, as if by magic, another stroke of luck.

Ruby bought a new fine-fangled gadget known as a mobile phone. It felt like magic. It felt like it might sort everything out. Nobody else in our neighbourhood had one, but Ruby felt it was imperative for her as a go-getting businesswoman. It was going to sort everything out for me.

And hopefully sort her out, too. That bitch, Briony.

It was Halloween. I've always been drawn to the dramatic. And I had used my paper-round money to buy a Ku Klux Klan fancy dress outfit from The Wizard's Sleeve joke shop and fancy-dress place in town. I had no need for Briony's dad's ladders now, as I had a new plan.

And it was pretty fucking good, actually.

Once I heard Ruby shutting her bedroom door and going to bed, I quietly got out of mine and got dressed. It was half past eleven. This was perfect timing. I took my specially prepared bag and crept as quietly as I could down the stairs. I went to the pantry, lifted out our two-tier stepladder and let myself quietly out of the back door.

I hurried down our back entry, and across to the street that was two parallel to ours. Ashfield. And then down that back entry, till I was behind Briony's house. I then unzipped my bag and pulled out the KKK outfit, and slid it over my head so it dropped down over my shoulders. I took out the torch from the bag, and the mobile phone. I extended out the stepladder and checked it was steady. I then climbed to the top of it and – *bingo* – my head poked above the wall of Briony's back yard.

I placed the torch under my KKK outfit, and switched it on. I had checked this look in the bathroom mirror at home without the lights on, and it was pretty scary. Light beamed from the eyehole slits, and the whole thing went luminous. Excellent. I then pressed the number I had previously entered into the phone.

I heard it ring in the house before I heard it through my phone.

It seemed to ring for ages.

Eventually, the light went on in Briony's bedroom. Her curtains lit up, an oblong of light against the rest of the dark house. Finally she answered.

'Hello?'

I took a deep breath. I was suddenly nervous.

'Hello?'

Shit, I'd better say something before she hung up.

'Go to your bedroom window.'

'What?'

'Look outside.'

'Who is this?'

'Go to your bedroom window, Briony. Look outside.'

She said nothing. I could hear movement. Was she walking to the window? The heat from the torch was now making my face hot. I wished she'd hurry up.

Then I saw her silhouette through the curtains.

'Good girl, Briony.'

'Who is this?'

Excellent. She sounded like she was about to cry. Superb. Her voice was tiny, high-pitched, quivering.

'Open the curtain!' I said, teasing, like this was all a big joke.

She opened the curtains and I saw her frown, eyes adjusting to the change in light. And then as I saw her register seeing me, peering over her yard wall, I crowed into the phone in the croakiest voice I could muster for my half-broken, twelve-year-old voice.

'I'm going to rape you, Briony. Till your fucking kidneys poke out of your eye sockets, you prick-teasing cunt.'

I then switched off the torch, jumped off the ladder, grabbed it and the bag, and ran.

I snuck quietly into the house, returned the ladders to the pantry, deleted Briony's number from Ruby's list of dialled calls and took off my disguise. When I went to bed, I slept like the dead.

I had planned that manoeuvre with military precision. I had planned that sentence so it flowed beautifully and scarily.

I'm going to rape you, Briony. Till your fucking kidneys poke out of your eye sockets, you prick-teasing cunt.

It was like poetry.

I was very proud of myself.

Except . . .

A word to the wise. I was very young. I was naïve. And I was pretty stupid to think I could outwit Briony. Nowadays, I'd know. I'd know all phone calls can be traced. But I honestly thought mobile phones were different back then. As it turned out, all it took for Briony to trace the call was to dial 1471 after I'd called.

Two policemen arrived the next day, wanting to speak to Ruby. And when it became obvious that Ruby had not made that threatening phone call, the finger of suspicion pointed towards me.

The shit had hit the fan.

I don't wish to go into too much detail about what happened after that. I certainly never showed my face again at school, whether they believed my claim that I'd done it as a joke or not, and soon Ruby decided that I'd gone off the rails too much. I was overwhelming her. It was decided that it would be best all round if I left Liverpool and went to live with her cousin in London. A fresh start. A clean page. A new life.

But then something happened that sent my life in a different direction.

Aunty Gina, who I was now living with in Brixton, had to go away for four days, and as I was only twelve I was returned home for a few days to stay with Ruby. As she would not let me out of her sight, she insisted I go with her to the funeral of an old lady who lived down the road. When I heard who it was I was keen to go, actually, as I knew the woman's granddaughter had been a friend of Jocelyn's. I wondered if she might hold some clue to her whereabouts. She didn't. But she came up trumps another way.

Her name was Kathleen. She got drunk, and she told me who my dad was.

Or so I fucking thought.

Sorry. I know I shouldn't swear.

Why am I apologizing to myself? I must be the only person in the world who does this. Must be my strict upbringing. Or is it in my genes? Hmm. Some genes.

Oh, it took her a while. I could see she was fishing, in her stupor, to see what I knew about my heritage and what I had been told. So I just came out and said it.

'I know Jocelyn's my mum.'

And the relief on her face was tangible. Like she'd been holding in the biggest fart, and finally she'd been allowed to let it out.

'Do you know who my dad is?'

She did indeed. My father was a man called Mark Reynolds. She reckoned he was making a bit of a name for himself in the world of politics.

She was waylaid then by people passing on their condolences to her and her father, and when Ruby saw that the father was there, she said we had to get back to check on some teasmade orders. I went with her, forming a plan in my head as to how I might find out more about this man called Mark Reynolds.

The next day was my final day in Liverpool before heading back to Aunty Gina. I told Ruby that I had promised to run some errands for Kathleen. She seemed surprised and raised some objections, but I laid it on with a trowel about how poor Kathleen had just lost her granny and how she needed a hand with sorting a few things out. Just for an hour.

A slow nod of the head said it was sanctioned.

I had already stolen a sweaty five-pound note from Ruby's handbag. I went to the garage by the railway bridge on Picton Road and bought the cheapest display of tulips I could find, then dropped by to see Kathleen.

She was still in her dressing gown, and looked like shit warmed up with sugar on top. She was delighted with the flowers, as I knew she would be. My strict upbringing came into its own as I continued to be charming with her, asking how she was and explaining that although she'd spoken at the service, I just wanted to check she was OK, as I knew what a friend she'd been to my mother in the past. I could see her practically preening like a peacock. She liked the sound of this. She was so typical of most of the grown-ups I knew. So susceptible to a compliment.

Women, eh?

Looking back, she was surprisingly flirtatious with me. Flicking her hair this way and that. Telling me how she was an international traveller thanks to her new job as an air stewardess, about how exciting it was to travel the world. She then turned to one side and asked me what I 'thought of her profile'. I had no idea what she was talking about and when I hesitated, she threw her head back and laughed – at this point I wondered whether she had been on the sauce that morning already – and explained that she'd recently had some 'minor reconstructive cosmetic surgery' and it was 'one of the benefits of international travel'.

At this point, I thought Kathleen was actually a bit of show-off.

I then said I mustn't delay her any more, and stood to leave. I could see the disappointment in her eyes. *Going so soon?* She stood too to follow me out, and thanked me for the flowers and told me what a charming young man I'd grown into.

I then did a double-take sort of head jerk, and said, 'Oh. What we were discussing yesterday . . .'

Like I'd forgotten. As if!

'. . . Would you have any idea about how I could get in touch with Mark Reynolds?'

Her eyes lit up, as if relishing the challenge. Well, how could she deny a boy who'd been so polite to her in her hour of need?

'No, but I'm sure we could find out.'

An hour later, we were sitting side by side in an internet cafe in town and Kathleen had brought up a new search-engine page called Google. I had no idea what this was, but she confidently typed the words MARK REYNOLDS into a box at the top of the screen and then hit return. She did a few more clicks before proudly announcing, 'Well, Billy. It would appear that your father lectures in politics at the City Lit.'

Once I'd returned to London, I stopped going to school (Aunty Gina was none the wiser, and her handwriting proved very easy to forge where an absence note was concerned) and made it my duty to track down my father.

'Father'.

When actually, nothing could have been farther from the truth.

God, I'm clever.

I know it was rather ungodly of me to be missing school, but I reckoned that even Jesus would think finding a bond with my dad would be a worthwhile thing.

The City Lit turned out to be located down a side street near Drury Lane in Covent Garden. For the majority of my first morning's searching I hung around outside the New London Theatre, where *Cats* was showing.

An ironclad smash! one of the adverts said.

I was trying to work up the courage to go round the corner to the actual college. For once, though, my nerve was failing me. My mind was full of what-ifs. *What if he doesn't know anything about me? What if he doesn't want to know me? What if he turns out to be a knobhead?*

What if that man walking past me now was him?

It made no sense to just go up to a man and scare him by saying, 'Hello, I believe I am your son.'

But what would I say instead?

I didn't know.

But I knew I had to meet him.

The only security at the City Lit that day was a middle-aged woman with a Sixties beehive, sitting knitting at what looked like a picnic table as you walked in. She looked rather taken aback when I said I was here to see Mark Reynolds. After all, what would a thirteen-year-old schoolboy be doing seeking out a politics lecturer? But when I added I was a friend of the family, she happily directed me to his office and returned to her knitting needles.

My first glimpse of Mark was as he was coming out of his office, as I was approaching. He was everything I'd feared he might be. He had a look of Paul Weller, and was suitably dressed like a mod, even though that was far from hip at the time. He had a pretty, pale, almost feminine face, slender hips, very generous of lip, and sideburns that fell in front of his ears like spaniel's ears. These days you might regard him as a hipster.

I had no idea what I was going to say. But what I said was something like . . .

I'm sorry to bother you, Mr Reynolds, but I thought you might be able to help me.

Oh yes, and I added a faint Liverpool accent for good measure. To make him feel at home. Even though mine had been zapped out of me at an early age.

We don't do politics at my school and it's what I want to do for a living. I'm looking for a private tutor. I can't pay coz my mum's ill with cancer but . . . I'd be an eager student and . . . well, I've heard from people back in Liverpool that you're the best. The best. I'd only need an hour of your time every now and again, but . . .

He practically screamed I'LL DO IT. There and then.

Men, eh?

I had appealed to his vanity. He had not thought it at all odd that so young a boy was seeking his company. He was happy to be seen with me in public.

Not sure that would have been quite so easy today.

Not only did Mark take it upon himself to educate me about politics, but he decided to educate me about the finer things in life. We met in bohemian cafes in Soho, tea rooms at the Criterion, subterranean drinking dens below Leicester Square. And in these places, one thing became obvious. Mark Reynolds LOVED the sound of his own voice.

I had to say so little. I'd sit there pretending to take notes while he hit the coffee and spouted forth his ideologies about everything from Churchill to Thatcher to Blair to social housing to . . . you name it, he loved talking about it. And he never really asked my opinion, he just seemed to think I was going to learn everything by osmosis.

One day he asked how my mum was. I got flustered, and said she was feeling a lot better. And wanted to meet him. Why didn't we all have supper on New Year's Eve?

He'd never fall for that, surely.

But fall for it he did.

And then . . . the rest, as they say, is history.

Maybe I've been saying some of this aloud. My therapist is pointing out, 'But this was a very long time ago, Billy.'

'Fifteen years,' I agree.

And she encourages me to reflect on my feelings for Jocelyn now. I hear myself saying, 'Mixed emotions, really.'

I hear myself milking it. 'I mean, she was so horrible to so many people. But at the end of the day, she was my mum.'

One thing I appear to have been very good at is erasing people from my life. Once I knew that Mark was not my father and that I wasn't going to find some sort of happy-ever-after with him and my so-called mum, it was no problem whatsoever to wipe her from my mind and from my life. She'd never been that integral to it to begin with. Why did she have to be a part of it now?

She was easy enough to blank out. I just avoided the magazine she wrote for every time I went to a newsagent's. Oh, it caught my eye, don't get me wrong, but it wasn't exactly my first choice for reading anyway. And then I noticed it was no longer being stocked in the shops, which was when I discovered that it had stopped being published. And from then on she was even easier to ignore, as she was no longer making any noises anywhere that might grab my attention.

If there was one good thing to come out of the ill-fated night at the pizza restaurant, it was this. I appreciated that I was self-sufficient enough to need neither a father nor a mother. I was thirteen. My future was my destiny, not theirs. Ruby had cared for me, and now Aunty Gina. In many ways, their presence had been a blessing. Imagine if Jocelyn had taken me to London with her and tried to raise me while she was posing topless, or singing those dire songs, or being caught having sex on planes, or writing her sex advice column. I was far better off without her.

And as the years went by and I matured into a young man rather than a boy, I realized that the anger I had felt towards Jocelyn I had taken out on girls and women, and that really was not acceptable. The church said that Jesus would forgive me. Well, good on him – so I threw myself into my church-going with such a vengeance that word got back to Liverpool, and even Ruby became proud of me.

I had pangs, now and again, about how I had treated that girl at school. But surely I was acting out towards her all the anger I felt about my mum? That's certainly what my pastor felt. He also said, if I asked for forgiveness from the Lord, then forgiveness would be mine. If I promised to Him that I would never again be so horrible to a woman, then everything would be OK. I promised, and I meant it. But something still gnawed away at me, because somewhere in Liverpool was a girl who I had scared with my threatening campaign of intimidation and my freak-show behaviour. I carried the shame and guilt around with me for a long time.

Eventually my pastor advised me to write a letter to Briony, apologizing for my threatening behaviour. It was difficult to do, but I did it. He also warned me not to expect anything in return. But he said that the act of writing it would 'lift my soul'. It didn't, and the subsequent silence compounded my negativity. She had received the letter, but didn't forgive me, or else she would have replied. I had sought forgiveness from God and got it. I had sought forgiveness from my victim, and not got it. I withdrew into myself for the longest time.

The upside of this was, it enabled me to be industrious at school and sixth-form college. It was like I had come full circle. I had turned into the little boy I'd been before I'd discovered what I discovered that time in the sweet shop. If my world had turned upside down that day, then it felt like it had been righted now.

Back to square one.

The boy who wouldn't say boo to a goose.

Yes sir, no sir, three bags full, sir. That was me.

And then – something bizarre happened. As if my life hadn't been a succession of bizarre occurrences already.

I was in the college canteen. I often went in before the start of the college day, as the powers that be at sixth form were a lot less frugal than Aunty Gina and therefore didn't mind having a few radiators on every now and again to keep out the chill. I would sip my cheap coffee and scour the day's news-papers that they left hanging around for us to read.

A headline in the *Express* caught my eye. It was about the premiership footballer Isaiah Jacob. He had been involved in a drunk driving incident, and had crashed into three cars on the M6. The press were baying for his blood, of course. The most horrific detail about the case was that three members of the same family had been killed in one of the cars he had crashed into. They were named as the Adlington family from Liverpool. Gerry, 42, wife Monica, 40, and their eighteen-year-old daughter Briony, who had been driving.

There was a picture of them.

It was her.

I should've cried. Of course I should have cried. This was a tragic story. A whole family from where I grew up, obliterated in the blink of an eye.

But I didn't. Instead, I felt as if a weight had been lifted from my shoulders.

Yes, something terrible had happened to her. But it meant that she was no longer suffering because of anything that I had done to her.

Yes, OK, that sounds twisted. And of course I told those closest to me in the canteen how sad the story was, and how I'd known her at school, and – OK, so I lied, and that's bad – she'd been my date for the school disco. And outwardly I was the model of decorum and sadness and mourning and shock, and . . .

But deep down inside, I was punching the air. I felt elated. I no longer had to feel guilty. Isaiah Jacob had put paid to that. He had done something infinitely worse to her. He had killed her. What's a little rape threat compared to that, huh?

Hand that man a medal.

Actually, no. Don't hand him a medal. That would be crass and insensitive, cruel.

But I had prayed to God, and my prayers had been answered. Briony's suffering was now over.

I finally felt like a free man. I finally felt like I could face the future and not be shackled by the errors of the past. I had promised God I would be good and behave, and not be mean to people, and he had listened, and now it was up to me to keep my side of the bargain.

'Billy? Billy, you're not saying anything,' my therapist says.

Oh, FUCK OFF, BITCH.

Oh dear. Naughty me. Naughty Billy.

Tut tut tut.

'I find it very difficult to talk about Jocelyn,' I say as a get-out. Well, partly a get-out. It's true. I do.

And so I turned over a new leaf with renewed vigour. The model teenager becoming the model man. The model Christian. The model student. The model everything. Everyone's friend. Everyone's favourite neighbour. And I kept on with that, and it would have lasted forever. It would. Jocelyn had disappeared off the face of the earth, seemingly, so her face wasn't on newsstands to taunt me.

And then, many years later, I heard of this thing called Twitter. And I took a look at it.

It wasn't for me. I thought no more about it.

But as the years advanced, it seemed to gain in importance.

And soon the papers were talking about the new Queen of Mean, and how she had made her presence felt through her non-stop tweeting.

Jocelyn was back.

How much longer could I keep up my act?

KATHLEEN AND ADAM

2005

From: Kathleen O'Hara (kathleenohara1970@hotmail.co.uk)
Sent: 13 June 2005
To: Adam Ferguson (adam@kenzimanagement.com)
Subject: HOWDY

Dear Adam

Howdy!

Long time no speak. Think I'm pretty much in the doghouse
with you as I've not heard from you in so long. Fair do's.
Listen, I don't want to take up much of your time but I
wondered if you had an email address or phone number or
even postal address for Jocelyn? I owe her a massive apology
and would like to get in touch. Any thoughts where she might
be? Hope you are well. Love to your mum. K xxxxx

P.S. Remember the Loft Club?!

From: Adam Ferguson (adam@kenzimanagement.com)
Sent: 15 June 2005
To: Kathleen O'Hara (kathleenohara1970@hotmail.co.uk)
Subject: Re: HOWDY

Dear Kathleen

Thanks for your email. I have checked with Jocelyn and I think it's safe to say she'd rather you didn't get in touch. (Polite version) I'm sure you can understand.

Best wishes
Adam
Adam Ferguson
Agent
Kenzi Management

From: Kathleen O'Hara (kathleenohara1970@hotmail.co.uk)
Sent: 15 June 2005
To: Adam Ferguson (adam@kenzimanagement.com)
Subject: Re: Re: HOWDY

Dear Adam

Ah OK, so we won't mention the Loft Club.

I sense from the tone of your email that you too are unhappy with me. I'll be honest with you. I'm not in a very good place right now and I'm going through a lot of shit. But it's all self-inflicted so this isn't an email requiring pity or sympathy, but I guess it's truth time.

I may have upset you. I may have hurt you. Or you may just be siding with Jocelyn. In either case I wouldn't know. And why wouldn't I know? Because the last few years have gone by in a blur of alcohol. I'm not passing the buck. No-one made me pour that much alcohol down my neck, no one had a gun to my head. I did it. Me.

Anyway. I am writing this from a rehab clinic place in the Derbyshire hillside. It's pretty outside, but pretty bleak inside. Funny, that.

Adam, whatever I have done to hurt you in the past, can I just say I am so, so sorry. Part of acknowledging we have a problem here is to try and make amends to those we have hurt through our addiction in the past. I tried to reach out to Jocelyn, not even thinking I might have hurt you, bizarrely. I now appreciate that this was blinkered of me and God, Adam, I'm a knobhead.

Listen, if you don't want to get back to me it's fine. Honestly. I've fucked everyone else off in my life, you will be part of a very long list. But I do love you. And I am sorry.

Your friend

Kathleen xx

From: Adam Ferguson (adam@kenzimanagement.com)
Sent: 15 June 2005
To: Kathleen O'Hara (kathleenohara1970@hotmail.co.uk)
Subject: Re: Re: Re: HOWDY

Oh Kath, I am so so sorry to hear this. I'm sorry if my last email was a bit abrupt and cunty but I just didn't know what to say if I'm honest. I felt a bit caught between a rock and a hard place really. Yes, I am still mates with Jocelyn, but it's a bit more complicated than that. She was all over the place after what happened between you and Leon, and it brought us closer I guess. For the first time she kind of let her guard down and wasn't the big hard-faced piece she'd always been.

But I also grew closer to Leon and now I work for him. I am a hair and make-up agent like him – well, trying to be. So my life and relationships and work are all a bit intertwined at the moment – I even feel a bit guilty writing to you, like I'm going behind their backs and fraternizing with the enemy. I think that's how they'd see it anyway. But you're having a hard time and I can't pretend that doesn't get to me. How bad is it? How are work coping with you having time off?

All I'd say to you is this – and yes, as a former founder member of the Loft Club – just don't be too hard on yourself. Yes, you fucked up with Leon and that's kind of inexcusable – you couldn't have been pissed off your head the whole time you were seeing him. But . . . and it's a big but. Just remember what a shitty start you had in life. I know you're not one for massive navel-gazing and feeling sorry for yourself, but Jesus, girl, cut yourself some slack. You were brought up by your nan, God rest her soul, after your mam pissed off to Australia with some fancy piece. Your dad was in and out of prison. YOU HAD A SCHNOZZLE THAT BIG EVERY TIME YOU CROSSED THE ROAD THERE WAS AN ECLIPSE. (!!!) (And I know you've taken care of that.) In the big scheme of things, you have a lot to feel sorry for yourself about. Not that you do. And maybe the hurt from all that, and your nan dying, maybe that all led to you being in the place you are today.

Oh God, Kath, there's a million things I could say to you right now but I have to go to dinner with one of my clients. Get me! But stay strong and speak soon.

A xxxx
Adam Ferguson
Agent
Kenzi Management

From: Kathleen O'Hara (kathleenohara1970@hotmail.co.uk)
Sent: 16 June 2005
To: Adam Ferguson (adam@kenzimanagement.com)
Subject: Hoorah!

Oh Adam, you don't know how relieved I am that you're being so nice to me. I really don't deserve it, but it is very much appreciated. Your description of my (former) nose made me actually spit out my toast. We are allowed toast here. As long as it's not got vodka spread all over it.

Argh, you ask me how work are coping. They're not. That's part of the reason I'm in here. I lost my job. They booted me off when I got pissed on a flight and had a row with my purser. Well, I say row, I actually called her a 'fat fucking rice queen'. I have no recollection, but by the time we hit Heathrow my P45 was waiting for me on the runway. I have also since had the phrase 'rice queen' explained to me. I'd heard a few of the gay boys at work using it on a trip to Thailand and I just thought it was a general insult for someone who likes carbs. I know better now.

Well, that was a pretty big wake-up call, obviously. And with no money coming in I lost my flat and, listen to this, ended up moving in with my dad back in fucking Liverpool. Well, that was pretty disastrous as you can imagine, and I just woke up one morning and thought, 'Enough is enough.' Well. Admittedly I woke up in hospital after having my stomach pumped. I wouldn't mind, but I'd only gone out the day before to a kid's third birthday party.

I know. The shame.

I got a stern talking to from an A and E doctor and the hospital referred me here, and hey presto. Apparently I'm an alkie. Who knew? (Answer: everyone.)

I can't believe you're an agent. I have to be honest and say I still don't really know what a hair and make-up artist's agent actually does, but I always knew you'd achieve great things. Like, who writes a bleeding nativity play when they're fourteen or however old we were? And then *Supper with Sam*! I LOVED *Supper with Sam*. The next one (I have forgotten the title. Sorry!) was good too but *SwS* was just gorgeous! AND I WAS IN IT! AND I DIDN'T HAVE A DRINK IN MY HAND! Sometimes I cling to that memory, there was a time before the madness descended.

Oh God, I have to go. They're ringing the bell for dinner. It's very Agatha Christie in here.

I wish it was that exciting.

Big love

K xx

From: Adam Ferguson (adam@kenzimanagement.com)
Sent: 16 June 2005
To: Kathleen O'Hara (kathleenohara1970@hotmail.co.uk)
Subject: er . . .

Far be it from me to cast aspersions but you did have a drink in your hand in that scene where they were all getting pissed in the loft, before Sam arrived. But hey, they were fictional characters so don't give yourself a hard time. (That's my job.)

x

Adam Ferguson
Agent
Kenzi Management

From: Kathleen O'Hara (kathleenohara1970@hotmail.co.uk)
Sent: 16 June 2005
To: Adam Ferguson (adam@kenzimanagement.com)
Subject: Oh God . . .

That is hilarious that I'd wiped that scene from my mind.
D'you remember Jocelyn got all weird after the show and just
got off without so much as a by your leave?

Xx

P.S. What is a by your leave?

From: Adam Ferguson (adam@kenzimanagement.com)
Sent: 16 June 2005
To: Kathleen O'Hara (kathleenohara1970@hotmail.co.uk)
Subject: NO FUCKING IDEA LOVE

Xx

P.S. And even though she acted weird. THERE WAS NO NEED
TO SHAG HER BLOODY BOYFRIEND KATH!!!!!!!!!!!!!!
P.P.S. I'm so vile.
P.P.P.S. Like you care.

Adam Ferguson
Agent
Kenzi Management

From: Adam Ferguson (adam@kenzimanagement.com)
Sent: 21 June 2005
To: Kathleen O'Hara (kathleenohara1970@hotmail.co.uk)
Subject: Hello?

Hi K

Not heard from you for a few days, so just wanted to check everything was OK? Let me know anyway.

A x

P.S. I've met a man. He's GORGEOUS. Details on request!

P.P.S. Hands off.

P.P.P.S. That was a joke by the way.

Adam Ferguson

Agent

Kenzi Management

From: Kathleen O'Hara (kathleenohara1970@hotmail.co.uk)
Sent: 23 June 2005
To: Adam Ferguson (adam@kenzimanagement.com)
Subject: MEN

SORRY SORRY SORRY for the radio silence. Oh, the shit hit the fan here big time. Apparently I've been inappropriate by forging, let's just say it was a sexual relationship, with another inmate in here. God, Adam, you should see him. His name is Ethan (I know, isn't that such a cool name? People called Ethan only exist in American youth TV shows, right?) and I thought he was in for drugs, I didn't bother to ask, but he's not in my group therapy and because he's so gorgeous I didn't like to ask him what he was in for as it felt a bit rude and nosey and would have made me come across like I was obsessed with addictions, which I'm not, and . . . well, who

wants to talk about how you fuck things up when you're
flirting with someone? Oh yeah, that's going to give me the
biggest horn . . . 'And then I nearly died. Had to have my . . .'
fingers a tomato juice suggestively, licks finger – 'stomach
totally pumped . . .' EXACTLY. Not exactly a turn-on is it? I
worried for a bit that he wasn't as hot as I thought he was
because every other fella in here looks like Marty Feldman on
smack and like they've not washed their hair, or any other part
of their anatomy, for months. So to have him walking in all
spruced up, like a cut-price Keanu – no wonder he set my
pulse racing.

One of the women in here claims to be a folk singer. Her
name is Jess and she rocks a lot of knitwear. She's the sort
that's always plucking away at a guitar every night when the
rest of us are shouting at Tracy Barlow on the telly. Anyway,
one night she informed us she was going to give a concert
in the dining room, and the way the knobheads in here were
behaving you'd think that Coldplay themselves had been
booked. Anyway, the concert was of course a bit of a bore
with her self-penned hits – one was called 'Sobriety Society'.
I was a little bit sick in my mouth. Anyway Ethan kept on
looking over at me, so I kept pulling these 'I'm going to be
sick' faces, which really made him laugh, and I did a sort of
'hacking at my wrists' mime, which made a few people tut as
I'd forgotten that Jess is always slashing her wrists. Anyway,
the next thing I know Ethan is nodding towards the door. Then
he gets up and leaves. And so I took my courage in both
hands and followed. Next thing I know – God it happened
quicker than in a porn film and my washing machine had
broken down – we're making out in the bushes outside. And
so we continued for a few days until one of the counsellors
found out (Ethan reckons from Jess) and then the shit hit

the fan because . . . oh God . . . turns out Ethan is in for sex addiction.

I know. Sex addiction.

And it made me feel a bit weird because I was basically porn come to life for him. And although in some ways that's flattering, it turns out he wasn't exactly being exclusive with me. He was also doing self-harmer Helen, cocaine Caitlin and – ye gods – Peter the drinker. Any port and lemon in a storm, basically. And so he was in trouble, and I was in trouble, I'm sure Helen, Caitlin and Peter were too, but God, it was only a couple of shags. According to my counsellor this shows just how addictive my behaviour is, as this is cross-addiction. I give up. I really do. So I have had to have extra sessions (of therapy, not down the pub) and I wasn't allowed access to my phone or the wifi. When I said this was barbaric they said I needed to do a lot more work on my sense of entitlement. To which I replied, 'Am I entitled to tell you to fuck off?'

You can imagine how well that went down. Especially here in Colditz for junkies. And so I have been in purdah ever since.

Now. As your life is bound to be much less of a car crash than mine, I demand to know who this new man is.

In the meantime this period of isolation has of course really been making me think and working out where I go from here. And what I've been stressing about is finding a job where it doesn't matter too much that I've screwed up. That I've lost my job and ended up in some sort of nuthouse. And maybe there is a line of work where not only is this nothing to be ashamed of, but maybe it's a badge of honour that'll make you better at the job. Now you used to say to me what a good listener I was, remember? And so, thinking about the treatment I've been receiving in here, I've been thinking that maybe I will train as a counsellor.

I'm not going to tell any of the therapists or counsellors here that that's my plan, as it'd give them too much . . . oh, I don't know, smoke up their arses. They'd either love it – 'Oh look at me I'm so amazing and have helped you so much that you're going to train to become like me' – or they'd hate it. 'Only I can do this job. I am untouchable. I am GOD.' So I think it's best to keep it to myself and keep that zipped.

Be honest with me, Adam. Do you think that's a completely bonkers idea? It might of course just be that I've had too much time on my hands and I'm surrounded by therapists and counsellors at the moment, so it's the only thing I can think of, etc.

I thought I could find myself a little job in retail and become a Samaritan, to get some experience. At least that way I can be volunteering and not spending any money on courses etc. And I will be able to see if it suits me and if I am suited to it. What do you think?

God, I'm treating you like my bleeding careers advisor!! Sorry!

Hey. I've just thought. We have an open day next week. It's where friends and family can come and visit. We show them around and show them all the good work we're doing. If you fancy a day off and a trip to Derbyshire let me know, and I'll send you a visiting order.

(it's not really a visiting order)

Lots of love and TELL ME ABOUT THIS MAN

K xxx

From: Adam Ferguson (adam@kenzimanagement.com)
Sent: 1 July 2005
To: Kathleen O'Hara (kathleenohara1970@hotmail.co.uk)
Subject: Knackered but happy and GOSSIP

Oh Kath

It was so lovely to see you today, and you are looking so well. What a hoot. The place isn't half as horrendous as you'd led me to believe, and what views! Amazing. And it was like the years had slipped away. I don't care if we're thirty-five. When I see you again I'm fifteen.

But . . . oh GOD. Guess what?!

I got back and there was a message on my voicemail on my landline and it was Jocelyn and she'd somehow found out I was going to visit you and she was absolutely furious. I will see what Leon has to say when I go into work but she was calling me everything under the sun. 'That bitch fucked Leon and you're siding with her and . . .' well, most of it's not to be repeated in polite company. Oh, and it ended with 'Never speak to me again. Ever.' And then she hung up.

It was five years ago, love. Get over it, and yourself.

Hutch up, babe. There needs to be room in that doghouse for me too.

Speak soon

A xx

Adam Ferguson

Agent

Kenzi Management

From: Kathleen O'Hara (kathleenohara1970@hotmail.co.uk)
Sent: 1 July 2005
To: Adam Ferguson (adam@kenzimanagement.com)
Subject: SHITE

Oh no, that's awful. How on earth did she find out?

Xxx

P.S. I thought Jason looked hot in that photo you showed me.

From: Adam Ferguson (adam@kenzimanagement.com)
Sent: 1 July 2005
To: Kathleen O'Hara (kathleenohara1970@hotmail.co.uk)
Subject: Re: SHITE

I have a new PA. Remember I told you about her? We have to be nice to her because her dad's this really big photographer. Well, she has been known to have a big gob and she's the one who booked the trains and the driver for me, so it can only be her who blabbed. I'll fucking kill her. xxx

P.S. He totally is!
Adam Ferguson
Agent
Kenzi Management

From: Kathleen O'Hara (kathleenohara1970@hotmail.co.uk)
Sent: 1 July 2005
To: Adam Ferguson (adam@kenzimanagement.com)
Subject: WOW

Keep me posted. So sorry. xx

From: Adam Ferguson (adam@kenzimanagement.com)
Sent: 2 July 2005
To: Kathleen O'Hara (kathleenohara1970@hotmail.co.uk)
Subject: Leon

Leon was fine with me today, though he took me to one side
and said he had no intention of getting dragged into our row.
I told him I wasn't rowing with anyone and he just did a
small laugh. Clearly J is making his life hell at the moment.
I phoned her at lunchtime hoping to keep the peace but she
was having none of it. 'I thought I told you never to contact
me again. Well, I meant it, now fuck off.' And hung up. God,
she's got some brass neck.

   Oh well. I didn't see her for years. A few more ain't gonna
be a problem.

   Poor Leon, having to put up with the likes of that all the
time.

   Onwards and upwards . . .

   xx

   Adam Ferguson
   Agent
   Kenzi Management

From: Kathleen O'Hara (kathleenohara1970@hotmail.co.uk)
Sent: 2 July 2005
To: Adam Ferguson (adam@kenzimanagement.com)
Subject: I know . . .

He'd've been much better off with me. x
(Did I actually say that out loud?!)

From: Adam Ferguson (adam@kenzimanagement.com)
Sent: 2 July 2005
To: Kathleen O'Hara (kathleenohara1970@hotmail.co.uk)
Subject: You're incorrigible.

xx

    Adam Ferguson
    Agent
    Kenzi Management

From: Kathleen O'Hara (kathleenohara1970@hotmail.co.uk)
Sent: 2 July 2005
To: Adam Ferguson (adam@kenzimanagement.com)
Subject: Incorrigible . . .

Like him off the Sound of Music. x

From: Adam Ferguson (adam@kenzimanagement.com)
Sent: 3 July 2005
To: Kathleen O'Hara (kathleenohara1970@hotmail.co.uk)
Subject Re: Incorrigible.

DON'T GET KURT WITH ME.
    Xx
    P.S. Jason has asked me to move in with him. Well he
hasn't, but he has given me a key to his flat SO IT'S AS
GOOD AS.
    Adam Ferguson
    Agent
    Kenzi Management

From: Kathleen O'Hara (kathleenohara1970@hotmail.co.uk)
Sent: 4 July 2005
To: Adam Ferguson (adam@kenzimanagement.com)
Subject: a KEY?

Fuck me you'll be doing anal next. x

From: Adam Ferguson (adam@kenzimanagement.com)
Sent: 4 July 2005
To: Kathleen O'Hara (kathleenohara1970@hotmail.co.uk)
Subject: KATHLEEEEEN!

You are outrageous. I remember when you were nice. What
happened?! X
   Adam Ferguson
   Agent
   Kenzi Management

From: Kathleen O'Hara (kathleenohara1970@hotmail.co.uk)
Sent: 5 July 2005
To: Adam Ferguson (adam@kenzimanagement.com)
Subject: Seriously?

I discovered vodka. x

From: Adam Ferguson (adam@kenzimanagement.com)
Sent: 7 July 2005
To: Kathleen O'Hara (kathleenohara1970@hotmail.co.uk)
Subject: Call Me.

Call me when you get a minute. I have news. Leon has
dumped Jocelyn and kicked her out of his house. And the

gossip round the office is that he found out she was (still) working as LISTEN TO THIS – a hooker behind his back!!

She told me not to tell anyone but she did confide in me that she used to be a high-class hooker with some big posh agency and that's how come she was so loaded. She said Leon was dead understanding about it when they got together but she told me she had knocked it on the head when they got serious.

So according to Leon's PA he was sent a link to an escorting website and it was her page and she had some sort of false name. So to double-check and catch her out, he booked her using a false name and arranged to meet her in some hotel. Only, when she got to the hotel room he was waiting for her with a load of her stuff, and told her to get to fuck. And she apparently didn't even apologize, just got all huffy that she wasn't going to be paid!! Can you believe that?!

Babes, do you need somewhere to live when you get out of there? What are your plans? I was thinking you could use my flat as a base if you fancy, till you get on your feet. I'm going to be round at Jason's quite a bit so you'd have the place to yourself most of the time. Just a thought anyway. It's not the biggest flat in the world but it's nice and is near some shops in Tufnell Park and it's got a nice big bath! Let me know what you think. I won't be offended if you don't fancy it, or of course if you have other plans. I wouldn't want any rent as it wouldn't be for too long anyway. Have a think and let me know anyhoo.

xx

Adam Ferguson
Agent
Kenzi Management

From: Kathleen O'Hara (kathleenohara1970@hotmail.co.uk)
Sent: 8 July 2005
To: Adam Ferguson (adam@kenzimanagement.com)
Subject: WOW

What did I ever do to deserve a friend like you? That is so
SO kind of you Adam. I promise I won't outstay my welcome.
Oh how wonderful. YIPPEEE!!!

Thanks for everything!

K xx

P.S. I keep re-reading your email determined to discover
that all that stuff about Jocelyn was a joke but I realize you're
being completely serious. That is going to take me a while to
get my head around. A fucking PROSTITUTE?!?!?!?!?!?!?!

From: Adam Ferguson (adam@kenzimanagement.com)
Sent: 17 July 2005
To: Kathleen O'Hara (kathleenohara1970@hotmail.co.uk)
Subject: Tomorrow

Great to chat just now. Just to reiterate I will be waiting for
you at Euston when your train gets in and we can get a cab
back to the flat from there.

Let this new chapter of our lives . . . commence!!!!

Love you

A xxx

Adam Ferguson

Agent

Kenzi Management

JOCELYN

London, 2015

At first I didn't think he'd still be living on Josephine Avenue in Brixton. Not after all these years. Who would move to London to stay with relatives, and still be there fifteen or so years later? But a quick online search told me he was still on the electoral register there, and so that is where I went.

I could have asked my private detective. I could have asked him to track down my online troll, Darius D'Eath, on my behalf; but my gut told me, my instinct told me, I already knew the answer.

I'll be honest. I had called my private dick with the intention of getting him to find out who was sending me those hideous messages, but when we finally met up for me to set him the assignment, I had bottled out. Instead I found myself telling him about the old Polish man from the cafe, the strange woman who was taking his money. It was a big ask, but could he find out who she was? A few days later he emailed me some pictures of the woman, asking if it was her; a few days after that, he informed me that she was Alfred's prodigal daughter.

'You'd be surprised,' he said. 'But the answer so often is family.'

And that's when it crystallized in my mind, this thought that Billy was Darius D'Eath.

I mean, I could, of course, be completely wrong. Who's to say it's not Kathleen? Or Adam.

Who's to say it's not Mr Billericay, or Mr Love, or Finty?

Leon.

They all have reason enough to want to put the shits up me, but something keeps bringing me back to Billy.

Which is why I now find myself walking along Josephine Avenue, wondering what I will say when I see him. After all, this is hardly a 'Ding dong, Avon calling!' kind of moment.

In the movie version in my mind, which I've played time and time again in the run-up to this day, it would all be so straightforward. I would hang about in Brixton and he would magically appear. I would confront him, he would break down, apologize and all would be almost forgiven. What's a little murder or rape threat when it's amongst family, hmm? We would move on. We would progress.

But of course, no matter how much pacing up and down I do, he doesn't magically appear like Mr Benn's shopkeeper. So I go and find his house. And ring the bell. Which is when I discover there is nobody in.

Oh well. Plan B.

Plan B involves going off to do some shopping for a few hours, and coming back later. Which is what I do.

Then I ring the bell again.

This time, success.

The shock of seeing him in the flesh after so long, despite having traced him on social media, despite knowing what he looked like. To see it in online photos was one thing; in the flesh it is completely another. It's like seeing a celebrity for the first time, someone you are so familiar with but in the flesh there is difference of some sort. The difference with Billy being that the last time I saw him, that inauspicious night in Kettner's, he was a boy. And now he is definitely a man. The realization makes me falter. And when he realizes who I am, he falters too. Then I go in for the kill. I am not going to let the fact that he is a grown man, towering over me, stop me from having my say. And in order to be persuasive I have to be confident and convincing.

'Why did you do it?!'

'Jocelyn . . .' he gasps. And it's not a greeting, it's his mouth making noise before his brain tells him to stop.

'I know it was you. I know it is you.'

'What's me?'

And in that moment, I know I'm right. If he didn't have a guilty conscience he'd be instantly more combative, he'd tell me to piss off or get lost and send me on my way, or at least ASK what I'm doing here now, after all this time. But no, he joins in. He plays ball. I've got him.

'I don't know how you worked out I was Jamie-Lee, but you did. Well done.'

'I don't know what you're on about.'

'And guess what, Billy. I may have spent a lifetime showing you up, embarrassing you; well, you got your own back now.'

'I don't . . .'

'You think I'm sick and twisted? Well, the apple doesn't fall far from the tree. I've got every mind to go to the police.'

'You've got no proof!'

Ah, the confident veneer is cracking. Good.

'My private detective traced your IP address. Good work, Billy.'

His face freezes. I know I've won. I know he will now stop. I don't know whether to hit him or hug him. Instead I turn and walk away. It's a bright day, sunny. Light bounces off car roofs, workmen on scaffolding have their tops off. I could stop for a second and wonder at how I produced a son so capable of sending such hideous messages to a woman, intent on scaring her. Well, he picked on the wrong woman there. I could punish myself and say, well is it any wonder, after he was lied to for so long? But I won't let anything crack my veneer today. The traffic on Brixton Hill is at a standstill as I amble down towards the tube. I put my sunglasses on so no-one will recognize me. But then, this is Brixton. I will blend in just fine.

But then someone shouts from a car window, 'OI! CUNT! YOU BRING SHAME ON OUR COMMUNITY!'

I don't even look, though I am tempted to say, 'The juxta-position of the vulgarity of the word "cunt" and the preten-tiousness of "our community" is really rather sweet. Well done.'

Instead I hurry into the tube station. I swipe my card over the Oyster reader before descending into the bowels of hell: just another sunny day underground. The air is full of the smell of BO and the sound of an announcer warning us to always travel with a bottle of water, and my head is swim-ming. I have got away with it. I have got away with winging it with Billy and being correct about who was out to hurt me, and I feel kind of invincible. This feels good. My gut instinct was correct, and now I have put an end to it.

I don't need him in my life so I don't need to protect his feelings – he's certainly never protected mine – so I don't see why I should worry about any ongoing conflict between him and me.

He will do well in life, I'm sure. He has to, he has my genes. He was well dressed when he opened the door. Nicely turned out, groomed. He smelt of scent, soap. I have nothing to worry about there.

There is a tube about to depart. As the doors go to close I jump on, and someone follows suit behind me. They seem to get caught in the closing doors. I turn to help them.

It's him.

He wrestles free of the door, and it whizzes shut quickly. The carriage is full. The train lurches into action. We are almost glued together in the corner by the door. He leans in to me and speaks quietly. I don't know why I am so scared. I am amongst people, I am not alone. He can't hurt me when so many can see, surely? But the fact that he has followed me and I didn't realize unnerves me. And makes me wonder what else he is capable of.

'Can you blame me?' he asks.

I say nothing.

'My mother, the whore. Spouting all that bullshit to earn herself a dime.'

'A dime? How very transatlantic of you.'

'I mean. She can't even tell me who my dad is. That's how much of a slut she really is.'

He can see he is getting to me. He smiles.

'What's the matter, Jocelyn? I'm only doing what you do for a living. Saying it how it is.'

'You want to know who your dad is, little boy?' I spit back.

And now it's his turn to stay silent.

'OK then. I'll tell you.'

KATHLEEN

London, 2010

'Happy fortieth birthday, Kathleen!!'

The clink of glasses filled the air. I'd've liked to have said you could hear the pop of champagne corks drowning out the pianist, but as most of these people were my buddies from AA, it was more the fizz of Diet Coke bottles being unscrewed. Still, the buffet looked nice, if a little vegan-y. Lot of pulses. And a cheese and pineapple hedgehog because, as someone kindly pointed out, I was a child of the Seventies. We were in a room above a restaurant in Clapham and the jukebox was belting out Seventies classics to make me feel really at home. I vaguely recognized some of them. Oh God, this could be dreadful.

No. Come on, Kathleen. Relax. Enjoy your lentils. Enjoy yourself.

Life, finally, was good. After screwing around and screwing everything up, I had finally got things back on track. I had a job, working in the womenswear section at House of Fraser on Victoria Street. I had my own flat, renting from a glorious couple I'd met through AA, and I'd not had a drink for almost five years. And do you know what? It felt good. For the first time in as long as I could remember, I woke up in the

320

morning and my first thought wasn't *Oh SHIT. Who do I have to call to work out what I did last night?*

And I was finally getting some experience with counselling. I had gone on the Samaritans training course but they hadn't felt I was ready to join their ranks, and they'd asked me to return when I'd had a year out of rehab. Anyway, one night at AA I heard one of the members talking about a new telephone counselling service that had been set up to rival Samaritans. Going on the assumption that a lot of people got lonely or upset late at night, Late Night was now up and running in a few centres in London and around the country. I looked them up online, applied for an interview and then spent a few weekends doing their training courses. They didn't seem to mind that I was fresh out of rehab, and I'd been volunteering for them for nearly five years now.

I got a lot out of my time at Late Night. I volunteered once a fortnight and the service ran from eight at night to eight in the morning – spurring me to comment at the first training session I went to, 'Late night and early morning might be a better name.' Which had actually got a huge laugh, as if no-one had ever said it before. Now you might understand why I got so much out of volunteering there. They thought I was fecking hilarious!

Mostly, what I got out of working there was a satisfaction that I was doing something in life other than taking. I was giving something back. It might well have been a cliché, but for me it was true. I hoped that I was helping our callers in some small way, the way I had been helped by others over the years. There was a lot to be said for random acts of kindness, and there was a lot to be said for just listening when someone was in a bad way.

Life really had never been better.

The thirty-year-old me would have found the forty-year-old me deeply annoying, probably. I travelled everywhere by retro pushbike and always tried to do at least three random acts of kindness a day. I looked in regularly on some local old people, and I walked the dog of someone who was going through a nervous breakdown.

And guess what? It made me so happy.

It was on one of these dog walks that I met Harry. He had an elderly Jack Russell called Ajax who was on his last legs. Ajax had gone blind, and I thought it was so sweet because Harry spent the whole time on their walks ringing this cowbell thing to show Ajax which direction he was walking in. The kindness of it made my heart melt. For a few weeks we just exchanged the odd nod and pleasantry. And then eventually he asked me out for a drink, and I blurted out, 'I can't. I'm an alcoholic!' – which I hadn't meant to sound like the biggest knockback ever, but sadly, it did. So the next time I saw him I asked him out for dinner and he blurted out, 'I can't. I have an eating disorder!' and I kind of gasped, and then he laughed and I realized he was joking and it broke the ice, and now six months on I was about to move in with him, and everything was rosy.

See what happens when you keep your powder dry and do random acts of kindness? The universe pays you back. And it had paid me back with Harry Monroe. See? He even had a movie-star surname.

One of my AA pals came over, Viv. She was quite a bit older than me but one of those women who could quite easily have been forty-five or nearly sixty, you just couldn't tell. And she was extremely competitive. If you had a headache, she'd had her head amputated. Anyway, she was really into this Random Acts of Kindness thing and was always showing off about how she'd fed a small principality with the leftovers in her fridge and stuff, and it looked like tonight, even though it was my special party, was still going to be played on her showy-off terms.

'Hey, Kitty Kat.'

She always called me Kitty Kat. It really got on my twitty twat.

'Hey, Viv.'

Air kisses. Of course she air-kissed!

'Hippety-hoppety-happy birthday, presh!'

Yes. That was how she spoke.

'Thanks, hon.' Usually I detested people who used the H word, but she brought out the worst in me.

'I know it's your birthday and stuff, but have you done your randoms today?'

'Yeah, I went and bought a homeless guy a coffee from McDonald's,' I said.

She pulled a face. 'Poor thing, McDonald's coffee is hideous.'

'How about you?'

'My cleaning lady was telling me how her juicer had broken? So I gave her my old one. She actually cried.'

'Oh, that's so sweet of you, Viv.'

'I know. I've just become really altruistic since I knocked the old boozy-woozy on the head.'

'Well, guess what?' I said, knowing I was going to TROUNCE her out of the ballpark.

'What?!' She looked concerned. She knew I was going to one-up the tits off her.

'I'm leaving my own fortieth birthday party to go and volunteer at Late Night. You know? The counselling service I volunteer at?'

She paled. She looked like she might vomit. Then she rubbed my arm and I could see her thinking, *I have to let it go, it's her fortieth.* She rubbed my arm. 'Saint Kathleen of the telephone counselling.'

I'll have that, I thought.

The party was soon winding down. The good thing about a load of alkies is that even though they're on the Diet Cokes, they're usually knackered by the time most normal parties are about to kick off. And I'd purposefully had my party in the afternoon so it kept me free to go to Late Night. I know most people thought I was mad to be volunteering there on the night of my actual birthday; but when the rota had come up and I saw I'd been allocated this slot, I was going to cancel it, but then I thought, oh sod it, why not? I enjoyed it. If it was a quiet night I got to watch a bit of TV and stuff my face on chocolates, and if it was a busy night the minutes and hours flew by.

Late Night was the brainchild of a woman called Angela-Dawn, who wore brightly coloured kaftans and had dyed green hair. If you Googled 'stereotypical tree-hugging bleeding heart' you'd probably come up with a photo of her. You didn't see much of her once you were working there, but her presence could be felt throughout. Everything about the offices was touchy feely. There were inspirational quotes painted on the walls. Things like, *Small lights have a way of being seen in a dark world.* Alongside a photo of a tealight.

The offices, such as they were, were above a kebab shop on the Holloway Road. They comprised three main rooms – one where you took the calls, one containing two single beds for volunteers to sleep in, and a meeting room in case callers dropped by. And there was a tiny bathroom and toilet.

You only ever worked in pairs. One man, one woman, so

that callers always had someone of a gender they felt comfortable talking to. This particular night my colleague was a guy I'd done several shifts with, Noel, a mixed-race guy with a soft Scottish accent. He was reading a newspaper when I arrived, tutting and shaking his head.

'What's up?' I asked.

'Oh, this Wikileaks thing.'

'Oh yeah, that.' I had no idea what he was talking about.

'All the stuff about the war with Afghanistan, amazing.'

'I know, right?' Again, still no idea. 'Right! What's on the telly?'

And I switched on the portable that sat on our mutual desk. I flicked through the channels. 'Let's hope it's a busy night, then, there's fuck-all on.'

He gave me that look – as if to say he wasn't sure if I was joking or not, but rather hoped I was. So I came over all Viv with him, and leaned in conspiratorially. 'Ignore me. I'm just a bit bonkers coz it's my birthday. And it's quite a big one.'

'Fifty?' he said, a bit too quickly.

I shook my head. I clearly looked horrified.

'I'm only joking!' he said – again, a bit too quickly. Which told me he had not been. BASTARD. So I busied myself with the log book, as I told him about my amazing birthday party.

Basically, Angela-Dawn liked us to keep a log of every call we took. Although we claimed to be a confidential organization, she felt we should write down in as much detail as possible what each caller said and how we helped them. It meant that we could keep an eye on regular callers, of which there were several. It was also meant to help us process the call and the effect that it might have had on us. For me, also, it made a great read when I arrived for each session. It was better than *Valley of the Dolls*!

I was just getting stuck into a written description of some-one who had phoned up while clearly masturbating, when the phone rang. Noel and I looked to each other. He held his hand out, indicating that I should answer.

'Well, it's your birthday,' he said, sarcastically. Which I didn't like. But I answered it anyway.

'Late Night, Kirsty speaking. How can I help you?'

Angela-Dawn's rule was we all had to have false names, just so the callers couldn't track us through Facebook and kill us or something.

The person on the other end of the phone was crying.

'Take your time.'

It was a woman. She sounded very distressed. I stood, and took the phone into the bedroom so that Noel wouldn't put me off, and so that he could put the telly on if he wanted. I must have waited a good minute or so before she finally spoke.

I recognized her voice immediately.

It was Jocelyn.

And she talked away. She talked away, because as far as she was concerned, this was a confidential call and my name was Kirsty. Why wouldn't it be?

'What's your name, my love?' I asked, like a concerned mother. All soft and gentle.

When she said 'Lindsey,' I still knew it was her. If I could be Kirsty, she could be whoever she wanted. It was, it was her.

I asked her why she was upset.

'I have this boyfriend. Mr Billericay. And he puts this pres-sure on me.'

Mr Billericay? What kind of a name was that?

'And I should just tell him what happened to me in the past, because . . . oh, what's the point? It's like . . . like I can only cope with bastards because of what happened to me back then.'

'Aha?'

What did happen to you back then? I let space hang in the air. I knew she would fill it, and she did.

'I come from Liverpool. I know you can't tell by my voice. But I had to go back to Liverpool this week for work, and . . .'

She started crying again.

Liverpool.

Lovely.

I should have stopped the call at that point. I should have explained that I thought I might know who she was, and that I needed my colleague to take over. But I didn't. I didn't even get excited. I just relaxed. I lay back on the single bed. And went along for the ride.

'I've not really been back there since . . . since . . .'

'Since what, Lindsey?'

'Since I ran away.'

'And why did you run away, Lindsey? What was making you so upset? Take your time. But there must've been something.'

God, I was going a bit off-piste with my responses. I was sounding almost accusatory. But she didn't seem to mind.

'I had a child. A little boy. And I left him there with my mum. She wanted to bring him up because I was so young. She made out he was hers. I've hardly seen him since.'

'That must've been tough, Lindsey.'

'Sometimes.'

Oh. Bit hard-faced.

'And the other times?'

'Other times it was easy. I looked and him and hated him. Because he reminded me of . . . he reminded me of . . .'

And there she went again, with her crying.

Maybe I should fill in the blanks, I thought.

Because he reminded you of Mark Reynolds, love? Is that it, Lindsey?

That would've freaked her out.

And then she said it. Quietly. Quickly. But it was out there.

'I was raped.'

I sat up quickly, my stomach lurching.

'I'm sorry?'

'I was raped,' she said again, louder this time, and sounding maybe a bit pissed off.

'Who raped you, Lindsey? Your boyfriend?'

'No.'

'D'you think it would help to tell me?'

'It was my mum's boyfriend.'

I tried to cast my mind back to all those years ago. I couldn't think of who her mum was with at the time. And then I remembered: that's why Adam surmised that Jocelyn's mum hadn't been pregnant, because she didn't actually have a boyfriend.

'He'd just come out of prison and was kind of hiding out in our house.'

My stomach lurched again.

'Mum was sort of seeing him, and then he took this shine to me. I didn't want anything to do with it. But he forced himself on me. She walked in on it. And she had the cheek to kick me out, and not him. My own mum found me being raped, and took his fucking side.'

Prison?

I now had to physically stop myself from being sick.

Jocelyn started to cry again. 'And what made it worse was that he was my friend's dad. So I couldn't tell her. I couldn't tell anyone. And they wouldn't have believed me anyway. Like she never believed me. They had me down as the local slut. And then Mum came up with this plan. To hide it all, and say the baby was hers. I wanted nothing more than to get rid of it. I wish I had got rid of it. I lost so much that night. I lost everything.'

I dropped the phone. I ran to the bathroom, threw myself on the floor and vomited into the toilet.

Noel hurried in. 'You OK?'

I shook my head, kneeling by the toilet.

Could that be true? Had my dad hid away at Jocelyn's house after getting out of the nick? Had he been sleeping with Jocelyn's mum, and then raped Jocelyn?

I was sick again.

'Is it food poisoning?' Noel asked.

I nodded my head. 'Fucking party caterers,' I said. 'The caller's still on the line.'

Noel nodded, then hurried into the bedroom. I heard his reasonable tones.

'I'm so sorry, but Kirsty has been taken ill rather suddenly. Would it be OK for me to talk to you? My name's Neil. What's yours?'

I stood. I washed my face in cold water. Dried it on one of the dayglo towels that Angela-Dawn had decided would stop us all from getting depressed. And then I walked out of Late Night, and I knew I would never go back.

I stood outside on the busy, smoky street. *It is my fortieth birthday*, I think, *and I've just discovered my dad is a rapist.*

My dad raped my friend from school, and she was only fourteen.

This was too much for me to handle. This was too much of a coincidence. I happened to be doing a shift at Late Night and I get a phone call from an old mate, and she tells me that? Oh, I got it. It was one of those TV prank shows. Someone was going to step out from behind that phone box over the road, laughing. A camera crew would file out of the kebab shop. Noel would come out behind me, pissing himself. Jocelyn would pull up in a limo, switching off her mobile, screeching *You fell for it! Oh that was TOO MUCH! Oh Kathleen! You are funny!*

I waited. I looked around. No-one came.

I forced a smile in case anyone was watching, filming. I even did a laugh, hollow though it was, as if to convey that I wasn't stupid and I had got the joke.

And I wasn't stupid.

And it wasn't a joke.

But coincidences like that didn't just happen, did they? Might Jocelyn have known I was working there, and . . . but how would she have known? It was a confidential service. I hardly told a soul I went there. I don't think I'd even told Adam, though I couldn't remember. And even if she did know, how would she have worked out when I was doing a shift? And that my name was 'Kirsty'?

It was just too weird for words.

Hearing her voice, hearing her cry, hearing her.

Too, too weird.

And what she'd told me. How could that have happened? How could that have happened and I didn't know? Say what you like about my dad, but he wasn't a rapist.

Was he?

According to Jocelyn, he so was.

Was it a one-off thing? Did he make a habit of it? Had he done it to other girls? Was this the real reason that my mum had left? Had he got into trouble with someone else and she'd had enough and just . . . scarpered? Was this one of the reasons he'd spent so much time in prison over the years? Not so much armed robbery as sexual assault?

I had so many questions, and nobody to ask. My nan was long gone, and Dad was currently back inside for . . . God, that was bad; I couldn't even remember what he was in for.

But one thing was sure. What Jocelyn had said had a strong whiff of authenticity about it. Whereas some rape allegations, people think, *Hang on. Rewind there. Are you sure that's what happened?* – I knew. I just knew.

I believed her.

I tried to figure it all out, but it was too much for my head to handle. I was a phone with too much on the memory card. I was about to implode.

Something across the road caught my eye.

The Mother Red Cap. A pub. It looked so warm, so welcoming. I was shaking. I knew I would go in. I ordered a large vodka and tonic, and downed it almost in one.

There was a folk singer sitting on a small stage at the far end of the pub, hunched over a guitar and a microphone. And – oh, as if this couldn't be any better stage-managed! Surely this was a set-up too – he was singing that song about fathers and sons, 'Cats in the Cradle'. About dads being a good role model, and being busy, and the sons growing up to be like them, and . . .

'Oh why aren't they just singing "I've Written a Letter to Daddy" and have done with it?' I said, to no-one in particular. And then I added, with a desperate giggle, 'Or "Thank heavens for little girls"!'

Because there was no getting away from it. If he had forced himself on a schoolkid, we all knew what that made him.

And yeah, OK, so Jocelyn had been, let's just say, well

developed for her age, but there was no getting away from the fact that she was not a grown-up. She was a kid. Which made him . . . I couldn't even say it. I couldn't even admit it to myself. I certainly doubted I would ever be able to say it out loud.

I turned to leave. I needed air. And then . . .

THIS HAD TO BE A SET-UP. BUT WHERE WERE THE CAMERAS?

There was a man approaching the bar dressed in fancy dress, as Jimmy Savile.

'Oh, come on. A joke's a joke. What's going on? I can't take any more of this!' I said to him.

WHERE WERE THEY? COME ON, CAMERAS!

'Sorry?'

'Yeah, I'm talking to you, Jimmy Savile.'

'I don't know what you're talking about.'

'Oh, come on. The bleached bob. The sunglasses. The shell suit. The guide dog.'

Oh. This person had a guide dog. And had quite a high-pitched voice. I then realized it wasn't someone in fancy dress, it was just a blind woman in a shell suit with dreadful hair.

I'd just told a blind woman she looked like Jimmy Savile. Time to find another pub.

Oh well. It had been a traumatic night. But the vodka had done the trick; I was starting to feel better. And the jumbled thoughts made more sense in my head. I had another.

Jocelyn must have been raped the night before her birthday. So that when Adam and I called round for her, and her mother was distressed, and claimed Jocelyn was in Toxteth . . . oh my God. My dad must've been inside there, too. We'd heard raised voices. She was probably rowing with Dad about . . .

And then Jocelyn had had nowhere to turn apart from

the one place she associated with being a safe haven. She couldn't come to my house – my dad had just attacked her. She couldn't go to Adam's because his mum was the biggest gossip in the area. But she could go to the loft at the church. And maybe she went there in tears, and Mark looked after her. Or maybe she didn't tell him. But she went there, and would have been in no fit state to have sex with him, as we assumed she had the next morning.

My dad had returned home that day. He had had bruises on his arm. He had had a long soak in the bath . . . was he washing the evidence off him?

And poor Jocelyn. Her mum hadn't believed her. Her mum had . . . what . . . accused her of seducing her boyfriend?

And Billy. As well as being her son, he was my bloody brother. Half brother. Sired by a father I couldn't even remember the last time I'd seen.

And there me and Adam had been, convinced she'd been fooling around with Mark that night. Mark who I was in love with. She HADN'T ignored my feelings and got off with him. Yet all these years, I'd been convinced she had. I'd even gone as far as to sleep with her man, so she'd get a taste of her own medicine. And she'd been the innocent party all along.

But the worst thing. The worst thing was all those promises we'd made. That night in the loft. With the bauble. The three of us, frozen in time in a glass ball, like the Wise Men and . . . one for all and . . .

She'd not been able to tell her two best friends that she had been raped.

Great friends we'd turned out to be.

Actually, *was* that the worst thing?

The worst thing, surely, was that I'd found out my father had a penchant for raping kids. He had done that thing that most people considered worse than murder. And what was even worse was I didn't know if he was still doing it. I didn't know if Jocelyn had been a one-off. But I couldn't believe it had been.

I mean, if you had the brass-necked arrogance to force yourself on a kid, thinking they'd never tell anyone, well surely if you could do that once, you could do it more times? And over the years, how many times had he done it? He hadn't done anything like that with me, at least I could thank my lucky stars for that. But how many times had he robbed other girls of their childhoods? He was. He was a robber of childhoods, a killer of dreams, a squasher of confidences.

Oh, why dress it up? Why be poetic about it? There was nothing, NOTHING poetic about what he was. He was a child rapist.

I had never felt this strange before. Never felt this repulsed. I had never felt this ashamed. I could feel the shame prickle round my body like an angry rash that I wanted to scratch. It's true, I wanted to claw at my skin. Rip off my clothes and tug at my flesh, peel my epidermis off and somehow get myself cleansed, but I didn't know how. I felt my stomach contracting in tiny, tight spasms and before I knew it I was doubled over in the gutter, retching my guts up. It was like I was puking up my pain, vomiting up my shame, but the sad thing was that neither disappeared as the bile swilled in the gutter.

I wiped my mouth with my sleeve, dabbed my eyes with my hands and staggered to my feet.

There was only one thing for it. Only one thing that could numb this pain.

I pushed my way into the next bar I arrived at. It was a Mexican place called El Grande Burrito. Someone was dancing on a table. Looked like fun. I walked through the crowded bar, smiling at strangers like they were old pals. This time I got a tequila to go with my vodka. Well, you know, when in Rome. Or Cancún. Or whatever the capital of Mexico is.

I liked tequila. I'd forgotten just how much.

Before long, I felt slightly less ashamed. My prickly skin was soothed. I didn't think of my dad raping Jocelyn all the time.

I even managed a smile.

Oh well. Looked like I was drinking again.

ADAM

London, 2015

Jay-Jay Velazquez bounded into my office, red with fury, brandishing a tabloid, which he slapped down on my desk.

'Have you seen this? The BASTARD. What a BITCH!'

Jason popped his head round the door with an 'I let him in. Sorry!' look on his face.

'What's happened, Jay-Jay?'

'Your so-called friend.'

'Jocelyn? What's she done now?'

'Your piss is gonna boil. Read it. READ IT!'

I didn't think I'd ever seen him so angry.

'Call her. And tell her she's a cunt from me.'

And with that, Jay-Jay stomped off back into the hall. A few seconds later we saw him through the French window, out in the garden, lighting up a ciggie.

'I see he's back on the fags again,' Jason commented, then we both peered at the paper.

And there it was. Jocelyn's latest column.

GAYBIES? PUT THE HOURS IN, FELLAS!

Listen. I love a gay as much as the next fag hag. They're the perfect accessory. No party is complete without one. Who else is going to start the bopping off to 'It's Raining Men' and 'In the Navy'? Your GBF (gay best friend), that's who. And yeah, sure, I'm all for gay marriage (though if I hear any more about it then I might have to take a machete to my own skull, pur-lease!) and . . . OK . . . I agree, two guys bringing up a little 'un is really sweet and appealing, and I'm sure they can do it as well as us heterozies.

Heterozies? What the . . .

But . . . let me give you an example here. I heard of some chums of mine. And they were so desperate to appear normal (pur-lease, what IS normal? It's just a cycle on my washing machine, bitches) that they wanted to have an ickle baby.

Well, you know how much I love them, mofos!!

And yes, give them their due, they didn't rent out a designer vagina to sire one of their own lookey-likey offspring. Instead they did the decent thing, the socially wonderful, generous thing, of adopting. And before you could say, 'Whoops, you is gonna get baby puke on dem Prada trainers, fellas,' they had a baby in da house.

But GET THIS.

Do they look after this kiddywinkle themselves?

No.

Because guess what.

They have . . . A NANNY.

'How the fuck does she know?' I gasped, looking at Jason. He was biting his bottom lip with fury. He shrugged.

'Leon might have told her?'

'Leon doesn't speak to her. He wouldn't piss on her if she was on fire.'

'Maybe she has other friends who . . .'

'I mean, she's not really our friend any more.'

'We can't be the only gay couple who . . .'

'Even if it's not aimed at us, it's still bang out of order.'

Before I could read any more of it, Jason had crumpled it up and dropped it in the bin.

'Where does she get off?' I said.

'She doesn't. She doesn't ever get off. She just stays on board the HMS Cuntiness for the rest of time.'

He leaned in to me, and pecked me on the forehead.

'Don't let her get to you.'

'I'll kill her.'

'No, you won't.'

'I'd like to.'

'Bit of a queue ahead of you. Every decent person in this country she's offended already.'

He had a point.

'Anyway. As we gave our nanny a month off to go visit her rellies in Australia, I'm going to take him to school. Shocking, eh? Jocelyn Jones?'

'Shocking,' I agreed. And he headed out.

I looked to the bin and realized I was shaking with anger. How dare she! How dare she be so . . . so demeaning about what we had gone through? We had given Denim a much better life than he had ever had before and now he was fed, clothed, watered and loved. If she'd bothered to ask before spouting forth I could have told her that we agreed to have a nanny to fit the criteria of what his social workers wanted. That there'd be a female influence in his life as well as ours. It was yet another hoop we'd had to jump through. But oh no, she just went mouthing off for money. And whereas usually it felt like her articles were outrageous for the sake of it – that she'd say what she liked for the shock value and you were left wondering whether she actually meant it – this one felt weirdly authentic.

I knew what had happened to Denim before he was taken into care. It was the sort of stuff that would make your hair curl. But then, I remembered, Jocelyn was the sort who had abandoned her child as well. Only this mother didn't leave him in his crib while she went off gallivanting. She left him in Liverpool, being brought up by his grandmother, while she went off getting up to all sorts.

But then. One night she'd hinted at something. And I couldn't tell if it was attention-seeking or her being truthful. Well, she'd hinted that one of her mum's boyfriends had abused her and . . .

Oh, she was probably lying.

Don't make me out to be a bad parent, Jocelyn. I'm a million times better than you. And I always will be.

I thought of Kathleen. We'd not spoken in a while. Actually, now I came to think of it, we'd probably not spoken in a few years. But I remembered I had meant to call her a few months before, when Jocelyn did that piece that was so obviously aimed at Kathleen. When she went on about never trusting people who'd had plastic surgery. That they got a new lease of life and fucked your husband. I'd meant to get in touch, but then worried that maybe she'd not even seen the article, so maybe it was best to let it lie.

Why would Jocelyn be attacking us in this way? What had I ever done – apart from visit Kathleen when she was in Jocelyn's bad books – to hurt her? Very little, from what I could work out. And yet here were these poisonous attacks.

And then there was the whole passive-aggressive air to it. All the 'oh look I really support the gays but . . .'.

I looked out of the window again. Jay-Jay was lighting up his second fag.

I snatched up my phone. Scrolled through my contacts. Then called her.

It rang out for a while, to the point where I thought it would go to voicemail. Good. I would give her what for in an angry voice message, the way she'd given ME what for all those years ago.

But then she picked up.

And was all sweetness and light.

'Baby boy! What a gorgeous surprise!'

'Don't you fucking baby boy me, missy! I've seen your newspaper column. I know you're having a go at me.'

'Which one?'

'Which one? Which one? You know which fucking one, Jocelyn. Well, I'll have you know that in order to get this kid in our care we had to prove that there'd be a female influence in his life, and thank God that influence was our nanny and not you.'

'You've got a baby?'

'Don't come the innocent with me, arlarse.'

'I had no idea.'

'Oh fuck off, Jocelyn.'

'I didn't. I'm so sorry. When I write those columns I just . . .'

'D'you know what, Jocelyn? Like you said to me when you told me never to contact you again, just coz I went to see someone in rehab: I'm not interested in your lies and excuses. You've done your worst. I've said my piece. Now let's go back to the status quo where we never speak to each other again.'

She said it again, quietly. 'I'm so sorry.'

'Coz if you don't shut up about my kid, I'll go to the press about yours. Now do I make myself clear? Never EVER criticize my parenting skills again. Or you know what'll happen.'

And before letting her say anything else, I hung up. And heard a round of applause.

I looked over and saw that Jay-Jay had come into the room.

'Go Adz!' he said, then stopped clapping.

I couldn't help but smirk. I felt so much better for my little rant.

'If you were gonna kill someone, Jay-Jay, how would you do it?'

'Ooh, I like this game. Let's walk and talk.'

We walked down Kentish Town High Street. When I'd first moved here ten years ago it had been a rough-and-ready mix of native working-class folk and the odd pretentious wannabe. In recent years, as all over the London, the wannabes had taken over and created the asylum. Where once an underground public lavatory sat, it has now been converted into a subterranean wine bar that served cocktails in those pretend-jam-jar things. It was called Ladies and Gentlemen. And as I pointed out to Jay-Jay, I'd had a much better time there when it had been a pissoir extraordinaire.

Jay-Jay cackled, and then fixed me with a glare.

'You asked me how I'd kill someone. I like games like this.'

'Who said it was a game?' I countered, provocatively. He liked it when I was cheeky.

'I have the perfect way to kill someone,' he said. 'I'd employ them to send out my Christmas cards. So they had to lick hundreds of envelopes.'

'Sounds ominous. I send out your flaming cards.'

'I know, but I don't hate you. And then I'd lace the sticky bit on the envelopes with something like hemlock.'

'Hemlock?! How old-school!'

'I know, right?'

We chuckled for a bit.

'Hemlock kills people in the following way. It acts as a paralytic that keeps the mind awake. It takes out the muscles, then attacks the respiratory system. Death comes from, get this, waking asphyxiation.'

'You seem to know a lot about it.'

'When you've ingested as many chemicals as I have, you get to know a thing or two.'

'I'm never coming to you for my blue rinse. I'd be leaving in a wooden box.'

'Why? How would you kill someone?'

'Oh, I'm a bit boring, really.'

'What, bore them to death?'

'I'd make it look like suicide. Set it all up so they look like they had a reason to do it. Then just do it for them. Gunshot to the head, food poisoning.'

'I like your style.'

'Or, you know. Push them from a tall, tall building.'

Our laughter grew guttural as we turned onto Highgate Road.

JOCELYN

London, 2015

It's hot on the tube, and sweat is forming in the crevice above his top lip. I wanted to see him sweat, the way he made me sweat. But now I've told him, I feel nothing but guilt.

'I don't believe you. You're lying. It's . . . it's a sob story.'

'It's not *The X Factor*, Billy.'

'Do you really want to hurt me that much?'

'I did, yes.'

'Yeah, so you made that up.'

'Why would I make something as sick as that up?'

He looks angry. He actually looks like he might hit me.

'You know,' I continue, 'I used to wonder how you could be so evil to me. But I guess you were born of evil, so it's coming out now.'

'Don't say that.'

'I'm only telling you the truth. It's what you wanted to know, isn't it? Who your bloody dad was? Well, now you know. So you see. I wasn't a slut, I wasn't a whore. I was a fourteen-year-old girl and that dirty bastard forced himself on me. Now I'm sorry, Billy. I know it's not what you wanted to hear, but it's the truth. And it's why I had to get away. Because every time I looked at you, I was back there. That night. And it was too much for me to handle.'

The energy between us is so intense. The tube is now packed and we are speaking so firmly but quietly that, although nobody else can make out what we're saying, people are looking over. It's obvious there's some major disagreement going on.

'Is he hassling you, love?' a stranger asks.

'No. No, he's not.'

'You sure, love?' someone else asks.

They might not be so nice if I didn't have my shades on so they can't see who I am. I look back to Billy. We're pulling into King's Cross now, and this is where I change.

'I get off here, Billy.'

He says nothing. But when the doors open and I step off, I am aware that he is following me still. And when I get on the connecting tube, I see him step into this carriage with me too. He sits a few seats down from me and avoids eye contact. It's like he can't help himself. He can't bear me but can't bear to be away from me, now that he knows the truth. Maybe he's working out his feelings. Maybe he is realizing for the first time that I am not all bad. But also, maybe he is hating himself. It must be the most awful thing imaginable, to learn that you weren't born of love or even carelessness. That you were born of evil. That must be some cross to carry.

He asked for it.

He did.

It's what he wanted to know, and now he does. He knows the truth.

When I get off at Westbourne Park, he is following me still. As we get to the flats I turn and look at him.

'What do you want, Billy?'

'A glass of water.'

I buzz us both up.

He looks round the flat silently.

'Thought it'd be posher than this.'

'Nothing is ever quite as you imagine, eh?'

He rolls his eyes and does the most sarcastic laugh. I get him a glass of water from the fridge.

'Bottled. Now that's posh.'

'Not really.'

He downs it in one. He sits on my sofa. This is not quite how I envisaged today panning out.

'Well,' he finally says, 'there's one way I can work out if you're telling me the truth or not. I mean, for all I know you seduced this fella.'

'I certainly did not.'

'Who was he? What was his name?'

'I'm not prepared to tell you that.'

'I'll find him.'

'How?'

'I'll ask the woman from the sweet shop.'

'Dorothy? Adam's mum?'

'She usually knew everything, from what our darling sisters told me. Or I can ask them. Or Grandmama. I'll find out, Jocelyn, you know I will. "Who was Mum seeing when Jocelyn got pregnant?" It won't take long. So you may as well just tell me now.'

'My word not good enough for you?'

'Of course not. You lie for a living. I bet you don't believe half the bullshit you write.'

'I didn't write this. It happened.'

He goes and looks out of the window.

'That's quite some view. Can I go on the balcony?'

I unlock the door, and he walks out. He peers over the concrete wall.

'It's a long way down.'

He is unnerving me.

'Davey,' I say. 'His name was Davey O'Hara.'

He looks at me and smiles. 'Thank you.'

He asks for my phone number. Says he'll want to be keep-ing in touch. I give it to him. He'd only find another way otherwise. He leaves.

KATHLEEN

London, 2015

You see, the thing is, I wish I could remember where I was. That night. That night that Jocelyn died. But I can't. And I hate myself. And of course my biggest, biggest fear is that I killed her. That I pushed her off the top of the flats and ended her life.

It's night time now. Adam left first so thinks I was just going to finish off tidying up and sorting a few bits and pieces, but here I am, sipping a glass of wine, standing on the balcony, looking at the last view she saw of London before she went down.

You'll go down for this. That's what they used to say on the docks in Liverpool. Isn't it?

My nan was married to a docker. She told me. She must have.

Oh no, they used to say, *There's nothing down for you.*

See? I can't even remember phrases right.

What did they do? That's it. They used to put the names of the dockers on a piece of paper and nail it to the wall and the dockers would come, and if their name was on the list they'd be working that day. Bit like a zero-hours contract. And if they hadn't made the list the others would say, *There's nothing down for you.*

I can't remember if I have been to this flat before.

I can't remember if I killed my friend.

If I did, I appear to have got away with it.

And yet . . . and yet . . . something about this building feels so familiar. As if I've seen it in a dream. As if I've seen it in a drunken stupor.

I've been drinking to forget for so long now that I've almost forgotten what I'm trying to forget. And sometimes that's felt nice. But since Jocelyn died it's brought it all back in sharp focus. So the booze and the occasional sleeping pill makes the edges fuzzier and that's much preferable.

Why would I have killed her? I had no reason to kill her. Unless I was being belligerent and I was in her flat, and we were rowing, and I pushed her. But does that really sound like me?

I always think I'm a nice drunk. But then I remember the shame of Harry telling me how horrible I was to that waiter, that time in Pizza Express. He was in tears, I was so vile. And of course, I have no recollection.

And there is a whole period of time unaccounted for on the night she went. I remember drinking in Soho and rowing with someone on a street. Vague memories of being kicked out of a cab. Dried mud on the ground. And then I woke up in a flat I didn't recognize. There was a man lying next to me. A black guy. I had no idea who he was, though admittedly I didn't see his face. I was so mortified, I dressed and fled. I appeared to be in Brixton. No memory of going back there.

So maybe I didn't go to Jocelyn's. Maybe I got kicked out of the cab and this black guy rescued me. I don't think I slept with him in the physical sense, as I was fully clothed and so, I think, was he. But I know what I get like with the devil inside me. Let's just say I can get quite . . . amorous.

So I don't know who my angel was. And it's doubtful I ever will.

Maybe I should start doing random acts of kindness again.

Well, I've done one today. I've started sorting out Jocelyn's flat. But I know deep down I wanted to come here to see if anything here was familiar. Outside, it was. But I don't know if that's just from looking the flats up online.

If I drink more, I might remember. I will be in the state I was in that night, and maybe it will spark some memory.

I want to stay here forever. I have nowhere else to go. I could hide away here, barricade the door, and it could be Jocelyn's gift to me, her legacy. But then, what does she really owe me? She owes me nothing. I treated her appallingly, and all she ever did was try to protect me. She never once told me what had happened between her and my dad. She could have, so easily. To hurt me, to spite me, to bring me down a peg or two. Especially bearing in mind everything I did to her. But no, she kept her counsel. And it must have bothered her, it must have plagued her. So much so that five years ago she called a telephone counselling service to discuss it. I would like to think that eventually she found some peace. But if she killed herself, clearly she was tormented.

I've drunk all the wine. It lasts such a short time.

I want to pick out landmarks on the horizon. But they seem to have shifted. Maybe I'm more pissed than I thought I was, but I can't see the things I saw earlier. It's gone dark. Maybe they're not lit up. But I can't remember what it is I'm trying to see.

I look over the balcony. I can see the parched mud way, way below. I dangle the empty wine bottle over the side, then release it from my grasp. It falls silently. And then eventually it smashes. I hardly hear that noise, it's so far away. And then

I think how wonderful it must feel, to fall silently. To smash, and nobody hears you.

That must have been what it was like for Jocelyn.

Who said death was an awfully big adventure?

It was somebody.

Maybe it was me.

Was it Peter Pan?

How glorious that Jocelyn fell like that. Silently. And then smashed.

I consider following suit. It would be so easy. I wouldn't make headlines like she did. Not many would come to my funeral, like they did hers. I lean over and stare. It would only take seconds. And then all this suffering would be over. I get it. I get it now, why she did it.

And then I feel a hand on my shoulder. It pulls me back forcefully. Adam must have returned. But how did he let himself in? I turn to ask, and see that no-one is there.

Was it you? I wonder. *Was it you, Jocelyn?*

But of course no answer comes.

I go through to her bedroom and climb into her bed. I want to feel close to her.

It's nice she tried to stop me. Well, she did stop me. It's like she forgives me.

Her sheets are crisp still. They smell like summer meadows. Actually, I don't know what summer meadows smell like, but I imagine it's like these sheets. Maybe it's Lenor, or something. Anyway, it's nice.

I feel myself drifting off. Sleep time.

A thought makes me surface. A thought I have often now. If I didn't come here that night, I wish I had. I'd always wanted to tell her that I knew. And in some way, offer up an apology. I know what my dad did wasn't my fault, but he is my kin and

I owed her something, surely. And to apologize for not being there for her. And for her not feeling able to tell me. To tell her I knew, and I was on her side. If I had come here that night, that's what I would have said. And I don't know if I did. And now she's not here to ask. I have this strong feeling now that I didn't come that night. And I really wish I had. Maybe I could have stopped this from happening. If I had told her, maybe she wouldn't have killed herself.

I switch the light off. That's a positive thing. That's what normal people do. They don't wake in the middle of the night, full of fear, the lights still on.

Tomorrow I will do a random act of kindness, and things will start to get better.

JOCELYN

London, 2015

Everything has spiralled out of control. Me, the control freak, no longer in charge. And now that I have told Billy, all those old feelings have returned. The shame, the revulsion, the self-hatred, the anger. God, the anger. The fear. Nothing positive could ever come out of this, not even a baby being born, because he would always be my ghost child, my memory box, a trigger for my nightmares.

I can't even close my eyes any more for fear of seeing myself back there in Alderson Road, pinned to the bed, suffocating in my own pillow. Wishing myself dead rather than wishing it to be over. The blood. Fuck, the blood, and yet my mother still insisted I'd started it. He's back in my dreams, and I just want it to stop.

And now I hate myself even more, because this is more now of my own making. Nobody asked me to become a public figure. Nobody asked me to become the Queen of Twitter. Nobody asked me to write those ghastly columns. OK, so Ross put pressure on me, but all it would have taken was for me to say no.

And now the tinderbox is going to set alight and explode. And I'm going to get burnt. And Billy, and Kathleen, and . . .

What's going to stop Ross leaking the story, anyway? Oh-holier-than-thou woman actually had kid out of wedlock. Maybe I should have told him the truth about what really happened that night. I've convinced him that it was nothing to do with Mark Reynolds, but I know that won't stop him spreading the story anyway.

And I've pissed Adam off, and he knows about my days with Black Orchid.

And now I've really fucked up Billy's life by telling him the truth. What must that be like for him? You can't sugar-coat a rape. You can't say, 'Daddy loved Mummy but Mummy didn't love Daddy.' There was no love involved in his conception. Only hatred and power, the misuse of.

I should have trusted my instincts. I should have just run away and had the abortion, and then none of us would be in this position today.

All the bad things I have done stem from that night, and that night alone. I know I'm not blameless in a lot of things, but that's what's rotten to the core about me. What happened that night. And I just want these horrendous feelings to end. I can't pretend any more.

My phone rings. I check the caller ID and see it's a Liverpool number. It must be Mum! The last time I phoned home and said nothing, she knew it was me. And she apologized. I know over the years she has reflected on what happened and has altered her opinion – she fucking APOLOGIZED! She'll put a stop to this. She'll make me feel better. She'll wash away the pain as only a mother can, and everything will get better. I will get better.

I click 'answer'.

'Hello?'

A man speaks. 'What the fuck did you say all that to Billy for?'

And I feel like my insides have fallen out onto the carpet.

'How did you get my number?'

'How d'you fucking think? Billy give it me.'

'I don't want you calling me.'

'And I don't want you going round saying I'm a rapist.'

'If the cap fits.'

'The cap doesn't fit, you lying bitch. Coz I'm not. Look. I know it's all trendy to go round saying everyone was abused by grown-ups and celebrities in the eighties. But you and I both know what happened.'

'You raped me.'

'I did no such thing.'

'Then how d'you explain Billy?'

'You give me the glad eye, you did. Hanging around in your short skirts, batting your eyelashes. Being all flirty.'

'I fucking wasn't.'

'I fucking hate it when birds swear. You give me the come-on. I responded.'

He is making me feel sick. How could he? How fucking could he?

'You came into my bedroom at night and . . .'

'Yeah, and then you bottled out – well, tough. You were gagging for it at one stage.'

'I was fourteen.'

'I've a good mind to go the papers about this. Miss High and Mighty. Tell them what you're really like.'

I say it again. Slowly. 'I was fourteen.'

'You were very well developed.'

'So you raped me?'

'Fourteen going on forty. And you can't rape the willing, love.'

'You wouldn't dare go to the papers. I'll just say you're a rapist.'

'If I raped you, why'd you keep the baby?'

It's pointless arguing with him, but I can't help it. Adrenalin is pumping round my body. I am shaking, sweating, my voice is rising. 'That wasn't my decision.'

'Oh, behave. I know what happened that night, even if you've forgot.'

'Oh, fuck off.'

'No, I won't fuck off. And d'you wanna know something else?'

'What?'

'You were a crap shag. It was like thingy. Necrophilia.'

And then he hangs up. My vision turns cloudy. My tears are blinding me. I need an escape. I look to the balcony.

I slide the door open. Fresh air hits me, makes me brave.

I know what I have to do now.

ADAM

London, 2015: That Night

I don't know why I've come here. I was in the area, had dinner with Jay-Jay and then I remembered. The flats I could see on the skyline, looming over us. That's where she lives.

I've come to have it out with her. I've come to tell her she can't keep hurting those who love her. Or loved her once upon a time. I've come to tell her she's a hypocrite and that if she doesn't stop being so repugnant about so many people, up there on her high horse, I have enough contacts in the media now to let them know about her secret kid, about her sordid past with the agency.

I stand in front of the flats. I look up.

A woman is looking down at me.

It's her.

BILLY

London, 2015: That Night

I've come to apologize. I should never have given her number to that horrible man. I was angry, confused. She will understand. I have prayed on this and I see she is the injured party, like me. I will apologize, she will forgive me, I will forgive her and we will move on.

Well, that's how I feel right now. I fluctuate.

I stand on the parched earth amongst the trees, working up the courage to go and ring her bell. I see a man lurking. He's clearly gay. Oh God, is this a cruising ground? But he is ignoring me. He doesn't seem to know what he's doing, pacing. And then he looks up through the trees.

Right. I am going to go and ring the bell and be contrite.

I have a lot to ask forgiveness for.

I move forward, then hear something fall behind me. I look. A white woman in party clothes has tripped over and is giggling. I go to help her up. It's her. It's Kathleen. It's the woman who . . .

THUD.

I look round to see where this hideous noise has come from.

And that's when I see her.

The other man. The gay one. He moves forward, stares at Mum for a second. Then he runs away.

ADAM

London, 2015: That Night

I don't know why I'm running away. I should have stopped, stayed with her. But it was obvious she was dead. I run as fast as I can through streets I am unfamiliar with.

I do know why I'm running. It's because part of me wanted to scare her when I went round. A part of me wanted to hurt her. It's so wrong to want to hurt a woman, but that's the feeling she brings out in me. Especially recently.

So it's like I made it happen.

I stop to get my breath back. I hear a siren wailing. From now on I will walk, in order not to arouse suspicion. I walk with a stitch in my chest, sweat pouring down me, panic rising.

I run into a back alley and puke my guts up.

BILLY

London, 2015: That Night

Dear God,

I am lying in bed with this strange woman who shouldn't be strange at all. She snores lightly and I stroke her hair. She is really rather beautiful as she sleeps. She has a beautiful nose. I try to see myself in her, but much as I try, I can't.

I now realize I should have stayed, gone with Jocelyn in the ambulance maybe. But it was obvious to any fool that you can't drop that distance and survive. That would be some kind of miracle, and my guess is you didn't love her well enough for that. I know you love all your children, but she was quite a character. Not exactly your best calling card.

I have left the curtains open, and I enjoy my tiny bit of sky. The street lamp. The roof. A bit of tree. Black sky and one star. Like the star when you were born, Lord. One bright star showing where you were. And tonight feels like a rebirth of sorts, as well. A time to start again. Maybe that is the gift that Jocelyn has given me. Maybe that is her legacy. Not that I want to rewrite my past, but . . . oh, I am tired. I am not thinking straight.

I wonder whether I would ever force myself on a woman like he did. And I think I would not. Especially now I know what a man can truly be capable of. I used to think like those

360

posters think. *Ladies! Girls! Don't wear that short skirt on campus, you're asking to be attacked.* Now I know they have it arse about face. The posters should be aimed at the men. *Men, fellas, don't drink too much tonight and get lairy, and keep your hand on your ha'penny. AND DON'T RAPE ANYONE.* That would be a much better advertising campaign.

I guess I could work in advertising. I could do so much really, instead of my boring job at the council. A pen pusher, they call me, which in itself is an outdated term; I am rarely away from my keyboard. Yet what have I achieved? Very little, really.

But then I think: unlike Mommie Dearest, I'm still here. And that, for now, feels like some kind of liberation.

I have always found discussing my family quite difficult. I never knew what I was allowed to say and what I had to avoid. And who was in on the story, and who wasn't. And there was never anyone really to share it with; for Ruby and the twins, it was too dangerous. Too fraught with 'don't say that for fear of upsetting them', and so on.

And yet this woman who lies beside me is part of that history. And she is someone that maybe I can share a history with. It's kind of nobody else's but ours. Neither of us chose this history. We are the innocent ones. And out of it might even come some good, some healing.

Of course, there is the possibility that she doesn't know any of this. After all, she is the one who got tipsy at her grandmother's funeral and insisted Mark Reynolds was my father. But something tells me – call it intuition, whatever – that she does know now. Why else would she seem so troubled? Her sleep is troubled.

Mind you, she is probably poisoned from all that drink. She really hums with it. But that's OK. Maybe I will be someone to help her veer away from that path and onto a better one. One where she doesn't fall over.

Two falls tonight in such close succession. My, my!

I really can't sleep. Too pumped, too wired. I pull my arm away from my sister, ease myself gently off the bed and return to the kitchen. I open the drawer next to the oven and pull it out.

It's a photo. I don't know why, but I stole it the other day when I was round at her flat. She didn't see me take it, and God knows why I did. Sorry, you know why I did . . . but it was there, and it was an act of anger more than anything . . . but you know what, Lord? I'm glad I took it.

It shows Jocelyn with two friends. They look about twenty. Their faces are fresh and trouble-free, and they look so full of optimism and excitement. One of them, I now see, is Kathleen. The other, a gawky-looking white lad with a snub nose. Jocelyn is holding up a purple Christmas bauble with gold figures in it, and they are all laughing. They appear to be in a nightclub. It makes me happy. And it means I now have a picture of her looking happy, instead of the morose, anger-filled creature I grew familiar with and who I eventually, sort of, got to know, albeit briefly. It's fading; well, it's an old picture. But I'm sure I can scan it and play around with it on my computer and bring it back to life. When Christmas comes I might even hang it on my tree. I'll have a tree this year. Maybe Kathleen will want to come round. We will drink grape juice and say, 'To the future!' and then talk about our shared history.

I'm feeling sleepy now. The photograph has calmed me. I slide it back into the drawer and close it.

I go back to bed and lie next to my sister.

I will sleep, I'm sure.

Amen.

ADAM

Dear Kathleen,

It was so lovely to see you yesterday and catch up. You're looking so well. You must be right, not drinking suits you. I was going to drop you an email but what I want to express feels too intimate for that, so a good old-fashioned letter it is! I'm so grateful you told me what you did. It must have been an awful burden to be carrying around all this time, but you know none of it is your fault. None of it. You're not your father and you hardly knew him growing up so he didn't even have that much influence over you. I'm glad you're forging some sort of relationship with Billy. But like I said yesterday, tread carefully. Though his selflessness in letting us scatter the ashes on our own was pretty remarkable. Like you said, he'd thought it through and thought it more appropriate if it was just us. In stark contrast, of course, to Ross, who just washed his hands of the whole thing. Some boyfriend, eh?

I loved that we did it on her birthday. I loved that we *did it* somewhere as pretty as Parliament Hill. I was less keen when the wind changed and we both got a mouthful of Jocelyn, but I kind of think she'd have loved that. I think that would have tickled her pink.

I've thought about what you said. About us staying friends but only seeing each other occasionally, and you're absolutely right. Times change, life moves on, and we're different people from when we were teenagers. It doesn't mean we don't care about each other, and it doesn't mean we can't just strike up where we left off when we do see each other. I get it. I get you. I get us, I guess.

I'm glad I told you where I was when she died. We know everything now. Well, as much as there is to know. We know enough.

It's funny, getting to this age. I often feel the best bits are behind me. Sad, isn't it? Oh I know I have a great future with Him Indoors and Denim and wherever he might take us. But I can't change my foundations now. That's my history. It's written, done.

I hope you manage to have a gorgeous, peaceful Christmas and who knows. Maybe we'll see each other in the New Year.

I meant what I said yesterday. I didn't know. Oh yes, she'd dropped hints. But she never ever mentioned your dad. Truth be told I dismissed it, thinking she was attention-seeking. You can imagine how proud of that I am now. Exactly.

Oh well. Guess we just have to keep on keeping on.

It really was a lovely day. I hope there'll be many more.

Please don't feel you have to reply to this.

Take care of yourself Kathleen.

All love

Adam xx

All She Wants

———————

There are some things in life you can always rely on.
Living in the shadow of your 'perfect' brother Joey,
getting the flu over Christmas, and your mother
showing you up in the supermarket.

Then there are some things you really don't count
on happening: a good dose of fame, getting completely
trashed at an awards ceremony, and catching your
fella doing something unmentionable on your
wedding day.

This is my story, it's dead tragic.
You have been warned . . .

Jodie X x

'Utterly original, sharply written and very funny'
JOJO MOYES

The Confusion of Karen Carpenter

Hello.

There are two things you should know about me:

1) My name is Karen Carpenter.

2) Just before Christmas my boyfriend left me.

I'm not THE Karen Carpenter. I just have the most embarrassing name in Christendom. Particularly as I'm no skinny minny and don't play the drums.

I can't even sing. I'm tone deaf. I work in a school in the East End. (Where I came third in a 'Teacher we'd most like to sleep with' competition amongst the Year 11 boys.)

My mum's driving me mad. She's come to stay and is obsessed with Scandi crime shows and Zumba.

Oh yeah. The boyfriend. After eleven 'happy' years he left me. No explanation, just a letter Sellotaped to the kettle when I got in from work. I think I'm handling it really well. I don't think I'm confused at all.

What was my name again?

'I enjoyed it HUGELY . . . a total page-turner, very entertaining, then very moving'

MARIAN KEYES

The Girl Who Just Appeared

LONDON – THE PRESENT

Holly Smith has never fitted in. Adopted when just a few months old, she's always felt she was someone with no history. All she has is the address of where she was born – 32B Gambier Terrace, Liverpool. When Holly discovers that the flat is available to rent, she travels north and moves in. And in the very same flat, under the floorboards, she finds a biscuit tin full of yellowing papers. Could these papers be the key to her past?

LIVERPOOL – 1981

Fifteen-year-old Darren is negotiating life with his errant mother and the younger brother he is raising. When the Toxteth Riots explode around him, Darren finds himself with a moral dilemma that will have consequences for the rest of his life.

Moving between the past and the present, Darren and Holly's lives become intertwined. Will finding Darren give Holly the answers she craves? Or will she always feel like the girl who just appeared?

'Absolutely delightful. Jonathan Harvey writes with all his heart and all his soul.'
LISA JEWELL

The Secrets We Keep

It's hard being *that* woman, the one whose
husband disappeared. It's made me quite famous.
I just wish it was for something else.

He went out five years ago for a pint of milk and
never came back. So here I am with a daughter who
blames me for all that's wrong in the world, a son
trying his best to pick up the pieces and a gaggle of
new neighbours who are over-friendly, and incredibly
nosy. Then we find a left-luggage ticket in the pocket
of one of his old coats and suddenly I'm thinking
. . .What's if he's not dead? What if he's still out
there somewhere?

You think you have the perfect life, the perfect
kids, and then it's all turned inside out. What if I
don't like what I find? And is it a chance I'm
willing to take?

It's time to relax with your next good book

THEWINDOWSEAT.CO.UK

If you've enjoyed this book, but don't know what to read next, then we can help. The Window Seat is a site that's all about making it easier to discover your next good book. We feature recommendations, behind-the-scenes tales from the world of publishing, creative writing tips, competitions, and, if we're honest, quite a lot of lists based on our favourite reads.

You'll find stories and features by authors including Lucinda Riley, Karen Swan, Diane Chamberlain, Jane Green, Lucy Diamond and many more. We showcase brand-new talent as well as classic favourites, so you'll never be stuck for what to read again.

We'd love to know what you think of the site, our books, and what you'd like us to feature, so do let us know.

 @panmacmillan

 facebook.com/TheWindowSeat

WWW.THEWINDOWSEAT.CO.UK

extracts reading groups
competitions books new
discounts extracts
competitions
books
new
events
extracts
books
interviews
events extracts
new
books
discounts
new books events
events new
discounts extracts discounts

www.panmacmillan.com

extracts events reading groups
competitions books extracts new